P9-EMH-764

The Price of Silence

Also by KATE WILHELM

THE UNBIDDEN TRUTH
CLEAR AND CONVINCING PROOF
SKELETONS
DESPERATE MEASURES
DEATH QUALIFIED
THE DEEPEST WATER
NO DEFENSE
DEFENSE FOR THE DEVIL

KATE WILHELM

The Price of Silence

ISBN 0-7783-2216-5

THE PRICE OF SILENCE

Copyright © 2005 by Kate Wilhelm.

All rights reserved. Except for use in any review, the reproduction or utilization of this work in whole or in part in any form by any electronic, mechanical or other means, now known or hereafter invented, including xerography, photocopying and recording, or in any information storage or retrieval system, is forbidden without the written permission of the publisher, MIRA Books, 225 Duncan Mill Road, Don Mills, Ontario, Canada M3B 3K9.

All characters in this book have no existence outside the imagination of the author and have no relation whatsoever to anyone bearing the same name or names. They are not even distantly inspired by any individual known or unknown to the author, and all incidents are pure invention.

MIRA and the Star Colophon are trademarks used under license and registered in Australia, New Zealand, Philippines, United States Patent and Trademark Office and in other countries.

www.MIRABooks.com

Printed in U.S.A.

First Printing: October 2005
10 9 8 7 6 5 4 3 2 1

The Price *of* Silence

Prologue

The Bend News, July, 1888

> *Four people perished in a fire that destroyed the Warden House last week in the town of Brindle. Dead in the fire were Mrs. Michael Hilliard, Mr. Joe Warden, the original founder of the historic inn, Mr. Harold Ivers, a traveling salesman, and Miss Dorothy Conway, an employee at the inn. Surviving the blaze was Mr. Michael Hilliard, and Daniel Warden, aged eight. The cause of the fire is unknown.*

The fire bell woke me up that night. I ran to Ma's room, but they weren't there, and I ran outside. Ma was in the street, and across the way I could see the fire. The flames were shooting up high, with great showers of sparks. People were running everywhere, dipping water from the creek, throwing it on, other people were screaming and yelling. Horses were going crazy, plunging into the creek, up the other side. I stood next to Ma and she put her arm around my shoulders and held me tight. I wanted to get nearer, but she wouldn't let me go.

The roof crashed down and made a geyser of ashes and sparks. The smell was terrible and the smoke made my eyes tear and I felt I was choking. Mostly I remember how afraid I was.

Pa came and when he saw me, he told me to get back in bed. He sounded mad and I ran back in and got in bed. But in a little while I got up again and listened to what they were saying. Pa said Brother McNulty would keep Daniel Warden with him, raise him with his own children. But Joe Warden, Janey, one of the girls and a traveling man had been in the building. "Gone," he said. "God's judgment, His punishment."

I ran back to bed before they saw me. I knew Pa would give me a whipping if he found me up again. And I thought about Janey and another girl burning up. I had never heard of Janey, and I hadn't known another girl lived right there in that house.

The next day Ma kept me in the kitchen with her most of the time. Because of the revival, and Reverend McNulty and his family, we were feeding a lot of people every day, and I peeled potatoes until I thought my fingers would fall off. It was so hot with the fire in the stove all day, my hair was sticking to my head, and my skirt sticking to my legs. I asked Ma who Janey was and she pinched my arm and said I must never mention that name again.

After we ate dinner and washed the dishes there was the tent revival and Reverend McNulty talked about sinful women and hellfire and brimstone. He was red-faced and yelled a lot, gesturing while he preached. He scared me. And it was so hot in the tent, it was like we were getting a taste of hellfire.

The day of the funeral everyone from town went, and folks came in from the countryside and even Bend. Pa talked about Joe Warden first, then Reverend McNulty talked a long time and Pa said a long prayer. Men lowered the coffin all the way and Pa threw in a handful of dirt and said, "Ashes to ashes, dust to dust."

No one had much to say over the traveling man, just things like God rest his soul.

I thought they'd go on to the other two graves already dug, but Pa told me to get back in the wagon. I waited until he went to talk to somebody else and asked Ma if they were going to bury Janey and the other girl, and she pinched my arm harder than she ever did before. She said, "I told you never to say that name. Now get yourself to the wagon and wait."

I climbed up in the back of the wagon and waited a long time. A hot wind kept blowing grit and dust everywhere, and there wasn't any shade. Just the dry dirt and sage and rocks. I was itchy all over and so dried out I couldn't have cried even if I'd wanted to. Since Pa was the regular preacher, it always seemed like everyone wanted a word with him, and we were almost the last ones to leave. The horse had just started to walk when I saw Mr. Hilliard standing by one of the other open graves. The men brought the coffin and put it in and began to shovel dirt on top. Mr. Hilliard just stood there. I don't think anyone said a thing. At least no preacher said anything.

At first I thought Mr. Hilliard looked funny in his long black coat and a stovepipe hat, but then I felt sorry for him because he looked lonesome all by himself by the men shoveling dirt. I didn't know whose grave was being filled in.

Our house was crowded again all afternoon until dinner time, and then there was the revival in the tent that was like an oven. I was glad enough to get to bed that night, and Ma said she was ready to drop.

But I woke up again, freezing cold. All the feather beds were put away for the summer and I went to ask Ma for a cover, but they weren't in their bed, and I heard Pa's voice in the sitting room. They were on their knees and he was praying about God's judgment, but Ma was crying. She had on her robe with a blanket around her, but she was shivering and crying, and I started to cry too. I ran to Ma and she pulled me under the blanket with her. She was shaking all over and I was, too. I never had been so cold in my life, even in the winter, and I thought we were dying.

I must have cried myself to sleep, sitting on the floor with Ma, wrapped in the blanket. When I woke up again, I was in bed and it was already hot.

I didn't get an answer to my question about Janey until I was a grown woman and married. My friend Eliza whispered that Janey had been married to Mr. Hilliard, but she was one of the bad girls at that House, and she either drowned her own baby, or else she was with a man when the baby wandered out to the creek and fell in.

I can't remember that anyone ever said her name out loud, and I know I never did after that.

This is what I remember about the fire and the days after. Annabelle Bolton. November 5, 1943.

One

Todd drove into the parking lot behind her town-house apartment building that sweltering afternoon in August and braced herself for the next few minutes. She knew Barney was already home; she had spotted his truck parked back in the separate section reserved for oversize vehicles. He would greet her, hope lightening his face, and she would shake her head. Then he would try to cheer her up. They spent a great deal of time trying to cheer each other up these days, and that was about as futile as her going out for yet another job interview.

Overqualified, today's idiot had said; they could start her at nine dollars an hour at best. But, he had added with the perfected personnel director's smile she had come to loathe, they would keep her résumé on file for a possible future opening.

She pulled away from the back of the seat, where her blouse was plastered to the leather. Neither of them was using air-conditioning, not in the car and truck, not in the apartment. Trudging up the flight of stairs to their apartment, she drew in a deep breath and straightened her back, ready to smile and wave away the disappointing interview as inconsequential, just like the others.

The apartment was as hot as outside, the only sound was that of a whirring fan. She took off her shoes and, carrying them, walked to the door of the second bedroom, Barney's studio. He had fallen asleep in a chair, his notebook and pen on the floor, a book on his chest. With his curly hair stuck to his forehead with sweat, he looked like a little boy worn out from softball practice.

"It isn't fair," she whispered, backing away from the door. Barney had worked his way through college, taking summer jobs, odd jobs, whatever he could find, and now, with his dissertation to write in the next two years, they were two weeks away from real desperation. In two weeks her unemployment would run out, and they couldn't survive on Barney's job in a book distributor's warehouse—exhausting work that paid very little and left him too tired to work on the dissertation when he came home.

It wasn't fair, she thought again, as she went through the spacious and beautiful apartment to the master bedroom. There were scant furnishings, not because they had been unwilling or unable to buy furniture, but because neither of them had wanted to take the time to shop. A bed, a chest of drawers, a few other pieces from Goodwill that they had bought when they first married three years earlier. Now she was more than grateful that they were such poor shoppers. What few new pieces they had acquired had gone on credit cards—an overpriced sofa, a good chair, Barney's desk.... She could admit that they had been like kids in a candy store with a dollar to spend, buying on impulse with no thought of tomorrow.

When they rented the town house, sixteen months earlier, they had given little heed to the price. Her job had paid too well to consider cost. They had bought her Acura and his truck, and now owed more on both than they could realize by selling them. In February her company had been taken over, and she had not worked since.

But they had a great view of Mount Hood, she thought, eyeing it out the bedroom window as she stripped off her sodden interview clothes, and put on shorts and a tank top. Silent with feet bare, she wandered out to the kitchen to make iced tea. Barney had brought in the mail and she glanced at it listlessly as she waited for the water to boil. Bills, pleas for money, offers for credit cards... She picked up an envelope addressed to G. Todd Fielding, the name she used on her résumés, and frowned at the return address: *The Brindle Times.* From Brindle, Oregon.

"Where the hell is Brindle, Oregon?" she muttered, opening the envelope. She had sent her last résumé to a box number. She sat down at the kitchen table and read the enclosed letter, then read it again.

"The person we are looking for must have editorial skills, computer skills, and the ability to lay out a newspaper as well as periodicals. From your résumé and the journal you submitted it appears that you have the necessary skills. You would have to relocate, however. If you are interested, call any afternoon and we can arrange for a telephone interview."

The letter practically quoted her own résumé, she thought in wonder. That was exactly the kind of work she had done for nearly three years. Her hand was shaking as she reached for the telephone, but she drew back. *Where the hell was Brindle?*

She located the town on the state road map, and had to fight back tears. On the other side of the mountains, south of Bend. Barney had to teach two classes during the coming year. It was bad enough to have to drive from Portland to Corvallis, as he had been doing this past year, but across the mountains?

She finished making tea, then sat and read the letter one more time. It *was* her job, she thought, exactly right for her, made to order for her.

She considered the alternatives. She could not support them on the kind of money she had been offered in her job search. If Barney had to work even part-time while teaching his classes, he would not be able to finish the dissertation in the next two years. His adviser would retire, and, university politics being what they were, he might be stranded.

They had already cut frills, everything that could be cut, and were still left with car payments, student loans, health insurance, rent, utilities, food. They could not afford the town house, but neither could they afford to move with first and last months' rent payable in advance, plus a cleaning deposit. She knew to the penny how much they had to have each month, and even if both of them worked at entry-level jobs they probably couldn't make it.

All right, she thought angrily, don't go down that road again. She had traveled it so often, she could do it sound asleep, and frequently did. No more recriminations about past stupidity, she and Barney had agreed, think alternatives instead.

If Barney could arrange his two classes for consecutive days, go over one day, come back the next… One long commute a week… He could stay in a motel one night a week… Have the rest of the week free… What he needed was access to a library—their apartment was crammed with the library books he needed for his research—and time. A lot of time without exhaustion from menial labor and, more important, without worry about money.

She picked up the letter and went to the bedroom, closed the door softly, then sat on the edge of the bed and dialed.

In the office of *The Brindle Times*, Johnny Colonna was glaring at his mother, who was holding the weekly edition of the newspaper and shaking it furiously.

"It's a shambles, a mess, a loathsome unholy mess!" she said again. "I won't have it, Johnny. I'm telling you, I won't have it! I'll shut down before I let a mess like this go out again!"

He looked relieved when the phone rang. "Yes," he snapped. "Who?" He held his hand over the mouthpiece. "It's that woman, Fielding, the one who sent her résumé last week."

"Tell her we'll call back in five minutes. And I'll do the talking."

He repeated the message and hung up. "Mother, I thought we decided on Stan Beacham. Why bother talking to this one?"

"I haven't decided on anyone," she said. "That man's a twit. He'd stay just as long as it took to find something better. And he doesn't know any more about computers than you do. I'll get her résumé and make the call in here."

Ignoring the sullen look that crossed her son's face, Ruth Ann marched from his office, crossed the outer office to her own and picked up Todd Fielding's folder. None of the three women in the outer office dared glance at her on her first trip across their space, nor on her return. When Ruth Ann was in a snit, it was best to look very busy.

Ruth Ann was eighty, and from the time of her father's death when she was twenty-one, she had published, edited and, for much of the time, written every word in the newspaper. And, she had decided that morning, reading the latest edition, she would be damned if she would see it become a piece of crap. *Crap,* she repeated to herself. That was what it was turning into. Ungrammatical, words misspelled, one story cut off in mid-section, strings of gibberish… Crap!

She placed the call herself, seated at Johnny's desk, while he took up a stance of martyrdom at the window. He blamed it all on the computer system he had installed the previous year. They would get the hang of it, he had said more than once. It just took time. Everyone knew it took time. Well, time had just run out, she thought as Todd Fielding answered the phone on the first ring.

"Ms. Fielding, my name is Ruth Ann Colonna and I'm the publisher of *The Brindle Times.* I was quite impressed by your résumé. And by the quality of the trade journal you provided. I have to tell you up front that we could not pay you the kind of salary you were receiving previously, however there is a house available rent-free through another party, therefore not to be considered part of your pay package. You would be responsible for property taxes and insurance, roughly a thousand or a little more annually. We offer excellent health benefits."

Ruth Ann watched Johnny stiffen, wheel about and shake his head. She ignored him. "I'd like to ask you a few questions about the journal," she said.

* * *

It was a long interview. Ruth Ann asked questions, and Todd answered in a straightforward way. When Ruth Ann asked what Barney's dissertation was, Todd said, "The Cultural, Political and Religious Movements that Account for the Fluctuations in the Ascendancy of Rationalistic Belief Systems."

Ruth Ann laughed. "My God! That's a mouthful. A philosopher, for goodness sake! I didn't know anyone studied philosophy these days."

When Ruth Ann finally hung up, she regarded Johnny thoughtfully. "She'll do," she said.

"Mother, be reasonable. You can't hire someone you never even met on the basis of a phone call. And whose house are you offering a stranger?"

"As for the first part, I believe I just did," Ruth Ann said. "And the house is Mattie and Hal Tilden's. Mattie begged me to put someone in it. Their insurance has quadrupled since it's been empty, and she knows an empty house invites trouble. But you're right about strangers. The Fieldings will come over on Friday to meet in person. And, Johnny, I suppose you haven't even glanced at that journal, or paid much attention to her résumé. I suggest you look them over carefully. She's had art training, and studied all sorts of computer technology, software and hardware, whatever that means. You don't know a pixel from a pixie, and neither do I, but she does. She can edit, and she's a good writer. She has excellent recommendations. If you take the press in the direction you're thinking of, you'll need someone just like her."

She walked to the door, paused and said, "I want to see every word, every paragraph, every ad on paper before you go to press next week. Every goddamn word."

* * *

In her bedroom Todd disconnected and carefully put the phone down on the bed. She stood up, flung her hands in the air and screamed a Tarzan yell of triumph, then raced from the room, only to meet Barney in the hall. He looked sleep-dazed and bewildered.

"What's wrong? Are you okay?"

"It's going to work! I've got a job! Oh, God, you're wearing too many clothes!" She began to pull at his shirt. "We need to celebrate! Right now!" Giving up on his shirt, she yanked off her tank top, and started to wriggle out of her shorts.

Two

On Thursday morning Todd sat cross-legged on the floor, both arms crossed over her breasts, fingers crossed on both hands. When Barney glanced at her as he started to dial, she crossed her eyes.

Sputtering with laughter, he hit the disconnect button. "Stop that!"

"Can't. This is how I work magic."

He turned his back and dialed Victor Franz's number. Victor was his adviser, his mentor, a father substitute who treated Barney like a protégé.

She listened to him explain the situation, and then could make no sense of his monosyllabic end of the conversation. "Yes.... No.... Sounds good.... No problem...."

He hung up and turned around to her, his eyes shining. "You're a witch," he said. "Classes on Thursdays and Fridays.

He'll arrange it. And no motel. He said I should plan to use one of his kids' rooms."

Victor's three children were all grown and gone, and he and his wife were keeping a big farmhouse with several acres of apple trees until he retired in two years. They also had two big, shaggy Australian shepherd dogs and numerous cats.

"But there's a catch," Barney said, pulling Todd to her feet. "Once a month I have to stay over until Sunday while he and Ginny go to the coast to visit her folks. I have to dog-sit, cat-sit and house-sit."

"Oh no!" she cried in mock dismay. "And have his library at your disposal! Merciless man!"

Barney laughed and drew her closer, biting her ear not at all gently. "Witch! I think we need to celebrate again."

They were both subdued when they approached Brindle on Friday. The Great Basin desert stretched out to infinity on one side of the highway, and the Cascades loomed on the other. One looked as dead as a lunar landscape, the other, thinly populated here with ponderosa pines, was as unmoving as a painting. The only signs of life were the cars and trucks on the road.

"You'll be bored to death out here," Barney said.

"Won't. I'll take up bird-watching. I wonder if there are birds? But you'll be miserable."

"Nope. I'll wander barefoot in the desert, grow a long beard, have visions and become a revered prophet."

"We are arriving," she said a moment later. On the left, a mammoth greenhouse seemed ridiculously out of place considering that the temperature was 101. A motel, a gas station with a small convenience store attached, a Safeway… Another store, general merchandise, a tourist-type souvenir store, another motel with a café, a rock shop... It looked like a movie set waiting for the actors. Behind one of the gas stations, a group of manufactured homes stood baking in the sun.

"We turn right on First Street," she said. It came up fast and Barney made the turn. Now a larger building came into view, a two-story hotel, with a lot of well-maintained greenery visible, and a few more shops. "Right again on Spruce," she said. Brindle had turned into a real village with houses and yards, green things growing, a restaurant, a few people going on about their business. She spotted the Bolton Building with a neat sign: The Brindle Times, and Barney pulled to the curb and parked.

"Ready or not," he murmured, and patted her thigh. "Just don't go into your magic pose. Okay?"

"I'll try to restrain myself," she said, uncrossing her fingers.

She had told Ruth Ann Colonna that they would arrive between one and two, and it was ten minutes after one when they entered the building. A pretty, round-faced young woman met them.

"Mrs. Fielding? They're expecting you. I'll tell Johnny you're here. Just a sec." She was wearing jeans, a T-shirt and sandals. She crossed the outer office, tapped on a door, then entered another room. Two other women looked them over as they waited, an older woman, possibly in her sixties, and a lean young Latina.

The door across the room opened and the one who had met them reappeared, followed closely by a thick-set man with straight black hair. He had a dark tan and big brown eyes.

"Ms. Fielding? Mr. Fielding? Johnny Colonna. Glad to meet

you. Come in, come in." He clasped her hand briefly, nodded to Barney and led the way into his office, where he introduced Ruth Ann.

Todd had assumed that Mrs. Colonna was his wife, and was surprised to meet the old woman. She was taller than Todd and as straight as a stick, without a hint of extra fat; her skin was weathered and wrinkled with a tan as dark as her son's, and her hair pure white and straight, cut short. Her eyes were startling, green with flecks of amber. She looked sinewy, tough, impervious to the elements. She was wearing faded chinos and a cotton shirt.

Todd was beginning to feel overdressed in her interview clothes—skirt, blouse, panty hose.

Waving Todd and Barney to chairs, Johnny went behind his desk to his own chair, cleared his throat, and then said, "I was impressed by the journal you sent us, but I'm afraid that we're not doing anything quite like that. We have a weekly newspaper, and a few circulars, nothing like you're used to working with."

Without glancing at him, Ruth Ann handed Todd a copy of the latest edition of the newspaper, the one that had infuriated her. "Can you tell by looking it over what went wrong? Theodore, our editor, swears that he edited the copy himself, and he's been quite good in the past. And I know beyond any doubt that my own editorial was letter perfect." She sat in a chair close to Todd's.

As Todd began to examine the newspaper, Ruth Ann turned to Barney. "Do you have computer expertise also, Mr. Fielding?"

Barney shook his head. "Not a bit. I use a word processor and when I goof, as I do all the time, she fixes it." He nodded at Todd, who was frowning at the newspaper.

She turned to the last page, then looked at Ruth Ann. "It's lost the formatting. And the columns aren't set. Also, someone tried to use text and graphic boxes without setting the parameters." She would have continued, but Ruth Ann held up her hand.

"If I edited all the paper copy and someone put it in the computer, would it end up garbled like that?"

"Until the program is straightened out, the errors fixed, the formatting reset, things like that, it would probably come out about like this."

Ruth Ann's lips tightened. "What are those strings of gibberish?" She leaned over and pointed to a string of codes.

"It looks like different programs were used and codes from one ended up in the text without being translated."

"Ms. Fielding—may I call you Todd? How long would it take you to straighten out the programs, fix things, print a decent edition if you had the copy?"

Johnny made a throat-clearing sound and Ruth Ann turned to snap at him, "Have you understood a word she's said?"

"You know I don't know anything about computers."

"And neither does anyone else in this office. That's the problem." She looked at Todd again.

"I could run off an edition in a day or two if I had all the prepared copy. But it would be makeshift. To fix things the way they should be fixed? I can't be sure until I know what programs are in use, how many people have access to them, if there are templates, or if they have to be set up. It could be a matter of days, or it could take several weeks. And after all that, your people, anyone who uses the programs, should be trained. I can't say without more information."

"When can you start?"

"I thought you said you would want someone by the first of September," Todd said.

"I want someone now, today, Monday. Todd, if you can start sooner, I would appreciate it. We will cover your relocation expenses, hire movers to come in and pack your things, haul them down here. Meanwhile you could stay in the hotel, Warden House. Would that be acceptable?"

Startled, Todd glanced at Barney. He nodded at her and stood up, then said, "Mrs. Colonna, I think Todd and I should take a few minutes to talk about this."

"Yes, you should," she said. "Come along. I'll take you to my office." She led the way back through the outer office to the opposite side and opened a door. "My room," she said. "This is where you'll be working, Todd, at least until Theodore leaves in September. When you're ready, just come back to Johnny's office. Take as long as you like." She looked around, shrugged, then left, closing the door after her.

It was a bigger office than Johnny's, and while his had been neat and tidy, this room was cluttered—an old desk, two old chairs, boxes on the floor, papers all over the desktop. A separate desk held only a computer.

"Barney, we can't just abandon our stuff," Todd said.

"Honey, that old lady is desperate," he said softly. He looked at the vintage desk, faded framed photographs on the wall, wooden file cabinets. "This is her baby," he said. "She has to save it, and she can see a savior in you. We won't abandon anything. I'll take care of stuff in Portland and you can go to work. Do you want to start right away? That's the only question."

She crossed the office to a tall window with venetian blinds, wooden blinds. She hadn't seen blinds like that since… Never, she realized. She had never seen blinds like that. Barney had pegged Ruth Ann Colonna exactly right, she thought then. She had been considering the work aspect of the interview, but he had seen through that to the person who had not actually pleaded with her to start, but had come close.

In Johnny's office again, Ruth Ann sat down and said, "We have to do something now. We can't afford another issue like that one. How many complaints have you fielded so far?"

He rubbed his eyes. "Plenty. I know we do. It's just the expense with money so tight."

"How many times have you brought in a consultant this past year? At fifty dollars an hour. They come in, spend three or four hours fixing things and for a week or two everything seems to work and then it turns into garbage again. We have to have someone in house to keep things working right and to train everyone here."

"I'm not fighting you," he said, holding out both hands in a placating gesture. "See. I agree. But, Lord, they look like kids, both of them."

"They are kids," she said. "Pretty, precocious children who understand the world they're inheriting, which is more than I can say for myself. All right. I'll take them over to the Tilden house and leave the key with them, and afterward I have to go see Louise. And, Johnny, see to it that Shinny behaves himself. She's to be the editor in charge and he has to accept that."

Lou Shinizer called himself a reporter; she called him many things but never that. In her opinion he was incapable of writing a yard-sale sign, and in fact he did little more than run around and pick up handouts from various sources, but someone had to do it. He fancied himself a ladies' man. She was certain Todd would swat him down fast. Shinny did not like to be swatted down.

That evening when Ruth Ann arrived home, she went straight to the kitchen to mix herself a tall glass of bourbon and ice water. Maria Bird was dicing onions, and she looked up as her husband Thomas Bird entered by the back door carrying a Jack Daniels' carton.

"What's that?" Maria asked.

At the same time Thomas Bird asked, "Where do you want me to put this?"

"With the others," Ruth Ann said, sitting down at the kitchen table. "Papers," she said to Maria. "And don't ask what kind because I don't know. Louise insisted that I stop by her house and pick up that stuff. She's fading away, Maria." Thomas Bird walked past them with the box.

"I know," Maria said. "And she's ready. But you have no business running around all day in this heat, or you'll be in the same shape she's in."

Maria was five feet two inches tall, stocky, with lustrous black hair done up in intricate braids laced with red ribbons. She had come to help out when Johnny was born, a teenage girl fresh out of high school. Leone had called her "the little Indian girl." He had left them all when Johnny was two, as if he had fulfilled his duty here and it was time to move on. Maria had stayed. A few years later, Maria had brought Thomas Bird in to introduce him, almost as if asking permission to marry him. He was not much taller than she was, and powerfully built.

Ruth Ann had no illusions about who ran her household—they did. She had told them fifteen years earlier that she had named them in her will. They would get the house, Johnny would get the press. She had few if any secrets from Maria, and Maria, no doubt, shared everything she knew with Thomas Bird.

Sipping her drink while Maria prepared dinner, Ruth Ann told her about Todd and Barney. "Shaggy chestnut hair, big eyes like milk chocolate, and a brain. She'll come back on Sunday and start on Monday and Barney will see to things in Portland and come along in a couple of weeks. He's like a curly-haired boy, maybe a little younger than she is, or at least he looks younger. She's twenty-eight. They loved the house, but it needs to be cleaned."

Maria nodded; she would see to it.

"I reassured them," Ruth Ann continued, "that the Tildens will likely be away for years." Their daughter had been widowed by an accident that had left her partially paralyzed, and there were three young children. She knew the Tildens were not going to return to Brindle until the youngsters were grown. Ruth Ann sighed. One after another of her generation, leaving one way or another. Louise, whom she had gone to see in the nursing home, was eighty-eight, on her way out. She took another sip of her drink.

"Anyway, Louise insisted that I go over to the house and pick up that box. Deborah was supposed to bring it around weeks ago, but she's been too busy and kept forgetting. If I'm going to write the history of Brindle I need that material, Louise said. Strange to be so lucid, and she is, and so weak. She's entirely bedridden now."

Maria tightened her lips. It didn't pay to dwell on the natural order of things, she sometimes said, and didn't repeat it now, but Ruth Ann got the message and did not continue. She would write Louise's obit that weekend, have it ready. She would kill Lou Shinizer before she let him touch it.

From the kitchen table she could see that the sun had cleared the mountains, and shadows were forming out on the patio. She picked up her drink and walked to the door. "Can I do anything in here?" she asked. Maria said no, the way she always did. Ruth Ann went out to the patio and sat down again. The air had cooled rapidly as the sun moved on its westward track.

Seeing her old friend that day, knowing her end was so near, had stirred up too many memories, she mused. She had suddenly remembered with startling clarity the last time she had seen her father alive, sixty years ago. Stricken with pneumonia, he had struggled for breath under the oxygen tent they used in those days, only a few years before the penicillin that would have saved him. He had said something about the paper, or papers, save the paper…something. Today Louise had said almost the same thing: she had saved the papers.

After her father's funeral, Ruth Ann had gone back to Eugene, to the women's dorm to pack up her belongings and go home again, to take charge of the press, to save the paper. She had worked with her father from the time she was a child and knew exactly what had to be done, while her mother was totally ignorant of every aspect of it.

For years after that, she had lived with her mother in their little house on Spruce Street, two blocks from the Bolton Building that her father had built to house the newspaper. And then Leone had entered her life. She smiled faintly. She had been thirty-eight, in love for the first time, captivated by a pretty face and a charming accent. Leone had done two good things: fathered a child, and built the house Ruth Ann lived in now. A good house, he had said, a Mediterranean house, stucco, with a red tile roof, and wide overhangs to keep out the summer sun, let in the winter light, spacious rooms, this semi-enclosed patio. She took a longer drink. Leone had believed she was wealthy, she had come to realize, and when he learned that she wasn't, he had pouted like a child. Johnny had his beautiful eyes and some of the same gestures, which she didn't understand. He had no memory of his father, how could he have learned those gestures? One of those riddles jealously guarded by the genes. She finished her drink.

She brought her thoughts back to the question of papers. After her mother died, Ruth Ann had gone to Spruce Street to pack up the house, and she had found half a dozen boxes of papers that she had never known existed. Now she wondered if her father had told both of them to save the paper, or papers, and if her mother had done so without ever mentioning it. Ruth Ann had moved the boxes to one of the empty rooms and they were still there.

Three

Wednesday night, Todd was dreaming. The presses were running, newspapers shooting out like disks from toy guns, flying out randomly, falling in heaps here, there, everywhere. When she tried to catch one, it eluded her, and she ran around a cavernous room pulling switches, jabbing buttons, trying to stop the press gone wild. An arctic wind stirred the papers, blew them around in a blizzard that blinded her, threatened to smother her.

Abruptly she woke up, shivering uncontrollably, struggling with the sheet and thin coverlet on her bed. The room was freezing. Groping for the light switch, she sat up amid the tangle of bedding. She had turned off the air conditioner earlier and opened a window; now she wrapped the coverlet around her shoulders and crossed the room to close the window. She didn't even have a heavy robe, not in August, she thought in disgust. The air-conditioner control was set to Off; she turned it to Heat, but the cold was penetrating, unrelenting. She went to the bathroom and turned on the hot water in the tub. When she looked in the mirror, she saw that her lips were pale, not quite blue, but close, and she couldn't stop shaking. In the tub of hot water, gradually warming up, she decided she had to get out of this creepy hotel, go to the house that was to be her home for the next two years.

At first, she had been charmed by the hotel lobby, its vaulted ceiling, the intricate pattern of inlaid wood flooring, the marble counter at the registration desk, all turn-of-the-century elegance. But the suite she was in was not charming. Two small rooms that had seemed quaint, cozy and inviting had changed, become oppressive. Now this. Air-conditioning gone crazy, and no one to call at two-thirty in the morning.

She closed her eyes as the steam rose from the hot water. She wanted to be home with Barney, feel his warmth next to her, feel his arm over her, his legs pressing against hers. Realizing how close she was to tears, she shook her head angrily. Not her style. She missed him, and she was tired. That was all it amounted to, fatigue and loneliness.

Ruth Ann shivered and pulled the cover up higher, vaguely aware of Maria, who had entered her bedroom. Maria put an electric blanket over her and plugged it in, then sat in a nearby chair, wrapped in her own woolen blanket. Ruth Ann slid back into a dream-laden sleep. She was examining the newspaper with a screaming banner headline: Murder. She looked at the text, but it dissolved into a blank white space before she could focus on it. She turned the page; again the text melted into whiteness when she tried to read it. She could see pages of dense, crisp black text on white, but wherever she paused and tried to read, the text vanished. "I can't see it, Dad," she said plaintively.

"I didn't have time to write it," he said from somewhere behind her. When she turned to look at him, he vanished just as the print had done.

"Hush, Ruth Ann. Hush," Maria whispered. "Go back to sleep now."

Gradually the warmth of the blanket stilled her shaking, and she slipped deeper into sleep. When she woke up again, the electric blanket was gone and her room was pleasantly warm. She tried without success to recall her dreams, gave it up, and reflected instead on the miracle Todd had wrought. This week's newspaper was fine, perfect, the way it should be, and she had told Todd to take the day off, to relax and get some rest, exactly what she herself intended to do. She felt as if she had run a marathon, which in a sense was what they had done over the past three days.

Todd checked out that morning, loaded her bags into the Acura, and then went to the newspaper to look over the computer programs. Once there, she stopped by Johnny's office. His door was open and she tapped lightly and entered. He beamed at her.

"I thought you were taking the day off," he said. "You deserve it."

"I am. I just wanted to get an idea of what all was installed on the computer. It's a real mess, jumbled with stuff you don't need, and missing a few things that you do. You really should have a firewall and a better utilities program. I'm going to have to uninstall just about everything down to the operating system and then reinstall things. It would be best if I do that after office hours. If you have no objection I'll network my laptop into the system, back up everything onto it, and do a lot of the work at home and try not to disrupt things here while I'm at it."

He spread his hands. "Say no more. Todd, whatever it needs, do it. Blanket permission, no questions asked. Good enough?" He grinned at her. "Just don't tell me about it."

She laughed and turned away from the door, paused and said, "Good enough. Is this place locked up tight after hours?"

"I'll get another key and drop it off at the hotel for you."

She shook her head. "I'm moving into the Tilden house today. I have to see to the electricity and phone, transfer them to our name, things like that. I'll drop by here later and pick up the key."

Mildred, the round-faced woman who handled the classifieds, smiled broadly at Todd when she left Johnny's doorway. "You've put him in the best mood he's had in months," Mildred said in a low voice. "Good job."

Toni, the accountant, nodded and mouthed the same words: "Good job."

Todd felt buoyed when she left the building and looked around. "Good job," she repeated to herself, pleased with the praise, with her acceptance. "It really is going to work," she said under her breath.

She took her time getting to her new home, winding in and out of the streets slowly. Back here, away from the highway, it was a pretty little town, with neat houses and yards, not a lot of greenery, but not desert, either. That changed as she drove north on one of the streets, where the houses ended and the desert took over. It was about another half mile to North Crest Loop; although the street had been finished all the way to it, building had stopped, and the continuation of the street was in poor repair. Scattered pine trees had achieved mature growth, and there was a lot of sage and rank grasses. It was like that on Juniper, her street, and apparently that way on all of them, as if the planners had anticipated development to continue north. Instead, it had moved south, on the other side of Brindle Creek, and east on the other side of the highway, leaving this end of town barren. There was a park along the creek front, a block wide, several blocks long with shade trees, picnic tables, a playground. Children were playing there now, a few women were on benches chatting.

Brindle, she had learned, had been named after the small stream that bisected the town. Joe Warden had ridden this far and stopped when his horse, a brindled mare, went lame. The stream, no more than ten feet across and shallow, flashed silver against black and brown lava, colored like his horse. He called it Brindle Creek, and years later, when the town was incorporated, the name stuck. There was a footbridge at the park, and she had heard there was another one up farther. She had not seen it yet.

It didn't take long to explore the town. She headed for her house, repeated it under her breath, "Her house." She loved it—the juniper paneling, polished plank floors, bay windows, fireplaces in two rooms.... But she had to buy opaque shades for the bedroom—Barney woke up if any light hit his eyes—and dishes, a few at least until their stuff was delivered, sheets to last until they got their own, a towel or two.... Wandering through the house, she made a list, and then headed for Bend, a discount store, the utility company, telephone company....

It was nearly five when she returned to the office, and very hot again. She was not sweating, to her surprise, and realized that the air was so arid that perspiration must evaporate as fast as it formed. She felt parched.

Johnny was chatting with another man in the outer office when she entered. "Todd," Johnny said, smiling, "I was beginning to think you'd gotten lost in the great metropolis of Bend. Come meet our doctor. Sam Rawleigh, everyone's doctor in these parts. Todd Fielding."

Dr. Rawleigh was tall and very handsome, like a television personality or a movie actor. Dark wavy hair, touched with grey at the temples, regular features, even a square chin with a slight cleft. As a young man he must have been a knockout, she thought, shaking hands. Now, fifty-something, he was still one of the handsomest men she had ever met. His eyes were dark brown, eyebrows with enough of an arch to suggest flirtatiousness, and a tan that was so smooth and even it looked like a salon tan.

"Todd, I've been listening to your praises," he said. "But no one mentioned that you are also beautiful. It's a pleasure."

She felt the heat rise on her cheeks. God, she thought, he must have to fight off his female patients with a baseball bat.

"We were on our way across the street for a drink," Dr. Rawleigh said. "Join us."

She started to shake her head, and he added, "What I prescribe for you is an iced double espresso. You look as if you've had quite a day in heat you haven't yet become accustomed to."

"Good heavens!" she said. "That sounds irresistible. Just like that, you talked me into it."

"I'll pick up that key for you," Johnny said, and strolled back to his office.

They crossed the street and sat under an awning at Carl's Café, where Todd could smell pine trees, desert and heat. She hadn't realized heat had its own particular odor, but she was certain that was what she sniffed in the dry air. Both men ordered beer and she had her espresso, then sighed with contentment at her first sip. Just right.

"You didn't like our hotel?" Dr. Rawleigh asked after taking a long drink.

"It isn't that," she said. "I want to get the house in order, get settled—but I have to admit that having the air conditioner go crazy in the middle of the night was not a real inducement to try another night there."

"It wasn't the air conditioner," Johnny said. "We get a crazy inversion or something now and then and a blanket of cold air settles over the whole area, then dissipates after a time."

"In August?"

"Any month. No one has really explained it, but it happens."

"Have you felt the water in the creek?" Dr. Rawleigh asked. "It's like ice water year round. Up at Warm Springs it comes out hot, here it's ice water. The inversion is sort of like that—except that it's air, not water. The volcanoes around here are strange, not like other mountains. That frigid air mass has been happening ever since I've been around, off and on, unpredictable. I was here for months before I experienced one. You're here less than a week and there it is. Go figure."

"Surely a meteorologist can explain it," Todd said. "I never felt cold air like that before in my life."

"We've had a couple come in," Johnny said, "and nothing happens. They leave again thinking we're all balmy. We're okay. This land is what's crazy."

He laughed. "For a good look at our crazy land, some time after the weather cools a bit, you and your husband should take a day hike up to the creek head," Dr. Rawleigh said. "Great view from up there. It's a good hike, five or six miles up and back. Up Crest Loop to a narrow bridge, and take the left road, a dirt road. The Loop winds on around a while, past my place, and eventually back down to the highway, but the dirt road turns into a trail up a ways and eventually you'll come to a big boulder, and gushing out from under it is where Brindle Creek begins. It isn't a difficult hike, but watch out for rattlesnakes. They're up there this time of year. Anyway, it's dry as a bone above the boulder, nothing to indicate that it's the source of pure ice water. You can fill your water bottles, perfectly safe up there. You don't want to do that down farther, but it starts out absolutely pure. The creek comes tumbling down the terraces, through town, under the highway bridge, and on for another mile or two and then takes a dive. Gone."

"What do you mean, gone? Gone where?"

"Underground. The Great Basin is jealous. No water that goes in ever gets out again. Just the way it is."

"Curiouser and curiouser," Todd said. She finished her espresso and picked up her purse. "I have to be going. It's nice meeting you, Dr. Rawleigh. Thanks for the prescription. It was exactly right."

"Please," he said. "Just Sam. The little kids call me Dr. Rawleigh because their moms make them, then it turns into Dr. Sam, and before you know it, just plain old Sam. We're all on first names here, even us outsiders."

"You're an outsider?"

"Going on twenty-one years now. Came, married a local girl, stayed, but I'm an outsider. An observer. You get used to it."

Although Johnny looked a little uncomfortable, he did not dispute the doctor's words. He shrugged and waved to the waitress for the check, and Todd left them at the table, bemused. So far everyone had treated her exactly the way she would have expected, kindly, with friendliness, without a trace of suspicion or distrust.

That night she called Barney and told him about her day and he told her about his, then said huskily, "The movers will come on Tuesday, and the minute they're out the door, so am I."

Just as huskily she said, "Good. Then I will try to be patient and not run away with the handsome doctor."

When she hung up, she closed her eyes tight and drew in a long breath. She had never been so lonesome in her life.

Four

"And on your left, is the one and only Coombs greenhouse where at this very moment an acre of tomatoes is getting sunburned, or sun dried, or something. The Coombs girls are both in their sixties." Todd was the tour guide, pointing out the must-see sights to Barney as they strolled. They had been there a month, but this was the first weekend free of settling-in chores. "I have to take pictures at their mother's funeral, at least at the cemetery, on Monday. Half the county will be there, according to Ruth Ann." Sobering, she said. "Ruth Ann wrote a very touching obituary. She's really a fine writer. Anyway, coming up on the right is Miss Lizzy's gift shop, where you will find plates with the map of Oregon, Chief Joseph's last stand, some of the loveliest carved or sculpted birds I've ever seen, a rendition of the Oregon Trail on bark—" She frowned at Barney, who had started to laugh.

"Sir, this is a serious business."

"You're babbling."

"I know. You have to remember that as one of four children, and just a girl, no one ever paid any attention to anything I said, so I stopped saying much of anything until I found you— Oh, look. There's Sam's Explorer. He's going into the rock shop. Come on, you can meet him. The owner is Jacko. No last name. Just Jacko." She hurried him along.

During the past month, she had made it a point to enter every business establishment in town and introduce herself. Her cause, she had explained to Barney, was to be known so that if anything happened, someone would think to tell her. Also, she had said, Shinny, their star reporter, didn't know the difference between a grocery list and a news story. So far the most compelling bit of news he had reported had been the town-council meeting; they were debating where on the highway to put a traffic light. North end of town, or at Crest Loop? The debate, she had added, had been raging for two years.

Jacko's shop was a single room with aisles barely wide enough to maneuver in, crowded on both sides by bins of rocks, baskets of rocks, a long counter so cluttered with rocks there was never enough space to fill out a receipt, a showcase filled with cut and polished rocks, and another one with rocks that had been carved, inset into wooden frames, rested on black pedestals, or simply tumbled about. An agate-framed clock said nine fifteen, and always said nine fifteen, but its snowflake agate was beautiful. It was dark blue with white flecks that looked adrift throughout. In the rear of the shop was a workbench crowded with lapidary equipment.

When Todd and Barney entered the shop, Sam was leaning

on the counter, where he and Jacko were examining something. Both men looked up.

"Hi," Todd said. "This is Barney. My husband." After the introductions, they all looked at a geode on the counter. The hollow rock was as big as a grapefruit, and had been cut into two pieces.

"I never saw one that big," Todd said. "It's awesome." It was neatly halved, the cavity filled with glittering crystals of quartz streaked with pale blue. She looked at Jacko. "Is it for sale?"

"Ask him," Jacko said, jerking his thumb at Sam. "He found it and sawed it open. He brings in stuff like that to rile me." Jacko was short, no more than five feet five, and his head was totally bald, but he had a great beard with enough hair that if it had been amply divided between his pate and his chin there would have been hair left over.

Barney was examining the geode. "Wow, that is a beauty. How did you manage to saw it like that?"

Two big crystals had been split almost exactly in half, and the cut edges smoothed and polished to a mirror finish.

"Just luck," Sam said. "No way of knowing what you're going to find until you open one of them, and I happened to hit it right. I thought I'd have them made into bookends, juniper wood, curved like a wave breaking with these set in. If Thomas Bird will carve the stands, they'll make a pretty pair."

"A fantastic pair," Barney said. "Where did you find it?"

Jacko snorted and Sam grinned, then said, "Does a fisherman tell where he caught the fifteen-pound trout? Out there." He waved his hand generally toward the vast desert.

"You have equipment to cut rocks and polish them, all that?" Todd asked.

Jacko made his peculiar snort of laughter again. "He's got stuff that makes mine look like a kid's first tool kit." He motioned to Todd to follow and started to move away, saying, "He had to build a special room to house his equipment. Look, I got some new crystals in last week."

While she looked at the new crystals, Barney and Sam chatted about the desert and rock hounds. "It gets in the blood," Sam said. "You always think that next time you'll find something even better, or you find a streak and have to force yourself to leave it, hoping no one else will come along before you get back to it. Come up to the house sometime, let me show you my collection."

Todd shook her head at Jacko. "I'm waiting for a clearance sale." Turning to Sam she said, "We took that hike last weekend, up to the start of the creek. It's beautiful up there. Thanks for telling me about it." She glanced at her watch. "We should be going," she said to Barney. They were on their way for a cookout with Jan and Seth MacMichaels.

Outside again, heading toward the manufactured houses where Jan and Seth lived, she said, "Chief Ollie Briscoe began calling Seth Sonny, and now almost everyone does, and he hates it. So don't call him Sonny."

"I wouldn't have thought of it until you told me not to. Now, I don't know. What if it pops out?"

"Ollie also said he's a loaded gun looking for someone to shoot. So watch it. That's all I can say."

They both laughed. Jan worked at Safeway and Seth was fulfilling a two-year contract as a police officer in Brindle, his first job after finishing police academy. Eventually he wanted to work as a investigator for the state police, she told Barney, but he was too young and green, and with the budget cuts they had endured, the department wasn't hiring anyway.

It was unfortunate, Todd thought a few minutes later, but Seth did look like someone who should be called Sonny. He was tall and broad, built like a football player, a high-school varsity player, with a lot of reddish-blond hair, a big open face, and candid blue eyes. He was sunburned, as if he never really tanned, but burned again and again. His nose was peeling. Jan was dimply and cute with masses of dark curly hair, heavy eye makeup, and a Barbie-doll figure.

They were seated under an awning at the rear of the house that was radiating heat, as was the concrete slab of a deck. "Bake in the summer, freeze in the winter," Jan said. "I can't tell you how jealous I was when I heard you got a real house. It wasn't available when we were looking." She took a long drink of beer from a can. Seth was grilling buffalo burgers. "When we get back out in the real world," she said, "I intend to go back to school. I think it's terrific that you've hung in there like you have."

"To study what?" Barney asked.

"I don't know. Something to do with people. No computers, and no numbers."

Barney grinned and held up his beer can in a salute. "My sentiments exactly."

"These are about ready," Seth said. "Hon, you want to bring out that tray?"

Jan stood up and went inside, came back with a tray of salads from Safeway. "Chow," she said. "I hope you don't mind store salad. It's too hot in there to cook. Thank God, it's not as hot as last month, and by this time next month we'll be freezing. That's Brindle for you."

After a bite or two of the buffalo burger, Todd said it was delicious. "Have you given up on beef?"

"Not if it's local," Seth said. He told them about a butcher shop out of Bend, local beef only. "If it comes from Grace Rawleigh's ranch, you know it's going to be great. Have you met her yet? She's a direct descendant of the town's founder, Joe Warden."

They hadn't. "You're in for a treat," Jan said with more than a touch of malice. "And now that her daughter Lisa's in town for a visit, it's like a two-scooper treat."

Seth gave her a stern look and she grinned and shrugged. "Just repeating what I've heard. I haven't met Lisa," she said to Todd. "But from talk I hear at the store, she's a bundle of fun. A ballbuster, if you get what I mean."

Seth put his can down. "Jan, cut it out."

"Okay. I'll keep it clean. She and her ex are having a big fight over the spoils of a divorce, her third. From what I've heard, Lisa doesn't feel like she's met a man until she's slept with him. And she's a serial marrier who believes in marital freedom." She rolled her eyes and grinned at Seth. "Clean enough?"

"Jesus," he muttered. Before Jan could say more, he said, "Lisa lives down in L.A. She's into movies, maybe produces or directs, something like that, not as an actress. She comes back every few years for a visit and sometimes, they tell me, there's trouble while she's here. And that's all we know about her." He gave Jan a warning look.

For a moment she met his look with an expression of defiance. Then she averted her gaze. "Plus she has mysterious plans for Brindle. She's thirty-five. And that's really all we know about her."

But it wasn't all, Todd thought. A new tension was in the air, the silence uncomfortable. "Are Sam and Grace still married?" she asked. "They don't seem to live together."

"They don't," Jan said promptly. "He lives in that big ugly stone house on Crest Loop, the one that looks like a gargoyle looming over the town. It's Grace's house but she hangs out at the ranch when she isn't traveling. She's gone a lot and hardly ever gets over here except to lay down the law about this or that. The hotel is hers, too. There's a general manager or something who runs it. Mort Cline."

"It seems to me that in such a small community, where everyone knows all about everyone else, there shouldn't be any crime to speak of or any need to lay down the law," Barney said.

Seth kept his gaze on a bun he was slathering with mustard as he said, "Just last week I had to break up a brawl. Three eight-year-olds in the park going at it. And yesterday I had to go tell an old man to stop burning trash outside. A real crime wave." He put a burger on the bun and bit into it.

"Aha, so there's more to Brindle than meets the eye," Barney commented.

Jan looked at him, suddenly all traces of cuteness gone, her eyes narrowed, her face pinched. "Brindle is rotten to the core," she said. "There's something really foul about this place. I hate it!"

Seth put his hand on her arm and she drew back. "Sorry. Anyone, more beer?"

Walking home later, Todd asked, "What did you make of them?"

"Cute couple."

"Come on, don't be coy."

He had his arm around her waist and hers was around him, but when they turned off First Street, lit with street lamps and shop windows, onto darker Juniper, his hand slid down to rest on her buttock. He said he liked to feel her muscles as she moved.

"Okay. She's miserable, and he's chomping at the bit, bored out of his skull. Enough?"

"More," she said. "Something to do with Lisa. I guess we're too new to let us in on whatever it is. Are you bored here?"

"No time to be bored."

She believed that. He was working hard, and to her eye he was more contented than she had ever seen him.

"What about you?" he asked.

"No time," she said. "Since the newspaper is in pretty good shape now, I'll also be working with Ruth Ann on the centennial edition. Scanning stuff, enhancing old photographs. My kind of thing. And tomorrow we'll meet the alluring Lisa and Grace. I'll be watching you, kiddo. No funny stuff."

He laughed and squeezed her bottom.

Seth scraped dishes as Jan loaded the dishwasher. "You can't leave it alone, can you?" he asked, opening a can of beer.

"I thought he should be warned, or maybe she should be. Whatever."

"You know nothing happened."

"Not her fault."

"Jesus, let's drop it."

They had been in Brindle three months when he'd seen a Corvette, speeding on the highway, make a squealing turn onto First and drive into the hotel parking lot. He had followed, and the memory of the encounter was still vivid.

"Miss, may I see your driver's license?" he had asked the young woman walking toward the lobby. He already had his ticket book in his hand.

She stopped and turned, a thin young woman, blond, blue-eyed, who looked him over, then smiled slightly. "I'm afraid I don't have it with me," she said. "Are you the new policeman? Are you going to arrest me?" She held out her hands, as if waiting for handcuffs, smiling. "Or maybe we could go somewhere and talk it over. Privately."

He backed up a step, her invitation as blatant as a prostitute's in any red-light district. He felt his face flushing, heating. Then Ollie Briscoe, the chief, came from the lobby.

"What's the problem?" he asked, drawing near them.

"He's going to arrest me," Lisa said. "Take me to a back room somewhere and...interrogate me." She kept her gaze on Seth, her smile deepening.

"She was doing sixty coming into town, fifty pulling in the lot," Seth said.

Ollie Briscoe waved him away. "You run along, Sonny. I'll handle this."

"Sonny," Lisa said. "How adorable. I'll be seeing you, Sonny." She gave him another long appraising look, nodded, and repeated, "I'll be seeing you."

He had avoided her for the several days that she was in town, and now here she was back again. He took a long drink from his can, wishing that he had not told Jan about the incident. Her comment had been that if Lisa got anywhere near him, Jan would pull every hair out of Lisa's head one by one, either before or after she scratched out her eyes.

Five

The alluring Lisa was a disappointment, Todd decided when they met at Ruth Ann's house on Sunday. Lisa was too thin, brittle in a curious way with jerky movements, and if her jeans had been any tighter, she would have been immobilized. She had on high-heeled boots and a red silk shirt that could have been buttoned higher. Her hair was bottle platinum-blond, styled in a way that was meant to suggest no styling, pulled back over her ears, unevenly cut. When she met Barney, she held his hand too long and swayed toward him, moved in too close.

"Do you ride?" she asked. Her voice was low, throaty.

He extracted his hand, shaking his head. "Nope. Never was on a horse in my life."

"What a shame. You'd be so handsome on a horse."

Todd suppressed a smile as Barney moved out of Lisa's range. She realized that Jan had been warning them about Lisa. But

Grace Rawleigh, Lisa's mother, was the real shock, she thought. She looked much older than Sam, and she was fighting it. Her hair was strawberry blond and carefully styled. Todd suspected more than one face-lift in her past, and the makeup she wore did little to hide the lines at her eyes or the vertical grooves on her forehead, and nothing at all for the look of disapproval that turned her mouth down. She smiled briefly at Todd, but the smile did not get beyond her thin lips.

Todd was relieved to see Johnny's wife enter the living room. She liked Carol Colonna, a comfortable, handsome woman who had a very successful real-estate business in Bend. Carol smiled at her, then said, "Maria says brunch is up and waiting in the dining room."

Ruth Ann was watching her guests with an amused expression. She had seen Lisa's pass at Barney, and Todd's dismissal of it as well as Barney's polite withdrawal. And she liked the way Todd had behaved, like a well-bred, confident young woman. She knew Sam had watched his stepdaughter go into her act with annoyance. But Sam was always annoyed with Lisa, and usually did not even try to conceal it. He and Grace had exchanged brief nods when she had arrived, as if of recognition, and that was that. At least Grace had not found a reason to yell at him. That would have been awkward. Families, she thought, and led the way into the dining room.

She had told Maria to keep it simple, but Maria had done exactly as she pleased. Planked salmon, thin slices of beef in a sauce in a chafing dish, spiced shrimp, fruit salad, green salad, a platter of cheeses... It didn't matter. The leftovers would make a good dinner. The food was on a long table, buffet style, and they started to help themselves.

"You'll have to come out to the ranch," Lisa was saying to Barney, her hand on his arm. "I'll teach you to ride. We'll have a real western barbecue. Next Saturday. Okay?"

He grinned and shook his head, moving as he did on down the buffet. "Thanks, but I'm afraid not. I'll be in Corvallis until late Sunday."

"Another time," she said. "I'll get you out there and on a horse. You'll see."

He filled his plate and went to the dining table where he sat next to Todd.

Johnny seated himself next to Lisa at the round table. "When do we announce it?" he asked her.

"You mean formally? As in the newspaper? Or just start a rumor?"

"Formally," he said, turning to Todd and Barney. "We're talking about turning Brindle into a destination resort. I'm building the mountain resort, and Lisa and Grace are considering a new hotel across the creek from Warden House. We'll have wilderness hikes, skiing in winter, desert treks."

"A mammoth heated swimming pool, a water slide, a wave machine," Lisa said. "Live music, a dance floor. And we'll have a dude ranch out at the ranch. We'll coordinate it all, have a theme destination resort. We'll put Brindle on the map." She picked at her food, but ate little. "I'm all for putting up false fronts on the buildings on First Street, and maybe on Spruce, too, to recreate an old western town. I still think we should have horses in the park." She put her fork down and said, "Llamas! We'll have to use llamas as pack animals for the wilderness hikes. People love llamas!"

"You'll have a part to play," Johnny said to Todd. "We'll need brochures, fancy proposals, all sorts of things. We'll work that out at the press."

"Don't be ridiculous!" Lisa said. "We'll need a real ad agency. I know just who to get when we're ready."

Todd felt Barney's leg nudging hers, and on the other side of her Sam said, "Last time Lisa was in town she had a scheme to bottle water and start a business to compete with Evian. Now it's Disney in her crosshairs."

Lisa gave him a contemptuous look. "Some of us have visions, dreams. This hellhole of a town is going to shrink down to nothing and blow away in the wind unless someone does something. Not that it would be a great loss."

Sam put his napkin on the table and stood up. "Thanks, Ruth Ann. Marvelous brunch as usual. But I have a patient I'm monitoring closely. I have to run."

He nodded at the others and walked out. For a moment there was silence, then Carol began to tell Grace about a new development being planned on the outskirts of Bend.

A little while later, Todd felt Barney's hand take hers under the table, and squeeze three distinct and separate times. She suppressed a smile and returned the signal. They did not linger much longer.

When they left, Lisa and Johnny were huddled talking and Ruth Ann looked tired, or perhaps simply bored. Grace and Carol had begun to talk about a dude ranch in a way that implied Grace was serious about it.

The day was pleasantly cool. They had walked up, and now took their time walking down Ruth Ann's winding drive to Crest Loop. The road was narrow, with a gorge on one side, and the mountain rising like basalt stair steps meant for a giant on the other. At a curve before the footbridge, there was a view of the entire town, pretty and postcard peaceful. The creek, fifteen feet down, tumbled and splashed over rocks in a little waterfall, causing a spray that glittered like diamonds in the sunlight.

"What did you make of them?" Todd asked.

"Grace is an embittered woman," Barney said. "You didn't feel anything around Lisa, did you?"

"Like what?"

"Or sense anything either, I guess," he said. "You don't have the right receptors. She walks in a cloud of pheromones. And she knows it."

"Well, there's no love lost in that family, that's for sure," Todd said. "I don't think Sam even spoke to Grace. And you saw the look Lisa gave him."

They reached the footbridge and crossed the rushing creek, on its way to nowhere, she thought. All that busy rushing only to vanish in the desert. "Do you think they'll carry through with plans for a resort here?"

"No idea." He laughed and took her hand. "But no matter, you're out of it. She wants a real ad agency."

"And you would look handsome on a horse."

He laughed harder. Then he said, "I wonder why Ruth Ann invited us."

"She said so that we could meet a few more people," Todd said after a moment.

He said, "Um," in a noncommittal way. "Well, this life in the fast lane, high society, upper-crust brunches, it's taking a toll. I feel a nap coming on."

They were skirting the park where some boys were flying kites.

"Why are we walking so fast?" Todd asked.

"All those pheromones floating around. They gave me ideas."

This time she laughed.

After Grace and Lisa left, while Carol helped Maria carry dishes to the kitchen, Johnny turned to Ruth Ann. "Why did you invite Todd and Barney? You knew I wanted some time with you and Lisa. We have to talk about this idea."

"I got the impression that it was all settled. Is there anything in writing yet?"

"No. This is preliminary, the planning stage. We'll get to that."

Carol came back and picked up the last chafing dish. "I won't be long," she said to Johnny. "I want to get that shrimp recipe."

When she was out of the room again, Ruth Ann said, "Johnny, just a suggestion. Watch your step. Don't get too wound up with Lisa."

He stiffened. "What exactly does that mean?"

"I think you know as well as I do what I mean." For a moment neither of them moved, then he jerked around, faced away from her. "I know, Johnny. I've always known. And I know what it did to you before."

"We might become business associates, Mother. Nothing more than that. Business."

"Good," she murmured. "I'll see if I'm needed in the kitchen."

If she had been honest, Ruth Ann reflected after all her guests had left, she would have told Johnny that she had invited

Barney and Todd to protect him. She smiled slightly as she imagined his indignant reply. But it would have been truthful. She had seen Barney and Todd together enough times to consider Barney safe from Lisa, but she was not at all certain Johnny was. Lisa had snared him once when she was twenty and he was single and twenty-seven, home from college, home from a couple of years of knocking around, uncertain what he intended to do. He would have followed her to California, Ruth Ann knew, but Lisa had met an actor and no longer had time for Johnny. He had been devastated, possibly suicidal for a time. Within a year, he and Carol were married with a child on the way.

It was a good marriage, she knew, and Johnny was a faithful husband. But then there was Lisa. And she had gravitated to Barney as a filing to a magnet, just as Ruth Ann had suspected she would. Ruth Ann had seen her eyeing Barney speculatively as she picked at her food, and even later, gushing about plans for Brindle, she had kept an eye on him. Lisa probably wouldn't linger more than a week or two, she rarely did, and although she might be planning a campaign to add Barney to her collection, he was safe. Todd would see to that even if he wavered.

Briefly she wondered how Lisa reacted if she failed to bag her catch. More uneasily, she wondered if Lisa had ever failed. She was glad that Barney would be away most of the coming week.

Six

After the mourners began to drift away from the cemetery Monday morning, Todd lingered to stroll among the grave markers, some fairly elaborate, more of them modest stone or even wood. The wooden ones were weathering badly, most of the words illegible on many of them. A harsh wind was blowing out of the north, and she was cold, but she didn't want to join the caravan of cars crawling along back to Brindle.

The cemetery was bleak, with a few clumps of sage, some tough-looking grass, shards of black obsidian gleaming in the sun, and a spray or two of plastic flowers on some of the graves. A marble headstone marked the grave of Michael Hilliard. Next to it was a smaller marble headstone: Jane Marie Hilliard, 1862–1888, then: Rachel Emmaline Hilliard, 1878–1880.

Todd gazed at the tombstones sadly. To lose a child only two years old must have been tragic. Jane Hilliard had been only sixteen when her child was born, only twenty-six when she herself had died. How lonesome it must have been out here a hundred years ago, just the desert, a few people in the way station, an occasional traveler.

The wind whipped a piece of paper past the graves, sent it skittering into a clump of sage where it clung for a second or two before it was released and blew off into the distance. Todd shivered, turned and left the cemetery. Warmer clothes, she was thinking, which meant a shopping trip on Thursday. High on her list was a warm hat, one she could pull down over her ears.

Ruth Ann was shivering when Thomas Bird stopped the car to let her and Maria out at the front door of the house. Thomas Bird drove on around to put the car in the garage.

"Coffee," Ruth Ann said inside the house. "Strong and hot." She started to walk toward the kitchen, but Maria took her elbow and turned her toward the hall.

"You go lay down and cover up. I'll put on coffee and start some lunch." Maria was dressed in her formal clothes, a long black dress and a heavy black woolen shawl. Today the ribbons in her braided hair were also black. She looked as broad as she was tall, but she was warm.

"Todd's coming up with some pictures," Ruth Ann said, yielding to the tug on her arm. "I won't go to bed now, but I do want coffee. Let's have lunch after she's gone. Point her to the sitting room when she comes."

Maria looked surprised, then nodded. Very few people were ever allowed in Ruth Ann's sitting room. "I'll bring coffee when it's ready, and a cup for her. She looked frozen out there."

"It's the wind," Ruth Ann said.

Maria agreed. "Change of season. It will blow awhile and settle down again. Summer isn't done yet. Go on now. I'll be in directly."

Ruth Ann often thought of her house in a phrase her mother had used in the distant past: preacher-ready. Maria kept the large living room preacher-ready, the sofa, several chairs, a coffee table, end tables, all so clean they looked unused, and practically were unused, forever ready for the preacher. She entered her sitting room, and it was what the entire house would be like if left to her. The room was cluttered, with books, magazines, photographs of her two grandsons, of Johnny at every stage of his life, his and Carol's wedding pictures, Maria and Thomas Bird's wedding, odds and ends various people had given Ruth Ann over the years. A snow-scene paperweight, vases, ashtrays that she actually used now and then, a few very good paintings on the walls, an assortment of polished rocks from Sam, half a dozen beautifully carved birds, a gift from Thomas Bird. She had brought her old school desk to the house and it was in the sitting room, heaped with papers and photographs she had been sorting through. Her kind of room, she thought, sinking into a reclining chair bathed in sunlight. Leone had been right about the windows. From now until spring, the sun would enter this room and it was welcome.

After a few minutes she stood up, took off her coat and tossed it on a chair. Maria came in with coffee and arranged a carafe and cups beside the recliner, drew another chair closer, poured one cup of coffee, and on her way out picked up the coat. Ruth Ann knew that Maria would have this room preacher-ready in a minute if she permitted it.

When Todd arrived, she gasped at the room. She loved Ruth Ann's house, but she had always thought it was almost too neat and tidy; in contrast, this room was perfect. She hoped she would be allowed in another time when she could linger and examine every object. She suspected that a story lay behind each one of them. "Your parents?" she asked, pointing to a studio portrait of a man and woman stiffly posed, unsmiling. The portrait was in an oval, carved metal frame, the glass bowed slightly.

Ruth Ann nodded. "Why do you suppose they always seated the man and had the woman stand in those old portraits? And they never smiled, did they? My mother was very beautiful."

"I can tell," Todd said. "Even without a smile, she's lovely."

She began to unpack her laptop. After she had it plugged in and positioned on an end table, they looked at the pictures she had taken with her digital camera at the cemetery. "I thought you would be able to see them better on the monitor than on the small camera screen. After you decide which one you want, I'll put up the front-page layout with it in place."

"You have the newspaper on your little computer?"

"Not really. Just on a CD, a compact disk. That's how I can work at home. And the laptop is small, but it has even more room on the hard drive and more power than the computers in the office."

Ruth Ann was impressed. She had known that Todd did much of her work at home, but she had assumed it was on a standard computer like hers at the office. She picked out the funeral picture to go with the obituary, and watched as Todd slid in a CD and opened a screen with the front page, then added the new picture. It looked like magic.

After Todd left, and lunch was over with, Ruth Ann thought again about how Todd was able to take old faded photographs and do whatever she did with them to make them as sharp and clear as if they had just been taken. The photograph of Louise when she was a teacher at the one-room school, faded, yellowed and brittle with age, had come to life again with Todd's tricks. No wonder the new generation loved their toys, she mused.

But she was really thinking of the photographs she had come across in Louise Coombs's box. She had a box just about like that of her own, as well as whatever her mother had preserved of her father's papers. At first she had been thinking of no more than a simple print special edition for the centennial, perhaps a one-page insert, but she was reconsidering. Old pictures of the town as it had been, from its first days on. The people who had lived here, even letters… Todd said she could scan anything on paper, digitize it, enhance it, reproduce it.

Second by second, a much more elaborate special edition was reforming in Ruth Ann's mind.

Usually Todd and Barney cooked dinner together, but since Monday, Tuesday and Wednesday were her only really busy days, on those nights he most often made dinner and had it ready when she got home. That night, chilled again by the strong wind, she entered the house, then called out, "Fe, fi, fo, fum. That smells good and I want some."

"Maniac," he said from the kitchen. "Lasagna, ten minutes. Wash your hands."

They ate at the kitchen table and she told him about the funeral. "There must have been a couple hundred people there. And I was freezing. That wind was brutal today."

"I know. I walked down to Safeway. We need to get out our winter gear. Summer or winter here, no in-between apparently. Guess who I saw at Safeway."

"I give already. Who?"

"Miss Sexpot herself. She wanted me to buy her a cup of coffee, to warm her up, she said."

"Oh dear," Todd said. "You'll have to come by the office to borrow my whip and chair."

"I told her I was mentally conjugating Greek verbs and couldn't be distracted. You might try that line with Shinizer. It worked with the sexpot."

"Two problems," she said, shaking her head. "He wouldn't know what conjugating means, and he doesn't know a verb from a velocipede. Anyway, after I told him that what he claims is friendliness the law considers sexual harassment, he hasn't come within ten feet of me. Deal. You take care of the sexpot and I'll take care of the bum. I can, you know."

"I know you can, tiger. Deal. What's a velocipede?"

Grinning, she said, "It's a two-wheeled horse that little boys rode in Victorian novels."

He looked doubtful and she laughed and started to clear the table.

Todd was dreaming. She was standing on a vast dun-colored plain with not a landmark in sight, no grasses, no rocks, nothing, just the endless plain. A strong wind was blowing granules of ice at her and no matter how she twisted and turned, they kept blasting her in the face. She ducked her head and tried to protect her face, her eyes, but the wind was too strong. "Don't cry," she told herself. "Don't cry." Tears would freeze on her cheeks.

"Todd! Wake up!"

"Don't cry," she whimpered, struggling against the wind, weeping.

"Todd! Come on, wake up."

She jerked awake with Barney's hands on her shoulders. She was shaking with cold.

"A door must have blown open," he said. "Where's another blanket?"

She couldn't stop shaking. "Closet shelf." She pointed and pulled the covers tighter around herself. Barney hurried to the closet and yanked another blanket from the shelf, wrapped it around her. He was shivering, too.

"I'll go close the door. Be right back." Pulling on his robe, he left the room. She huddled under the covers, drew herself up into a ball, and realized that she was weeping, her face was wet. Even with the covers over her head, she couldn't stop shivering, and she couldn't stop crying.

Barney was back. "Come on," he said. "This bedroom is like an icebox. I put a log on the fire. We'll be warmer there."

He had moved the sofa in front of the fireplace, where a hot fire was blazing. They sat holding each other on the sofa, wrapped in a blanket, not talking. Gradually the warmth reached her and the shivering subsided, with only an occasional tremor coursing through her. Barney got up and left, returned with a box of tissues. "Are you okay?" he asked. At her nod, he said, "I'll make us some hot cocoa. Be right back."

She didn't know how long they sat on the sofa before the fire, sipping the sweet hot cocoa. Eventually they moved the blanket away, but they didn't get up.

Then, warm through and through, even sweating a little, she said, “There wasn’t an open door, was there?”

After a moment he said, “No. Why were you crying?”

“I don’t know,” she said in a low voice. “It wasn’t just me. You were freezing, too, weren’t you?”

“I was pretty damn cold,” he said, “but you were like ice. And crying. You were dreaming, crying in your dream. Do you remember the dream?”

Miserably she shook her head. She had to fight back tears, because sitting there with the fire, with Barney’s arm around her shoulders, safe and comfortable, she felt a nearly overwhelming sadness, a loneliness such as she had never experienced before. “Let’s go back to bed,” she whispered.

Ruth Ann was dreaming that she was a small child in the old press room where the machinery was gargantuan, high over her head, making ogrelike growling noises. Her father spread blank newsprint on the floor and she began to help him paste up the news stories, crawling over the paper on hands and knees. She had a paste pot and a brush and carefully brushed the paste on an article, then crawled around trying to find where to place it. Her mother said, “For heaven’s sake! Look at you. You’re all over ink.”

Ruth Ann stood up and looked at her knees and both hands, then stamped her foot, and her mother said, “Don’t you stamp your foot at me, young lady.”

She stamped her foot again and her father laughed as the newly pasted news stories came unstuck and scattered.

She woke up when the cold descended, and this time when Maria glided into the room carrying the electric blanket,

Ruth Ann had already put on sheepskin slippers and a heavy wool robe.

"I won't be going back to bed until this air mass moves on," Ruth Ann said. "In fact, I was going to go make a cup of tea. I'll make two cups."

"It's the shadow," Maria said. "It moves out when it's ready. I'll put this on your bed in case you want it later." Maria had on a heavy robe, but her feet were bare.

"I can't understand why you don't get cold when this happens," Ruth Ann said in the kitchen a few minutes later, seated at the table sipping the tea she had insisted on making herself the way she liked it, black and strong, and in a big mug. Maria had a cup, half tea, half milk, the way she liked it.

"I get cold, but not like you do," Maria said. "And Thomas Bird, he hardly notices it."

"Strange," Ruth Ann murmured. "I was thinking earlier how many things are strange. People think that when you get old you suddenly get smarter, or at least wiser, and I doubt that. You just have more memories."

"Isn't that what wiser means? More things to compare and weigh with?"

"You won't get smarter," Ruth Ann said. "You're already too smart for your own good."

"What other strange things were on your mind?" Maria asked.

Ruth Ann drew her robe tighter. She was very cold, but the tea was helping, and she knew the cold spell would not last very long. It never did. "Earlier," she said, "when Todd was here we were looking at that picture of my mother and father, and I began to realize one of the reasons I like Todd and Barney so much. They remind me of my parents. Isn't that strange?"

"Not how they look."

"No. No. They don't look at all like them. How they act, how playful they are together, trusting and honest. Things like that. Their attitude, I suppose." She held her mug of tea, the heat felt good on her hands. "My parents were like that," she said softly. "Laughing, playing, teasing a little. I think funerals make you think of such things." Then more briskly she said, "Maria, it's two-thirty. Go to bed. I'll be awake a bit, but you should go on to bed."

Even this was strange, Ruth Ann thought when Maria agreed that she was tired. People probably thought of them as mistress and servant, but she knew that they were simply two old friends who could share a cup of tea and chat easily at two o'clock in the morning.

Back in her sitting room, Ruth Ann stood before the portrait of her parents. She wished that they had smiled for the photographer. She had never seen her father looking that stern, he certainly had never directed such a look at her. Now she felt as if his eyes were looking through her. That's how they posed them in those days, she thought, but he was looking at her, demanding, commanding....

"Tomorrow, Dad. I'll start tomorrow." She had saved the newspaper, and her mother had saved the other papers. It was time to see what was in them.

Todd snuggled close to Barney, comforted by his deep breathing, by the warmth of his body next to hers, but she couldn't go to sleep. Usually they both fell asleep almost instantly, the way children do, the way she had done most of her life, but she was wakeful that night. She had been crying in her sleep, she thought, disturbed by the idea that a dream could have induced real tears, even sobbing, and then vanished from memory leaving no trace.

She knew that hers had been a fairly easy life compared to most people she knew, especially compared to Barney. Nothing terribly traumatic had ever happened to her; she had loving parents, loving brothers even if they had teased her unmercifully, three living grandparents. The last time she had cried like that, she recalled, had been when the family dog, Dash, had died, and they all had cried over him. She had been eight.

She never had minded the cold before. Growing up in Colorado, she had skied and ice skated, enjoyed winter sports most of her life—but the cold air that had invaded the house was not like any cold she had ever known. Barney had felt cold, too, although nothing like the chill she had experienced twice now, or the feeling of loneliness and desolation that came with it.... It had started in the hotel that night. If she had not stayed in the hotel, maybe it would not have found her, targeted her. She tried to banish the thought, but it persisted. The cold had targeted her.

Not just her, she told herself. Others felt it, too, an inversion setting in and then dissipating—in what, the wind? That made no sense at all. No door had been open that night, and no wind had been blowing back in August the first time. She knew this kind of thinking drove Barney wild. It was exactly what he was struggling to denounce in his dissertation: superstition, fear of the inexplicable, feeling targeted by the unknown.

There is always an explanation, he would say, even if we

don't know what it is yet. She closed her eyes tight. If he had felt it the way she had, he wouldn't be so certain of that.

She remembered Jan's vehemence when she said there was something rotten about Brindle, how she hated it. "She's right," Todd heard her own voice in her head. "There's something rotten here, something wrong, something evil."

Seven

Mornings in the Schuster house were always hectic after Mame Schuster left for work. Jodie scurried around making sure the boys were up and getting dressed, making sure they didn't settle in front of the television, that they ate breakfast. She tried on one shirt after another, not satisfied with the results, and finally pulled on a sweatshirt that she would wear all day no matter how hot it became. She had never worried about her body until this semester, her first in high school, when all her friends were getting real figures. She was saving money to buy a padded bra, but she had decided not to tell her mother. Saturday she would go to the mall with her best friend Kelly and buy it.

She yelled at her little brothers to get moving or they would be late, and for Bobby for heaven's sake to tie his shoes. His socks were not matched, but he liked it that way. Half the kids in his second-grade class would have mismatched socks. They thought it was cool.

"And put your dishes in the dishwasher!" she called on her way to the bathroom to give her hair a final brushing. She was putting her algebra book and spiral binder in her backpack when the boys left. They would ride their bikes down to the field across Brindle Creek where the school bus would come. They liked to get there early to fool around with the other kids. She checked the table, wiped up a little milk. Bobby always managed to spill a little.

She was worried about one of the algebra problems, certain her answer was wrong, but it was the best she could do. Algebra was hard for her. She closed her backpack, grateful that this year she had one with wheels. It was time for her to leave.

They always used the back door, as she did that morning. She stepped out, maneuvered her backpack over the sill, reached past it to shut the door, and someone grabbed her from behind, an arm hard around her chest, something cold pressed on her face. She tried to kick, but she was being held too tight, and she couldn't breathe. Her struggles weakened, then stopped.

She moaned and twisted her head, trying to escape a bright light that hurt her eyes. Her head ached and her tongue was thick and dry. After a moment she opened her eyes and, shielding them with her arm, she sat up. She was on a bed. A wave of nausea rose. She thought she would vomit and closed her eyes again, but it passed. After a moment she cautiously opened her eyes just a little, squinting in the bright light.

It wasn't a real bed. Just a mattress on the floor. And her clothes were gone. She was wearing a dress of some sort, pink and soft, and nothing else. No underwear, no shoes or socks.

Memory rushed in and with it a tidal wave of fear.

"Who's here?" she said faintly. "Where is this place? Where are you?"

She pulled herself to her feet, shaking, holding on to the wall behind her, and looked around. She was in a long narrow room with lights in the ceiling. Everything was pale yellow, the walls, a carpet on the floor, the ceiling.

There were two doors, one partly open. She hurried to it and pushed it open farther. A bathroom. She ran across the long room to the other door. It was locked. Frantic, she looked around the room again.

There was a table with two chairs. A television was high on the wall, out of reach, with a remote control on the table. A bookcase, books, magazines. A small refrigerator. No windows on the smooth walls.

She was breathing in long shuddering gasps, as if she couldn't draw in enough air. She ran to the table and tried to lift one of the chairs. Break down the door! The chair was bolted to the floor. The table was bolted down, the remote on a chain. Desperately she looked for something to use to break the door. There wasn't anything. She ran back to the door and tried the doorknob again and again, then pounded on it with her fists, yelling for help. She turned to face the room once more, rising panic making it hard to breathe. Her fear gave way to terror. She began to scream.

Above the door a red video camera light had gone out; Jodie was out of range. On the underside of the table, a tape recorder taped every scream until she collapsed, exhausted, when it turned itself off.

Eight

"Come on back," Ruth Ann said on Thursday when Todd arrived. It was eleven o'clock, and Todd was ticking off the chores to be done, including checking in with Ruth Ann, before she left for shopping in Bend. A stocking cap, she had decided. One she could pull down over her ears when the wind started up again—but her choice of hat was far less pressing than it had seemed the day before. Today was like summer with a soft warm wind and hot sunshine.

Ruth Ann led the way to the dining room, where, to Todd's surprise, there were a number of cardboard cartons on the floor, and one opened on the big dining table.

Ruth Ann waved toward the boxes. "My source material for the history," she said. "I can't lug all this stuff down to the office and go through it there, so I'll set up shop right here. Are you through at the newspaper for the day?"

"Yes. Thursdays are pretty light."

"I know. That's when I usually did my shopping, that's why I asked you to come up today. Todd, what I want to do is have my own computer here, one like yours, small, compact, and powerful. With a scanner and a good printer."

Todd could see her point. Her office in town was too cluttered to handle the boxes on the floor. "We could move a computer over here," she said.

"No, no. Those are all linked somehow, and even if I want to be tuned in from time to time, I don't want anyone messing around with my copy. Sorry, Todd, I know you've done a wonderful job down there, but still I prefer a separate system." She smiled ruefully, shook her head, then added, "Actually, I don't want Johnny to know yet what I'm planning. He's thinking of a one-page story for the centennial, but it keeps growing on me. That's off the record, by the way."

"Okay. What can I do?"

"Buy my computer and the other things I'll need and get it up and working, teach me how to use it. I'm a good typist and that's all I know how to do on a computer, treat it like an expensive typewriter. I hope it isn't too much of an imposition."

Todd grinned. "I had a long lonely weekend facing me," she said. "This is much better. Let's talk about what you'll need, what you want to do, how much you're willing to spend, if you'll want the Internet, cable connection, DSL, or dial-up. . . ."

Ruth Ann had a feeling that this all might take more than just a few days. They went to her sitting room and began.

When Todd left with Ruth Ann's credit card, Ruth Ann told Maria they would invite her to dinner.

"With that table in such a mess?" Maria asked. She scowled first at Ruth Ann, then at the dining table.

Ruth Ann scowled back. "We'll eat in the kitchen. Don't be a scold."

Maria was not appeased. She called Ruth Ann's sitting room "creeping chaos," and seemed to think that the chaos was in full gallop, threatening to run over the preacher-ready rooms. When Ruth Ann asked Thomas Bird to move a lamp stand to the table, Maria's scowl grew fiercer.

It was after nine before Todd was ready to leave Ruth Ann's house that night. She had done a lot with the new computer system, but more remained to be done. "Just don't be afraid of it," she said. "Play around, try this and that. Short of taking a hammer to it, there's nothing you can do that I can't undo." She would put in a few hours at the office tomorrow and come by around one to finish installing things, she added at the door.

She hesitated, then asked, "When that mass of cold air comes in, do you feel it up here?"

Ruth Ann, sitting at the computer, became very still for a moment. "Yes. Was it terrible for you?"

"Pretty awful. I was freezing and I couldn't get warm."

"How about Barney? Did it affect him?"

"Some, just not the way it hit me. It's...it's weird."

"Todd, no one has been able to explain it, and it's been around all my life, just like last night. It doesn't get worse, but it doesn't stop, either. It appears that some of us are more affected by it than others, possibly we're more sensitive to the sudden change. Usually outsiders hardly notice. Another sweater, or turn the thermostat up a notch and that takes care of it."

More slowly then, she added, "Some people feel depressed, or have other emotional reactions." She was watching Todd closely and saw her swift expression change, not to relief, exactly, but perhaps reassurance that she had not overreacted. "It used to distress me profoundly, but now I just get very cold until it passes. Don't be alarmed, my dear. We seem to have a local phenomenon without an explanation. Like the Vortex Houses, something like that, I imagine."

She knew she had gone too far when Todd's expression changed again to one of polite disbelief that came and vanished quickly.

"Good enough," Todd said. "I'll see you tomorrow."

Ruth Ann sat without moving for a long time after Todd left. She thought of her as almost a child, she mused, although when she was twenty-eight she had believed herself to be highly sophisticated and smarter than most people she knew. Now twenty-eight seemed still in the development stage. But Todd had felt more than cold, she knew. Her expressions hid little of what she was feeling. Still malleable, impressionable. Susceptible. Why her, an outsider? She shook herself.

For a long time she had believed the cold to be supernatural, but she had abandoned that idea when it persisted through the years without changing, without doing anything. If it was supernatural, what was its point? she had demanded of herself one day, and almost immediately after that she had gotten rid of all the books she had collected on ghostly phenomena. The cold air in Brindle didn't fit any of the patterns, and it didn't do anything. It just was.

But her question kept repeating: why Todd? Why had Todd felt more than an Arctic chill in the air, the way she herself always did?

* * *

Walking to the Bolton Building the next morning, Todd saw a sheriff's car parked in front of the police station down the block from the newspaper. She entered her own building. "What's going on with the police?"

Lou Shinizer was at his desk reading a Bend newspaper. He always looked hungry, with prominent cheekbones, somewhat sunken eyes, but his undernourished appearance was contradicted by a paunch. With black hair worn Prince Valiant–style, and steeply arched eyebrows that she suspected he kept trimmed and shaped, he looked like a man past his prime who thought he qualified for a position as a rock star or a TV personality. He hardly glanced up at her that morning. "Nothing," he said and continued reading.

"Jodie Schuster didn't go to school yesterday and didn't show up last night," Mildred said. "Her mom called the sheriff and Ollie."

Todd glared at Shinizer. "Why aren't you over there finding out what's going on?"

"Told you. It's nothing. Kid's staying out of sight a day or two. If there's a story, they'll tell us."

She wheeled about and walked out, seething.

She had described Ollie Briscoe to Barney as the Pillsbury Doughboy done in shades of red-brown, and that morning he was more red than brown when she walked into the police station. He was at his desk, and a deputy sheriff was sitting across from it.

"Morning, Todd," Ollie said. He turned to the deputy. "This is the new girl over at the newspaper," he added, as the deputy stood up and nodded at her.

"What's this about a missing girl?" she asked.

"Nothing," Ollie said. "Kid had a hassle at school, boyfriend made eyes at another girl, or her mother gave her what-for over something. She's at a pal's house, or her aunt's place. Happens. Sonny's out asking around."

"How old is the girl?"

"Now, Todd, let's not make a big deal out of it. Kids do this. We ask around, they show up, get time out or something. Happens."

"How old is she and when did she go missing?" Todd's tone sharpened.

Ollie heaved a big sigh and stood up, came around his desk, and took her by the arm. "If anything turns up, we'll give you a call. There's nothing here for you. Now you run along. You're doing a real fine job over at the paper. That was a nice piece about Louise Coombs." He was propelling her toward the door. "You just go on about your business, and we'll get on with ours."

She stopped moving and twisted around to look at the deputy. Fortysomething, thick in the chest, very clean looking and fair, with an expression that told her nothing.

"Why did the mother call the sheriff's office?" she asked him. "She must think there's more to it than a kid off pouting."

He shrugged. "She got excited, maybe. Mothers do that."

Todd looked from him to Ollie, then shook off Ollie's hand on her arm and walked out stiffly. They weren't going to tell her a damn thing, she thought furiously.

When she entered her own building again, Ally looked up from her desk, held her hand over the mouthpiece of the phone; Mildred stopped whatever she had been doing, and

Toni stopped keystroking to look at her. From his desk, Shinizer said, "Hold the press! Our interpid girl reporter just came in with the scoop. *Little green men snatch local—"*

Todd kept walking toward her own office. Behind her, she heard Johnny say sharply, "Cut the crap, Shinny." Todd entered her office with Johnny right behind her. He closed the door.

She walked to her desk and sat down. Johnny went to the window, looked out, glanced at the papers on her desk, at her monitor with a screen saver of the sphinx morphing to a pyramid, and finally took a seat opposite her desk.

"We have a new ad," he said. "Germond's furniture store in Bend. Advertising is on the upswing."

She nodded, waiting for the real purpose of his visit.

"Look," he said, "you've been here some weeks now. What's there to do here for teenagers? Anything? It's a great community for little kids, safe as heaven for them, but for teens? Nothing. They see TV, videos, movies, magazines. They know what's out there and they want theirs." He looked past her at the wall. "Ollie says about eighty thousand kids a year take off. Just take off. Pictures on milk cartons, all that. Some of them come from here. Ten, twelve over the past dozen years. Gone a few days, months, even longer, then most of them check in again. A phone call begging for money, a note or postcard, or the girls show up with a baby. Some get picked up here and there on vagrancy charges, drug charges, soliciting. Name it."

He stopped, as if waiting for a response. She didn't move, watching him.

He stood up. "Okay, my point is that there isn't a story here. We get mixed up in it and sooner or later the girl is picked up and brought home, and there's juvenile court, the children's services agency, foster homes, a goddamn mess, and no one thanks you for butting in."

"What if it's more than that?" she asked when he paused again. "What if she didn't just take off?"

Johnny shook his head. "They look for evidence. You know, blood, signs of a struggle, a menacing stranger hanging around, the usual suspects." His grin was a feeble effort as he spoke. It came and went quickly. "Absent any sign like that, it's a runaway, just like thousands of others. You can't make a federal case of eighty thousand kids!"

He went to the door, where he stopped and said, "How long do you suppose any outsider would go unnoticed in Brindle on a school morning? People going to work, kids on the way to the school bus. They'll find her in a girlfriend's bedroom, or in someone's rec room, a relative's house. Bring her home, tears all around, no media circus, and life goes on. Or else in a week or two Mame will get a call or a card or something. She'll be embarrassed, apologetic, or boiling mad. What are you going to do, chain kids to the water pipes?" He gave Todd a hard look, opened the door and said, "Just leave it alone unless something develops."

Todd sat at her desk for several minutes after Johnny left. Leave it alone. Don't rock the boat. Keep it in the family. Mum's the word.... By next week when the newspaper came out the girl would be back home, back in school, all forgiven, forgotten. She pulled her notepad closer and jotted down two names: Jodie Schuster and Mame Schuster.

At last, she began to look over the papers on her desk—Shinizer's school board meeting minutes, the water commission meeting, birth of twins to someone or other.... It was no use.

Drivel, she thought, gathering the notes and items together and stuffing them into her computer case. Homework. She needed something to occupy the late hours while Barney was away, and with a weekly it didn't matter where or when she did this kind of work as long as she had it ready by Wednesday. She decided to go to Ruth Ann's house and do something that might take her mind off Jodie Schuster.

By late afternoon, she felt that Ruth Ann had mastered enough to be comfortable using the computer to write her history.

"I thought I knew the history pretty well," Ruth Ann admitted, "but there are too many blanks. When exactly did Joe Warden arrive, for instance? No one ever said to my knowledge. How did the two men, Joe Warden and Mike Hilliard, become partners? Why? Another blank. We know Joe Warden had a son but nothing about the child's mother."

"How did Jane Hilliard die?" Todd asked, recalling the sad tombstone.

"That I do know," Ruth Ann said. "She died in the fire when the original hotel burned to the ground."

"She was so young," Todd said. "Well, if you run into trouble, give me a call. And I'll be around to do the scanning when you're ready."

"It may be a while," Ruth Ann said, indicating the boxes. "I have just a bit of reading to do, and notes to make."

"Just a bit," Todd agreed, glad that she wasn't the one to start plowing through all that old material.

Todd had talked to Barney and rewritten Shinny's notes about meetings and a flu clinic that would be at Safeway in two weeks and then sat looking at the two names she had written earlier: Jodie Schuster, Mame Schuster. She knew about the bands of young people in Portland, hanging out at the malls, congregating downtown, forced to move on with nowhere to move on to. But ten or more runaways from a small community like Brindle? And no one was doing anything about it?

There really wasn't anything in town for them, no swimming pool, no rec hall where they could get together and listen to music, dance, just fool around. No doubt the school held dances now and then, and there were team sports, maybe a drama group put on a play once or twice a year. But they needed more than that, a place of their own where they could get together regularly.

An editorial, she decided. She would write a series of editorials, research what other small towns did for their young people. Not until Jodie Schuster checked in, she thought, remembering Johnny's words. Evidently the newspaper had run a story about a runaway, only to be subjected to a lot of criticism for it when the kid turned up again. Maybe, because Johnny had been stung, he had exaggerated about how many kids had run away from Brindle, trying to make it seem commonplace, not worthy of a story. Okay, she told herself. First research, information, then a series of editorials. And have something just a little more interesting than school board meetings and flu clinics in the newspaper.

She could not account for, or even identify, the tingle that passed through her as she picked up her pen to make a note about the missing children of Brindle.

Nine

On Saturday, Todd found many photographs aligned on the dining table. "I tried to put them in chronological order," Ruth Ann said, "as much as possible, anyway. Most of them don't have dates, of course. But that's the original Warden's Place in the early years, maybe at the start. There are several photos of it, some with him and Hilliard, one with Janey with them. They all lived in it." The pictures were fanned out, and she spread them a bit so that each one was visible. She put the one with Janey aside. "I know I'll want that one, but I haven't decided which of the others I'll use. The first church," she said, pointing to the next set. "My grandfather was preacher there."

She pointed to several other photographs, the first one-room school with a teacher in a rigid pose and six children who looked petrified. Four of them were barefoot. She put that one aside, also. "In," she said.

"I'll skim through the diaries and letters and try to get a clue about who all those people were," Ruth Ann said, "and date them if I can. I want to use pictures with people as much as possible, but only if I can identify them."

"They all look so grim," Todd said. The children's clothes looked either too big or too small, smock dresses on the girls, shapeless pants and shirts on the boys. Women were wearing high-neck dresses with long sleeves, aprons or shawls, and what seemed to be laced boots. So much for the glamorous west of moviedom, she thought.

"I suppose they were grim for much of the time," Ruth Ann said. "It was a hard life. One of the diaries says that it was an all-day trip to Bend, another day to stock up on staples, then a whole day coming home again. No running water, no electricity, no plumbing. A hard life and a lonesome one."

She had put aside four of the photographs for Todd to start working with, the others to be decided upon later. She went back to resume reading the diaries in her sitting room, and Todd went to work on the pictures.

She was so young, Todd was thinking a few minutes later, working on the photograph of Janey with Mike Hilliard and Joe Warden. Her hair was parted in the middle, drawn back, probably in a bun; her hands were clasped before her. Standing between the two men, she looked diminutive, frail and frightened. Todd remembered what Johnny had said about the runaways—what was there in Brindle for kids to do? What had there been for Janey? Sixteen, with an infant, in a wilderness, alone with two much older men who both looked stern and rough, staring at the camera as if it were the enemy.

Todd was working on the picture with the school children when Ruth Ann reappeared from her sitting room, yawning.

"I fell asleep," she said. "Bad poetry put me to sleep. Todd, stop for the day. You've been at it for hours."

"Let me show you what I have," Todd said. "Here's the photo of Janey with her husband and Warden."

Ruth Ann studied the printout, then nodded. "I think she had a dimple," she said.

"I think so, too. She was only a kid, almost a child herself."

Ruth Ann put the printout down and shook her head. "From all accounts she was a prostitute," she said. "They started a cathouse in Warden's Place, and it seems she was a working girl there. It was rumored that she was carrying on with a customer when her daughter drowned in Brindle Creek."

Todd stared at her, then at the printout. How could she have left a two-year-old child alone by that ice-cold water? "Is that what you're going to write about?"

"Only if I can verify it. You young people don't know what real censorship is these days. No one, to my knowledge, has ever openly talked about what really went on in the early years. Mothers whispered things to daughters or to each other. Not outright. Coded. They invented coded language. Men, no doubt, talked among themselves, told things to their sons perhaps. Whispers. Innuendos. Hints. Sex was the ultimate dirty word, one that no decent person uttered. I think it's time this town learned the truth about Warden and the Hilliards."

"Why?" Todd said. "It's a hundred-year-old scandal. Why rake it through the ashes now?"

Ruth Ann's expression had become as grim as those in the photographs. "Every few years someone brings up the idea of a monument to our founders," she said. "Grace Rawleigh is pushing for it and this year, the year of the centennial, she intends to force it through. She can afford it, but she intends for the town to foot the bill. I intend to stop that. This town needs a lot of things, and a monument in the park to feed Grace's ego isn't one of them."

"A youth center," Todd said. "That's what the town needs. Did you hear about Jodie Schuster? A runaway girl?"

"Yes. Maria told me."

"Do you know anything about her? How old she is, when she took off? Anything?"

"She's fourteen," Ruth Ann said. "Her mother's a nurse at the hospital in Bend. She left Jodie and her two little brothers at home when she went to work on Thursday morning at six-thirty. Jodie gets the boys off on their bikes at about seven-thirty, and then she walks down to catch the school bus. That morning she didn't get on the bus, and no one has seen her since."

Only fourteen! Todd thought in wonder and dismay. She hesitated a moment, then said, "Whose permission do I need to run a series of editorials about runaway children, youth centers, things of that sort? Yours or Johnny's?"

"I'm still the publisher," Ruth Ann said sharply. "Do it." She started to gather the photographs together, then added, "Don't count on any of the council members for cooperation, not Ollie Briscoe, and probably not Johnny. They all would cage the devil and put him on display if they thought it would bring in a tourist dollar."

Todd walked home deep in thought. Seth, she decided. If she could talk him into helping her find local information, that would be step one. She couldn't use only national statistics, she had to tie her editorials to the local community, to these people here and their runaway kids. She got her Acura out and drove to Safeway. It was five minutes before six and she knew that Jan got off at six on Saturdays.

She parked, then waited until a minute or two after six before leaving her car as Jan was coming out of the store.

"Too late," Jan said as Todd approached. "We're closed."

"I was really looking for you," Todd said. "I wanted to ask you and Seth to come to dinner tomorrow night."

Jan's smile vanished and she said in exasperation, "Wouldn't you know it. Nothing happens all the time and when it does, it's all at once. We have pals coming through tomorrow on their way to Vegas for a vacation. How about a rain check? And a cup of coffee with me right now? I'm heading for the Terrace Café for some coffee, or maybe a glass of wine, to wait for Seth. He's still at the station. When he comes we're off to Bend, have a bite to eat, and see a movie. Our big night on the town."

Perfect, Todd thought in satisfaction. She couldn't have arranged things better. They walked to the motel café with Jan chatting about her friends from Portland. They were both sipping chardonnay when Seth joined them.

The waitress was at his heels. He ordered a draft beer and sat next to Jan in the booth. "How are things?" he asked Todd.

"Pretty quiet," she said. "Any news about Jodie Schuster?"

He shook his head. "The chief said I'm not to talk to you about that."

"I know. He gave me the bum's rush when I asked him about her. What do teenagers do around here for fun? You guys can take off to see a movie, but what about kids too young to drive? What do they do?"

"They drive," Seth said. "Pile in one of their dad's trucks, take shotguns out on the desert and shoot jack rabbits or coyotes. Sheriff business," he added. He sounded bitter and defensive.

The waitress brought his beer and after she left, Jan said, "I've heard that years ago, when Lisa was home on a visit, she was full of ideas about building a theater here, to show first-run movies and have a film festival every summer. Like Sundance. I wish she'd done it. Going up to Bend to see a show is a drag, and like you said, the young kids can't do it alone."

Todd told them about her plan to try to raise interest in a youth center. "I'd need local stuff. You know, the kids who have taken off from here, their families. Like that," she said. "Ollie won't give me the time of day, but, Seth, you could help."

His big open face took on a blank expression.

"What I want," Todd said, "is a list of the runaway kids over the past ten to fifteen years. Names, how old they were, how the cases were resolved. I won't use names, but I'd try to interview some of them who have come back, get their side of the story. Why they took off, things of that sort. It isn't just about Jodie. It's runaways in general."

He shook his head. "No can do. Not without authority, which I have as much chance of getting as a snowball in you know where."

"Yes, you can," Jan said, leaning forward. "You're alone in the station half the time. There's a copy machine. Take out a file, make a copy, put it back. You don't even have to hand anything over to Todd. I'd do that."

"I can't be forced to reveal any source of information," Todd said. "Unwritten law of journalism. Confidentiality of sources. Holy writ or something."

Even as Seth began to shake his head again, Jan said fiercely, "God, it's a chance to shake up these zombies. It's like being in a town of Stepford people, men and women, all Stepford zombies."

"We could make a difference, Seth. Think about it." As she spoke, Todd realized their waitress was hovering nearby. Todd finished her wine and pushed back her glass. Raising her voice slightly, she said, "Well, I'm off, shopping to do."

The waitress began to move away as Todd pulled a five-dollar bill from her purse and stood up, saying, "Have fun at the movies." She put the money on the table, nodded at the waitress and left.

Had the waitress been listening in? How much had she heard? Todd doubted that her own voice had carried, but Jan's might have. And did it matter?

Ruth Ann's eyes were tired that night. It was nearly eleven when she finished the last diary and put it back in its box. She had put several items aside for possible inclusion in her history, and now had only two packets of letters left to look through, and she would be finished with Louise's box. Most of the material she had collected so far had been for human interest, nothing really newsworthy, except for some of the early photographs. She regarded the packets of letters with mounting impatience. Skip them and go on to bed, she told herself, but she wanted to be done with all this material. With a sigh she picked up the first of the letters.

More violet ink on stationery that had become brittle and an ugly tan. It was dated July 7, 1888, and signed "your loving daughter Mary." Skimming it, Ruth Ann realized with a start that Mary had been on her honeymoon with Raymond McCormack in Portland, and the letter was all about the magnificent fireworks display they had watched. She smiled faintly at the thought of writing to her mother while on her own honeymoon in San Francisco. She had written a postcard, and had handed it to her mother on her return.

She skimmed the second letter, this one about a paddlewheel boat ride. The third one stopped her when she saw the name Hilliard. She backed up to read it more closely.

> *. . . Two nights before my wedding, unable to sleep, and unwilling to disturb my dear sister, I put on my cloak and walked out to clear my mind of my anxiety. As I walked near the corral I saw flames in the windows of that House. I ran, thinking to ring the fire bell, to raise the alarm. I saw the Warden child coming from that House, staggering and running like a blind person. He fell down, lifted himself to run and fell again. Then I saw Mr. Hilliard step out of a shadow and hasten to the child. He lifted him and started to carry him back toward that House. Others began to call out and Mr. Hilliard stopped and turned and it appeared that he was carrying the child away from the inferno. I was very afraid and I hurried home. I was so greatly afraid that I said nothing. I am sorely troubled, Mama. Raymond said I must put it out of mind, it is not fitting to dwell on such matters. However, I find that I am unable to do so. When I return you must advise me, dearest Mama.*

Her fatigue forgotten, Ruth Ann returned to the letters, but there was no other mention of the fire or Hilliard.

"They told her to keep her mouth shut," she muttered when she finished them all. And she had done so. Hilliard had been acclaimed a hero, risking his life to save Joe Warden's son.

Mary had been Louise Coombs' grandmother. From mother to daughter, she thought, or daughter to mother, the rumors lived on in whispers, in hushed conversations, in letters bound with ribbons for more than a hundred years.

Ten

Late Sunday afternoon Ruth Ann was smiling over her father's journal account of his courtship of her mother when Maria entered the sitting room to say that Sam had dropped in.

"You want me to bring him on back here?" she asked, eyeing the disorder with disapproval.

Ruth Ann glanced around, then stood up. "No. I'll come out." Normally she would have visited with him in the sitting room, but Todd and Barney would also drop in, and four people would be a crowd. The room was more cluttered than usual with open journals and her notebooks on two tables, a half-empty cardboard carton on a chair, another box of pictures on a different chair....

She met Sam in the foyer, held out her hands to him, and turned her cheek for his kiss.

"You're looking chipper," he said. "Am I interrupting something?"

"No, of course not. I've been reading my father's journal. Courtship back in 1920 was not lightly undertaken or carried out." She motioned toward the living room. "Sit down. Scotch, bourbon? You look like a man in search of a drink."

He laughed. "Scotch."

He went to the living room and she to the kitchen where she mixed his Scotch and water, and a bourbon and water for herself.

When they were both seated in the brocade-covered chairs, he took a long drink. "This is the only place I know where I can have a drink without everyone watching to see if I'll stagger when I stand up," he said.

"And if I have a drink with my doctor, Maria can't scold," she said. "*Salud.*" After a sip or two, she put down her glass. "You look tired. Hard week?"

He shook his head. "It's those two women. Grace and Lisa. I know I shouldn't let them get to me but, damn, they do. Grace insisted on a meeting. They're off to Portland now and in a couple of days Lisa will fly back to Los Angeles, but she had to give the pot a stir before leaving. I think I irritated her over here last week. Get-even time. She's as vindictive as her mother."

"Oh, dear," Ruth Ann said in sympathy. "Now what?"

"She told me to start looking around for an apartment or something. When she finalizes her plans for the destination resort, she'll turn the house into a historical museum."

Ruth Ann waved it off. "You know as well as I do that in a month or two, she'll have an altogether different scheme cooking. Or she'll marry a Saudi prince and start wearing a veil, or be into saving endangered chipmunks."

Keeping his gaze on his glass, he nodded, then said in a low voice, "I also know that eventually some guy is going to strangle her, or put a bullet in her head. I wish to God he'd just go ahead and do it."

"Sam! Don't say things like that." His words had been spoken with a quiet intensity that was more alarming than a loud harangue would have been.

"It isn't just me," he said, then took another long drink. "She has it in for your pals Todd and Barney, too. She doesn't like being blown off, and he did it to her. Now she's saying he begged her to go to Corvallis with him, but she doesn't have any use for schoolboys who play around while their wives work to pay the bills." He finished his drink, set the glass down and rubbed his eyes.

"Good God," Ruth Ann said in consternation. "It's so unfair, isn't it? They're good kids, both of them. Todd's been here for only a few weeks and she's already trying to do something good for the town, and Lisa... She spends her life tearing things down."

"She'd like nothing better than to get between those two. What's Todd up to?"

"She thinks someone should start a movement to create a youth center, to keep kids from running away, give them something of their own, a place to meet, dance, listen to music, whatever youngsters do these days. Raise people's consciousness about being so nonchalant about a runaway now, as well as those who ran away in the past."

"She won't get any thanks for poking them in their conscience," Sam said darkly. He stood up. "I'll be on my way. I'm in such a foul mood I'm not fit company for anyone. Thanks for the drink."

She rose and went to the foyer with him. As she opened the door, Todd pulled into the driveway. When she and Barney got out of her car, he was carrying a large bulging paper bag.

"Apples," Todd said. "Hi, Sam."

"I thought you meant a few," Ruth Ann said. "That's enough for five families."

"They'll keep," Barney said. "They're a little green, but Victor said pickers will come next week and I should fill the box he provided. I filled the box. I'll take them on back to Maria." He walked past them, and Ruth Ann closed the door.

"Sam, would you like some apples?" Todd asked. "I'll give some to Jan and Seth, and take some to the office, but we have an awful lot."

He grinned. "A few maybe. By few I mean three or four. Not a big bag."

Barney returned, carrying a smaller plastic bag. "Actually, the apples are by way of a bribe. I wonder if you'd mind if I put up a portable weather station here?" he asked Ruth Ann.

"What is it?"

"I talked to the fellow who teaches earth science, a geologist, who also does a class on meteorology now and then. He's inclined to think that our little bit of a freeze was more psychological than physical. Something like the effect of a sirocco wind that is said to cause nervous breakdowns in susceptible people. A very strong front came through the last time the cold came in, but when I mentioned that it also happened in August when no wind was blowing, he suggested I set up these." He pointed to the bag. "It's a pair of high-low thermometers that record the temperature daily for a week. One for inside and the other one for outside. After a week you reset them and they do it again, and you have a daily record of changes. Someone has to make a note of the time when the cold hits and how long it lasts. I'm setting them up at our place, too. He wants two records." Barney grinned. "I don't think he believed a word I said."

"No one ever does," Sam said. "Good luck with it. I'm on my way. Good seeing you both." He waved to them all and left.

"It's been happening as long as I remember," Ruth Ann said. "My mother used to say they'd done something to the weather, and these days anyone saying that would be right. Set them up anywhere you want. I'll note the time it starts and stops. But you understand that it might not happen again for months?"

"We'll be ready if and when it strikes again," Barney said. "We'll want a shady spot out back somewhere."

Maria and Thomas Bird watched with Todd and Ruth Ann as Barney installed one of the thermometers on the side of the garage, and the other on an interior wall, then explained how to reset them both.

"What difference will it make if your professor at the university knows what we already know?" Maria asked when it was done.

"Maybe none at all," Barney said. "But it will add to the knowledge of what makes the weather behave as it does, why things happen the way they do, and the more we know about nature, the better we are equipped to deal with it."

"Your instrument won't tell you why it happens," she said with a slight shrug. "Just that it does, and we already know that."

She turned and started to walk back to the kitchen, and Barney followed. "Maria, hold on a second. Do you have an explanation?"

She faced him, then looked hard at Ruth Ann and gave another searching look at Todd. "It's the shadow," she said. "And it speaks loudest to those who can hear it best." She smiled slightly. "Is that explanation enough?"

"It's no explanation at all," Barney said. "What does it mean?"

Maria's smile widened and she shook her head. "It's the best I can do. I have to start dinner. Will you and Todd have dinner with us?"

Todd had felt herself stiffen with Maria's words, and was only vaguely aware of Barney's polite refusal to her invitation. She was recalling with startling vividness the feeling of desolation and despair and, even more, the loneliness the cold had brought. Ruth Ann's hand on her arm jolted her.

"I'm afraid Maria's bought into the great American mythos of the enigmatic Indian," Ruth Ann said briskly. "But of course, you're welcome to have dinner."

"No," Todd said. "We have a lot to do. I won't be back probably until Thursday, but if you have a problem please give me a call." She was walking to the front door as she spoke, in a hurry now to be home, in her own kitchen putting something on the stove, doing something meaningful.

Even as she thought this, she knew it was not true. What she really wanted was to go home, go to bed, merge her body with Barney's and feel his arms around her as tight as he could hold her.

After seeing them out, Ruth Ann returned to the living room and retrieved the drink she had barely touched earlier. She took it to her sitting room and sat down, mulling over the last hour or so. The university professor had put his finger precisely on the spot, she realized. He knew, as she did, that no matter how cold the air became outside, it should not have any effect on the air inside a well-built modern house. Of course, she thought, sipping her drink, his purpose was to refute the unreliable witnesses to the phenomenon. She smiled wryly and drank deeper.

"Refute away, Professor," she said under her breath. If he came poking around asking questions, she would sic Maria on him.

Eleven

It was a typical late Tuesday afternoon. Ally was explaining to Shinny why she couldn't keystroke in his sports column. Toni's computer had crashed again. And Mildred was in a long conversation with someone who wanted to put an ad in the classifieds, even though the deadline for the current week's edition was ten in the morning on Tuesday. Mildred looked at Todd beseechingly and Todd, working on Toni's computer, shook her head.

Johnny came in from wherever he had been and snapped at Shinny, "Type your own damn copy. Todd, when you're done, come in for a minute." He went into his own office and closed the door.

Todd got the computer back in order. "I'm sure it's nothing you did," she said. "It happens sometimes. You lost a few entries, not much."

Toni looked at the computer with stark hatred. "I was fine with a calculator," she muttered.

"And you'll be glad you have this when it's income tax time. I reset the automatic save for you. All yours." She stood up and went to Johnny's door, tapped and entered when he called to come on in.

He smiled at her. "I just wanted to tell you the Schuster kid checked in. A postcard came in the morning mail. Like I said, she got an itch and took off." He looked smug and, while not gloating exactly, pleased with himself. "I told you not to worry and go jumping to conclusions. Sometimes the old-timers, like me, know the locals pretty well."

"Thanks, Johnny," she said. "That is good news. That poor kid. Where is she now?"

"She didn't say, just told her mom not to worry, that she's with a friend. She needed space," he added. "Her words, she needs some space." His expression sobered then. "Ollie thinks she was romanced on the Internet by some guy and went off with him. They've sent her picture to stations in Portland, Eugene, up and down the whole West Coast, and sooner or later she'll be spotted, the guy will be arrested, and she'll come home older and wiser. Internet predators," he said bitterly. "The down side of something that should have been only good. Who ever dreamed of such a thing in years gone by?"

That night after Todd finished rewriting Shinny's sports column—she no longer pretended she was simply editing it—she sat at her desk, thinking of what had to be done the following day and making notes to remind herself. Ten-hour days three times a week, then two- or three-hour days and done until it repeated the following week. She liked the hours, even if she was wrung out by Wednesday night. But she liked working at home, and for once she and Barney had plenty of space for them to have an office within hailing distance of each other. That was nice, too. Barney had brought home a new stack of books and was busy reading, making his own notes.

She glanced at the notepad on her desk and was startled to see that she had written *Jodie Schuster* and *Mame Schuster.* She had no memory of writing the names.

Barney passed by her open door without glancing in, and in a moment passed again going in the other direction. She admired the way he could focus on what he was doing, what he was thinking through. If she were standing on her head, he probably wouldn't notice, she mused, and was surprised that the thought was followed by annoyance and even frustration.

They always talked about things, everything, but when she had brought up the missing girl, his attitude had been almost exactly like Johnny's: people around here knew the kid, maybe this had been simmering for a long time, and it wasn't uncommon for kids Jodie's age to take off when the hormones kicked in. It wasn't as if she had been dragged away kicking and screaming, and in fact there were absolutely no signs of violence. She had just walked. All that was undeniable, Todd had to admit. But they hadn't really talked about it. She knew very well that if pressed, he would have said there wasn't anything else to say. What was the use of speculating? That was both endless and pointless.

And they hadn't talked about what Maria called the shadow, the cold air that entered the house when it shouldn't have been able to. And the tears and loneliness it brought with it. Again, what was there to say? Neither of them understood paradoxical weather, and anything beyond what was known was simply speculation. She stopped the line of thought, surprised again, this time, that she was becoming angry, and uncertain whether her anger was directed at Barney or at herself.

He was probably immersed in Abelard's Paris, she thought. He had done the rational thing, set up an instrument to take measurements, and there was nothing further that was rational to say about the matter. "Then say something irrational," she muttered. "Say something!" Recognizing that she was growing more and more angry did not lessen her frustration. If he walked past one more time, she thought suddenly, she would scream.

Abruptly, she jumped up before he could pass again, hurried across the room and closed the door, then stood holding the doorknob with her eyes shut. She had never closed him out before, had never even thought of closing a door on him before. She had never been so angry with him before, either, and she didn't know why she was so angry now. "What's happening to me?" she whispered, shaking as if with a chill.

She returned to her desk and stared at her monitor, where camels were making their way across a vast desert with pyramids in the background. She looked again at her notepad, at the two names, Jodie and Mame Schuster. Slowly she picked up her pen, intending to cross them out, but instead circling them. Then she wrote: *Talk to Mame Schuster.*

After waving goodbye to Barney on Thursday morning, she walked to the office to check in, attend to anything that had come up, and then go see Mame Schuster. After that, she would work on Ruth Ann's material, and that night begin to sketch out the series of editorials. Talk to some of the high-school teachers, she had added to her notes. Maybe Sam. He must have treated most of the runaway kids, but he might not be willing to discuss patients. Nothing specific, she had added to her notes, keep it in general terms. She would save him for later, she decided. The one she really wanted to talk to was Seth. She had given him time to think about helping her, and he had not been in touch, a bad sign.

She made another mental note: Did police files come under the Freedom of Information Act? She doubted it, especially where juveniles were concerned. If the newspaper hadn't printed a word about the previous runaway kids—except for the time that Johnny evidently had been burned—there was no point in searching through archives, and that meant she would have to ask a lot of people for names and dates.... Or talk Seth into cooperating.

In her office she studied a wall map of Brindle, and located the Schuster house, just two blocks from hers, at the end of Poplar Street. Not at the end, at the developed end, she corrected herself. Looking at the map, she saw how simple it would have been for someone to drive in by way of North Crest Loop, meet Jodie, drive out. She made another note: Where was the postcard mailed?

At first she had thought to walk to Mame Schuster's house, but then decided that could be a mistake. She would avoid going public as long as possible, not give anyone cause for speculating prematurely about what she was up to, and someone probably would notice if she walked. Instead, she walked home, got in the car and drove toward North Crest Loop. The street deteriorated quickly, with pine trees, sage and clumps of ragged grasses on both sides. At the junction with the loop, her house was hidden by the shrubs in the yard and other growth. She drove two blocks and turned onto Poplar. No one on the loop would have seen a car as far down as the Schuster house.

She had deliberated on whether to call first and had decided not to. It was easier to say no over the phone than in person. The house was a two-story frame building, the yard neat with dry-looking shrubs and a cottonwood tree, and scant grass that looked more dead than alive.

She went to the porch and rang the bell; the door was opened almost instantly by a tall, slender woman, in her early forties, probably, but she looked older, haggard, with red-rimmed eyes and deep hollows beneath them. The woman looked at her, then past her, and her expression changed from hope to despair.

"Mrs. Schuster?" The other woman nodded and Todd introduced herself, then said, "Can we talk a few minutes?"

"Why? What about?"

"I'm the new editor at the newspaper," Todd said. "I want to write about the kids who have run away in the last few years."

"You want to write about Jodie?"

"I'd like to include her, yes."

"She didn't run away! She didn't!" She held the door open and motioned Todd inside. "Will you write that? That she didn't run away."

"Will you tell me about her?" Todd asked.

"Yes. Yes. They don't believe me, Ollie, that sergeant, no one believes me. I talked to a lawyer and he said to let the police look for her. They have ways, he said, but they don't believe me." She drew in a long breath, then motioned to chairs.

They were in the living room, comfortably furnished, but untidy with a boy's sweatshirt on the couch, newspapers on a coffee table, books on the floor by another chair, a glass on an end table.

"Did you talk to any reporters?"

"One. He said their policy is not to write about runaways." She closed her eyes briefly, then said, "I showed them the postcard, but she didn't write it, not willingly, and they acted as if they wanted to pat me on the head and say something stupid. 'There, there, don't take on.' Something like that." Again she closed her eyes hard, as if trying to keep tears at bay. "I don't know where to turn. I was going to be on television, beg the man to let her go, try to speak to her, just beg. They got in touch with Ollie and he said she was a runaway, and that was the end of that. I thought about a private investigator, but the lawyer said all he'd do is take my money. It needs manpower, a lot of detectives to find anyone. I've called everyone I know, everyone she knows. I don't know where to turn."

"What about the postcard? Why do you think she didn't write it willingly?"

"I'll show you." She jumped up and hurried from the room, returned with the card and handed it to Todd. "See? She wrote *Mom,* and she never called me Mom in her life. Not once. From the time she could talk she called me Mamie, always Mamie, never Mom."

Todd read the card: "Dear Mom, please don't worry. I have to do this. I have to have space. I'm ok. I'm with a friend, and everything's fine. Love, Jodie."

She turned it over to see the postmark. Sunday, mailed in Bend.

"It isn't how she writes," Mame said almost helplessly. "It doesn't sound like her. She wouldn't have written okay like that. She had it marked wrong on a school paper. She doesn't make the same mistake twice. And who would she go to Bend with? She's only fourteen. She doesn't know boys with cars outside of town here. Where would she have met someone with a car? They say someone over the Internet, but she wouldn't go off with a stranger."

She began to weep then and had to stop the torrent of words. After a moment, she got up and ran from the room. She was longer this time and when she came back she had a box of tissues. "She didn't write that willingly. She didn't!"

"Do you have a computer here?" Todd asked.

"Yes, they play games, go to chat rooms, things that kids like to do. Play music. Ollie said she probably deleted messages, that's why I couldn't find anything."

"Didn't they examine the computer?"

"Ollie did, but he didn't see anything and said she probably deleted it."

"Mrs. Schuster, maybe I can find out for sure," Todd said. "I know how to search for deleted material. Would you permit me to have a look?"

"God, yes! There isn't anything because she knows better than to give personal information or get involved with someone that way. She's a smart girl. She knows better than that."

She stood up. "It's back here, in the den." She led the way through the house to the den, and watched as Todd began a methodical examination of the computer.

"Is she a hacker? Does she know how to program, do things like that?" Todd asked after a few minutes. She had seen no signs of such activity.

"No. They play games, she and the boys, and e-mail friends, things like that."

Todd finished her search and stood up. "You're right. There's nothing to indicate that she was in touch with a predator of any sort."

Mame Schuster had been pale, but now she turned almost gray, as if a lingering hope that her child had simply gone away with someone, a hope not voiced, never admitted, had vanished, and there was the devastating conclusion left behind: she had been abducted. Without a struggle, without a sign of violence, without leaving a shred of evidence, someone had kidnapped her daughter.

Todd touched her arm, as cold as marble, and shook her slightly. "Let's sit down and talk a little," she said.

Moving like an automaton, Mame led the way to the kitchen and sat down in a chair at a small table, staring ahead, oblivious, as if facing internal devils more demanding than Todd or anything else.

"I'll make some coffee," Todd said, almost in despair. She didn't know what to do for Mame, how to shake her out of what looked like a state of shock.

She found the coffeemaker, coffee, filters, and made the coffee, took a cup to Mame, another for herself to the table and sat down. "Mrs. Schuster—Mame, please, let's just talk a little. Are you all right?"

"I kept thinking that if she left with a boy, she'd be back soon. Then I knew she hadn't just left like that. And the card. She's such a good girl. Still more like a child, no boyfriends or anything yet…"

Her voice was low, a monotone, the words disjointed as she talked on in a discursive monologue. Jodie made good grades, she had just started her menses in August, a slow developer, just as she had been, loved her little brothers, like a mother….

Listening attentively, Todd waited for the coffee to cool enough not to be dangerous, then put a mug in Mame's hands. She seemed not to notice and rambled on. Paul, her husband, had died four years ago, an accident, insurance put away for the children's education, live on her salary as a registered nurse, Jodie like a second mother to the two boys, getting them off to school…

Very slowly Mame seemed to come back from whatever safe haven her mind had taken her to, and she looked at her hands wrapped around her coffee mug, then across the table at Todd. "We have sugar, cream," she said faintly.

"I'm fine," Todd said. "Have you been sleeping at all?"

"A little. I'm very tired." She looked at the table as if surprised to find herself in the kitchen. "See, Sam brought me sleeping pills." She pointed to a small pharmacy bottle, a pharmaceutical company sample, not for sale. "He said I have to pull myself together, for the boys' sake. I…what if the phone rings and I don't hear it? Or the doorbell…"

"He's right," Todd said. "You have to sleep and eat, make meals for your sons. Tonight, after they're in bed, take a pill, get some rest. You'll hear the phone or doorbell. Your heart will see to it that you do."

She remained a while longer, and when she got up to leave Mame gave her two pictures of Jodie, her current school picture, and one taken during the summer of the girl in shorts, her long hair blowing in the wind; she was holding a tennis racket in one hand, an ice-cream cone in the other, smiling.

"You'll write about her, about Jodie?" Mame asked at the door.

Impulsively Todd embraced her and held her close for a moment. "Yes," she said. "I'll write about Jodie."

Twelve

Mame's words about Jodie had stirred up long-dormant memories, Todd realized when she got in her car. She was remembering what it had been like at home with two younger brothers, and one older one. How fiercely protective she had been with the two little boys, how much she had loved them both and later, when they outgrew her, how that protection had switched sides, but the love endured undiminished. She had read to them, played silly games with them, had sent them back to wash their hair when they didn't meet her standards. Their mother had taken a job when the baby, Lyle, was four, thinking even then of college costs for four children, and Todd had become a second mother to the two little boys. Most men looked on it as too much responsibility, enough to send a girl flying away at the first chance she saw, but Todd knew it had not been like that. The bond of love had been strong, perhaps even strengthened by responsibility. She never would have abandoned them.

She started the car and drove out the way she had come in, back along the ruined street to the loop. At her own street she hesitated, then continued straight through to the highway, and on to Brindle where she stopped at the supermarket. Jan was on duty at the checkout counter. Todd picked up a loaf of bread, and waited for another customer to be checked out as a woman got behind her with a cart.

"Hi, Jan," she said when it was her turn. "I have some apples for you. Barney brought them back from the valley last week but I've been too busy to deliver them. Will you be home tonight? I'll bring them around."

"Sure," Jan said. "All evening, any time after six-thirty or so."

Todd paid for the bread. "See you then," she said. The woman behind her averted her gaze when Todd glanced her way. She shrugged and left the store. On to Ruth Ann's, a few hours scanning pictures, a quick sandwich or something, then a serious talk with Seth, she was thinking when she got back in her car.

Ruth Ann had set aside more pictures and pages of text. There were several documents with much of the text illegible due to creases in the papers, or faded ink, or the greediness of time, which swallowed the past when it could.

Todd looked over everything and said, "The photographs won't be a problem. But the text might be trickier. We'll give it a go, but no guarantees."

Ruth Ann nodded. "That's all anyone can promise, I suppose. Would you mind starting on the documents?"

Although she would have preferred to put that off for

another day, when she was not quite so preoccupied, she said sure.

Ruth Ann was as distracted and preoccupied as Todd was that afternoon, and she returned to her sitting room and remained there reading for the next several hours while Todd worked. She opened her door and watched later, but Todd was concentrating and she did not interrupt. Even if she couldn't get all the text, Ruth Ann thought, partial text, her father's words, the courthouse records, that would be enough. She wondered what Todd was making of the text she was working on. Without the background it probably made little sense, she decided, picking up her father's journal and resuming where she had left off.

In fact, Todd was not reading text at all. She was looking at lines, at broken lines, at contrasting black, gray and blank spaces. With the contrast at the limits of her computer, some of the blanks yielded spots and new parts of lines emerged enough to link them—those were the spaces she could fill in pixel by pixel, to make a whole line again.

One of her art teachers had stormed at her class: "Stop interpreting! Learn how to see what is there, what your eyes see, not what your brain is telling you it means!"

Rebelling, Todd had muttered under her breath, "I see a candle and a candlestick, you ninny!" But one day in that class two bananas, a pear and an apple had disappeared and in their place there had been curved lines, spaces, dark areas, blank areas. An epiphany, she had come to realize, understanding what the teacher had meant all along. See what is there, not how you interpret it. Now she was seeing lines, broken in places, and she was working to restore the breaks.

When she had done all she could with the first document, the new, restored lines were in place with the original text, not all of it filled in, but most of it. She was jolted by Ruth Ann's hand on her shoulder.

"I'm sorry, Todd. I didn't mean to startle you. That's a wonderful job you've done. Can you print it out now?"

She had no idea how long Ruth Ann had been behind her, watching. She printed out the document.

"Time to stop for the day," Ruth Ann said then. "It's five o'clock, and Maria has fixed us a little snack. Not dinner, just a snack. In the kitchen." They walked through the house to the kitchen.

There was a tray with cheese and crackers, rounds of dark bread, thin sliced ham, and apple fritters steaming hot. "We have so many apples," Ruth Ann said, "we decided you have to share them. Would you like a glass of wine?"

"I'd better not," Todd said. "I just remembered that I didn't stop for lunch today." She was eyeing the tray hungrily.

"Coffee, then," Ruth Ann said. "Help yourself."

Maria brought coffee and seated herself at the table. The first time she had done that had been a surprise to Todd, but now it seemed perfectly natural. Todd helped herself to ham and cheese with spicy mustard on bread.

Ruth Ann had made herself a bourbon and water, and Maria had coffee; they both ate cheese and crackers. When Todd finished with her first open sandwich, she didn't hesitate to make a second one just like it.

"Did Mame have anything of interest to tell you?" Ruth Ann asked then.

Todd had been in the act of taking a bite. She stopped and looked hard at Ruth Ann. "How did you know I was there?"

"We saw your car," Ruth Ann said. "I had business in Bend and Thomas Bird drove me. They won't let me drive on the highway anymore, afraid I'll run over a truck or something. Anyway, when we were coming home, up at the top of the loop, we could see your car."

So much for going unnoticed, Todd thought. She hadn't considered how visible her car would be from up there. Barney ran the loop two or three times a week, two miles in all, and he had said the whole town was visible from the top. He had picked out their house with no trouble, and she had forgotten that. Although little on top was visible from below, the town was spread like a panorama from up there. She took the interrupted bite while trying to decide how much to tell Ruth Ann and Maria.

"Mame thinks Jodie was kidnapped," Maria said flatly. "But no one believes her."

"Why don't they? Why don't they talk about it?" Todd asked. "Why a wall of silence if kidnapping's even a possibility?"

"Fear," Ruth Ann said. "It works both ways. If she ran off it was because of sex, and if she was kidnapped, no child is safe. They prefer to think it was sex, and they can't talk about that openly, not when a fourteen-year-old girl is concerned."

Todd looked from her to Maria, back. "They think it will just go away if they don't talk about it? Good God, that's insane!"

"If they talk about it, admit it, maybe one of their own children will take a notion to run away with a boy, or for an adventure in the big city," Ruth Ann said evenly. "What they'll do is keep a close watch on their own children for the next few months, the next year, however long it takes for the fear to subside, and then regard it as another case of a girl gone bad.

They'll begin to remember signs that no one paid attention to before—she was a bit of a flirt, played with boys too long without supervision, didn't always go straight home from school. That sort of thing."

Todd stared at her, aghast. "What if she really was kidnapped?"

"That's an even greater terror because they would have to admit that it must be someone local. No outsider could have gone in there and kidnapped her without leaving a trace. But, you see, they have already decided that she ran away. They don't have to face a local monster." She regarded Todd with a steady gaze. "If there is such a person, he probably thought he was safe, with no suspicions, no rigorous investigation. Case closed. Your editorials might shake his self-confidence."

"Why doesn't someone do something?" Todd cried. "Why don't *you* do something?"

"I did once," Ruth Ann said. "Some years ago. I wrote about the girl and later she came home again, and her parents threatened to sue. Defamation of character or some such thing. It scared Johnny out of his skin. What you're going to do is different, link them all, runaways, victims, all of them. I didn't think of that. And it seems so obvious now that I should have. I blame myself for not seeing it at the time. But you've come to do it. Maria says that's why you were sent here."

Todd looked at Maria, whose expression was indecipherable. "I came here because I needed the job. I was not sent."

Maria smiled at her. "Have you tried the apple fritters yet?"

And Ruth Ann asked, "Is Sonny going to help you?"

Todd looked from one to the other, and felt that she had blundered into a madhouse, with a whole town of mad people, but especially these two mad women, who to all appearances knew her every move.

"I don't know," she said.

"You might mention to his pretty little wife that it could be a stepping stone to the position he wants with the state police," Ruth Ann said, as she picked up an apple fritter. She laughed gently at Todd's confusion. "Maria and Thomas Bird hear so much down in town, and they tell me most of it, I think."

Carefully Todd pushed her chair back. Rising, she said, "I'd better go now. Thank you for the snack."

"I have something for you," Maria said, getting to her feet. "More fritters. Just wrap them in paper towel and nuke them a few seconds, they're better warm." She picked up a paper bag from the table and handed it to Todd.

Todd thanked her again, then said to Ruth Ann, "I'll be back tomorrow, get to more of those papers and pictures."

Ruth Ann nodded, and remained at the table while Maria walked to the door with Todd. When Maria returned, she sat down again and picked up a fritter. "She believes Mame," Maria said.

"I know."

"Why didn't you tell her what they're saying about Barney?"

"Later," Ruth Ann said. "She has to get Sonny's cooperation before she copes with gossip about Barney. Have you made any more headway with that list?"

Maria shook her head. "I know some of their names, but no dates, no new addresses for those who have moved away. She needs the police files."

Ruth Ann nodded, picked up a piece of cheese, and stood up. "Well, back to my reading. Call me when it's dinner."

Thirteen

What was that all about? Todd kept wondering as she drove back down Crest Loop to the highway, waited out a bit of traffic to make her turn, crossed the bridge, then turned back into Brindle. It was more nuisance to drive than to walk. Everything was so close here that walking was even faster than driving in most instances.

She couldn't fathom Ruth Ann at all, she thought, turning onto her own street. She felt certain that there had been a purpose behind the little snack in the kitchen, the cozy companionship of three women who trusted one another and could talk freely. Was it that simple?

The house was darker than outside, and she turned on lights as she went to the kitchen. She set the thermostat up a little; it cooled off fast these days, as soon as the sun went behind the mountains. She should remember to leave a light on, and the porch light, too, if she planned to be out after dark. In the kitchen she regarded the bag of apple fritters with a frown.

Maria had had them ready for her, as if she had known that Todd would leave abruptly, without even tasting the ones she had served. She sat down to consider that scene in Ruth Ann's house. Long ago she had learned not to question exactly why anyone did anything, since she rarely had been able to come up with a reason, but rather to look at the results.

One, she thought, Ruth Ann would be supportive of Todd's efforts to draw attention to the runaway kids. But she had already said so earlier. Two, the fact that no one was likely to talk about any of it—that was old news. Three, Maria, at least, accepted Mame's story. No one had said as much, but it had been apparent. If Maria did, did that imply that Ruth Ann did, also? Four, there was the hint about how to get Seth to cooperate, which she would follow. And five, a warning that her movements would be noticed. She shivered and drew her jacket closer around herself with that next thought: There could be a "local monster" in the area, and she might shake his self-confidence. She could become a threat.

She rose and deliberately went to the back door, made certain it was locked and turned on the outside light, then went to the front door to do the same thing. She drew the drapes in the living room, pulled down the shade in the kitchen, and finally removed her jacket and put on coffee. She didn't want to eat anything yet. Later, after she talked to Seth. She had planned to walk over, but it would be dark by the time she returned home, and she would do no more walking about after dark. If a warning had been part of Ruth Ann's little plan, it had been received, and she would treat it seriously. Even if Ruth Ann had not consciously thought of her words as a warning, Todd realized now that if Mame was right, whoever was responsible for Jodie's disappearance would know very soon that Todd was asking questions.

At seven-fifteen she rang the bell at the manufactured house. She had not been inside before, and was surprised at how spacious the interior appeared to be. There was one large room with a dining area and living room combined, separated from the kitchen by a wall of cabinets on the kitchen side and a wall of shelving on the living-room side. Knickknacks and books were crowded on the shelves. The house smelled of onions, garlic and roasted peppers. It smelled good.

"We just finished eating," Jan said, taking the bag of apples. "Thanks. Fruit from the valley. Yum. Coffee coming up. Will you have some with us?"

Seth greeted her pleasantly enough, she thought, accepting the offer of coffee and hoping her stomach would not start a clamorous demand for food. As Jan left, Todd took off her jacket and tossed it over a chair. Jan returned with a tray, cups and the carafe. She and Seth sat on a couch and Todd in a low-slung chair, a coffee table between them.

As soon as the coffee was poured, Todd asked, "Have you given some thought to what I asked for? The files on missing kids."

Seth shook his head. "Sorry, no can do. Jodie's case is closed and the other files are off-limits." He gave her a shrewd look. "Why are you interested in all this? Getting involved? Inviting trouble?"

She shrugged off the question. She didn't know why. "I talked to Mame Schuster today," she said. She suspected that Seth was not surprised. "Mame's convinced that Jodie was taken by someone, and I believe her."

He shook his head again. "Look at it the way the investigators do," he said. "Paul Schuster was killed in an accident a few years ago. Lonely widow. A lot of stress in that house. Too much responsibility dumped on an adolescent girl. She misses her father, needs a man in her life, sees a chance to duck out and takes it. The card was the clincher."

Todd regarded him levelly. "The card is the clincher that she did not leave willingly or write it willingly."

"You're talking about her calling her mother Mom. But no one believes she'd send a card using a baby name for her mother. She's all grown up, on her own, free, no more baby talk." He sounded bitter and angry. His big open face was drawn in hard lines now. He spread his hands and shrugged. "Like I said, case closed."

"It isn't just the name," Todd said. "Why not a phone call? Easier than a postcard, it works like a public announcement that she's okay—that everyone can breathe in relief and go on about their business." Seth's expression did not change. "If you saw Jan walking toward you from a block or so away, long before you could see her features, would you recognize her?"

"Sure."

"How?"

"The way she moves, the way she holds herself, how her arms swing, a lot of little things. What are you getting at?"

"Style. Mame said the card doesn't sound like Jodie. She's talking about style, although she didn't know how to express it. Also, there's a mistake on the card that Jodie got marked down for in school. She wouldn't make that mistake again. It's a matter of style. The card is in her handwriting, not her words."

Seth picked up his coffee and sipped without responding.

"Mame said Ollie and a sergeant talked to her. State police? Sheriff's office? Who was he?"

"State. Mame called them. He came, Sergeant Dickerson, talked to her, talked to Ollie and Sam, examined the card, and agreed that there isn't a case. Sam said Jodie's depressed, but no more than other kids her age, angst or something, whatever it is that makes them as jumpy as fleas."

"Why wasn't there an Amber Alert for her before the card came?" Todd asked.

"Her age. By fourteen, fifteen, they go of their own accord, they don't get snatched without leaving a trace of physical evidence. A broken window or forced entry, blood somewhere, something."

Todd reached into her purse and withdrew the two pictures of Jodie that Mame had given her. She put them on the coffee table. "Look at her, Seth. One taken in August, the other in September, her school picture."

Seth glanced at them without touching either one. Jan picked them up and after a moment, she said, "She's just a little kid, as flat as a boy, practically. No boobs yet." She thrust the August picture at Seth. "Look at her!" she said. "I don't care if she's fourteen, she's just a little kid."

He snatched the picture from her hand and threw it on the table, looking at Todd, not the picture. "You're going to make a stink about this, aren't you? The damn case is closed. There isn't a case. We checked out people, teachers, others on the block, no convenient handyman lurking around, no stranger cruising. If anyone went in there by the back way, it was by an arrangement with her. There's no way an outsider would know how to get to her house. The goddamn case is closed! Ollie would hand me my head in a basket if I got involved." His face had become flushed and a vein throbbed in his temple. Both hands were clenched and he was leaning forward as if ready to leap.

Todd remembered what she had heard: that he was a loaded gun looking for someone to shoot. Quietly she said, "I'm going to make a stink, with your help or without it. I intend to make this goddamn town face the fact that their kids are running away, that they're turning their backs on those kids, putting them out of mind. It could be your head, or it could be a giant step up the ladder for you if there is a case and you're the one to crack it open."

Seth jumped up and walked to the kitchen. There was the sound of running water. But Todd had seen the change that came over Jan, a stillness, an awareness. Todd picked up the two pictures and replaced them in her purse, then stood up and put on her jacket. "I guess there isn't anything else I can say. I'll be seeing you guys."

She was almost to the door when Jan caught up to her.

Jan opened the door, touched Todd's arm. "I'll talk to him," she whispered.

At dinner that night, Ruth Ann had paid little attention to the food on her plate, her gaze on something very distant, something very ugly.

"Ruth Ann," Maria said, sitting opposite her, "your eyes look tired. You should stop reading all that old stuff and rest your eyes."

Ruth Ann brought her mind back from the hundred-year-old puzzle she was working through. "It was all a swindle, Warden and Hilliard were swindlers from the start. One big land grab, that's what they were into. Using fictitious names to stake parcels of land, selling those parcels to themselves, going on to more land. One big land grab."

"It's done with. Over," Maria said. "That's why you went to the courthouse, checking things? What for?"

"That's why I went to the courthouse. I checked enough to know Dad was on the right track. He started all this sixty years ago but died before he could finish it. I seem to be finishing his story for him."

She considered Maria's real question: why was she doing this? No matter how the land had been acquired, it belonged to Grace now, and no fictitious heir of a fictitious previous owner could take it away from her.

She became aware of a silent dialogue taking place between Maria and Thomas Bird. They did that. A communication of some sort, a decision, and not a word spoken. Maria shook her head slightly and then got busy clearing the table.

They had coffee and apple pie, and Ruth Ann said, "You're trying to fatten me up."

"You could use a little fat," Maria said. "You're just skin and bones."

"And you're getting too fat," Ruth Ann said lightly. "It evens out."

Later, in her sitting room, Ruth Ann lingered before the portrait of her mother and father. "Why did you get interested,

Dad?" she murmured. He stared at her with that stern commanding gaze and did not say a word. She returned to her chair and picked up the latest interview she had been reading.

> ...Warden was as bad as Hilliard, watching over Janey like a hawk...if one of them girls took to talking to Janey, they'd get slapped to hell and gone. And he damn near beat a traveling man to death when he caught him making eyes at her. They kept her on a tight rein, both of them.

Her father had not noted his questions, but Ruth Ann had little trouble supplying them from the answers they had elicited. Now she read:

> She never worked the trade. They would of killed anyone that touched her. Then Joe got the notion that it was time to get the boy out of there, he was getting on, and noticing the other girls. You know. So he started the house up on the crest, and he began hauling stuff up there as soon as there was a roof and four walls. And some of us noticed that he was hauling some of Janey's stuff up there, too.

The interview ended there. Ruth Ann put down the sheets of paper and gazed at the portrait across the room. "She was a prisoner, wasn't she?" she murmured. "They kept her imprisoned."

She rubbed her eyes and turned off her reading light, then sat in the pale light of the desk lamp, thinking of what she had read, what it meant. Janey, kept a prisoner by two ruthless men, unable to find companionship with the prostitutes and, without doubt, shunned by the virtuous women who were starting to settle down in Brindle. Janey was finally released from a living hell by hellfire when the hotel burned down.

Ruth Ann stood up and went into her bedroom but, not ready to go to bed yet, she simply turned on a light and returned to the sitting room, where she switched off the desk light and stood in semidarkness looking out her window at the town below. Most lights down there were already darkened, and one by one more vanished. She counted streets and found Todd's house and was gratified to see that there were lights on in front and back.

She lifted her gaze past the town, past the highway where approaching headlights appeared ghostly white, and receding lights were red. Past them to a few scattered lights, past the cemetery, dark with its buried secrets, and to the vast black desert that merged with the infinite sky. She was thinking of how it must have been a hundred years ago when the blackness started a few yards from a doorway, and stretched out forever.

She hugged her arms about herself and turned away abruptly. You can't right a wrong, she told herself. You can't undo the past. The thought followed swiftly: but you can feel pity. She voiced it softly, "You can feel pity."

Fourteen

There had been a heavy frost overnight. Ice crystals still sparkled on grasses and shrubs as Todd walked to the office on Friday morning. Some baskets and planters had been hit hard and had blackened petunias and drooping geraniums. Few people were walking in town that cold morning. Barney had said the night before that it was raining over in the valley. Todd yearned for rain, for misty fog, even, but the sun was bright, the sky nearly cloudless, with just a few cirrus streaks of filmy white high over the western sky.

When she entered the Bolton Building, Mildred was talking to a woman who had brought in an ad for the classifieds and Toni was scowling at her computer. Ally was at a file cabinet. None of them greeted Todd with more than a glance and a nod. Johnny's door was closed. She went through to her own office. There was never much to do on Friday mornings, check the schedule, see what Shinny was supposed to be doing, make certain he was actually doing it if she could find him. He was not around that morning.

Johnny had left copy for two new advertising clients, one a Mexican restaurant opening, the other a natural food store. She started on them.

That morning Ruth Ann had come across another interview, this one in her father's notebook. Her mother had made no attempt at organizing anything when she packed the boxes from her father's home office. Everything had gone in any which way. Newspaper clippings, whole newspapers, index cards, the little three-by-five spiral notebooks he had carried in his pocket at all times, the steno notebooks he had used for interviews and other stories, typed copy, even invoices for materials all jumbled together in cartons. Ruth Ann had been taking things out and reading or skimming through them as they came.

This interview was in her father's small, neat script, with many abbreviations. He had never learned shorthand and had substituted his own version at will. As a girl, she had transcribed many of his stories and over the years she had become familiar with his shortcuts. Now, looking over the interview, she had the unnerving feeling that time was playing tricks on her. She was that girl again, working with her father.

The interview started: "Nov 7 1943, Manly's Nursing Home Bend Or—"

Ruth Ann stopped reading. Her father had died on November 17, 1943. After a moment she resumed.

"Z Stith, 86, sick coughing. Good mem, luc just sick."

After glancing over the interview, Ruth Ann stood up and

went to the dining room, to the computer, and started copying the text. She didn't think of it as keystroking, it was just typing with a new machine. She caught herself reaching for the carriage return repeatedly, and she had forgotten how to set the double line space, and how to adjust fonts. She felt as if she had been transported in time to sixty years earlier.

Her lips got tighter as she typed. Stith had worked at the way station from the beginning.

> Then, along about 78, Hilliard and Janey come. The stage stopped there regular like, and she was the only lady on it that day. She got out first, and Joe was there to give her a hand, but she took one step and she would of fell but for him. And Joe, he says, Zack, saddle up and get the doctor in Bend.... And when I get back the next day they had a deal going, to be partners.
>
> And two weeks later the baby came along.... And one day Janey was out back holding her baby, tiny little thing, and Janey was crying and I went over and said what's wrong, but she didn't say nothing. Joe saw me talking with her and he said he'd kill me if I went near her again, and I reckon I knew what Hilliard had to trade.

There was a little more. He said he would sign it after it was typed. But it never got typed. Her father must have caught the flu there, in the nursing home, and he died ten days later. He got his story and it killed him.

At lunch with Maria that day, Ruth Ann talked a little about what she had been learning about the early days at Brindle.

"That's what I've been doing," she said, "gathering the material for a long article. So many people know a little, so few know how it's all connected."

Maria nodded. "Tomorrow," she said, "we will go to Thomas Bird's relative, the daughter of his mother's sister, and you will know more."

"What are you talking about?"

"Evelyn's grandmother has one of the missing pieces. I can't tell you, it isn't my story. And Thomas Bird can't tell you because it's not fitting for a man to talk of such things with a woman. But Evelyn's grandmother will tell you. Up near Redmond. I'll drive you."

Exasperated, Ruth Ann said, "Evelyn must be Thomas Bird's cousin. Does he know the story?"

"Some of it. Evelyn's grandmother will tell you." She set her mouth then and would say nothing more. It was not her story to tell.

They were still in the kitchen when Todd arrived, and Ruth Ann went to the dining-room table with her to show her the new material she had assembled to be scanned and enhanced.

"Wow," Todd said. "It looks like you have enough for a whole book."

"My father always said it's best to have far more than you will use, because you can condense and cut, but if you don't have enough you are tempted to start padding. I'll do a lot of condensing and cutting, I'm afraid."

Todd got started and Ruth Ann went to the sitting room, back to her father's journals. Reading his notes, his interviews, his thoughts had brought him back alive, almost as if he were in the next room, or behind her just out of sight, or pacing his office in thought, musing on the probability of a story he had heard and not quite believed. She smiled, recalling his impatience with imprecision, with simple stories that got embellished too much. She picked up the next journal.

At five o'clock Ruth Ann stood up, stiff and tired, and exclaimed at the hour. She hurried to the dining room, where Todd was concentrating on another document, oblivious of her presence until she spoke. "Todd, it's getting late. Stop for the day. I lost track of time, I'm afraid."

Todd hardly glanced at her. "Almost done with this," she said. "A few more minutes."

As before, Todd had been paying little attention to the content, seeing lines and spaces and broken lines to be filled in. Finally she drew back, satisfied, and waited a moment before she printed the document.

She heard voices and was surprised when she looked at her watch to see that it was twenty minutes after five. Barney would be home between six and six-thirty. She hurriedly gathered her own things, put on her jacket and walked to the living room where Ruth Ann was handing Sam a tall drink.

"Hi, Sam," Todd said. "Ruth Ann, I'd better be on my way. Tomorrow?"

"Wait a second, Todd," Ruth Ann said. "I was just going to ask Sam for a favor and it might concern you."

Sam laughed and said, "No free drinks. Is that how it goes?"

"Of course," Ruth Ann said. "Anyway, I've come across references to Joe Warden moving things to the Crest house before it was even finished. Have you seen boxes of papers, anything like that up there?"

Sam shook his head. "But God alone knows what all is up in the attic. I might have poked around a little twenty years ago, but I don't remember seeing papers. There are boxes that haven't been touched in a hundred years, probably."

"Would you object if Todd and I have a look?" Ruth Ann asked. "You know, for the history article I'm doing."

"Not you," he said quickly. "Dust an inch thick, I'd bet. Let Thomas Bird do it. I have no objection. Grace might, but what the hell."

"Thomas Bird is helping clear brush up at Wild Woods," she said. That was the resort Johnny was building up in the forest. "Todd, would you mind? You know the sort of thing I'm looking for. Maybe Barney would be willing to help carry a box or two if you find anything."

"Sure," Todd said. "Tomorrow?"

"Late afternoon," Sam said. "Three or so? I have some dust masks you could use. I'll show you my rock collection."

"Three tomorrow. See you then. I got through a lot of that stuff," she added to Ruth Ann. "It's all on the table in there."

After she left, Ruth Ann sat down to chat with Sam and have her own bourbon and water. "She's a wizard with the computer," she said. "I think that's the real generation gap now, those who know how to use the damn things and those who blunder through. I've crashed it half-a-dozen times already. She comes in and in a second has it up and running again."

Sam regarded her speculatively. "Just what are you up to with all that old material? I thought the history was pretty much known."

"I thought so, too," she said. "I was wrong. Everyone has been wrong. I think that when the time comes, when I have all my ducks in a row, I'd better have a little get-together, invite Grace and Johnny, and give a preview of what I intend to publish. You might want to bring smelling salts. Do they still use smelling salts?"

He laughed. "Grace isn't the fainting kind, but she might take a swing at you. It sounds as if it's pretty bad."

"Yes. It's bad."

"That reminds me. Have you had your flu shot yet?" She had not given it a thought. "Okay. I have to go by the hospital in the morning. I'll bring the stuff up and give you a shot myself. It's going to be in short supply again this year."

"That's what killed my father," she said. "He caught influenza, developed pneumonia and died."

"It happens more often than you want to think about, even now. I want to keep you in good shape, at least until after you write your true history, and I want to be here when Grace hears what you have to say. See, ulterior motives."

"Sam—" She stopped before she committed a social sin. You don't ask someone else why they got married or stayed married.

He looked at her expectantly.

"Nothing," she said. "It's good of you to be my personal doctor who makes house calls. I know people in big cities who would kill for such attention."

At home, Todd washed salad greens and put them in the refrigerator, then got out eggs, cheese, spinach, an onion. She would make an omelette, but not until Barney arrived. Then she watched the clock hands.

When he came in, he embraced her hard and nuzzled her neck. "Home from the student wars," he said. "I think we should celebrate my safe and sound return."

She forgot all about the omelette.

It was late when they had dinner, then over coffee and cookies, Todd told him about her talk with Mame and with Seth.

"I believe Mame," she said. "She's out of her mind with worry, and no one is doing anything."

"Did the girl take clothes with her?"

"Mame wasn't sure. Jodie's been in charge of her own wardrobe for the past year, shops at Goodwill now and then, or a discount store, and Mame stopped trying to keep track."

When he looked skeptical, she added, "It was like that with me. I did my own shopping. At a certain age girls don't want their mothers choosing their clothes. Also, they don't always show them things they know Mom wouldn't approve of."

"Okay. Look at it from a different angle. Realistically, what more should be done? They've posted her picture, sent it to the police up and down the coast, alerted local police to keep an eye out for her. They're satisfied that she left of her own accord. You're going to write editorials about runaway kids in general, try to start people thinking about the problem in terms they can deal with, a youth center, something like that. Realistically, what more can you do?"

"You mean I should be rational about this."

"I said realistically what more can you or anyone else do?"

"In your mind aren't the two words interchangeable? I'm being irrational if I think there's more?"

Barney leaned forward and put his hand on hers on the

table. "Honey, let's not argue about a girl neither of us knows."

"I'm not arguing," she said, but she was, and she wanted to keep arguing, make him understand. Understand what? she asked herself. She was the one so good with words, but she had none to explain her feeling that something was wrong, something evil, something totally irrational. A feeling, a sense, an intuition—whatever was driving her was beyond her ability to explain to herself, much less to Barney.

He, demanding demonstrable facts, verifiable proofs, was as incapable of accepting a gut feeling as a cause for action as she was incapable of denying her own feeling. She looked at their hands, his on hers, and slowly she pulled her own hand free. There was a line, she thought distantly, that neither of them could cross and remain whole, a line that could become a wall, but one that defined them for good or for bad. He could not accept belief unsupported by facts, and most of the time she shared that rational system. But she believed without a doubt that Jodie had been kidnapped, and she could not prove it. There was no hard evidence to point to, just a belief.

She felt very aware that she might be etching that line deeper, allowing it to take root, as she stood up and started to clear the table without speaking again. There was nothing more to say.

Fifteen

Driving to Redmond, Maria told Ruth Ann a little about Evelyn Poynter and her grandmother, Ramona Greentree. "Grandmother Greentree is legally blind—macular degeneration—but she can see a little." Evelyn, she continued, was a teacher, and her husband was an attorney who worked for the Confederated Tribes. There were two young sons, who would be out with their father.

It was a cold, clear morning, with dark clouds shrouding the Three Sisters mountains down to the tree line. Later those clouds might bring rain, or perhaps dry storms with lightning bolts that threatened fires in the parched forests. Ruth Ann hoped for rain. She still marveled at the bunchgrasses and bitter grasses, the sages, how they collected any drops of rain as soon as they fell, hoarded them, so that when the rain passed, the desert floor was as dry as it had been minutes before the water came, but the dun or gray plants would show green for a time. Nature's most efficient water gatherers, she mused.

Maria drove through the small, dusty town of Redmond. She turned onto a dirt road and drove slowly to a frame house painted pale green with red trim. Goats crowded a fence, curious about anything out of the ordinary, and a black-and-white dog came to greet them as chickens scattered. In the shadow of the house, hoarfrost gleamed on low juniper shrubs and a rock garden composed of show-worthy pieces of obsidian, jasper and quartz stones.

When Ruth Ann and Maria got out of the car, Maria retrieved a tote bag from the back seat. They approached the house as the front door opened and Evelyn welcomed them.

"Maria, come in. Come in. It is so cold." She was tall, with big bones and wide shoulders. A long braid was over her shoulder. She was dressed in jeans, a heavy sweater and boots. Several gold bracelets, gold hoop earrings and gemstone rings on four fingers looked almost incongruous on her.

They entered the house and Maria introduced Ruth Ann. Evelyn took their coats, hung them in a closet, then motioned them to follow, as she led the way into a back room.

"Grandmother," she said inside the door, "Maria has brought Mrs. Colonna."

Grandmother Greentree was sitting close to a woodstove. She put down knitting, and turned her head nearly sideways to peer at them from the corner of her eye. Her face was crosshatched with lines, and she had thin white hair and skeletal hands. A shawl was draped over her shoulders and a long black skirt went down to her feet clad in fur-lined slippers.

She enquired politely about Thomas Bird, then said, "We must have hot tea." Evelyn left to prepare the tea.

"Come close to the fire," Grandmother Greentree said. "I'm afraid it is winter already."

Although the room was almost too hot, Ruth Ann and Maria both moved straight chairs closer to her, nearly close enough to touch.

"Thomas Bird has sent you a small present," Maria said, reaching into her tote bag to withdraw a carving of an eagle. She put it in the old woman's hands. Grandmother Greentree did not try to look directly at it, but felt it carefully, running her thin fingers over the intricate wings and feet. Then she smiled broadly.

"Bald eagle," she said. "It is good. Thomas Bird is a good boy. I send him my thanks." She continued to run her hands over the juniper carving. She nodded. "It is good."

"And I have a small gift," Maria said. "Blackberry jelly." She brought out a jar of jelly and placed it on a table.

"Ah, my favorite," Grandmother Greentree said. "Thank you, Maria."

Evelyn returned with a tray and poured tea for them all, then seated herself in another straight chair.

Without preamble, Grandmother Greentree said, "When my grandmother was a small girl, her mother took her to the place called Brindle where the woman with the sky in her eyes was to bear a child. That was my grandmother's name for her, Blue Sky Eyes. For many weeks she was at her side, until the baby was born, a small girl.

"Two years passed and a rider came to say Joe Warden wanted my grandmother's mother again. My grandmother was happy. She had thought of Blue Sky Eyes many times, and she was eager to see the baby Rachel again, to see if she, too, had the sky in her eyes. They rode back to Brindle, and now Rachel was walking and babbling, and she had the sky in her eyes, just like her mother. My grandmother was told to take care of Rachel while Blue Sky Eyes was in labor with another baby. All day my grandmother took care of Rachel, but Rachel cried for her mother, and in the other room Blue Sky Eyes cried out many times. It grew dark and Rachel would not stop crying and calling for her mother and my grandmother could not quiet her. When it was very late in the night, Joe Warden came to the room and he put his hand over Rachel's mouth until she stopped breathing. My grandmother pretended sleep and did not say a word. When he left the room she ran and hid. After the new baby was born, a little boy, my grandmother's mother made tea in the kitchen and my grandmother crept in and whispered what she had seen. Her mother told her to go out the back way, not go near Mr. Hilliard who was very drunk and was throwing many things, then lead their horse out and walk quietly to a place they knew and wait there for her to come. My grandmother did as she was told, and when her mother came, they rode back home as fast as they could and they were hidden by their people. Two riders came looking for them, but they were hidden well. Joe Warden came looking for them, but they were hidden too well for him to find them. My grandmother told my mother, who told me. Now I tell my granddaughter."

No one moved when she stopped talking. Ruth Ann felt as if she had not breathed for a long time. She drew in a deep breath. "Dear God," she said faintly.

When Barney came in that morning from resetting the high/low thermometer, he was carrying a stack of new library books that he hadn't bothered to bring in the night before. "Got down to twenty last night," he said cheerfully on the way to his study. The inside thermometer had gone down to sixty, where they always set the thermostat at night. Now, with the sun melting the frost, the day promised to be mild, and if the clouds in the western sky moved in, possibly it would even rain.

"How about a movie tonight?" Todd asked, following Barney to his study door. He was arranging the new books on makeshift shelves. The room was crammed with books on shelves, on two low tables, his desk, some on the floor. When he hesitated, she said, "Or we could rent a couple of videos, and settle for a new Mexican restaurant in Bend. Cheap food, opening weekend specials."

"Sounds good," he said. "Burritos, home movies, popcorn, fire in the fireplace."

He would watch for a few minutes, become restless, and wander back to his study to start reading, she thought with resignation. She returned to the kitchen to clean up the breakfast dishes, and suddenly she was thinking how few friends they had made here. Few? None, really. Seth and Jan might become friends in time, but it hadn't happened yet, and might never happen if Seth believed she was trying to use him. She yearned for one of her friends, someone she could go have coffee with, chat and relax with.

Cut it out, she told herself, and went to her office where she called up ads and Shinny's copy to begin rewriting. She bit her lip. It was hopeless. She couldn't concentrate. Later, she told herself, and began to think of what a youth center should have. A pool table, Ping-Pong, game table, dance floor... Her mind skittered again and she considered calling Seth, gave it up. Let

Jan have time to work on him. And there was no point in calling Mame, tormenting that poor woman.

Realistically what else could she do? The answer came swiftly. Nothing. She needed information and no one was willing to give her any. Under her breath she cursed Ollie Briscoe for not cooperating.

Since she was accomplishing nothing at her computer, finally she got up to do laundry, maybe vacuum, dust a little.

At three that afternoon, Todd and Barney drove to Sam's house on the peak of Crest Loop. The garage door was open, his Explorer parked inside. When they got out of the Acura, Sam opened the door of the house.

"Hi," he called. "I thought I heard company. Come on in."

The house was two stories, built of gray stone with a peaked roof, imposing and ugly, just as Jan had said weeks earlier, like a gargoyle looming over the landscape. Tall narrow windows, a porch that wrapped around the building, gray stone stairs to the porch, some dry-looking sage in the front.

"Welcome," Sam said after they mounted the stairs. "Ugly as sin, isn't it? But remarkably comfortable."

Inside was a surprise. A crystal chandelier in the foyer was turned on, casting warm yellowish light on an Oriental throw rug in deep burgundy. An arched entry led into the living room, and another into a hall where a deep red carpet runner glowed. A wide staircase was carpeted in a rich forest green, and on the upper landing another light shone.

"I'll show you around," Sam said, taking their jackets. "I'm afraid that by modern standards it's pretty sybaritic."

It was, with luxurious Oriental rugs, a hammered copper

screen in front of a fireplace, good art on the walls, gold-and-forest-green sofa and chairs with scarlet pillows. Everywhere, precisely arranged, were cut and polished rocks. Through the hall, the kitchen was pristine and completely modern with a convection oven, a microwave, a stainless-steel double door refrigerator, a table and two chairs. A grocery bag was on the counter by the refrigerator, but no glasses, no cups, nothing else to indicate that someone actually lived in the house.

"Dining room over there," Sam said pointing to a door. "I use it once a year to repay all my social obligations at one time. My study, that way. Bedroom upstairs."

"It's all beautiful," Todd said. She felt as if she did not dare touch anything. It all looked as if he had placed every object carefully in exactly the right spot. Everything was scrupulously clean and gleaming.

"I like it," Sam said. "Well, up to the attic. I have the dust masks for you, and a spare lightbulb in case the light up there is bad. As I said, I haven't been up there in years. I use only one room on the upper floor and haven't poked my nose in any of the others for at least ten years." He handed Todd and Barney the dust masks and led the way up the stairs, then through another hallway to the attic stairs. The carpeting on these stairs was threadbare and dusty, the stairs narrow. He opened a door at the top, stepped inside and motioned them to enter.

"Dusty," he said, flipping a switch. A dim light came on. "Well, there you are," he said, putting the spare lightbulb down on a lopsided wicker chair. "I'm out of here. Too dirty for me. There's a lavatory off the kitchen. You'll need to wash up after you're done."

Todd looked over the attic with dismay after Sam retreated,

closing the door behind him. Trunks, boxes, odds and ends of furniture, a pile of shoes and boots. She put on the dust mask. Barney already had his on.

"I'd guess that anything Joe Warden put in here would be behind everything else," Barney said. "First in, last out, that sort of thing." He opened a trunk lid. "Quilts."

They had to clear a path to the back of the attic where boxes were stacked haphazardly. Quilting frame, a loom, picture frames, boxes of mismatched dishes... Everything they touched caused a cloud of dust to rise. At the rear wall, Barney lifted the topmost box from a stack and Todd opened it. At one time it had been taped, but the tape crumbled when she started to pull it loose. The box held books that looked as ready to crumble as the tape had done. Another box of books.

"Hey," Barney said. "A wooden box is under here." It was a small trunk. He opened it, started to close it again. "Clothes."

"Let's see," Todd said. He moved the trunk out farther and opened it. She pulled out a skirt. Gray and blue, faded almost to solid gray. "Janey's skirt," she whispered, remembering the picture of Janey between the two rough-looking men. The skirt had a waist small enough to fit a child. A blouse was in the trunk, high-necked, long sleeves, very plain, and again it looked as if a child could have worn it. A pair of tiny boots, gloves, another skirt and blouse, apron, a nightgown or two... A coarse, heavy coat. Todd was bewildered by the clothes. Why would Joe Warden have moved Janey's clothes? In the bottom of the trunk there were a few more books. Carefully she opened one, poetry. The next one had writing in it, a neat script illegible in many places. She did not try to decipher any of it in the dim light, but replaced everything in the small trunk. "We should take this to Ruth Ann," she said. "I think those are Janey's diaries." She felt the prickle of goose bumps on her arms and neck.

"Whatever you say. I'll haul that down and stash it in the car. Be right back." Barney lifted the trunk and made his way through the path they had cleared to the door. "You're okay alone for a few minutes?"

She looked at him in surprise, and nodded.

"You look cold," he said.

"It's a touch chilly in here. Not too bad." She realized that she had been rubbing her arms, no doubt leaving streaks of dirt. She reached for the next box.

When she moved it, she saw two more of the wooden trunks. She pulled the nearer one toward her and looked inside. A man's shirt, trousers, a sweater… Joe Warden's clothes, probably. That box held no books or papers, and she pulled the next one forward. It was locked.

The goose bumps were back, and she was shivering now. "That's it," she said under her breath, thinking of what Barney had said, first in, last out. That trunk might have been the first one put in, then hidden behind miscellaneous stuff for a hundred years.

Just to be thorough, she began to open the rest of the boxes, but found nothing worth retrieving. Barney came back and she pointed to the locked trunk. "It will have to be pried open, or something," she said. "It's the only one with a lock. There are a couple more to check and we're done up here."

"Good. All this old junk gives me the creeps."

He waited until she examined the last two boxes—cookware, some of which she couldn't imagine a use for, and a box of magazines from the early twenties. Some of them might be valuable, but they weren't on her list of things to take back to Ruth Ann. She closed the boxes again and straightened up.

"Let's get out of here," she said. "I'm getting a headache. Dust and bad air. Yuck."

Downstairs again, she washed up while Barney carried the trunk to the car. He had water sparkles on his hair when he returned. "It's raining," he said. "How about that?"

She hurried to the door to look out, drew in a deep breath of the freshened air. "Wonderful! Bet it turns to snow before it's done."

Behind her, Sam laughed. "Maybe. Usually it's just about enough to settle the dust. Come look at my collection."

"Be with you in a minute," Barney said, heading for the bathroom to wash his hands.

Todd followed Sam into the garage. The far wall had shelves, some of them backlit, and she exclaimed at the rocks on display.

"Picture jasper," Sam said, pointing to a rock on a stand. It was the size of a dinner plate, as thin as a quarter, and with the light behind it, a landscape scene was like a painting in the pale translucent rock. He pointed out other picture jaspers, agates: snowflake agate, blue streaked, some with red-gold streaks. Oregon opal in a fishbowl filled with water. Thunder eggs, some cut and polished, some uncut, just rough lumps; obsidian, black, black-and-orange, as clear as glass, Apache tears… Peridot, a small vial of gold dust and flecks. One shelf held only crystals, each one perfect, from an inch high to eight inches or taller.

Barney had joined them as Sam pointed out his collection,

and he was looking at the workbench with interest. A cutting wheel with clamps, another polishing wheel, a tumbler... A shelf held an assortment of finishing disks.

The wall next to the house displayed a big Oregon map with many markings on it, crosses, *X*'s, exclamation marks, underlines, small circles....

"Your secret hunting grounds," Barney said. "Is there a key to the marks?"

"In my head," Sam said, grinning. He went to the map. "I'll let you in on a one-afternoon jaunt that you and Todd might enjoy. Here, Glass Butte. Lots of obsidian in fields, along the road, everywhere, but if you go back on this little dirt road, follow it in for a few miles, then hike for another mile along this creek, it's good hunting for thunder eggs." He traced the path he was describing.

Next to the map was a rack of equipment: a heavy-duty spade, maul, rock hammer, pick. Todd looked the implements over and shook her head. "You won't need stuff like that," Sam said. "They're out on the ground, on the sides of the creek, yours for the taking. All you'll need is a good stout bag to carry your finds." He gave Todd a searching look then. "I hear that you're interested in starting a movement to get support for a center for the kids here."

She nodded. "I think it's about time they had something of their own. A place to meet, listen to music, maybe form a band, dance. Things like that. I've heard that every few years one of them just takes off, some come back, some are never heard from again. I can't imagine a community that doesn't even address the problem. I want to find some of the kids who took off and came back, get some interviews, and write about those who just vanish into thin air, like Jodie Schuster. But so far it's a blank wall."

Sam looked thoughtful, then said, "I can give you one name, at least. A patient. Andrea Corman, at least that's her married name now. She left, came back pregnant, and settled down. She lives in the Bend area." He shrugged. "That's how it usually goes. They get a taste of life in the cities, on the streets, and hightail it back eventually. Or not."

"It's the 'or not' that concerns me," Todd said. "I talked to Mame Schuster. She's convinced that Jodie didn't just take a hike. I believe her, but no one else seems to."

"Maybe they're going by past experience," Sam said. He sounded bitter then. "How many kids do you have to see come home pregnant? Or addicted? You know as well as I do how they support their habit. Or they stay long enough to dump a kid on their own mothers and take off again." He rubbed his eyes. "Sorry. Anyway, I agree that a center of their own would be a step in the right direction. Good luck with it."

"Thanks," Todd said. "We'd better be on our way. And thanks for the tip about the thunder eggs and letting us take up so much of your time today."

Sam assured them that it was his pleasure and they left by way of the double door in the garage. As they pulled out of the drive, the door slowly closed, and the house, so charming and even luxurious inside, once more was the ugly gray gargoyle.

"Well, let this be a lesson," Todd said. "Never judge a book by its cover, or a house by the outside. And now I know how Sam spends his spare time. Cutting and polishing rocks."

"I think there's a little more to it than that," Barney said. He started the engine and turned on the windshield wipers. "I glanced inside that grocery bag on his counter. A box of Godiva chocolates. A guy wants a bit of candy, he picks up a Hershey's bar. I'd bet that Sam has a girlfriend on the side."

She considered it, then nodded. "I'd bet you're right. He's too good-looking to be totally unattached. I wonder if Grace suspects."

There was a rumble of distant thunder, but the rain was already letting up, leaving the windshield streaked. Barely enough to settle the dust, Todd thought, disappointed. At least, she thought then, she finally had a name, Andrea Corman, a runaway who had come back. She would go have a chat with Andrea on Monday during her lunch hour.

Back at home, Barney went straight to his study and Todd to her office, but concentration was as elusive as it had been earlier. She gave up trying to work and thought instead of the name Sam had provided: Andrea Corman. It was only five o'clock, not too late to pay a call, she decided. But she didn't have a clue where Andrea lived, just in Bend. "Find out, damn it," she muttered and went out to consult the telephone book. There were three Cormans listed in Bend, without a hint of which one was Andrea. After making a note of the addresses, she went to Barney's study door. He had two opened books before him and his notebook in his hand. He didn't look up until she spoke.

"I'll run over to Bend and pick up a couple of movies," she said, "and I'll bring something to nuke later."

He grinned, obviously relieved. "Thanks, honey. Thanks a lot."

She drove to Bend and found the first address on her list. It was a small, nondescript frame house, possibly from the thirties era. A small woman who looked as old as the house came to the door.

"Hello," Todd said. "I'm looking for Andrea Corman. Does she live here?"

The old woman shook her head. "I'm sorry. No one by that name here. My name is Doris and my husband is Calvin. I don't know an Andrea."

Todd thanked her and left. After consulting her Bend map, she drove to the next address, in a cluster of frame duplexes. She knew the type; she and Barney had lived in such a place when they first married. Tiny, cramped rooms, no ventilation to speak of, and everything about it as cheap as the builder could get away with. She rang the doorbell.

The woman who came was about thirty, with dark hair in a ponytail, dressed in a T-shirt and jeans. She looked tired and drawn.

"Hello," Todd said. "I'm looking for Andrea Cor—"

"I'm Andrea," the woman said. "And whatever you're selling I don't want." She started to turn away.

"Please. I'm not selling anything," Todd said quickly. "I work for the newspaper in Brindle, and I'm interviewing people who left as teenagers."

"I don't have time," the woman said.

"I want to learn why they left so young. Raise interest in building a youth center—"

"Look, I'm busy. I don't care what you're doing. And I don't care what anyone's doing in Brindle. I don't care if they rot in hell."

"Could I make an appointment?"

Andrea Corman slammed the door.

Todd walked back to her car and sat without starting it for a moment. "Thanks a lot, Sam," she muttered. "For nothing."

Sixteen

They had wandered along a dry creek bed, where they found a few geodes and some nice pieces of orange-and-black obsidian, just like Sam's. Todd had picked up a large piece of black obsidian, for a fountain, she had said, putting it in the bag. Now they were on their way home. Already the sky was turning garish with the sunset: gold bands, cerise, navy, with an all-over peach glow that turned Barney's cheeks ruddy and added warm pink tones to the dun-colored landscape.

"I think I'm beginning to understand why people stay around here," Todd said lazily, tired from the day's hike and the brisk cold air. "Look." She pointed off to the side where antelope, as immobile as statues, were watching the truck. As she spoke, the small group turned as a unit and raced away.

"Good day," Barney said. "Let's do it every week or so. Explore the countryside bit by bit."

"I could sneak into Sam's garage and get pictures of his map."

"And I'll swipe some of his tools," Barney said. "At least a shovel and pick."

"I'm hungry."

"Me, too. First stop Safeway, for something quick and easy. One of their roasted chickens, maybe."

It was strange, Todd was thinking, that out here on the desert with no one in sight in any direction, just the scrub, sage, clumps of grasses that were bowing in the wind now, distant encircling mountains that were like a fringe between earth and sky, the feeling of loneliness was gone. For hours there had been no sound except their own voices, their boots on rocks, wind in the sage and grass, an occasional scampering of something unseen. And all she had felt was peacefulness. Yet, in town, with Barney nearby, or at the office with others around, the oppressive loneliness had threatened to bring tears again and again.

They reached the supermarket within minutes of closing time. The deli was shut down already, and they settled for sliced ham, Swiss cheese and salad greens. Jan was at the checkout counter.

"Hi, guys," she said cheerfully. "You both look windburned or sunburned or something. Out taking in the sights?"

"Something like that," Todd said. "Rock hounding."

Jan rang up the sale and as Barney counted out money, she said to Todd, "Oh, by the way, I've got those books you loaned me out in the car. I was going to run them by your house later, but you can take them now. I'm through here in—" she looked at her watch "—two minutes."

Todd started to ask what books, stopped herself. She had not loaned any books to Jan.

Jan had already turned to the next customer in line. "Hi, Susan. How you doing?"

"We'll wait outside," Todd said.

Jan waved and began ringing up the items on the counter.

Seth had come through, Todd thought with a surge of relief, walking to the truck. Unaccountably she felt her heart pounding.

Jan came out promptly at closing time with the last customer close behind her. She pointed toward the side of the parking lot. "I'm over there. Did you find anything neat today?"

"Geodes," Todd said, walking with Jan to her car. "A little obsidian. It was fun."

"Yeah, we've done that now and then." The other woman was taking her time getting in her car, casting surreptitious glances at Barney and Todd alternately. Jan unlocked her own car door, reached in and brought out a canvas tote bag. "I love those romances," she said. "Let's have lunch tomorrow or Tuesday." She handed the bag to Todd, waved again to the other woman, then got into her own car. "Give me a call," she said to Todd.

"How's it going?" Barney asked late that night, standing at the door to the dining room where Todd had spread out the pictures of nine adolescents.

She shook her head. "Nowhere. Nine gone missing in a twelve-year period. They fit a cross section of America's kids. Thirteen," she said, picking up the photocopy of a boy. He looked even younger than the age given. "To seventeen," she said, pointing to a girl's picture. Sullen-faced, heavyset, with too much makeup, she looked like a thirty-year-old. Andrea's picture was there, she had been sixteen when she ran away, and pretty. "Nordic fair to Hispanic dark, everything in between. Five accounted for—in foster homes, back home, picked up for vagrancy, one in jail for breaking and entering…"

Barney came in the rest of the way and put his arm around her shoulders. "Give it up for now. It's after eleven."

She gathered the files together and nodded. "I'm beginning to see Johnny's point," she admitted. "What can you do, chain them to the water pipes?"

She was too restless to go to sleep yet, she decided an hour later. Barney had fallen asleep easily, but she was starting to twist and turn, a bad sign, and she got out of bed, pulled on her heavy robe and slippers and went back to her office. At her desk, she opened the file folder with the copies of the police cases. Four unaccounted for, including Jodie Schuster. She found those four files and lined them up. Angela Diehl, sixteen, five feet three inches, one hundred and eighteen pounds, pretty with dark hair, dark eyes, she had made one phone call home from Los Angeles, nothing more. She put Angela's case aside and studied the other three, drew in a sharp breath. Jodie, fourteen, five feet tall, ninety-six pounds, blue eyes, blond, one postcard. Virginia Ward, four feet eleven inches, ninety-four pounds, blue eyes, blond. She had sent a postcard from Portland. Caitlin McCarthy, fifteen, five feet one inch, one hundred pounds, blue eyes, blond, a postcard, followed by a second postcard two weeks later.

"They could be sisters," Todd said under her breath, studying the pictures of the three blond girls. Immature, childlike, undeveloped. Or, as Jan had said, no boobs yet. She read the cases: Caitlin, vanished after a school concert let out at eight o'clock on a Friday, not missed until Saturday. She was to have gone to a friend's house for an overnight. Virginia, vanished on a shopping trip in the mall in Bend with friends on a Saturday afternoon. Jodie, vanished before school on a Thursday morning.

Todd leaned back in her chair with her eyes closed, seeing in her mind's eye the anguished face of Mame Schuster, hearing again her desperate plea: *Will you write about her, about Jodie?*

Slowly she nodded, opened her eyes and pulled her laptop forward on the desk and began to write: "Where is Jodie Schuster?…"

"What do you think?" she asked Barney the next morning at the breakfast table. He had read the editorial twice without a word, and he looked disturbed, even worried.

"You can't print that yet," he said at last. "Not until you have something to substantiate it. Her mother's word isn't enough."

"Let me show you something," she said, getting up. She went to her office and brought back the folder with the cases of the three girls who looked alike.

Barney read the cases, examined the girls' pictures, then shook his head. "All right, they're similar, but you don't know how many other runaway kids would fit that description. You're not going to write about them, too, are you?"

"Not yet. I have to find their families, find out if they ever checked in again. I can't go barging in on people and ask, by the way, did your daughter run away years ago? I know that." She was thinking of her reception from Andrea Corman.

"And maybe you should put off writing about Jodie. What if she calls next week? Or comes home pregnant or something. It could be trouble."

"What if she doesn't?" Todd asked in a low voice. "Anyway, I intend to do some research this week, find statistics on missing kids, how many per thousand, what kind of communities they take off from, what happens to them later, things like that. I want to get at least four editorials ready before I print the first one, but that's going to be first. Not this week, but soon."

"You're accusing Ollie Briscoe of negligence, along with the sheriff's office, the state police, right up the line. Tar-and-feather time."

"They are negligent! All of them. They can't just write her off like they're doing."

"You'll make enemies," he said. "Maybe lose your job."

"Barney! This isn't about my job. I thought you would understand, back me up."

She stood up and went to the sink and held it with both hands, shaken more than she would have thought possible.

"Honey, be reasonable," he said, coming to her side. "You know I'll be there whatever you do. But you have to step back a little and look at this in a rational way. You don't have a thing to go on except a feeling, an intuition, and a hysterical woman's disbelief that her daughter would run away. All I'm saying is that it isn't enough to start throwing accusations around. Right now you're the golden girl at the newspaper, but what would it be like if Johnny turned against you?" He touched her arm and she continued to stare ahead, seeing nothing out the window. "It would be hell for you," he said. When she made no response, he returned to the table and started to stack their dishes.

From across the room, with his back to her, he said, "You know my folks got divorced when I was thirteen. All my life they had been fighting and it reached a fever pitch. I hated them both for it and ran away. A pal hid me in his bedroom, sneaked food to me for three days until his mother found me. What I'm saying is that sometimes kids feel an intolerable pressure and the only recourse they can think of is to get the hell out. You grew up in a stable family and have no idea of what the other side can be like. And you can't tell by looking at them what some kids are going through."

She closed her eyes. She had known that his parents had fought, and finally were divorced, but he had never talked much about it. "I accept that," she said, "but you also can't judge them all by your personal experience."

"Fair enough. Truce?"

"Truce." She turned from the window then. "Barney, do you realize that this is the second time we've come close to a fight over Jodie Schuster?"

He nodded. "Yes. We can't afford to fight. You have no idea how it poisons the air. You have a loop in your head that plays over and over afterward. Mean, ugly words, unforgettable words. I don't want to fight with you over anything, much less a girl we don't know."

"But she's there. And she isn't going away."

"I understand," he said slowly. As if choosing his words with great care, he added, "Honey, you've always been used to a lot of people around, a high-powered job, stimulating people to talk to, challenges, and suddenly you're in a pretty low-level town with none of that, plus a job you could do with your eyes closed. Is it possible that you're grasping for something to add a little excitement to your life? Maybe you're reaching for something not really there?"

"Maybe it isn't just the shadows on the cave walls," she said just as slowly. "Maybe there's something between the shadows and the nuts and bolts you can weigh and measure. No one could see bacteria, microbes, viruses until a couple hundred years ago, but they were there. Before they were discovered, it was a case of shadows on the walls, curses, spells, malign spirits. Maybe we still can't see everything out there simply because we haven't learned how to look, or we don't have the right tools yet. Maybe we know things without being able to say how we know. We don't have the verifiable theories. But I know Jodie Schuster was taken by someone." She shook her head. "It's getting late. I have to go to work."

Mondays were hectic and she was busy until midmorning, when she remembered that Jan had asked her to call. Not just a social request, she had understood at the time. Weeks that Jan worked on Sunday, she was off Monday, Todd knew. She called her at home.

Jan answered on the first ring. "Meet in Bend somewhere?" she asked.

"Can't take that much time," Todd said. "Maybe Carl's Café?"

Jan hesitated, then said, "Why don't you just drop in at the house for a quick sandwich? I'll be home all day."

Todd called Barney and left a message not to expect her for lunch. He could be running the loop, she thought. At twelve-thirty she left the office and drove to Jan's house across the highway.

"Listen," Jan said at the door, "I'm not supposed to be telling you anything, but I don't work for Ollie. Come on in."

She had coffee made, and started to put sandwiches together as she talked. "One of Jodie's teachers is raising hell about the kid's disappearance, and there are a couple of people around town who aren't satisfied. Just a couple, but that's something."

"That's a relief," Todd said. "I thought everyone was taking it too calmly."

Jan brought the sandwiches to the table, poured coffee, and sat down. "I'm not done," she said, leaning forward. "Some people are talking about Barney, too. They're saying that he tried to get Lisa to go to Corvallis with him for the long weekend, you know, when he spends extra time over there. She turned him down flat."

Todd had picked up her sandwich. Now, she set it down hard. "That's crazy! She tried to get him to buy her a cup of coffee or something. Who's saying that?"

"She started the rumor herself," Jan said. "You don't turn down someone like Lisa and get away with it."

"That bitch!" Todd tore into her sandwich savagely. "It will blow over," she said after swallowing. "But what about the people who aren't satisfied about Jodie? Are they demanding a real investigation? Do you have any names?"

"Not the teacher," Jan said. She had the other two names and Todd made a note of them. One in Brindle, one up in the forest above the town. That woman, Jan said, worked with Mame, another nurse. "They aren't battering down walls, and they don't really know anything, but they know Mame and Jodie pretty well and they believe Mame. If you write something about it in the newspaper, they might start wanting more answers than they're getting now."

Todd knew Jan's motive in pushing for action, she just

wanted Seth out of Brindle and thought this might be the way to achieve that. If he got involved in a real investigation it might even work, if there was anything to investigate. "I have to talk to Seth," Todd said. "Not at the station."

"Something you found in those files?"

"Maybe. How can we set up a meeting? I don't want to get him in any trouble with Ollie."

"Yeah, there's that. He has orders not to talk to you. Nowhere in Brindle. Ollie would know in a second. You can't move in this dump without someone noticing and talking. We don't count, you and me, I mean. Just two girls talking about romance novels."

"In Bend, then. I'll spring for dinner for you. Some place with booths where we can have a little privacy and some light. I have something I want to show him."

Jan's eyes widened. "You did spot something, didn't you? I know just the place. I won't tell him we're meeting or anything, just that I want to go out to dinner. If I can talk him into it. And you and Barney happen to turn up."

"Give me a call at six to say if it's on. I'll come alone or with Barney, if I can talk him into it."

Jan grinned. "Husbands!"

Todd had no intention of telling Barney about the rumor concerning Lisa, and she didn't know exactly when she decided not to try to talk him into dinner with Seth and Jan, but when she got home at ten minutes before six, the decision had been made. No more scenes, or near scenes, about Jodie, about her obsession, she added to herself, certain that was how Barney regarded it.

"Dinner's going to be a little late," Barney said after his welcoming kiss. "I lost track of time."

"That's great," she said. "It works out for both of us. I have to go to Bend and talk to someone. It won't take long, and you go ahead and eat without me. I'll catch up when I get home."

"Overtime?" he said. "You're putting in long days."

"Just a few times a week," she said lightly. "It's okay. The person I need to talk to wasn't available earlier. More working people, story of our lives."

He had the dining table covered with school papers he was grading. She motioned toward them. "Speaking of long days, you should take up true-and-false quizzes. Or multiple choices. A snap to grade."

"I'll try to remember that," he said with a grin. "As it is, I could just sprinkle Cs or Ds randomly on them and be done with it."

"That bad?"

"That bad."

"Poor baby," she said. "That's what you get for being a tough teacher." The phone rang and she hurried to answer it. He patted her bottom as she passed his chair.

"It's on," Jan said, and hung up.

Todd held a mock conversation for another few seconds, said thanks and replaced the receiver, aware that Barney could hear every word.

"Okay, that's my party," she said then. "I need a couple of things from my office and I'm off. Won't be long." He was frowning over another essay.

Thirty-five minutes later, she pulled into the parking lot at Benito's Restaurant. There were few other cars in the lot, but she saw Jan and Seth's car already parked. She picked up the envelope she had brought and entered the restaurant. The food smells made her mouth water instantly. Long day, she told herself, and looked past a waitress to find Jan and Seth. "I'm meeting friends," she said, spotting Jan in a booth.

"Hi," Jan said as she approached. "We've ordered drinks. What do you want?"

Seth gave Todd a mean look and turned a murderous look toward Jan.

"This was my idea," Todd said. "You two go ahead and order, I'll just have coffee."

She waited until they placed their order, and the waitress left, then said, "Seth, I hate doing it this way, but I have to talk to you."

He made a grunting noise and his big face was set in hard lines.

"Let's wait until your drinks come and we have a few minutes, then hear me out. After that, I'll take off and leave you in peace. Deal?"

He shrugged noncommittally. They didn't have to wait long for the drinks and her coffee to be served, and when they were alone again, she asked, "Did you read those files?"

"No."

"Thanks for getting them to me. I want to show you three of them." She took them from her folder and passed them across the table.

At first his glance was no more than cursory, but she saw it change. He went back to the first photo and description, and studied it intently, then on to the next one, and the last. "Coincidence," he said.

"What if it isn't?"

"Jesus Christ," he muttered. "It has to be."

"Will someone please let me in on it," Jan said then.

Silently Seth passed the three files to her, then regarded Todd with a bleak expression. "It has to be coincidence."

"What if there's another one or two in the files from even longer ago?" she said in a near whisper. She tapped first one picture, then another one. "Six years ago. Eleven years ago. What if there are others?"

Beside her in the booth, Jan gasped. "They're all alike!" she said in a low voice. "Good God, they're all alike!"

"There wasn't any way for you to know," Todd said to Seth. "How long has Ollie been here?"

"Seven or eight years," he said.

"So he wouldn't have known about the first one, either. And he didn't connect the dots with the other two. Why would he? But what if there are others?"

Seth rubbed his hand over his face, then took a long drink of beer. He put the glass down and took the files from Jan, fumbled in his pockets for a notebook and made some notes. Names? Dates? He didn't say what he was noting. He passed the files back to Todd.

"Who is the teacher raising hell?" she asked.

"Bernice Seligman. She had Jodie in her drama class. She claims that Jodie was excited about a part in a play they're planning for the Christmas season."

"Thanks," Todd said.

"You know it could be just a coincidence. Girls that age often look pretty much like that." He sounded as if he were arguing with himself.

"I know they do," she said. "And it's possible that they've come back or checked in. Can you find out? And will you let me know if there are others?"

"Yeah, sure. Jesus!"

She didn't linger very much longer. At the counter she signed the credit-card slip for their dinner. "Whatever they want," she told the cashier, who seemed unsure how to handle such a request.

Her stomach grumbled. Soon, she promised it, and drove back home.

Seventeen

At three on Tuesday afternoon, Todd entered the consolidated high school near Bend. She had called Bernice Seligman for an appointment earlier, and was on her way to meet the teacher. All high schools were the same, she thought, following a sign to the office. The same kids, the same sounds, the same smells, an ever-changing population with different hairstyles, different clothes, but basically never-changing. Polished floors, pale paint, green, gray or ivory, lockers, young people scurrying here and there, flirting, acting disdainful, flippant, irreverent.

In the office, the woman at the desk was on the phone, but while Todd was waiting, another woman entered the office. Wizened, tiny, gray-haired and dark-eyed, using a cane, she came straight to Todd.

"Ms. Fielding? I'm Bernice Seligman. We'll go to my classroom."

As she led the way through the hall, now crowded between classes, she never hesitated or gave an inch to the hurrying students, and they carefully skirted her.

Her classroom was empty. She closed the door, limped to her desk and motioned Todd to a chair at the corner of it.

"You wanted to ask me about Jodie Schuster," she said then. "What can I tell you?"

"I understand that you are her drama teacher," Todd said. "And that she had a part in an upcoming play that she was excited about. Is that correct?"

"I'm an English teacher," she said rather sharply. "We don't have a drama teacher these days, but I volunteered to take it on. We are going to do a modified version of *The Dead Poets Society,* and yes, she had a part. No one has a large part, but everyone will be required to recite a bit of poetry. I urged Jodie to participate, to help her overcome her shyness. She agreed. If she was excited, I can't say, but she agreed."

"Ms. Seligman, is it also true that you don't believe that she ran away from home?"

The teacher regarded her for a moment, then asked, "Why are you asking questions about her? What is your role here?"

"I talked to her mother. I believe her. As I said on the phone, I'm the editor for *The Brindle Times* newspaper, and I plan to write about missing children, starting with Jodie."

"I see." She gazed past Todd and drew in a breath. "I've been a teacher for forty-two years," she said. "I've known a lot of children like Jodie, shy, introverted, slow to mature, and also very bright. She's a good student, mostly As, a few Bs. I saw the postcard they say she wrote, and I agree with her mother that Jodie did not write it willingly. Let me show you."

She wrote on a piece of paper, then passed it to Todd. She had written, "Okay is okay, and O.K. is okay, but ok is not okay."

Todd looked up at her.

"I wrote that on the top of a paper she turned in," Bernice Seligman said, "and she was embarrassed. I agree with Mrs. Schuster that she would not have written that again. I told the sheriff that, but he dismissed it. They think she was too excited to take care, apparently."

"But you're convinced?"

"Yes. There are students who will make the same mistake repeatedly, use the vernacular they are most familiar with, colloquial speech and so on, and there are others who pick up every nuance instantly and never repeat the same mistake. She is in the latter group. I had her as a student all last year, and for the first few weeks of this year. I feel that I know the child."

Driving back to Brindle half an hour later, Todd thought that Jodie Schuster was becoming more and more real to her: physically immature, intelligent, struggling with shyness, but making an effort to overcome it. She recalled what Barney had said, they were fighting over a girl neither of them knew, but she was beginning to feel that she did know her. Jodie was no longer just a name.

She began to rewrite her editorial in her mind to include a statement by Bernice Seligman. Not the word *ok* itself, she decided, she did not want to give a kidnapper a clue about what was wrong with the postcard, just that something was. She heard the words in her head—*a kidnapper*—and she shuddered.

"Time to show the boss the current newspaper," she said that night after she and Barney finished dinner. He had made a strange and wonderful chicken dish with a lot of hot peppers and sour cream, and she didn't want to move, just sit and digest.

He grinned. "First a surprise." He went to the oven, opened it and brought out a pan of brownies. "Peace offering."

"Oh, good heavens! I can't take another bite!" She sniffed the brownies. "Maybe a little bite, and later a big bite." She had never felt more guilty in her life as she ate a whole piece. He was making up, and she was keeping secrets, excluding him. "Heavenly," she murmured. "You're much too good to me. I can feel myself spoiling around the edges. It creeps in, you know, peripherally at first, then all over until the term *spoiled rotten* applies."

"You won't linger long at Ruth Ann's house, will you?"

"Nope. I show her the copy, she looks it over, and I leave. Johnny never reads a word until it's in print, except for the advertising, and he's on that like a hawk. I just feel as if I should get someone's approval before we go to press."

By the time Barney came home from Corvallis, the newspaper would be old news, and she doubted that he would even glance at it. Local football teams and high school sports were not his cup of tea, nor was the movie listing or anything else of local interest. Except the editorials, and she simply would not show him the one for this week.

Actually, Ruth Ann had made it clear that there was no need to show her anything before going to press, but Todd thought that this week that might not be the case. She had to show her the editorial. She collected her laptop and the paper copies and left.

Driving up Crest Loop, she told herself firmly that Ruth Ann would not object, that she was in agreement that the missing children no longer could be dismissed. She told herself the same thing several times, as if it were a mantra, until she pulled into the winding driveway and came to a stop. She mouthed the words once more before she left the car and went to the door to ring the bell.

Maria opened the door and called, "It's Todd. You look cold," she added. "You might want to keep your jacket on a minute until you warm up."

"In the dining room," Ruth Ann called back. "Come on in."

The table was more covered than before with notebooks, old newspapers, journals, photographs.... Todd didn't know how Ruth Ann could tell what was what in such a mess.

"You look a lot busier than I've been," Todd said. "I won't keep you long. Just some new copy. I still have to rewrite Shinny's report on the fire-marshal meeting, but I can't do that until I call them in the morning for anything new."

"Three or four new fires," Ruth Ann said. "That little storm we had was mostly dry lightning, and that's hell this time of year. Poor Shinny, he doesn't get any better, does he?" She shook her head. "He was full of promise when he came, fresh out of journalism classes up at Hood River Community College. He began sending out résumés the day he got here and kept it up for years, I imagine, but here he still is. I know why I kept him. I didn't want to go to those dreadful meetings, and someone has to. I'd rather rewrite his material than sit through them. Well, let's see what you have."

"This is what I really wanted to show you," Todd said, handing her a paper copy of her editorial. Ruth Ann hated to read copy on the monitor.

She read with pursed lips, and Todd's hopes crumbled when she reached for a pencil and underlined here and there. "You talked to Mame and the teacher? Got their permission to use their names, quote them?"

"Yes. Mame begged me to write about Jodie, and Bernice Seligman was very positive about using her name and quoting her."

"So that's all right," Ruth Ann said. "But Ollie can't be named. I would change that to *the investigators.* Everyone will know who you mean, but no legal problem. Ollie just might get his back up and decide to defend an honorable old family name in these parts. I used names without permission once and got in trouble for it. Andrea's mother threatened to sue." She looked at Todd. "Who is Seth MacMichaels? Oh, is that Sonny's real name? I didn't know that. Well, I'd leave his name out, too. Just to keep it clean with Ollie. Good editorial. Run it, with the name changes."

"Thanks," Todd said, after letting out the breath she had been holding. "I don't think Johnny will be pleased," she added.

"Dear, he will be furious." Ruth Ann leaned back in her chair and regarded Todd with a thoughtful expression. "He isn't a newspaperman at heart, you know. He wants to be an entrepreneur, a capitalist. He says he wants tourism, his resort on the mountain, another one down below, so anything that threatens to frighten off tourists is anathema to him. But you and I are newspaperwomen, and we're printing a newspaper, not a tourist come-on."

Todd wanted to kiss her. "You said the girl you wrote about was named Andrea. Is she Andrea Corman now?"

"I'm not sure. She was Andrea Yost then, but she's married, probably. Why?"

"It's a name Sam mentioned. I tried to talk to her Saturday but she booted me out."

"Forget it. I expect that's a chapter in her life that she would not want to revisit. She came home again, you know, with a baby, or one due. I forget which. And the town treated her very badly. Other girls were forbidden to talk to her and so on."

"One other thing," Todd said, getting to her feet. "Ollie's from around here? He has family here? I thought he just came in seven or eight years ago."

"Both statements are true," Ruth Ann said. "His family's from here, and he grew up here, then got a job as a deputy sheriff up in the Pendleton area. When his wife passed away, he came back, but he was back now and then over the years to see his parents and cousins and such. I guess it was about eight years ago that he applied for the chief's job when our last one left for greener pastures. Why do you ask?"

"To clear up a bit of confusion," Todd said. "I'm still trying to straighten out who's an old-timer and who's new around here."

Ruth Ann smiled gently. "Those who stay around are generally from old families, people who come in new tend to stay a year or two, then move on. Well, that's how it is."

It was a clear, cold night, with the smell of smoke drifting in from the mountains. Todd shivered in the car heading back down Crest Loop, thinking of coffee and a brownie, a warm house, Barney.... No point in waiting for the car to warm up. That wouldn't happen in the short distance between her house and Ruth Ann's. She had not yet reached the first major curve in the narrow road when she felt the car pulling in a strange way, and then the thump, thump of a flat tire. She cursed under her breath and slowed down, but there it was, the unmistakable thump of a flat. She let the car drift downward a few more feet, slowed more, examining the road ahead, a ditch on the right, the mountain climbing up behind it, and on the left the chasm cut by Brindle Creek. Beyond the curve another twenty or thirty yards she knew the footbridge crossed the creek. Closer that way than going back to Ruth Ann's house, she decided, and pulled to the side of the road as far as she thought it was safe.

She sat thinking of the dark road, an approaching car rounding the curve, smashing the Acura. And how dark it would be without the headlights, she added grimly. Would she even be able to find the footbridge? Her headlights would remain on for a few seconds after the engine was turned off. Enough time to get to the bridge? Scattered light, she thought then, that was all the light she would have. And how do you scatter light? Gather it in both hands, fling it about? She cursed again, at herself this time. She could change a tire, but not on a pitch-black road without any light on a steep grade with a dangerous curve ahead. From where she had stopped, she could see the house lights in Brindle, the streetlights on First Street, and a couple of other streets downtown, but they seemed very far away.

"Okay," she said grimly. "Do something." She put her envelope inside her computer case, picked up her purse, and opened the car door, thinking, just around the curve, then the footbridge. She had taken a dozen steps away from the car when she froze for a second, wheeled about and ran back, got inside her car and closed and locked the door.

She let out the hand brake and began to roll forward unevenly, aware that she was probably destroying her tire, maybe the wheel. She couldn't have said why she had made this decision, or even if it had been a conscious decision, but she had felt it imperative not to be on the dark road on foot. She rolled down the road, rounded the curve and stopped again, and this time she did not hesitate, but jumped out of the car, leaving the lights on, and ran to the bridge and across it. She was at the end of the park when the car lights went off, and she kept running for another block until she was within the lit area of the town.

She walked fast to the newspaper office, found the key Johnny had given her long ago, and let herself in, then leaned against the door taking long breaths, waiting for her heart to stop racing.

Someone was out there, she thought. She had not been alone on that road.

Eighteen

By the time they had changed the tire in the glare of the truck headlights and had driven home again, with hot coffee and the brownies at hand, Todd had convinced herself that her earlier fear had been like that of a child afraid to get out of bed in the dark. Monsters, as every child knew, dwelled under the bed. And on dark roads, she had added to herself.

But when she walked to the garage where she had delivered her car that morning, the attendant on duty said, "Ma'am, there wasn't a thing I could find wrong. Just went flat. They do that sometimes. Maybe the valve worked loose." Her fear rebounded.

"We need to get cell phones again," she said that night. That was one of the extravagances they had given up in their effort to save money. "Things are still tight, and if you'll notice I haven't bought a single thing on impulse for ages, but what if that had happened on the road to Bend, or out on the desert?"

"Long walk home," he said. "Want me to take care of it?"

"I'll do it while you're in Corvallis." She realized to her chagrin that she was dreading the two days he would be gone. She had never been afraid of anything in her life until now. Good family, safe neighborhood, good school... Nothing to fear, except the monsters under the bed. More than once she had started to tell him about it, and each time had bitten back the words. He would stay home, or insist that she go with him, or something. But he couldn't afford to stay home and she had to face the fireworks from Johnny, whatever fallout there might be from her editorial. Besides, there were people she had to see. She said nothing. And she thought with some bitterness, there was nothing very rational to say: she had become spooked. Period.

Barney—growing up in that fighting, brawling household with accusations flying, where he had been treated like a Ping-Pong ball bounced back and forth—disbelieved anything that he had not seen with his own eyes or had not been proven. He had no sympathy for baseless fears, superstitions, intuitions, hunches. And that was all she could use to justify her fear.

Thursday morning she waved goodbye as he headed out toward the north loop. He never drove through town on his way to Corvallis. He said the kids, convinced of their own immortality, were oblivious of traffic as they made their way to the school bus stop. Inside again, she took her time getting ready to go to the office, in no hurry to confront Johnny.

It was nine when she entered the newspaper outer office, where all three women averted their faces and appeared very busy on her arrival. Shinny was at his desk, the first time she had seen him in the office that early in weeks. He had a malicious smirk on his face.

"Todd, get in here," Johnny snapped, standing at his office door.

He stepped aside for her to enter and slammed the door behind her. "I told you that case was closed," he said furiously. "You deliberately crossed my expressed wishes to leave it alone. I'm serving you with two weeks' notice as of now."

The door opened and Ruth Ann walked into the office. "Good morning," she said. "Am I interrupting something?"

"You know damn well you are," Johnny said. "I'm firing her. She has no business printing an inflammatory piece without authorization. I won't put up with it."

Ruth Ann glanced at Todd with a faint smile. "That was a good piece. Strange how much better things look in print than in typescript."

"You saw that editorial in advance? She showed you instead of me?" Johnny cried, outraged.

"Of course," Ruth Ann said.

"Mother, there can't be two bosses running any business, and you well know it."

Todd had felt frozen by his first words, that he was firing her, and now she was beginning to feel invisible as mother and son ignored her and faced each other. Johnny's face had become livid and a vein was throbbing in his temple. Both hands were clenched. Stiffly he walked behind his desk, then banged his fist on it.

"This is intolerable!" he said. "Who's running this damn paper? Do you know what an article like that will do to a community like ours? It will tear it apart! That's what!"

"Johnny, first question first. Who is running this business, I believe came first. My understanding is that you're the managing editor, in charge of the presses, supplies, various equipment, overseeing all the staff to make certain their work gets done, and taking care of the advertising, except for the classified. Todd is the editor in chief, and she's in charge of the design and layout, the content of the news articles and such, and the editorials. And, dear, I am the publisher, and I believe that you all ultimately work for me."

She smiled again, at him this time, as color rushed to his face, turning it brick red. "As for the second part of your question, what this will do to the community, perhaps it will shake them out of their lethargy, their apathy, make them question the status quo and what they can do about it."

She had been standing as she spoke, and now she took off her coat and tossed it over a chair, then sat down in one close to his desk. "What I want to talk about is the special centennial edition," she said. "I'm thinking magazine size, an insert on high-quality paper since there will be a lot of photographs." She looked at Todd, who had not moved since Ruth Ann's arrival. "You don't have to stay for this," she said. "We'll be talking money and it's a touchy subject. Sit down, Johnny, this will take a few minutes."

Todd didn't wait to see if Johnny sat down. She fled. Walking through the office again, she was aware that everyone there was casting surreptitious glances her way and she ignored them all. Before she had crossed the space and entered her own office, she was grinning. She sat at her desk and thought, *My God! I want to be Ruth Ann when I grow up.*

She was at her desk later when Ruth Ann tapped on the door, opened it and said, "I know you probably have errands to do, but when you're finished, join us for lunch at the house. I'm afraid I have a lot of work for you."

Todd knew that it was quite deliberate, a message to the others who could hear every word. "I'll come up as soon as I take care of a couple of things."

She could almost feel sorry for Toni, Mildred and Ally, she thought when Ruth Ann left. They had to work with and for Johnny, but they all knew who was the real boss. Her sympathy did not extend to Shinny, who was so good at pretending to be working hard.

She left soon after that and headed to Bend to pick up a cell phone and arrange for service.

The work that afternoon was more of the same, scanning, digitizing, enhancing, saving, then printing out documents and old photographs. As before, Todd paid little attention to the contents, concentrating on the lines and spaces, filling in the blanks when she could.

"I think you have more than enough material for a full-length book," she said to Ruth Ann when she took a break for a cup of coffee late that day.

"I know. It keeps growing. I keep finding things I don't want to leave out." She sipped her coffee. Neither of them had mentioned the scene in the office. "I hope you had enough time to take care of your errands. I really didn't mean for you to rush over here."

"I didn't have much to do. I wanted a cell phone and took care of that. I never knew how much I'd miss it until last night." She told Ruth Ann about the flat tire. "It would have been convenient to just call home for a ride," she added ruefully.

"I'll have Thomas Bird check the driveway for nails, although I don't see how such a thing could have been there."

"They didn't find a puncture or anything," Todd said. She had gone back and forth with a sense of fear, and realized that she was on the right side of it again, having persuaded herself to believe the garage man had been right, just one of those things. It made too little sense for anyone to have flattened her tire, not knowing how she would react. And if anyone had done that, why not follow through and bean her? she had demanded silently. There had not been an answer.

Ruth Ann's mouth tightened, but she made no comment. "Tell me about the cell phone," she said. "I've read about them but I haven't used one. I haven't felt the need."

Todd showed her. "See, I can speed dial my own home phone, or nine-one-one, or anything else I put in. Or list numbers by people's names, and it will dial them up. I have the office in there."

"Is my number on the speed dial?" When Todd said no, she said, "Why not include it, just in case you want me in a hurry. Or if Johnny tries to pull rank again."

Todd smiled and added her number to the speed dial. She tried to imagine herself on the road to Bend, getting a flat and calling Ruth Ann for assistance. Or calling for help if Johnny had her on the carpet again.

Ruth Ann was not smiling when she said, "Todd, what you did today just might initiate a renewed investigation of Jodie Schuster's disappearance, and if that happens, someone out there might not be exactly thrilled. You know as well as I do, that if that child was kidnapped, in all likelihood she is now dead. And someone from around here is a murderer. There is that and, also, some people in town might not want to think about a possible kidnapper in their midst and might behave maliciously toward you. There is almost always someone in this house, Maria, Thomas Bird, or I, and if you need help for any situation, one of us will be available."

Todd felt the fear coil in the pit of her stomach again and she wished Ruth Ann had not articulated what she had refused to put into words: Jodie was probably already dead. There was a murderer.

It was not yet dark when Todd was ready to leave that day. Ruth Ann walked to the door with her, and there, with her hand on the doorknob, she said, "From now on, Thomas Bird is going to follow you home. Don't be alarmed if you see him behind you. He'll wait at your house until you go inside and flick a light on and off."

Ruth Ann's gaze was steady, her voice so calm she might have been discussing the weather. Todd tried to swallow, found that she couldn't. After a moment, she said, "People will notice. They'll talk."

"I want them to notice," Ruth Ann said. "Good night, Todd." She opened the door.

That night, Todd channel-hopped for some time before she gave up on television. She started to make a fire, decided not to. It wasn't worth the trouble when she knew she was too restless to settle down with a book in front of it.

She was pacing a few minutes later when the phone rang. It was Jan. "Todd, listen up. There are two more, just like the ones you spotted. One in 1984, and again in 1989. The same kind of postcards in each case. Each case closed when the cards came. Ollie's having a fit about your article and Seth's in trouble. He called the state police, a sergeant who was here before. I can't talk more now. He'll be back any minute. Just wanted to keep you informed."

"Oh, my God!" Todd said. "Thanks, Jan. Just thanks."

"Yeah, talk to you later." She hung up.

After a moment, Todd jumped up and hurried to the back door to make certain it was locked, then checked the front door again, and looked in each room to inspect the drapes and shades. In her office she added the two new dates to the ones she already had, then sat staring at them all. She was startled again by the phone, and this time it was Barney. She had not realized how late it had become.

He sounded cheerful as he talked a little about the tests he had handed back, but something in her voice when she responded made him cut it off abruptly. "Todd, what's wrong? Are you okay?"

"Sure. Chilled. I must have dozed and the house is too cold. I forgot to turn up the heat when I got home. Too busy all day, and I ate the rest of the chicken—"

"Todd, cut it out. What's wrong?"

"Nothing!" She heard the shrill note in her voice and made an effort to snap out of it. "Bad dream or something. It's okay. Honest. I got the cell phone, but I forget the number. Hang on, I'll get it." She held her hand over the mouthpiece and glanced at the cell phone on the table, counted to ten, then said, "Okay, ready?" She gave him the number.

"I'll be home early tomorrow, no dallying after class or anything. Honey, is the deep freeze back? Something like that?"

"No. Really, Barney, I'm okay, just cold from the lack of heat. Nothing mysterious or spooky going on."

On the whole, it was an unsatisfying call, and she knew when they hung up that he would now worry about her, even though there was nothing he could do. But she couldn't talk to him about the missing girls over the telephone. Tomorrow, she promised herself, tomorrow she would tell him all about it, five missing girls, all more or less alike. And monsters under the bed and on dark roads? she asked herself and closed her eyes tight. She couldn't answer her question. She was afraid that if he tried to rationalize it, she might scream.

She returned to her office and again stared at the dates she had written down. About five years apart each time. Why? Going back nineteen years. Why? What connected them all beyond similarity? Or was that enough? Had they ever checked in again? Were their parents still in the area?

She scribbled notes as questions arose. Not a single answer presented itself. Knowing she should go to bed, but too restless again to fall asleep, she made coffee, grateful that she was one of those people who seemed to be unaffected by it late at night.

She had just poured a cup when the chill descended. It wasn't a gradual cooling down, but more like moving from a warm spot into Arctic air. She started to shake with cold and goose bumps covered her arms, her back, all over. Taking her coffee with her, she hurried to the bedroom and grabbed her heaviest robe, then went to the bathroom to fill the tub with water as hot as she could stand. She put the cup within reach and stepped into the hot water. Waves of despair, of loneliness, desolation gripped her and she shivered in the steaming water and wept.

Nineteen

Todd felt dopey and heavy-limbed when she entered the office the next morning. Beset by dreams verging on nightmares again and again, awakening to find herself straining to hear something above or beyond every creak and groan of the house adjusting to the low overnight temperature, by the time she gave up, she felt as if she should have spent the night baking cookies, or doing yoga exercises. Either one would have been more profitable. No one in the outer office spoke when she arrived and she walked silently to her own office. Cold-shouldered again, she thought with a shrug. They weren't sure where she would end up and were taking no chances. Johnny's door was closed and Shinny was absent.

There was little that needed to be done that morning, a few letters, new advertising copy, nothing that she couldn't do at home. She didn't bother to open the letters to the editor. It was probably too soon for feedback about her editorial, she decided, and put them aside. From her desk, she could always hear the phone ringing in the outer office and that morning it was ringing a lot, call after call. Johnny was probably getting calls, too; she hoped his door would remain closed until after she left. She looked at her watch and added to herself, in ten or fifteen minutes.

Her own phone rang then and she regarded it with distaste, then forced herself to answer, and was surprised to hear Seth's voice.

"Todd, Chief Briscoe would like you to stop by the office at ten o'clock if that's convenient." He sounded very formal and distant, as if speaking in a room with others present.

"Sure, Seth. I'll come around." He said thank-you and hung up. After replacing her own phone, she mouthed, "Freedom of the press. I don't have to tell him anything! No sources, dude. So slap me in the can."

She walked to the station promptly at ten and was met by Seth, who looked grim and as distant as he had sounded on the phone.

"They're waiting for you," he said. "This way." He walked to a closed door, held it open for her, and they both entered an office.

Ollie was behind his desk, more red-faced than ever, and another man was present. He rose when Todd walked in. He was slender and looked wiry, in his forties, with thinning gray hair and a pale mustache. He stepped forward with his hand extended. "Ms. Fielding, Sergeant Clyde Dickerson from the State Special Investigations office."

They shook hands and he motioned toward a chair. "Please, make yourself comfortable. I'd like to ask a few questions about Jodie Schuster. You strongly hinted in your editorial that her absence is not voluntary. Why?"

No one suggested that Seth sit down and he remained standing at the door looking unnaturally stiff.

"I don't know a thing that the chief doesn't have," she said slowly. "I talked to Jodie's mother and to her teacher. From what they both said, I formed the same conclusion they reached."

"Let's start with the postcard," the sergeant said. "What's wrong with it? I have a Xerox copy." He passed it to her.

She repeated what Mame Schuster had said, and what the teacher had confirmed. "Let me show you what she wrote on Jodie's paper." She tore out a page from her notebook and wrote the lines, "Okay is okay and O.K. is okay, but ok is not okay." She handed it to the sergeant. "She is certain that Jodie would never make that mistake again."

Ollie muttered, "Bullshit! The kid was in a hurry, and that's the usual way to write it."

Todd kept her gaze on the sergeant, who was looking at what she had written. He studied the postcard.

"That's all?" he asked after a moment.

"No. Jodie is a very late bloomer, she came into her menses only last summer and is still asexual. She has shown no interest in boys yet. She is timid and shy and would never get in a car with a stranger, and there's absolutely no trace of an Internet romance on the home computer she uses. I looked, and I know how to find things like that if they're there. She babysits now and then, has a few dollars saved up, her money is still in the house, and she didn't take a toothbrush with her. I think that's enough to demand a real investigation."

"She's fourteen!" Ollie said. "That's exactly the age they get ants in their pants!"

Todd continued to ignore him and kept her gaze on Dickerson. He was regarding her with a thoughtful expression. "Also," she said, "I've been talking to quite a few people in the area, and apparently this case bears a remarkable similarity to others over the past years, down to the same kind of postcard."

No one moved or made a sound for what seemed a long time, until Ollie said in a low, grating voice, "We don't have any open cases! So help me God, if you print anything like that I'll throw you in jail and toss the key!"

Sergeant Dickerson held up his hand. "Ms. Fielding, at the present time, I agree that the circumstances of Jodie Schuster's disappearance warrant further investigation. It has already been started. This will be known throughout the area very quickly, of course. You indicate in your editorial that there will be a series of editorials and I urge you now not to mention a possible connection to any past disappearances. There shouldn't be a rumor, a suggestion, even a hint that anyone suspects there possibly is more than one case here. For one thing, it would complicate the current investigation. But more important, if Jodie Schuster was taken and if she's still alive, it might put her in more jeopardy than she's in already." He paused, as if waiting for a response from her.

Again, Todd thought, *If she's still alive,* with the assumption that she probably wasn't. She moistened her lips and nodded.

"Also," Dickerson went on, "for the same reasons I've given, it would be best if you didn't try to contact any of the parents of other missing children. That would be tantamount to a loudspeaker in the street, I'm afraid."

She could only nod once more.

* * *

When she left the station, she drove home, not ready yet to get immersed again in the history of Brindle, which was seeming more and more irrelevant. She needed to think about Dickerson. They had already started a new investigation. They hadn't needed information from her, and in fact she had not told them anything they didn't already know. Dickerson had not been surprised that she knew about the other girls; his message was for her to keep it quiet. She drew in a long breath. He must have concluded that all those cases were connected.

She felt a great sense of relief that the police were going to do something meaningful and, at the same time, a nearly overwhelming sense of dread thinking that someone had been preying on young girls for twenty years—and that he was still loose in the area.

She stirred herself, noticed the answering machine was blinking, and pressed the play button to hear the robot announce that there were four new messages. The first was heavy breathing; she hit the delete button. Next was dead silence and she deleted that one. Then Mame Schuster's voice came on: "Thank you, Todd. Thank you. God bless you." Her voice was thick and choked. The last message was a muffled voice: "Pack up your stuff and go back where you came from." She deleted it. Well, Ruth Ann had warned her, and she had been right. Not everyone was happy with her meddling.

Dinner, she thought then, and got out a frozen ham steak, washed two apples to bake, and scrubbed two sweet potatoes. Everything ready to start, with a minimum of fuss. Finally she headed for Ruth Ann's house.

* * *

She was studying an old photograph of Brindle Creek that afternoon when Ruth Ann came to tell her it was break time. Ruth Ann glanced at the picture. "After the big fire," she said. "It came within a few feet of burning down the whole town back in 1886. That's when they cleared all the trees and brush from the crest and started building the loop."

Todd put the photograph down and trailed after Ruth Ann to the kitchen, where Maria had coffee and sandwiches ready.

"I understand that the state police have reopened the case of Jodie's disappearance," Ruth Ann said at the table. "Are they considering the other similar cases?"

Todd looked at her, then at Maria, warily. How did they learn everything the way they did? She shook her head. "They don't want to link anything from the past just yet. They don't want to alert anyone that they suspect a connection."

Ruth Ann nodded. "Good. I was hoping that's how they would handle it for now." She took a bite of her sandwich, and after chewing and swallowing she said, "I imagine that Ollie is holding out for a runaway. He will until proven wrong, of course. Pride, stubbornness, a dislike of bad publicity, God alone knows what drives the man. He isn't likely to be cooperative, but Thomas Bird holds the sergeant in high regard. He thinks he's intelligent and that he will be thorough. He's seldom wrong about things like that."

"He knows the sergeant?"

"No, not really, but he was questioned, you see. Local handyman, one of the usual suspects."

Maria made a rude noise and Ruth Ann smiled gently at her. "That's part of being thorough. He'll question a lot of people, or his team will, and I wouldn't have it any other way." She looked at Todd. "People might be upset, being questioned, and they might hold you responsible."

"I know. Three messages already, a heavy breather, silence, and a get-out-of-town kind of message. It's okay. I can handle it."

"Good. Now, about the special edition. Johnny and I have agreed that the week before Thanksgiving is a good time to plan for it. After Thanksgiving there will be a lot of advertising for the Christmas sales, of course, and he doesn't want a distraction then. I've been making a rough outline of what I propose to write, and on Sunday I want to have Grace and Johnny here to tell them about it. Sam will come, too, and I'd like for you and Barney to join us. Next week I'll be writing, and on Thursday and Friday we can pick the photographs and start thinking about design and layout. Are you free for Sunday afternoon? And I insist that you both have dinner here on Sunday. Nothing for tomorrow, by the way. You and Barney need a little time to yourselves."

Todd assured her that they would be free on Sunday. Maria poured more coffee all around, and Ruth Ann said, "By the way, did you check your low temperature last night?"

Todd had forgotten to do it, and she had not given a thought to noting the time when the chill had started and stopped. She had been too cold to care.

"You might want a look at our thermometer," Ruth Ann said. "It's interesting."

Todd went out to the foyer to check. The temperature in the house was seventy-two, and the low needle was on sixty-eight. She returned to the kitchen. "I guess you didn't get the full effect last night," she said, sitting down again. "It was a lot colder than that at my place."

Ruth Ann nodded. "We don't turn the heat down low at night. Maria knows I'm up and down a lot and they don't want me wandering about in a cold house. Sometimes I feel like a child again, the way they fuss over me."

"Where do you set the thermostat at night?"

"Sixty-eight," Maria said. "Where do you set yours?"

"About sixty," Todd said. "Last night it felt more like thirty or even lower." She looked at her watch, ten minutes after three. "Well, I'd better get back to work. I think I'll be able to finish with the documents this afternoon. They're turning out rather well on the whole. I had my doubts when I started." She left them sitting at the table and went back to the computer and started.

As soon as she was out of the room, Maria leaned forward and said, "Are you going to clear up the dining-room table before Sunday?"

"Of course not. Not for the next two or three weeks."

"You invited company to eat in the kitchen!"

"Maria, for heaven's sake, don't be so…so puritanical, so much more proper than I am."

Maria stood up, muttering something not quite audible, and took the carafe and cups to the sink. Ruth Ann smiled to herself. Of course in the kitchen. She could think of no better place to talk about the kinds of things she intended to discuss with Barney and Todd.

When Todd left Ruth Ann's house, she drove to Safeway to pick up a bottle of cheap wine and the cheapest vegetable they had—cabbage. The cell phone had put a new dent in their budget, one she had not anticipated. She was thinking how just a year earlier they had bought six bottles of very good wine at a time, and never looked at the price of anything in the supermarket. If they wanted it, they got it. And she thought how little it mattered now, how unimportant that was.

Jan was not working that evening, and the woman at the checkout hardly glanced at Todd when she paid for her purchases. Cold shoulder, or just indifference? Todd wondered, and decided that didn't matter either. She had the sweet potatoes in the oven, the apples cored and filled with raisins, brown sugar and cinnamon ready to go in, the cabbage shredded, ready to stir-fry, the ham steak ready for the skillet, wine chilling. All prep work done, she decided with satisfaction, looking at the kitchen clock. He would be home any minute, dinner ready in about twenty minutes after he got there, and then a lot of talk. She felt bursting with things she wanted to talk about.

When Barney got home, she forced herself to contain the words that wanted to pour out. He kissed her, then held her shoulders and examined her face. "You worried me last night," he said. "You sounded strange. Are you okay?"

"Fine, fine," she said. "Wash up, stash your things, and we'll eat in just a few minutes. Trip okay?"

He nodded. "It's snowing in the higher elevations, a dusting on the pass, drizzle in the valley." He continued to hold her shoulders. "Let dinner wait. Tell me what's going on first."

"Oh, Barney, it's...it's awful! Worse than I thought. There's wine. Let's have a glass of wine."

Sitting at the table with wine before her, she told him everything. "I showed that editorial to Ruth Ann and she said to print it, and I did. Johnny hit the ceiling." She gulped a little wine. "There are five missing girls, all alike, like Jodie, and Seth called the state police and they're opening a new investigation, but no one's to mention anyone but Jodie."

Barney held up his hand. "Okay, okay. Slow down and take it from the top, first things first. You ran the editorial, then what?"

She drew in a deep breath and told it more coherently. "The first one was nineteen years ago, but they're all connected. Sergeant Dickerson knows that, but Ollie's still denying everything, including Jodie's disappearance. And apparently Seth is in trouble with Ollie because Seth's the one who called the state police."

This time when she stopped talking, Barney rubbed his eyes. "Jesus, five girls. And no one noticed? I can't believe it."

"The postcards," she said. "Each time, as soon as a card came, the case was closed. And they're separated by five years or even six. But I can't believe it, either. Are they insane around here? Are they blind?"

"Well, you've opened their eyes. I'm proud of you. Anything else?"

"Ruth Ann is having Thomas Bird follow me home from her house. In case I get another flat or something." Her voice trailed off when Barney took her hand in a too-tight grip.

"No. Come to Corvallis with me. You can hang out at the farm, shop in town, whatever."

"I can't. Two jobs, remember. Newspaper, and with Ruth Ann. I can't simply walk away from either one." His grip tightened, causing her to wince. "Thomas Bird will wait for a signal from me before he leaves, and after I get home I won't budge again. The whole town will know by tomorrow. No one's going to try anything, Barney." In a fainter voice, she said, "You're killing my hand."

He released her hand and stood up, crossed to the refrigerator and brought out a bottle of beer. "We have a few days to think about it," he said coming back to the table. "Last night you sounded so strange I was sure the deep freeze had hit again."

"It did, but later, after you called. I forgot about that."

"Did you check the thermometer?"

She shook her head, and he went to have a look. When he returned, he had a puzzled expression. "You haven't reset it, have you?"

"No. I forgot to look at it, even."

"The low outside last night was twenty-nine, and now it's forty-two. Inside low was sixty-two. Now it's sixty-eight."

She swallowed hard. "Barney, it was just like before. I was shaking with cold. I had to get in the tub to get warm. The thermometer must be broken. I was freezing, just like before! You know how cold it got before, how cold I was."

"I do know how cold you were, like an ice cube," he said. "I'll change the thermometers, bring the outside one indoors. I know it's working okay."

"Ruth Ann felt it too last night," Todd said in a low voice, "and her thermometer didn't register a low temperature, either. Barney, that's..." She swallowed hard again and left the words unsaid. It was too frightening to say out loud.

They were sitting side by side on the sofa later, both of them with an open book. Todd had not seen a word in hers for a long time, and Barney was gazing at the low fire, not reading. There were things they couldn't talk about, she kept thinking, not really because they were unwilling, but more as if they didn't know the words to use. They didn't have the right concepts, or frame of reference. Nothing in their past had prepared them and there were no memories to draw upon, nothing they could point to and say, see, it's like that. That penetrating chill wasn't like anything they knew. There was nothing to compare it to. A cold air mass that didn't register on the thermometer. An impossible thing.

"Tomorrow let's take a day trip," she said. "Pack sandwiches and stuff and stay out all day."

He jerked back from wherever he had been and closed his book. "Good idea. Where?"

"I don't care. I'll get that tourist folder." She went to her office to find the folder they had picked up weeks earlier and had not yet used. "Okay," she said, sitting down again. "Lava caves, a wildlife refuge. It says here they have pelicans. Do you believe that? Pelicans in the desert?" He shook his head. "Moving on. Painted hills, up around John Day, and petroglyphs in the area. Smith Rocks, a Grand Canyon-like formation. Dormant volcanoes, one at Fort Rock, one at Malheur—that's the refuge. You know, Thomas Bird saw pelicans somewhere, maybe that's where. Ice caves. Crater Lake. Lost forest. How can you lose a forest? I put it down here somewhere, can't rightly remember just where." She was talking fast, as if to fill the silence that had become too heavy.

Barney put his hand on her thigh. "Take it easy, honey. Let's go look for pelicans. As you said, Thomas Bird must have seen one somewhere."

She drew in a long breath. "He's a real artist," she said. "I told him he should sell his birds and he just smiled. I think he's said maybe a total of ten words in my presence, but he smiles a lot. Ruth Ann said he does sell a few, but only those he isn't happy with, his rejects. All those in the gift shop are rejects. Can you believe that? He gives away a lot of them. They questioned him today. Just one of the usual suspects. Did you see that crane he did in the living room at Ruth Ann's house? It's really beautiful. He always uses juniper wood because it comes out like silk or porcelain or ivory, something as smooth—"

Barney squeezed her leg gently. "Let's go to bed, get an early start in the morning."

"Will you make love to me for hours?"

"Good lord, woman! Insatiable hussy! I'll do my damnedest." He stood up and drew her to her feet. "I'll have you yelling uncle before this night is over."

Twenty

She was making sandwiches the next morning when the phone rang. Barney picked it up in the living room, and after a minute came to the kitchen. "We'll start a little later than I thought. Ollie Briscoe wants to ask me a few questions. Another one of the usual suspects."

"That asshole! I can see you swooping down on your bike to kidnap a girl nineteen years ago when you were all of nine years old." She tried to keep her tone as light as his had been but she was tight with anger. Ollie was determined to treat Jodie's case as a separate, single, possible abduction, one he refused to believe in, and she suspected he was simply out to harass them or to get a bit of revenge for her meddling.

By the time the doorbell rang, she had assembled everything for their outing. Lunch, coffee in a Thermos, water, heavy jackets, her stocking cap and paper bags, just in case they found nice rocks or something.

Ollie was accompanied by Sergeant Dickerson. He introduced himself to Barney, and they all went to the living room.

"Mr. Fielding, just a few questions I'd like to ask," Dickerson said, shifting in the upholstered chair he had selected as if to get it just right.

Barney nodded.

"You know the morning we're interested in, three weeks ago this past Thursday," Dickerson said. "I understand that you drive over the mountains every Thursday, teach classes or something at Oregon State University, then come home on Friday evening. Is that right?"

"That's right. Once a month I don't come home until Sunday. I house-sit for my adviser at the university. That's how it was that week."

Dickerson made notes as Barney answered his questions. "What's your usual routine? Leave at what time, leave the area by what road, like that?"

"I try to get away by eight, earlier if possible. It's a long drive. And I leave by the back road, the north loop, to avoid the kids in town heading for the school bus."

"A couple other people leave for work on the upper loop," Dickerson said. "Do you recall if you saw anyone that morning?"

Barney said no. "Not that I remember. Sometimes I do. A dark blue Chevy, eighty-four or eighty-five, about that old, a time or two, Sam Rawleigh's Explorer once. That's about it."

"On that Thursday? Anything that morning?"

"Not that I recall. But, Sergeant, I had no reason to remember that morning in particular, and there could have been someone on the road. I simply don't remember anyone at any particular time."

"Did you ever see anyone walking on your way out? That morning in particular?"

"Never. Not that morning or any morning. The kids head for town and the school bus the opposite way." Without prompting he added, "And no strange cars or trucks, but keep in mind that, with few exceptions, I don't know the cars people here drive. I wouldn't know a stranger from a local."

Sergeant Dickerson nodded and put his notebook in his pocket, and Ollie leaned forward. He had been silent and watchful before. Now he asked, "After you drive out, where do you go? Straight to the university? Where?"

"Usually to Victor Franz's house, a few miles out of Corvallis, dump my stuff there, and then go to the university. On the weeks I'm going to be there until Sunday, I always go straight to his house and leave my things before I head for school."

"Hmm," Ollie said, making a note. "What time are your classes?"

"Thursdays from one until three, Fridays from ten until twelve-thirty."

As Ollie asked question after question, Todd felt her anger giving way to indignation, then to a sense of dread and even fear.

"Five hours is a long time to allow," Ollie said. "Leave here by eight, class not until one."

"I like to have time for a bite to eat before I start," Barney said. "After class on Thursday there are office hours from three until about five, and again on Friday, office hours after class. I need time to use the library both days."

Ollie asked for Victor's address and phone number, the people Barney had seen during office hours that week, and whether Victor or his wife had been home when Barney arrived that Thursday, or when he left on Sunday. Had he seen or had he been seen by anyone outside of classes either day that week…?

Ollie's smooth red face never changed expression, impassive at the start, impassive as he asked questions, made notes. "You ever take a friend out to the farm to keep you company those long weekends you put in over there?"

"No."

Sergeant Dickerson was gazing at the fireplace in a contemplative way, as if he were not at all interested in the line of questioning Ollie was pursuing. Good cop/bad cop? Todd asked herself as she felt her tension increase. If Ollie had to accept Jodie's disappearance as a true abduction, he would still try to isolate it, make it a one-time criminal act, unconnected to the past. He would have to find a stranger to accuse, and Barney was as near a stranger as anyone could hope for. Gone on the right day at the right time, out of sight for several days on an isolated farm. No doubt Ollie had heard the accusation Lisa had made, that Barney had asked her to go with him to Corvallis. She wanted to yell at Ollie to leave them alone, to go look for the real kidnapper, to stop being an idiot. It was her fault, she thought then. If Ollie was seriously after Barney, it was her fault.

"You ever see Jodie Schuster out in her yard, walking in the neighborhood?"

"I don't know if I did or didn't," Barney said evenly. "I wouldn't have known her if I had seen her. There are kids walking around after school hours, on the weekends—she could have been one of them for all I know."

Don't scream, Todd warned herself. *Don't make a scene.* Then she was hearing Ruth Ann's words, almost as if they were being whispered in her ear: *People might be upset, being questioned. They might hold you responsible.*

She stood up. "If you'll excuse me, I'll put on coffee." Her voice was as calm and unruffled as Barney's continued to be. She left them in the living room, went to the kitchen and started a pot of coffee. Ruth Ann had warned her, she thought, tried to prepare her for this. She had not necessarily meant "people," she had also meant that Todd herself might be upset, hold herself responsible.

She turned on the coffeemaker, then said under her breath, "If he tries to pin a single case on Barney, I'll make such a stink he'll never wash the smell off. Five girls, Ollie! Five, goddamn it!"

When she returned to the living room to offer coffee, Dickerson got to his feet swiftly. "That would be good," he said. "I'll help you."

Ollie looked uncomfortable, possibly even embarrassed, and turned down her offer.

In the kitchen, Dickerson glanced at the tourist folder, at the bag that held lunches. "Planning a little jaunt?"

"We hoped to get to Malheur today."

"It's a long drive, two or two and a half hours from here, but worth it. It's on the migratory flyby path, so there should be a lot of birds right now. Be sure to drive back out to the highway before dark, though. You know about driving in the open range at dusk? Wildlife on the road, antelope, mule deer, jackrabbits, wandering cattle. You want to be most careful around dusk, and a couple of hours after."

He added sugar to his coffee as she fixed a cup for Barney with sugar and cream, another for herself, and they returned to the living room. Apparently Barney was answering another question.

"I didn't see anyone. I picked apples, played with the dogs, read, made class notes, ate, watched television. Sunday was much the same until I left the farm at about one. That's our deal. I hang out, take the dogs out for a run, lock them inside again and take off."

"Would you like some apples, Ollie?" Todd asked. "We have a lot and they're keeping beautifully." His face turned a shade redder and he shook his head. Dickerson raised his cup to his mouth, but she caught the little smile he was hiding.

Dickerson finished his coffee and put the cup down shortly after that. "Maybe we've kept these folks long enough," he said. "They were on their way to Malheur. A long drive." He looked at Barney and added, "After you turn off the highway, it's an unimproved road, and that can mean most anything out there. I'd take the truck if I were you."

Ollie closed his notebook. "A long drive," he said. "You'll be back later tonight?"

"Of course," Todd said. "It's too cold to camp out with the birds."

As soon as the two men left, Barney pulled Todd close, nuzzled her neck and said, "I keep being surprised by you. Three years and I'm still learning about you."

"I don't have a clue what you're talking about. Do you suppose Ollie thought I was trying to bribe him first with coffee and then with apples?"

He laughed and bit her ear. "For a while I thought you were going to pop your cork. You walked out like a soldier, and came back like little Miss Sugar Bun, all sweetness and honey. I think he was trying to rile you."

"I think you're right. Let's hit the road."

It was a long drive. Todd took the wheel for the first part. "You dodge the wildlife later," she said. "Mule deer, antelopes, jackrabbits, oh, my!"

A few clouds drifted across the sky, casting shadows on the ground that kept changing in appearance from hollows to mounds. There was little traffic on the road, for long stretches none at all. And no wildlife in sight yet. Ahead, the road stretched endlessly, straight and flat, but she knew that was deceptive. Their little jaunt to Glass Butte had demonstrated that. As soon as you turned off the highway, the land showed its true self with buttes and chasms, gorges, outcroppings of basalt here and there, black rimrock, lichen decorating rocks in shades of green, yellow, pink, white.

"I like this," Barney said after a long silence. "I didn't think I'd like the desert, kind of surprising to find it's growing on me." He pointed to a dust devil in the distance. "Something runs and leaves a trace in the air," he said. "Nothing hides out here."

At the small desert town of Burns, they bought gas, and then changed places to let Barney drive into the refuge. The unimproved road was dusty, but not bad, although in wet weather it might become impassable. Suddenly Barney braked hard, and Todd was jolted.

"Look," he said. Neither of them moved as a flock of pelicans circled a butte dead ahead, circled again lower, then vanished behind the low ragged mountain. "I'll be damned," Barney said in a hushed voice.

And that began what Todd thought of as the perfect day. They followed the road to a field station with several buildings, trailers in the background, cars in a lot, and drove on past it all to follow a road that took them to the shoreline of the lake. It looked like a sea of birds, she thought in wonder, with hardly any clear water visible. Ducks, geese, cranes, pelicans, birds she didn't know…

They scrambled in the wastelands of Diamond Crater, a lunar landscape of a dormant volcano, then climbed a steep trail to overlook the lake with a stream in the distance, more birds. They drove some more, hiked again and again, ate everything she had brought for lunch, wishing they had twice that much, drove, hiked, strolled….

"Let's come back when we can rent a canoe," he said, on a crest overlooking a relatively clear patch of water with a boat landing visible.

She nodded. "To be down there with the birds on all sides, close enough to touch. We need a field guide to birds, and field glasses. Look, an eagle." They watched it swoop down to the water, rise with a fish in its claws, fly away.

The shadows had grown long and were darkening when they started back down, then stopped again. Something was happening on the water below. There was a great stirring of birds, and the geese were setting up a loud cry that repeated, echoed, re-echoed, harsh yet melodious. They began to beat their wings, running on water to all appearances, and they were taking off, a few, more, dozens, then many dozens of them. They rose almost awkwardly, gained altitude and circled as more and more rose from the water to form an unorganized mass in the sky. Gradually they seemed to find a pattern as they circled about, and then in two straggling lines they began to fly higher and higher. The lines became straighter as their formation was reached, and they headed south, crying out, honking, rising in the air. The lowering sun caught them and turned them into a golden arrow speeding away before they were lost to sight, and only the distant honking was left, diminishing slowly until quiet was restored.

Todd and Barney had not moved as they watched. In silence they clasped hands and headed to the truck. It was time to start for home.

"We're surrounded by illusions," she said dreamily minutes later, on the dirt road to the highway. Behind them, a cloud of dust betrayed their passage, and at a distance someone might see nothing more than a dust devil swirling. Above them, the sky was in constant flux with a spectacular sunset. "We think of birds as free creatures—you know, free as a bird. Yet they're programmed in the genes, hardwired to behave as ordered. And you can't capture such a sunset in oils or pastels or on film because it's a process, not an event."

The sun had gone behind the distant mountains, while in the east, the clouds were alight with dancing fires. The ambient light was golden-peach tones as gathering darkness claimed the dun-colored desert floor.

She rested her hand on his thigh, and he covered her hand with his. The clouds were already losing their fire when they reached the highway and turned to the west, and darkness fell swiftly.

"You know I don't really believe in magic," she said a few minutes later. "I mean, spells and cauldrons, the eye of a newt, that kind of magic."

He squeezed her hand. “I know.”

“But today, watching the geese, seeing them respond to a signal they can’t comprehend or ignore, acting as one entity instead of hundreds of separate creatures, it was like witnessing true magic.”

“For me, too,” he said.

It was important, she was thinking, that they had seen the geese together, that he had felt what she had felt. Too sentimental to discuss, to put into words, she thought, but it was important.

Then, surprising her very much, he said, “We’re adding to that special storehouse of memories, shared memories. When we’re old and feeble in our rocking chairs one of us will say, ‘Remember when…’ and whatever follows will be ours alone. Our grandchildren will look at us with disbelief or possibly pity, and whisper, ‘There they go again, talking about the good old days,’ but we’ll know. We’ll know.”

She wanted to cry.

Twenty-One

"That's enough," Ruth Ann said to Maria on Sunday afternoon after surveying the side table in the living room where Maria had arranged coffee service, a bottle of Jack Daniel's and one of Scotch, a pitcher of ice water, an assortment of cheeses and crackers, glasses, napkins. "I'm not having a party, God knows."

"You have to offer guests something," Maria said. She had her mouth set in a stubborn line, and Ruth Ann shrugged and let it go. Maria knew what was right and a party was a party no matter what Ruth Ann chose to call it. Maria had told Thomas Bird to make a fire and bring in plenty of wood, and now the fire was burning, a novelty since Ruth Ann rarely used the living room. Maria looked around, straightened a cushion on the sofa, nodded in satisfaction and walked out. She returned in a minute or two with white wine in a cooler, a bottle of pinot noir and wineglasses, gave Ruth Ann a defiant look and left again.

Todd and Barney arrived promptly at four and hung up their own coats, then went to the fireplace to look at the lovely crane Thomas Bird had sculpted. Sam walked in while they were at the fireplace, and Johnny and Carol arrived moments later. Sam was chatting with Todd and Barney; Johnny hardly acknowledged their presence.

After greeting them as they arrived, Ruth Ann had remained sitting quietly in her armchair gazing at the fire. She stirred herself.

"Please, all of you, help yourselves to whatever you'd like," she said gesturing toward the table.

Sam was the only one who went to pour a drink. He made it light on the Scotch, sat down and regarded Ruth Ann with a faint smile. "A soiree," he said. "Cheers."

Grace came in, looked with disapproval at the assortment of bottles, then poured wine for herself. She and Sam didn't exchange glances, much less a greeting. "I really can't imagine why you thought this was necessary," she said. "But since we're here, let's get on with it. I want to be home before dark."

"I won't take long," Ruth Ann said. "I felt it important to give you a preview of the article I'll publish the week before Thanksgiving. I'll keep to the highlights, although my article will fill in background and reference sources. Anyone, a drink? Coffee?" No one seemed to want a drink. She suspected that they would before she finished.

They all seated themselves and she started. "In 1870 or thereabouts, a gang of cutthroats preyed on riverboat travelers in the St. Louis area. There was a trap set for them and most of them were either killed or arrested and hanged. Two men escaped, Timothy McHughs and Joseph Sloane. A year later

McHughs was shot down in New Orleans, but Joseph Sloane was never found. Three years later he arrived at Brindle, calling himself Joe Warden. He built the way station, and he put in a claim for the land around here."

Grace's mouth became a tight, nearly invisible, line. She was a descendant of Joe Warden. Before she could say anything, Ruth Ann continued.

"Meanwhile, in San Francisco, Jane Marie Carstairs and her mother were shopping in one of the stylish stores when Mike Hilliard first met them. He had studied law but didn't practice it, apparently. He followed mother and daughter home, and managed to speak to Janey. Her father was a school headmaster, and the family was quite respectable. Janey was fifteen, had always been sheltered, and she had no resistance when Mike Hilliard pursued her. She became pregnant, and when the fact was indisputable, she had to confess who the man was. After forcing a marriage, her father turned her out and threatened to make her a widow if Hilliard was caught in town again. He fled with Janey, and they ended up penniless in Brindle."

She paused when Johnny stood up and poured himself a drink of Jack Daniel's and very little water. He looked almost as grim as Grace.

"When Janey got off the stagecoach, seven or eight months pregnant, she fainted, and Joe Warden caught her and carried her inside. He was smitten. He sent for the doctor, and then he and Mike Hilliard struck a deal. Hilliard knew enough law to know how to get land grants and such, but that's all he had to bargain with, except for Janey. She became a prisoner shared by the two men from then forward, and they proceeded to build their empire. Most of the land they acquired was gotten illegally, one swindle after another."

Grace put her wineglass down hard and started to rise. "I think I've heard quite enough," she said furiously.

"You haven't heard the best parts yet," Ruth Ann said, as imperturbable as Grace was enraged. "Sit down and let me finish." Grace sat rigidly on the edge of her chair.

Ruth Ann waited while Carol helped herself to coffee. No one in the room was looking directly at anyone else.

"Hilliard and Warden brought in prostitutes, but, curiously, in the spring of 1880 they sent them away again, and two months later Janey gave birth to a second child, Daniel Warden. While she was in labor, Joe Warden smothered two-year-old Rachel Hilliard, and the following morning the child's body was found in Brindle Creek, presumably drowned. It isn't clear if he intended merely to quiet her screaming, or if murder was his intention. But he did kill her."

This time Grace jumped to her feet and started for the door. "If you print anything like that, I'll sue you. Lies, all lies!"

"I have notarized documents, diaries, statements, a wanted poster for Sloane. I can prove every word," Ruth Ann said quietly. She could well imagine the outrage and shock Grace was enduring, learning that she was a descendant of the notorious Janey. "Don't you want to hear the rest?"

Grace paused at the door, turned stiffly and sat down again. She was red-faced and her hands were shaking.

"They turned Warden Place into a brothel again, but Janey was kept isolated. She tried to escape once and was rebuffed when she pleaded with a minister of the new church for help. My grandfather turned her away," she said evenly. "Years passed.

Then Hilliard and Warden had a serious falling out. Warden had decided to take his son and Janey away, to lodge them in the house he was building, and Hilliard couldn't let that happen. As long as the ménage à trois was kept secret he was willing to share his wife, but even he could not bear the scandal if she left with Warden. Of course, financial gain must have played a part. He burned down Warden Place with Warden and Janey inside, along with their son Daniel, a traveler, and a prostitute. When Daniel escaped the flames, Hilliard caught the boy and would have carried him back inside, but by then folk had gathered and he couldn't follow through. A traveling preacher took Daniel away with him and kept him until 1904, when he returned, full grown. Two days later, Mike Hilliard was shot dead."

Grace stood up, shaking with rage. "I'm warning you, I'll see you in prison if you print a word of that!" No one moved as she hurried from the room, went to the closet and retrieved her coat, then left the house, slamming the door behind her.

The others began to stir, as if they had been released from a spell. Johnny poured another drink and Sam did also, this time not keeping it light. Barney got coffee for himself and Todd, and Ruth Ann got up and helped herself to the pinot noir.

"I won't let you print that," Johnny said after downing much of the drink he held. "She'll sue and clean us out."

"It's history, Johnny. All history should be open for inspection."

"For what purpose?" he demanded harshly. "Why do you care what happened over a hundred years ago? You can't undo it, change it. Leave it alone. No one alive today is responsible for what their ancestors did. Where would you stop? With Adam and Eve in the Garden?"

She shook her head and smiled faintly. "Not quite so far back. Just our own local history. A lot of people knew what was going on at Warden Place, and not a one of them raised a hand, raised an objection. They whispered the truth among themselves, mothers to daughters, fathers to sons. They were all complicit in the deaths of four people by fire, others by gunfire, and they were all complicit in the subjugation of a young woman who was no more than a sexual slave. My grandfather was one of them. Ruled by fear, by tradition, by gossip about the wanton Janey? I don't know what colored his actions, how much he understood, or if an unexamined past was used to justify his daily behavior. This is a sick town, possibly a dying town, and it may be that the truth will start a healing process." She shrugged. "Or the truth might tear it apart. But they will learn the truth. I *will* print my article."

Johnny had been standing by the fireplace, pale and visibly shaken. Abruptly he put his glass down on the mantel and motioned to Carol, who had not moved for a long time. "Let's go home," he said. Her relief was obvious when she jumped up and started across the room with Johnny close behind her.

Ruth Ann's quiet voice stopped them before they reached the door. "Johnny, keep in mind that once you know the truth you can't continue to walk forward blindly and claim ignorance. There are choices that truth imposes."

He turned to face her. "Now what are you talking about?" he asked coldly.

"The missing children. No more silence. No more secrecy, whispers that go nowhere, denied. It's time to raise hell about our missing children. This town has cloaked itself in secrecy far too long."

He took a step in her direction. A muscle was working in his jaw and his hands were clenched. "Mother, let me tell you what I'm thinking," he said in a low, intense voice. "I'm thinking of my own choices. To stay or to go and leave you with another vacancy to fill."

"I know," she said. "I do know."

As soon as Johnny and Carol were out of the house, Sam stood up. He crossed the room to Ruth Ann and put his hand on her wrist. She knew he was taking measure of her pulse and pulled away from him.

"Are you sleeping okay?" he asked.

"As well as usual."

"I'll drop off some sleeping pills tomorrow. Very mild, just insurance. Your heart is racing."

"Sam, I just had an emotional scene with my son, regardless of how quiet we both appeared to be. Of course, my heart is responding. Stop playing doctor."

He laughed. "Thanks for the drink. I'll take off now. But I will drop off some pills for you. Doesn't hurt to have them at hand." He waved at Todd and Barney and let himself out.

Ruth Ann stood up and went to the door. "If you will excuse me, I think I'd like to go sit quietly for a few minutes," she said with her back to them. "Just make yourselves at home. It won't be long before dinner."

"One question," Barney said. "Why did you ask us here today?"

She turned and gave him a searching look, then directed the same look at Todd. "I'm sorry if you were uncomfortable," she said. "As for why, two reasons. I really do want to talk with you both, just not at the moment. And the other reason, purely selfish, was that I thought Johnny would not say something irrevocable in front of others. He came close, but he held it in."

Todd seldom thought of Ruth Ann as old any longer, but at that moment she looked ancient, and very strained. She walked from the room, as straight as ever, with as firm a tread as ever. But she was eighty, Todd thought almost with surprise, and the past hour had taken a toll on her.

Silently she went to the fireplace and regarded the crane. It was three feet tall, the pale juniper wood as smooth as ivory. She reached out to touch the bird, drew back guiltily when Thomas Bird came to her side.

He poked the fire and added a stick to it. "You can stroke him," he said. "Crane likes to be stroked. He is pretending to be above all that, but he likes it. He's mad at me, but he'd like to feel your hands on him."

She stroked the bird. "Why is he mad at you?"

"Because he wants his mate and I haven't brought her out yet. She's still locked in."

She looked at him in wonder. "You have her locked in somewhere?"

"Come. I'll show you."

He motioned to Barney to come along and led the way past Ruth Ann's sitting room, through a hall to a part of the house Todd had not seen before. Their section, she realized when he opened a door and stepped aside for her and Barney to enter a studio.

A long worktable had heavy-duty clamps holding a block of wood. Smaller clamps were aligned neatly, an array of knives, a hatchet, a saw, sandpaper.... A shelf on the wall held an assortment of wooden birds: ducks, quail, songbirds, a pheasant.... There were two shelves of books, Audubon, several field guides to birds, a thick book titled *Ornithology*....

"She is in here," Thomas Bird said, laying his hand gently on a juniper log that was about four feet tall with one down-curving branch. "It took me a long time to find her and Crane is getting impatient." Gesturing with both hands now, he held one out with his stubby fingers close together, pointing in a downward direction. His arm had become the neck of a bird as he turned his hand this way and that. His other arm became a wing that moved up and down slightly as he took several mincing steps. "She is saying, you lazy good-for-nothing, where's some food?"

He had become a crane, Todd thought in amazement, and she laughed. He turned his hand in a peculiar way, like a bird eyeing her in reproach. The branch would be the head, the beak, and long curved neck, she realized, the rest of the log would be the elongated body and legs. He had found Crane's mate, and she was still locked in.

They admired the finished pieces in the studio, and just as Todd had said before, Thomas Bird smiled a lot. Evidently he liked to be stroked as much as Crane did.

While Barney checked the thermometers and reset them, Todd wandered into the dining room and surveyed the messy table. She didn't touch anything, and again wondered how Ruth Ann could cope with such disorder, but she had seen her go unerringly to whatever she was after several times. There seemed to be more pictures than ever in one pile, and in another the small diary she had glimpsed in Janey's box of belongings. She shuddered, thinking of the young girl, the life she had led.

Barney joined her, looking disturbed. "Just like at home," he said. "No real change in temperature."

"I know. You'll have some explaining to do to your meteorologist friend."

"Not quite yet," he said. "We'll give it some more time. Maybe he was right, it's psychological, not a physical event."

"Right," she said derisively. "I'll go see if I can help Maria with dinner."

A minute later she returned to the living room, where Ruth Ann was now seated, chatting with Barney.

"Did you get chased?" Ruth Ann asked.

"Well, she didn't exactly take the broom to me, but I feel as if I've been chased."

Ruth Ann smiled knowingly. "Barney tells me you went to Malheur yesterday. Such a lovely place. I've spent many hours out there, but not for the past few years. It seems my circle of wandering has been spiraling in on me. Ah, well. Sit down, Todd, and I'll tell you what's on my mind."

Todd sat next to Barney on the sofa, across the coffee table from Ruth Ann.

"Has either of you ever lived in a small town like this before?" Ruth Ann asked. They both shook their heads. "I thought probably not. For one thing, here there are so many entangled relationships, kinship by marriage, by birth. Scratch one and three others share the itch. In the beginning it all belonged to Warden and Hilliard. They made the rules and they enforced their rules. Then Hilliard was the boss for some years. When Daniel Warden came home, he took over. There's little doubt that he shot and killed Hilliard, but no charges were ever made. He was the new king, you see, and he owned the town, the sheriff, the land, just about everything. The king is dead, long live the king." She waved her hand as if to banish the past. "When the town was incorporated and it needed a mayor and a chief of police, councilmen, all the accoutrements of a real government, Daniel got busy and handpicked them. He also began selling off parcels of ground for housing and such, but even though he owned less land, no one doubted that he was still the king."

She smiled sardonically. "Things stayed the same no matter how much they appeared to change," she said in a musing way. "But it really didn't matter, because nothing was happening that called for a real government. And now, we don't have a king any longer—we have a queen."

"Grace Rawleigh?" Barney said. "I thought she stayed out at the ranch."

"She does most of the time, but when necessary she shows up to keep her hand in. The councilmen don't do a thing without her permission, and Ollie... Poor Ollie, he would be a good man if he dared, but it's mother-may-I with him, as well."

"How on earth can she control things now?" Barney asked. "I mean, wealth isn't everything. What can she do? Send in the dogs?"

Ruth Ann laughed. "What an idea. I wonder if she's thought of it. But how she can keep control is through the land. Almost all of downtown is built on her land, leased to the present occupiers, but it's still hers. Including the land the Bolton Building is on. She could find a way to void the leases and raze everything for blocks, and there would be little anyone could do about it. Few people have the kind of money it would take to fight her."

"Your house?" Todd asked. "Is this on her land?"

"No. Thank God. We decided it was not a good idea to build on someone else's land and we didn't want a lot down in the loop, anyway. Many of the houses are on privately owned land, just not much of the downtown area is."

Barney leaned forward. "If what you said earlier is correct, that many of the land deals were swindles, does she actually legally own it all? Can records that old be used to contest her ownership?"

"I'm not sure," Ruth Ann said. "After my special edition is published, I intend to find out. I wanted her to know that it's an option, and no doubt she'll be consulting her attorney."

"Is there anything she can do to stop you in the next few weeks?" Todd asked. "Short of starting an arson fire?"

"No. Nothing. Even if she tries to void our lease, it will take six months' advance notice. But you two have to be warned that she can be vindictive, and you're on her list now, just by being here today, and you, Todd, by virtue of working on the newspaper. You know about the rumor in town concerning Lisa?" she asked Barney.

He shook his head. "Not a clue. What rumor?"

Todd said angrily, "I didn't tell him a thing about it. What's the point?"

"He has to know," Ruth Ann said. She looked at Barney. "She claimed that you pleaded with her to go to Corvallis with you on your last long stay over there, and that she turned you down. If Ollie doesn't already know that, he is certain to be told, and if he is forced to look for an abductor, you'll be his first suspect. If he doesn't think of it himself, Grace or Lisa will almost certainly give him a little nudge."

For a moment Barney didn't move. Then he said, "Not will be a suspect. I already am, and that explains a lot." He told her about the interrogation. "He asked if I ever took anyone over there for those long lonely weekends."

"If he's forced into a corner, he'll do whatever Grace tells him to do," Ruth Ann said. "If it comes to charging you, I want you to know that the newspaper, and I, will do everything possible, including legal counsel for you. And we'll certainly bring up the other missing girls. This madness has to end."

Todd moistened her lips. "I don't believe Sergeant Dickerson will let it go that far," she said. "And Seth knows...."

Ruth Ann nodded. "I hope you're right. Meanwhile, both of you, take care."

Maria came to the door to say dinner was ready. She added in an aggrieved tone, "In the kitchen."

At the table a few minutes later, after several minutes of uncomfortable silence, Ruth Ann said, "They went out to Malheur yesterday. Were the geese still on the lake? This time of year they're often thick enough to hide the water."

"They were there," Todd said, grateful for something she could talk about. "And we saw them take off. What a racket they made, hundreds of geese honking, flapping their wings, splashing water everywhere. How they know when it's time to leave is a mystery, isn't it? One minute they're just idling along, then without warning, they begin to throw themselves into the sky. What makes them decide now's the time?"

"Great Goose tells them," Thomas Bird said gravely.

Barney grinned. "That's pretty weird."

"Or," Thomas Bird said, still straight-faced, "a synapse fires in them, setting in motion all their programmed, genetic instincts, and off they go." He looked at Barney. "Is that less weird?"

"Well, we think it's something like that," Barney said.

"And what tells that little synapse it's time to fire?" Thomas Bird asked, and then he laughed.

"You win," Barney said through his own laughter.

"Tell me something," Thomas Bird asked then, sobering. "Why do they follow the leader?"

Cautiously, Barney said he didn't know.

"Because he's in front." Thomas Bird laughed again, boisterously this time and Maria told him to behave himself.

Todd and Barney praised the dinner. "It's all wonderful," Todd said. She asked Ruth Ann if she ever cooked.

"Not for many years. Maria wants me to stay out of the kitchen. She says I make too big a mess."

Todd had no doubt that Maria was exactly right about that.

Later, driving down Crest Loop, Barney said, "Remember the day we came for the first time? Each of us thought the other would be bored out here. Are we bored yet?"

"God, I would welcome a little boredom, come to think of it. You know what her message really was? That my job might vanish in the not-too-distant future."

"Or that I could be charged for kidnapping."

"And that Johnny is faced with a real dilemma."

"Or that the terrible Grace witch might drive us all out of her town."

She laughed softly. "I'll go into my magic pose and scare her off her broomstick."

He chuckled. "That'll do it. You know, Ruth Ann is quite a remarkable woman. She's risking everything at her age to right a very old wrong. I wish I knew why."

After a moment Todd said, "She has to. For the same reason the geese have to fly. Great Goose tells them to go. And something tells her she has to do this. Maybe it's all the same something."

She thought, but did not utter the words, that perhaps that same something was what had compelled her to follow up on the Jodie Schuster disappearance. It was a disquieting thought. She much preferred to believe that she had chosen deliberately.

Twenty-Two

By Wednesday, Todd was on the edge more than she could recall ever being, even when money and bills were at a crisis point. She had no idea what Ollie was up to, or where Sergeant Dickerson was and what he was doing. She had to banish her fear that Ollie was seriously investigating Barney as it resurged repeatedly. Seth did not return her call, nor had she talked with Jan for days. No one in the office had spoken to her that week and she had not seen Johnny. If he had checked in daily and left again, she couldn't tell. She did her work, went home, ate the meal Barney had prepared, played with him, made love, talked about nothing consequential, slept restlessly, returned to the office the next day.

That afternoon, she took her new editorial for Ruth Ann to look over. The statistics had filled her with horror and disbelief. Ollie, as reported by Johnny, had been wrong in saying that eighty thousand kids were reported missing every year. The number was 139,100. Family abductions, non-family abductions, runaways, throwaways, lost, injured, otherwise missing.

Ruth Ann read the editorial with a grim expression, then nodded. "Print it."

The closing paragraph was almost a direct quote from the FBI site:

> ...114,600 children are the victims of attempted family abductions. Between 3,200 and 4,600 are victims of non-family abductions, and 300-plus children have been assault victims. One hundred of them are presumed to be murdered.

"The next one gets even uglier," Todd said. "I'll catalog the various ways kids are exploited after they've been abducted or coerced away from their families. International sex trade, child pornography, addicted to drugs and turned into slaves for the drug trade. They become diseased and are discarded, or busted and locked up for years, or shot—" Her voice broke and she stopped.

Ruth Ann had been sitting at the table at her computer. She stood up and went to Todd, embraced her. "And in the last one, you'll offer suggestions about how to combat this evil. That's all you can do, my dear. You're doing a very fine thing. I'm proud of you."

"Thanks," Todd said huskily. Then, buttoning her jacket, she asked, "If Johnny doesn't come around to look over the advertising copy, do you want me to bring it all up for your approval before we go to press?"

"He hasn't shown up?" Ruth Ann knew that Johnny had been

spending hours up at the resort under construction, but she had hoped that he was checking in at the office first. Thomas Bird, also spending time at the site, said things went much faster when Johnny stayed away.

"I don't think so," Todd said. "He doesn't usually pay much attention to a lot of the copy, but he generally wants to see the advertising."

"If you're satisfied with it, don't wait for him. I have no need to see it."

When Todd hesitated, Ruth Ann said, "I'll give Hank a call and tell him you're in charge for the time being. When you say go, he'd better scoot."

Todd couldn't hide her relief. "Again, thanks. I'll be here around ten tomorrow." She had no idea if Hank would have paid any attention to her order to go to print, or if anyone else in the office would pay any attention to an order or request from her. They were doing their work, as far as she could tell, but a direct order from her? She doubted her authority.

Ruth Ann sat brooding about Johnny for a long time after Todd left. If he was serious about leaving the newspaper, there was little she could do about it, but it was hard to accept. When he and Carol had first begun to think about a resort, Johnny had asked Ruth Ann to become a partner, and she had refused. What he really had wanted, she understood at the time, was partnership in the newspaper in order to get a loan. They had gotten financing through Carol's real-estate business eventually, but Johnny was in debt, deeper than Ruth Ann had ever been in her life, and while she could appreciate his concern about money, she had no intention of sharing it. She knew that the fairly generous salary he earned at the press was his only source of income until he had the resort up and running. Would he be willing to give it up? That was the question. No doubt Carol was making a great deal of money with her real-estate company, but was it enough?

The press did odd jobs now and then, brochures, flyers, various things, for which Johnny earned a commission, but it was sporadic, not a reliable source of income. She suspected that Carol's business was carrying much of the burden of the debt for the resort's construction, and no doubt that was an added frustration to Johnny. Meanwhile, the machinery at the press sat idle a great deal of the time available. She narrowed her eyes in thought, and was startled when Maria came in to tell her dinner was ready.

Maria had spent hours out that day, and at the kitchen table while they ate dinner, she told Ruth Ann what she had learned.

"There's a lady detective asking questions at school, kids, everyone who knows Jodie, teachers, everyone. And they're asking questions all over town, up and down the streets. Ollie took off on his own investigation. He's pretending to be a detective or something." She sniffed, then said, "And some people are starting to make noises about Barney, how if he couldn't get Lisa to go away with him, maybe he settled for Jodie."

Ruth Ann shook her head. "We knew it would happen. Just not when. Always suspect the outsider, isn't that the rule?" She looked at Thomas Bird. "Is Johnny staying up at the site all day long?"

He nodded. "Most of the day. Getting in everyone's way most of the time. He wants it to go faster, be ready by spring, and it isn't going to happen. Yesterday he put on a hard hat and picked up a hammer and three guys took off on their break until he put it down again." He said this perfectly straight-faced, but there was merriment in his eyes.

Ruth Ann never had quite figured out the relationship that had formed with the three of them: Johnny, Maria—who had been with him from the time of his birth—and Thomas Bird. Aunt and uncle? Pseudo parents? Big brother and sister? Maria had bossed him around when he was very small, then stopped that and instead made suggestions. The one time he had tried to give her an order, she had laughed and after a moment he had laughed also.

Maria made certain to prepare Johnny's favorite dishes when she knew he was coming for dinner, and Thomas Bird had given him and Carol several museum-quality sculptures. He had taught Johnny how to fish, how to hunt, do house repairs, maintain a car, everything a father was expected to pass on to a son, and often regarded Johnny's attempts with amusement, but always with encouragement. Ruth Ann suspected that Thomas Bird would see to it that Johnny didn't hurt himself or anyone else at the resort work site.

Meanwhile, the press would roll without him, at least for the time being. How long it could continue might become problematic, but not this week. Tomorrow the newspaper would appear as usual.

Barney had pleaded with her to go over the mountains with him, and she had put her finger on his lips. "That's all settled," she said. "Remember?"

"I won't linger tomorrow," he said, ready to drive to Corvallis. "Bring you anything?"

She shook her head. "Just be careful on the pass. Freezing rain or something up there."

"Right." He hesitated. "You'll be at Ruth Ann's all day?"

"Yes. Then straight home with Thomas Bird right behind me, lock the doors, pull the blinds, and keep warm. You gave me my marching orders already, remember?"

"You remember," he said. "Call me when you get home, okay?"

"Barney, come on. I'm a big girl now. You should go. It might be slow driving over the mountains today."

"Call me," he said again, holding her shoulders.

She nodded. "I'll call."

At least, she thought, trying to shake off her dismal mood after he left, this wasn't going to be one of his long weeks away. Victor and his wife had a social event or something and they planned to go to the coast the following week instead, over Halloween. She listened to the news, put dishes in the dishwasher, then left for the office, where she was greeted with a stony silence. Johnny's door was closed and Shinny was not there. She planned to stay no longer than it took to pick up the mail and look over the few things on her desk, and she didn't even bother to take off her jacket. When she walked outside again, Carl was sweeping the sidewalk in front of his café. Very deliberately, he turned his back when he saw her. She shrugged, got in her car and drove to Ruth Ann's house.

By lunch that day she had finished the many old documents, and she was glad. She still had no idea how much of the material Ruth Ann planned to use, but she knew there was too much for one article. Especially if she intended to insert diary pages, notarized statements, land deeds and journal entries. She didn't ask questions, however, and after lunch with Ruth Ann and Maria in the kitchen, she went back to start work on a new stack of photographs, some of them in color.

"Can you keep the color?" Ruth Ann asked at the dining table.

"No problem. I didn't realize your article would include color, though."

"A few color prints," Ruth Ann said. "From my own box of pictures. I was the official newspaper photographer, reporter and editor, and I even ran the presses more than once, so I have some historical photos of my own to add. I'm afraid some of the colors have faded over the years, though. Is it cheating if we restore them to their original spectacular Technicolor? Can you do that?"

Todd nodded. "I won't tell."

That day Ruth Ann was working on the laptop in her sitting room, and now and then she wandered out, muttering under her breath. It reminded Todd of how Barney worked. Read or write for a while, get stuck over something, and start wandering about talking to himself not quite inaudibly. When she got stuck, she tended to sit very still and stare at the wall.

Several hours later, she was sitting still and staring, not at the wall, but at a snapshot of Lisa and a man who looked familiar. Lisa was dressed in a blue lace floor-length gown with long sleeves, cut low in front. She was wearing a diamond necklace, and more diamonds sparkled on her fingers, in earrings. Her hair was pouffed attractively and she looked almost beautiful. Her eyes were the same color as the gown she wore. But it was the man who had stopped Todd. Then she had it. Greg Waverly, a movie star from years gone by.

Ruth Ann came to tell her to take a break, and she held up the picture. "That's the movie star, isn't it?"

Ruth Ann glanced at it. "Her first husband. They had a reception at the hotel to celebrate their marriage, which I think took place in Las Vegas. She had to bring him home to show off her catch to the locals. Three years later they were divorced."

Ruth Ann remembered the day vividly. Lisa had tried to dance with every man present and girls had swarmed around Greg Waverly. Carol had started to bulge by then and was sitting out the dances and Johnny had been staying at her side. From across the room, Ruth Ann had seen Sam join them at a table. The three of them were talking when Lisa approached and held out her hands to Johnny, leaning in toward him too far, obviously an invitation to dance. Her body language, her nearness, disregard of Carol and Sam, everything about the invitation was too blatantly intimate, too suggestive. An invitation to more than a dance. When Johnny shook his head, Lisa had looked Carol over, then laughed. Johnny and Carol had both stood up and, with his arm around her shoulders, they had walked out. Sam had followed. He had been furious, Ruth Ann recalled. Lisa had laughed again, then turned to someone else in an invitation to dance. An ugly scene, Ruth Ann thought again, as she had thought at the time, and a telling one. It brought to mind her concern about Johnny. Had he ever really gotten over Lisa? Did men get over her once she landed and discarded them?

"She looks pretty young, and he must have been at least forty," Todd said, putting down the picture.

"She was twenty," Ruth Ann said. "And he still looked good on a horse."

Todd was startled at the reminder, and Ruth Ann smiled. "She liked good-looking men then, and apparently she still does."

She was regarding the stack of photographs she had collected from her own box. "I won't use many of them, but I began looking and found I couldn't stop. Wait until you see the park decked out like a Hollywood set for Grace and Sam's wedding." She laughed softly. "An old fool and her pictures of the past. Anyway, I set aside the ones I know I'll use, and I'll think of the others for now." She indicated the short stack of those she had chosen, but still regarded the much larger pile with affection.

It was nearly five when Todd came to the wedding picture of Grace and Sam. Frowning at it, she shook her head. The background was beautiful, with palm fronds arched over them, flowers everywhere, a long table gleaming with crystal and silver, flowers in crystal bowls and vases, and a massive wedding cake. Grace was dressed in a mauve satin gown with a tiara studded with diamonds and tiny flowers, and Sam in a white tuxedo. She was smiling at the camera and she looked old enough to have been his mother, Todd thought with dismay. He was as handsome as she had imagined he was as a young man, but he appeared agonized, gazing off to the side.

After studying the picture for several minutes, she stood up. Taking the print with her, she went to Ruth Ann's sitting-room door and tapped lightly.

"Come in, it's open," Ruth Ann said. She was in the reclining chair in a patch of sunlight. "I've had it for the day, and no doubt you have, too."

"Well, I suppose so, but I really wanted to ask about this."

Todd handed the print to Ruth Ann. "Is it the only one you have of them at the wedding? He looks like a man with a toothache or something."

"And she looks triumphant, doesn't she?" Ruth Ann said after a moment. "It's the only one I found that has just the two of them. All the others have a lot of people clumped here and there."

"I could work with something like that," Todd said. "Keep that background, delete everyone else."

Ruth Ann looked bemused. "Pictures used to be the ultimate truth. Now? Delete what you don't want, add what you do. To be honest, I didn't even think of that. Leave it. I'll root through them and find something better. Poor Sam. It must have been close to a hundred degrees that day, and him in that tuxedo."

She stood up and stretched. "I keep forgetting how tiring it can be to do nothing but write for a few hours. Now it's time I have my daily drink. One a day, but I insist on it. You must have a glass of wine or something to keep me company, and I'll tell you what little I know of Sam and Grace."

At the kitchen table, Ruth Ann with her bourbon and water, and Todd with a glass of wine, Ruth Ann said, "He came here right from his internship down in Los Angeles. One of the older doctors in Bend was looking for a young partner, and Sam applied. At the time he believed it would be temporary, just a fill-in position while he decided where he wanted to head next. He met Grace and began to spend time out at the ranch, and a few months later they announced their engagement. There was a shock wave, as you can imagine. She had married young, divorced when Lisa was three or four, and had had nothing to do with any man since. And he was the most handsome young man to come down the pike in a long time. Everyone assumed he was after her money."

She paused and sipped her drink. "We could all see what she was after, the catch of the century, no less, but what was in it for him? Money was the only answer anyone came up with."

"Blackmail," Maria said from the sink, where she was peeling potatoes.

"Perhaps," Ruth Ann said. "Something from his past that she had investigators dig out? If so, it has never come to light, and he has shown absolutely no interest in her money, or in the ranch. Anyway, after the wedding, they packed Lisa off to boarding school and left on a long honeymoon on a cruise ship. When they returned in three or four months, they lived at the ranch for a short time, until Lisa rebelled against the boarding school. She demanded to be taken to Paris, or so I've been told, and Grace always gave in to her and did that time, too. Sam said he couldn't leave the practice again. The elderly doctor was not in good health and Sam was carrying most of the load. In any event, whatever was going on at the ranch, the result was that Grace and Lisa left. Sam moved into the house on Crest Loop and immediately began renovations, buying furnishings, and so on, and he has lived in it ever since. As you probably noticed here, they barely speak to each other now."

"I wonder why they stayed married," Todd said after a moment.

"And so does everyone else, or they did. Now they just accept it. Early, there were whispers that maybe he was a homosexual, but that passed. He's gained the respect of the community, the hospital, his patients. Never a hint of scandal, or misbehavior of any sort. He's a very good doctor. When

Louise Coombs was dying, he treated her as if she were his own mother."

"I think he has a girlfriend," Todd said. "When we went over there to get the Joe Warden material, Barney spotted a box of expensive chocolates, not the kind a man buys for himself, according to Barney."

"That may be," Ruth Ann said. "But if it's true, it's incredible that he's kept it a secret in such a close community." She shrugged. "I rather hope it is true and that they can keep it discreet. I shudder to think how Grace would react if she learned something like that."

Todd finished her wine and stood up. "I'd better run," she said. She turned down Maria's invitation to stay for dinner. "Laundry to do, but thanks. See you tomorrow."

She would swing by Safeway and pick up a frozen something to microwave, call Barney, do laundry and relax until bedtime, she had decided earlier. And three of the four items on her to do list sounded plausible, she had added grimly.

At the supermarket, Jan was on duty at the checkout, and smiled brightly at her when Todd put her few things on the counter.

Then, after a swift glance around, she said in a low voice, "If you're home tonight, I'll drop in. Around eight?" And raising her voice to match her cheerful smile, she asked, "Find everything you need?" Without waiting for the answer, she began to ring up the purchases, acknowledging Todd's slight nod with one just as slight.

With the dinner in the microwave, not yet turned on, Todd called Barney at Victor Franz's house. He sounded distant and stiff, with very little to say, as if other people were around, and when they hung up she bit her lip in frustration. On the other hand, she told herself, she hadn't mentioned that Jan was coming by, and probably he had thought she was as distant and stiff as he was. On the whole, another unsatisfactory phone call. She turned on the microwave.

At ten minutes before eight, she stationed herself at the window in the dark dining room, watching for Jan. She was surprised to see a car drive up before her house, and stop just long enough to let Jan emerge. She hurried to open the door.

"Who brought you?" she asked when Jan slipped inside.

"Seth. He doesn't want me to walk around alone at night. He'll swing back by in an hour. He's on patrol or something."

"Come on to the living room," Todd said. She had coffee in a carafe waiting for them.

Jan took off her jacket in the living room after glancing at the windows, as if to make certain the drapes were closed. She sank into an armchair, reached into her tote bag and withdrew a folder and put it on the coffee table. "The other two cases," she said.

"Does Seth know?" Todd opened the folder and gazed at the first picture, another blond, undeveloped girl, just like Jodie. The next one was similar.

"He sent them. He's mad as hell. He wants you to blow the whole thing out of the water. Ollie's an asshole, taking orders from Grace Rawleigh, and she wants to hang Barney, and probably you, too." She said this in such a rush that her words ran together.

"What's going on?" Todd demanded. "Why is Seth mad? What orders from Grace?"

"Right. Right. Coffee first."

Todd poured the coffee and after sipping hers, Jan set the cup down. "Okay. After your article came out, the one about Jodie, Ollie blew his stack, and Seth brought out the other cases and said they had to call in the state investigators. Ollie ordered him not to do it. He did, anyway, so he has a reprimand in his file now, and that ticked him off to begin with. Sergeant Dickerson came and started to open the cases again, then he changed his mind and said only Jodie's case would be considered now."

"Did he say anything more about them?"

Jan shook her head. "Listen, no one's telling Seth anything, and Ollie has him on his shit list, doing things like now, patrolling once an hour to keep order. I've never seen him so mad."

"What about Grace? What's with her?"

"Who knows? According to her, her people wouldn't kidnap a girl, so Barney must have snatched Jodie and taken her over to the valley and killed and buried her. She was yelling on the phone to Ollie, and Seth heard enough to know that was what she was screaming about. Then she told Ollie to hightail it over to her office at the hotel, and he left. That was Monday, and Tuesday he took off for the valley, probably to look for the grave or something."

"This is insane!" Todd cried. She motioned toward the girls' pictures on the table. "They can't just ignore all the others!"

"Seth says you'd be amazed at what they can ignore if they put their minds to it. Are you going to write about them all? Link all those girls?"

"That sergeant asked me not to. He said they don't want a possible serial kidnapper to realize they are on to him. God, I don't know!"

"Seth's afraid that if you wait until they charge Barney, it will be seen as trying to save his skin. You know? Stir up a lot of confusion and stuff."

Todd closed her eyes tightly and drew in a breath. "What else is going on?"

"They—the state guys—have been checking on everyone, where they work, if they got there on time that Thursday, stuff like that. So far, it looks like all they've done is make people sore up and down the line. And, boy, are they getting sore."

"They know it was someone local," Todd whispered. "No Internet predator, anything like that."

"Yeah, I think they've accepted that. They had someone go check out the computer at Mame's house, just like you did. Nothing."

At fifteen minutes before nine, Jan said she had to go outside and watch for Seth. They didn't want anyone to see her getting picked up here, and he didn't want to have to wait for her.

"I'll go with you," Todd said. "No going out alone at night, for either of us."

They stood on the front walk huddled in the dark. On Juniper Street there were no streetlights, and few house lights on, and even fewer visible on the other side streets. It was bitterly cold.

"I don't know what I'll do," Todd said as they waited. "I feel as if I've walked into a nightmare and there's no exit door."

"You can pass me a note at the store any time," Jan said. "Or call at night, but don't leave a message on the answering machine. Who knows who might hear it? We shouldn't be seen together anymore until this is all over. People are still talking in the store, but that will dry up if they think we're buddies. Ollie warned Seth that if he contacts you, he's fired, period. Asshole."

Seth's car rolled to the side of the street and Jan darted to it and got in. Todd hurried to her own front door. The car drove away slowly as she entered the house.

She was already dreading the long night alone.

Twenty-Three

Todd had been gazing at the five pictures lined up on her desk until her vision blurred. The girls could have been cousins, they were so similar. The first one vanished after a Halloween dance at the high school. The next one was believed to be sleeping over at a girlfriend's house with a group of girls, plotting how to get Greg Waverly's autograph before he left town. She never showed up there. Just like Jodie, gone, until a few days or a week later, the postcard was delivered, and the case closed.

One of the girls had her hair drawn back severely, in a ponytail or a braid. Put her in the right clothes, Todd thought, gazing at the thin-faced girl's picture, and she could have been Janey's sister.

She recalled what Ruth Ann had said about the relationships in the area, scratch one, three others shared the itch. Joe Warden's son, Daniel, with Janey's genes. Had he actually spread her genes throughout the community? She rubbed her eyes and shook her head. Don't look for connections that aren't there, she told herself. They're just of a type.

But her brain was not listening to her good advice as it kept serving up other connections. Twice that she knew of, Lisa had been in the area. Had she been around during the other disappearances? And who would know? The morgue? She had browsed through the newspaper archives a time or two out of curiosity. Do it again, she told herself, this time with a purpose.

And why was Grace Rawleigh intent on limiting the investigation to one case? Or was she even aware of the others? No doubt Ollie was keeping her informed, so she must know. If she was serious about starting a dude ranch, bad publicity would be the last thing she would want.

Todd realized that she was avoiding the real question of what she should do: write about all the cases, or follow the sergeant's directions and remain silent? Finally, exhausted and without an answer, she gathered the pictures, put them in an envelope, and put it in her laptop case. By Wednesday she would know. By the time they went to press again, she would have come to a decision.

But what if Ollie charged Barney before then? She had come full loop again, back to the starting place, she thought wearily.

Friday morning, after glancing over her desk, Todd went to the archive storage room, where rack after rack of newspapers were kept in deep drawers. At least they weren't on microfiche, she had been relieved to see on her first visit to the morgue.

The first of the two new dates yielded nothing. No mention

of Lisa. The second one made her catch her breath. On the front page was a story about the Halloween party Grace had given at the hotel. In the picture, Lisa was at Grace's side dressed as Peter Pan. Slowly Todd replaced the newspaper and closed the drawer.

Three times out of five. Coincidence? Lisa must have been in town many times when nothing happened, no girl went missing. It had to be a coincidence.

Todd retrieved her jacket and purse from her office and headed for Ruth Ann's house. To her annoyance, the phrase *three out of five* kept repeating in her head.

By four that afternoon, Todd had finished all the pictures Ruth Ann had put aside for her.

"I haven't found the right picture of Grace and Sam," Ruth Ann said. "But I will in the next day or two, and meanwhile I'll put an *X* where I think it should go. Over the next four or five days I'll finish the text, I imagine. Then the editing, formatting, whatever else for next weekend."

"Sounds good. That's Barney's four days away, so I'll have plenty of time."

Ruth Ann was eyeing her shrewdly. "You look tired. Are you sleeping? All this hassle is hard on you, I'm afraid."

"I'm fine," Todd said swiftly. "Maybe we'll take off a day or two, go to the coast and look for whales or something, and eat clam chowder."

She had not given a thought to such a thing, but suddenly it sounded irresistible. Away, just get away for a day or two, even if they could not really afford it.

Several times that day she had started to tell Ruth Ann about the five girls, and how Lisa had been in the area at least three times when the disappearances had occurred. Each time she had started to bring it up, though, she had held back. Ruth Ann was completely immersed in her own history article, but, more important, Todd wanted to talk to Barney first.

She had shopped for dinner, a dark ale for Barney, a chicken to roast, rosemary and garlic, green beans....

By six, the chicken was in the oven, the potatoes roasting, beans ready to cook, salad tossed, and she paced, full to bursting with everything she had to tell him. When he appeared finally, she drew in her breath.

"Are you sick? What's wrong?" she demanded at the door. He looked drawn and almost haggard, as if he had not slept since leaving on Thursday.

"No, and nothing. Something smells good."

"Come in and have a beer and tell me what's wrong," she said. "It isn't dinner yet."

He took off his jacket and flung it over a chair, then embraced and kissed her. "House rule," he said, "first things first. You mentioned beer."

She got the beer and his favorite stein, poured wine for herself, and they sat at the kitchen table. He took a long drink.

"Okay, it seems that good Chief Briscoe has raised my standing in the world to prime suspect. Is that the term they use? Anyway, he showed up at Victor's house on Tuesday with a cop in tow and asked if they could look around. Victor said not without a search warrant, and they left. They went back on Wednesday with a warrant, looked over the room I use, and spent several hours tramping around the farm. No doubt looking for a fresh grave or something."

She could almost feel the blood drain from her face as he talked. When he finished, she whispered, "He's crazy!"

"I'll drink to that," Barney said, lifting the stein.

The words that had seemed uncontainable now were forgotten as Todd realized that her decision had been made for her. Not an editorial—that was already set to go—but a front-page news story about five missing girls, their statistics, the facts of their disappearance, the similar postcards....

"Honey," Barney said in a gentle voice, "come back from wherever you are. Okay?"

She shook herself. "Right. Tomorrow, let's get away. Another day trip. I don't care where. I'm making a great big chicken, leftovers for lunch tomorrow. Let's not come back until late. Real late."

Barney had risen, and drew her to her feet, held her in a tight embrace. "Relax. This will blow over, but yeah, let's go somewhere. Crater Lake?" Then, more positively, he said, "Crater Lake. And neither of us will hint, breathe, or even think about this mess. Right?"

After a moment she nodded. In that other part of her head where ideas got thought through, where words became attached to ideas and images, she was starting to write her article.

On Sunday afternoon, Johnny called Ruth Ann to say he would like to drop in for a few minutes. Here it comes, she thought, one way or the other, he's ready to commit himself.

She surveyed her sitting room, shook her head. Johnny was not as compulsively neat as Maria, but he did consider Ruth Ann to be something of a pig, she well understood. The living room would have to do. She shuddered to think how he would regard the dining room that day. She had scattered things around even more than usual in her search for a good picture of Grace and Sam at their wedding. The whole table was covered with pictures.

When she heard the doorbell half an hour later, she went out to greet him in the hall. Maria had beaten her to the door, and when they entered the living room, she was not at all surprised to see a fire burning. Maria knew what was proper.

"Sit down, Johnny," Ruth Ann said, seating herself on the sofa.

He was pacing restlessly back and forth and seemed not to have heard her. He continued to pace.

"I guess Thomas Bird mentioned that I've been putting in time up at Wild Woods," he said. "Not working. Just out in the open where I can think. It's going pretty well. If it doesn't snow much, they might even get it finished by late spring."

At times he was so much like Leone, she thought watching him. Leone had paced like that when he had something on his mind. The day he said he was leaving, he had walked a mile back and forth, back and forth, explaining himself. "You, of course, my darling, are captivating, but this wilderness! Such isolation. I have to be in a city, with museums, theater, charming people to talk to. I am suffocating here." They had been here, in this room, with her on the sofa, and Leone pacing before her. The memory vanished when Johnny spoke.

"You know that Grace will put us out of business as fast as she can," Johnny said, his back to her as he paused at the fireplace.

"She'll try."

"She will. If not today, then tomorrow, or next year. She won't let it go. Eventually she'll pull the ground out from under us if nothing else." He looked at her then. "Mother, a newspaper like ours can't make it these days. We can't compete with dailies, television, the Internet, all of it. It's just a matter of time, and we're on the downhill slide."

"I know that," she said.

"Then why—? Never mind." He jerked away from the fireplace, walked to the window and gazed out, then turned to face her again, becoming a silhouette with the strong light behind him. "Anyway, up in the woods, thinking, I decided what the hell. We're in it together. If she pulls the carpet, we'll both tumble."

Ruth Ann exhaled softly. "Thank you, Johnny. Please sit down and let me tell you what I've been thinking."

Having said what was on his mind, he could sit still for a few minutes.

"I know the newspaper is small potatoes, but as long as I have my faculties, we'll put it out once a week. And with Todd on our side, I think we'll even function as a real newspaper again. Her editorials will get attention, wait and see. She could become a new Izzy Stone in time. Anyway, leaving that for now, I decided we have to move the whole company. Get out of Grace's reach. A piece of ground on the other side of the highway."

He shook his head. "Too expensive when there's such doubt about the future. We'll do well just to hang in there."

"The other part of my thinking has to do with the future of the whole plant. Johnny, tell me truthfully, do you look forward to running a resort, catering to well-heeled tourists day in and day out?"

He jumped up from the chair, strode to the fireplace, and gave the fire a poke, causing it to spark and flare. "It's a fine business," he said, not looking at her.

"I know it is for many people. I think Carol will be extremely good at it. But I asked about you. Put that aside for a moment. When we move the press, I think it's time to consider using our machinery for a second business. It's idle far too much of the time. And it's paid for. I think we should have a publishing house, maybe take in manuscripts from other publishers, print them, as well as some of our own. I thought High Desert Press would be a good name for it, but you might prefer something else. Wild Woods Press? A little publicity for the resort."

He had turned slowly and was regarding her with disbelief. "You want to start a new business?"

He didn't utter the words that followed, but she knew what they were: *At your age?* She smiled slightly. "No. I'm offering you the chance to start a new business. I have a business, the newspaper. Do you want to be the publisher of a small press? Print books for others? Take your wares to trade shows, talk to people—editors, agents, writers—about what you are equipped to do, show them beautifully printed books?"

"What books? Mother, what in hell are you talking about?"

"I've come to believe that the article I'm writing is really little more than an excerpt from a larger work, a whole book. A history that was repeated many times with variations throughout the West. You could start with that after I write it. And in a couple of years Barney will have his dissertation done, and you could print that. I understand it's quite difficult to find a publisher for dissertations on philosophy."

Johnny laughed. "I imagine there's a reason."

"I know, but it would be a book, and I have no doubt he would be pleased to have it published and would not demand much in the way of payment. Within the coming year we should be moved, settled in, functioning and soon after, there would be two books to show off. Todd taught me how to do research on the Internet, and I've been browsing a good deal. There are hundreds of small presses popping up everywhere, filling the niche the big houses are leaving vacant. Those small presses need printers, for one thing. We have the talent and the equipment to satisfy that need. If you are interested in taking it on."

"My God, my head is spinning. Mother, I can't take on anything else. I can't afford anything else."

"I can," she said. "Why don't you go get us both a drink? I think we have a lot to discuss." And he, she knew, needed a few minutes to let it sink in that she was offering him a chance to have his own business, one that he could control.

They talked for another hour and Johnny agreed to speak to their lawyer about how best to proceed with two separate businesses sharing equipment and space.

"I'd advise you to keep Todd in charge of the editorial department," she said. "She's very talented, you know."

"I admit that, but she's—" He hesitated a moment, then finished. "She's somewhere in between unpredictable and a loose cannon. And besides, she might not be available. You realize that Ollie is hot on Barney's trail, convinced that if Jodie Schuster was actually kidnapped, Barney's the culprit."

"He's a fool," Ruth Ann said. "Jodie's the tip of an iceberg, and he knows that. He also knows that Todd is aware of it and that she won't let the matter rest with the investigation of only one of them."

"What do you mean?"

"Jodie's one of several girls who all vanished in the same way, identical circumstances, postcards, everything. It goes back for years, long before Barney could have found Brindle on a map if his life depended on it. And, as for Todd, she put herself in grave danger publishing that editorial."

"How the devil—?" He shook his head. "Never mind. Your spies told you." His disbelief was evident.

When he stood up to leave, he said, "I've got my work cut out for me, don't I? Get Carol looking for the right piece of ground. Research. How much space will we need? What new equipment? A building to plan."

At the door, pulling on his jacket, he paused and asked, "If I had come to tell you I was leaving, would any of this have come up?"

She shook her head. "Not a hint. I would have given you my blessing, whatever direction you were heading, that's all."

He was grinning and his step was buoyant when he walked out.

Ruth Ann smiled after he left. Then she laughed aloud. "Good God," she said under her breath. "I've become a venture capitalist."

It might take most or even all of her resources, she mused, and she had little doubt that she would end up in debt, after all. Also, there were no guarantees that Johnny would succeed. She knew, however, that he never would have been a success at running a posh resort for tourists.

He had stood against the window exactly the same way

Leone had done that day with his altogether different message. The memory flooded in, sharp and clear.

"San Francisco," he had said in a low, intense voice. "You loved it two years ago. Remember? A new life. A different kind of life. Come with me, my darling."

She had shaken her head. "My roots are here, the desert's in my blood, in my heart, my soul. What would I do in a big city day in and day out, month after month? I loved it as a place to visit, but I can't leave."

"You can't leave and I can't stay," he had said. And with that, the matter was settled. A week later he was gone.

For months she had agonized over her decision. She stood up and crossed to the window where he had stood years ago, and where Johnny had stood hours before. From here she could see most of Brindle and for all its faults, its entrapment by the past, its unwillingness to face the truth, this was home, where she belonged. Born here, she would die here.

But not yet, she added to herself. Not quite yet. She had a book to write first.

Twenty-Four

Todd was dreaming. She was picking flowers, dazzling white daisies with golden centers, and taking them one by one to a table to arrange them. One more, she thought, just one more. When she returned to the table with one more, the other daisies were running away, scattering. She rushed to pick them up again, but they kept eluding her, dancing this way and that as she reached for them. "There are too many," she said. "I can't hold them all." From a great distance she could hear Barney's voice murmuring inaudible words, and her own voice, also unintelligible. She wished the voices would go away, as she ran here and there to collect the flowers that had escaped. She had to arrange them before the director came, or he would be furious, and she feared his anger.

The dancing flowers surrounded her, bobbing and weaving, flashing brilliantly in the sunlight. She became more and more desperate to get them all together again before the director came but wherever she reached, her hand closed on air. Behind her she could hear the surf pounding, great waves breaking against rocks with crashes like thunder. The wind started to blow, cold and harsh, and the flowers huddled against it, but the gusting wind stripped the petals and hurled them in swirling patterns until they were caught on inches-long cactus needles, impaled, sheathing the immense cactus in shimmering white. One kept flying higher and higher until it vanished against the sky. The wind was blowing her toward the giant cactus, and she could find nothing to grab, nothing to hold on to, as she was driven closer and closer to the stiletto-like needles. When she tried to call for help, the wind carried her voice away and no sound issued.

Then Barney's distant voice was in close to her ear. "Todd, it's all right. I'm here. You're all right."

She felt his arms, and the warmth of his breath and she sighed and plunged into dreamless sleep.

All day Johnny had been in and out of his office, joking with the three women in the outer office, grinning at Todd, and not a word about the problem Ruth Ann had presented him with concerning the history article. It was as if the past week had not happened, Todd thought, another mystery. The other women even smiled tentatively at her, although none of them spoke directly to her.

Johnny had left and she was ready to leave for the day when sirens suddenly began wailing on the highway. They kept going, gradually fading.

"Now what?" Todd said to no one in particular, shrugged into her jacket and went outside, just as Ollie's police car tore around the corner, with his siren at full blast.

She got into her own car and followed him to the highway and north. As she drove, she called Barney to tell him she would be late. "Lots of sirens," she said to the answering machine. "Don't know what's going on yet. I'll call back when I know something."

A few miles south of Bend there were many headlights, flashing police-car lights, even a flood lamp. She slowed as she approached. Ahead, Ollie was waving her to a stop.

"Just turn around and get back to town," he said. "Nothing here for you."

"What happened?" She could see a truck overturned on the highway, but too many other cars were blocking the view. She got out of the car and tried to look around Ollie.

"I told you to beat it," he said.

"Press, Ollie. Remember? I have a right to know what's going on." She pushed past him, and he cursed and went to a car that had followed her this far.

She saw Shinny with two other men. Shinny grinned at her. "If it ain't our own little Lois Lane looking for another scoop." He had been drinking. She ignored him and continued forward. Spotting Johnny and a state trooper talking, together she hurried to join them.

"What happened?"

The trooper moved away when his phone rang.

"Nothing's very clear yet," Johnny said. "Apparently a guy pulling a U-Haul swerved into the path of the log truck and it swerved, went out of control, and tipped over. Logs are all over the road up there."

"Anyone hurt?"

"I don't know. Sam's looking them over. He was on this side of it and came back. They won't let anyone else get closer yet."

Ollie finished turning several cars around, sending them back the way they had come, and now joined Todd and Johnny. He didn't acknowledge Todd, but said to Johnny, "Sonny put up a detour down around the trailer park. Won't be any more traffic this way for hours, looks like. It's a mess."

There was another siren from the north end of the accident scene. "Ambulance," Johnny said. Ollie started to move toward the trucks.

"Shouldn't we be getting names, more information?" Todd asked.

"Can't yet. Wait until the ambulance takes off."

"I'll see if I can get a picture," she muttered. This was insane, keeping the press away from the action, she was thinking angrily. She got her digital camera from the car and began to inch forward, paused, and then returned to the Acura and climbed onto the hood. She could hear Shinny whooping with laughter, but now, with the scene illuminated by a flood lamp, she could see a little something, and she began to take pictures. The log truck was on its side, the U-Haul crossways on the highway. There were clusters of men in shifting groups milling about the trucks, and logs everywhere. She spotted Sam coming her way and climbed down again.

"How bad are the injuries?" she called to him. Johnny joined them.

He shook his head. "Not bad. The U-Haul driver has a head injury, possibly a concussion, but I don't think so. He's conscious. He says he swerved to miss a deer. The other guy is shaken up, but not injured. They'll wait for an insurance inspector to come before they do anything about cleaning up the logs and getting that truck upright. Hours, many hours, looks like."

"Looks like I go back to Brindle and take the detour," Johnny said. He lived on a hill south of Bend. "Ollie says this road will be closed just about all night."

Other drivers were starting to back up, turning on the highway, to head south. Todd waved goodbye to Johnny and Sam and got in her car, then called home again. This time Barney answered on the first ring.

"Hi," she said. "I'm up the highway not far from Bend. Two trucks mixed it up and one's overturned with logs all over the place. No serious injuries. I'm waiting for a chance to get turned around and come home. Is it soup yet?"

"It will be by the time you get here."

She paid little attention to the other cars maneuvering on the road. When they were out of the way she would make her own turn. "I shouldn't be long. There's no need to hang around here for names or anything. Johnny will get that kind of stuff from Ollie tomorrow or the next day. Ain't non-deadlines wonderful?" After disconnecting, she turned her car around, and soon was driving back to Brindle.

Ahead of her, taillights were dwindling fast, and with no approaching headlights, she felt as if hers was the only car on this lonely road. She thought uneasily how dark the countryside was without traffic coming and going. Then, almost with relief, she saw headlights behind her. Coming fast, she thought, pulling slightly to the right, slowing a little. But it was a three-lane highway here, with plenty of passing room. The headlights were blinding in her rearview mirror. She adjusted it to reduce the glare, flicked her own headlights from high beam to low, back. The lights did not change and they were closing in fast.

My God, she thought with a rush of fear. *He intends to ram me!* She pushed the accelerator to the floor and shot ahead, but behind her the other vehicle took only a second to start closing in again.

She was doing ninety miles an hour, thinking just a few more miles, just a few more miles, over and over, when headlights appeared on the road ahead. Someone was coming her way. The lights in her rearview mirror vanished. A pickup truck roared past, but she was going too fast to see more than that. Although the lights did not come on behind her again, she didn't slow down until she got closer to Brindle. Approaching town at the speed limit, she saw Seth's car blocking the road ahead, with him in the highway, talking to a driver and motioning toward the detour. A second car pulled to a stop.

She turned onto First Street and braked in at the curb, suddenly shaking too hard to drive. Sitting, waiting for her heart to stop racing, for her hands to steady again, she watched to see who would drive into town. No one did. Very slowly, she drove the rest of the way home.

Barney met her at the door, and after one look took her in his arms. "You're pale as a ghost. What's wrong? What happened?"

Unaccountably she was shaking again. Barney loosened his hold and led her into the living room, guided her onto the sofa and sat next to her with his arm around her. "Calm down, honey. Long breaths. Relax."

After a moment, when she stopped shaking and drew in one

long lingering breath, she said, “Someone tried to run me off the road. I was doing ninety, maybe more. What if he had hit my car, nudged it even a little bit?”

Barney made a low throat sound and tightened his arm around her. “Start back further. You were at the accident scene. Then what?”

She swallowed hard and started further back and told him about it. “If that truck hadn’t come, he would have rammed my car. He was getting closer and closer.”

“Jesus,” Barney whispered. “Jesus Christ! Did you see anything beyond the lights?”

She shook her head. She had started to sweat and realized she was still in her heavy jacket. Together they unbuttoned it and took it off, but he continued to hold her.

“I couldn’t see past the bright headlights,” she said. “You know how they can blind you. I kept going faster and so did he.”

“We have to call Dickerson,” Barney said.

“Why? I didn’t see anyone. What can he do?”

“Whoever was driving that truck must have seen whoever was behind you.”

She had not thought of that, but of course they would have seen her car racing and the other one.

“His cell-phone number,” she said. “I left his card on the table.”

Together they went to the kitchen to find the card, and she stayed close to Barney as he made the call, then left a message for Dickerson.

“Do you want a drink or something?” Barney asked when he disconnected. “No telling when he’ll get back to us.”

“Coffee, that’s all.”

"Sit down. I'll put it on."

She sat at the table and watched him prepare the coffee. Again, she thought. First the flat tire, and now this. And nothing she could really point to either time.

They were still at the table with steaming mugs of coffee when the doorbell rang. Barney motioned for her to remain there and went to the front door; she jumped up when she heard him greeting Seth and Sergeant Dickerson.

"We're having coffee in the kitchen," Barney said. "You want some?"

"Sure would be fine," Dickerson said, and they came into the kitchen.

"Hope it's all right for him to be along with me," Dickerson said, motioning toward Seth, who was regarding Todd with a faint smile. "He's on patrol duty, and this is on his route, so I hitched a ride."

"That's my duty roster these days," Seth said. "Redirect traffic, patrol the town on the hour."

"And," Dickerson said, taking off his jacket, "since he seems to be collaborating with you, it seemed fair enough for him to hear what's on your mind."

"He knows I passed those cases on to you," Seth said.

Barney poured coffee for them and they all sat at the table while Todd repeated what she had told Barney.

"No truck went past the street blockade," Seth said when she finished. "It might have been kids in one of their dad's trucks, out through the North Crest Loop."

"Find them and find out what they saw," Barney said.

"If they were underage kids, illegal as hell to be out there driving in the first place," Seth said. "We can try."

"They won't talk to you," Todd said dully. "In this crazy town no one talks. Isn't that how it goes?" She looked at Dickerson. "Ollie and a deputy went to Corvallis looking for a grave at Victor Franz's house. Did you know about that? He intends to hang Jodie Schuster's disappearance on Barney."

Seth and the sergeant exchanged a quick glance and Seth shrugged. "He got the council to hire Gary Hanks as his temporary deputy and they took off. He didn't say what for or where they were headed. Not on my duty roster to know." He couldn't hide the bitterness behind the words.

Todd kept her gaze on the sergeant. "I'm going to publish that list of girls and the circumstances behind each and every case. We all know that wrongful arrests are made all the time and I don't intend to let it happen to my husband."

Barney put his hand on her arm and she stopped. "More to the point," he said, "I think that tonight was the second attempt to get at Todd. Someone out there is getting desperate and I want to know what you're doing about it."

"What other attempt?" Dickerson asked.

"She left Mrs. Colonna's house after dark and on the loop road she had a flat. Nothing was wrong with the tire, just a loose air valve. But they don't loosen themselves."

Todd felt herself stiffen and Barney's hand tightened on her arm. Sergeant Dickerson was regarding her with interest. "Why don't you tell me about that incident," he said.

She told him. "I just felt as if someone was there, but I didn't see anyone or hear anything."

"She let the car roll down to where the headlights were on the bridge," Barney said. "Whoever arranged for the flat couldn't have expected her to do that. A man wouldn't have done it. He probably thought she'd go back to Mrs. Colonna's house to get a ride home or to call me."

Dickerson looked thoughtful as he said, "Not much to go on, is there? Sometimes valves really do work loose and she didn't see or hear anyone. And tonight's incident, again, there's not much to follow through with. We'll see if we can find that truck and whoever was in it. But the guy following you could have intended nothing more than a malicious prank, someone out for a laugh. Or someone might have tried to make you lose control of your car, crash at high speed. Doubtful if anyone would try to bump you going that fast. Too unpredictable. Both vehicles might have spun out of control. It would have put a dent in his vehicle, or left red paint. But let's assume for a moment that you're right, it was deliberate. That raises an interesting question: I wonder what that guy thinks you know."

"I know there's more than one girl involved, but so do you, and Seth, Ruth Ann, Jan, Ollie, even if he won't admit it. And I don't know a thing you don't know," she said hotly. "This is insane."

"It's the articles," Seth said. "You stirred up a hornet's nest with them and he wants to quiet you."

"I haven't even started," she said grimly.

"I hope you'll reconsider." Sergeant Dickerson drained his coffee mug and set it down. "If there's a possibility that Jodie's alive, you don't want to be the one who finishes her off."

"That's foul!" she cried. "I know Barney's in danger, and she may have been dead for weeks now."

"Just think about it," he said, rising. "We'd best be on our way, lots of streets to check out. Oh, you might make a list of everyone you recognized at the wreck." He gave Todd a shrewd look. "And I hope you won't go racing around the countryside after dark for quite a spell."

Barney stood up to go to the door with them, with Todd closely following. At the door, Barney paused. "Tell me something, Sergeant. Is this still a local affair, or has the state officially taken charge?"

"It's local."

"So the kidnapper or killer thinks there's a possibility that you'll come up with nothing and pull out. Is that the scenario you're working with?"

Sergeant Dickerson gave him an appraising look. "Do your philosophy studies teach you to think like a cop? Interesting." He waved to Todd and when Barney still didn't open the door, he reached past him and opened it himself. "We'll be in touch."

"That's it," Barney said after they were gone. "They haven't come up with anything and they hope the kidnapper will do something really stupid."

"Like kill me," she said.

In the car as Seth began to drive, Sergeant Dickerson said, "Well, she knows something, or at least our guy believes she does. That might be a good lead. She's only been here a couple of months. How many folks does she have contact with?"

Seth shook his head. "Not that easy. She made it a point to meet everyone she could in the early weeks, in and out of shops, introducing herself, chatting with people. I expect she's talked to every businessman in Brindle. That might be all it's narrowed down to."

The sergeant said, "Better than nothing, and that's what we have so far. Something else. The timing of that first attempt."

Seth gave him a swift look. "You agree that it was an attempt?"

"Sure," Dickerson said. "But what's interesting is that it happened before her first editorial was printed. How many people knew what she was up to before that?"

Seth could think of only a few; he named them. "Ollie, everyone in Mrs. Colonna's house, I did, Jan. Mame might have told someone, or any of them might have, especially Ollie. He reports to Grace Rawleigh."

"Johnny Colonna?"

"I don't think so. He raised hell when the editorial came out and he would have fired her if Mrs. Colonna hadn't stepped in. She has Thomas Bird following Todd home every day from her place, by the way. He waits until a light goes on and off before he leaves."

"Interesting," Dickerson said. "So folks around here know that, and our guy does, too. That's real interesting. The guy is smart. That flat might have been his first mistake. Tonight's his second. Good track record. Any chance you can find out about the truck and who was in it? That could go somewhere. I want you to handle that. They might talk to you, and I know they aren't about to tell my crew anything."

"Maybe. But it won't be fast. In a day or two there'll be rumors about who had the nerve to head up there. They probably parked a good distance from the wreck and walked in. And they'll talk about it. They always do, after the fact." He thought a moment. "They might not have seen him. Todd said he turned off his lights when the truck was approaching. Dark car, pulled off the highway, excited kids."

"There's that," Dickerson said. "We'll keep an eye on her, but discreetly. It's good that he knows about Bird, but I don't want him to know we'll be keeping an eye out. He'll try again. The flat tire was planned. Tonight was opportunistic. He'll plan next time. And he's a good planner."

Seth's hands tightened on the steering wheel. Bait, he thought. Todd was the only bait they had.

They had eaten finally, the dishes were rinsed and in the dishwasher. "Is there anything you have to do that can't wait until tomorrow?" Barney asked.

She shook her head.

"You've had a long, tough day," he said. "Come sit down. I want to try something. Game?"

"Just maybe," she said. "No promises. No mental games. I think my brain cells are in meltdown."

"Right." He took her hand and led the way to the living room where a fire was burning low, making pleasant fire sounds and smells. "Let's sit here, and I'll tell you about it," he said, drawing her to the sofa, sitting beside her.

"You ever participate in the sleep lab experiments at school?" he asked, stretching out his legs, gazing at the ceiling.

"Nope. I know about them."

"Okay. I was a volunteer quite a few times. You know, twenty bucks here, twenty there, it was worth my while. What they do is wire you up before you go to sleep, electrodes here and there. You start REM sleep and they record it, and in some experiments they get you to tell them what you're dreaming. The theory is that your first dreams, when you go to sleep are closest to reality, a sorting of events in the order of arrival, something like that. Apparently they get wilder as the night goes by. I'm not sure they ever proved anything, but I went along with it."

She yawned in spite of herself. The fire, good food, comfort were all bringing relaxation that hadn't seemed possible such a short time before.

"Scoff, see if I care. Anyway, do you recall your dreams from last night?"

"Nope. I hardly ever do."

"Yeah, me, too. But you were dreaming, and I was still awake. You were pretty restless, tossing around in your sleep. I asked you what you were dreaming. Do you remember any of that?"

She shook her head, suddenly fully alert and uneasy that he had invaded her sleep, that he knew what she had dreamed even if she didn't.

"After you went into deeper sleep I got up and wrote down what you said," he continued. "Let's look it over and see if it means anything to you. Game?"

"Sure," she said unwillingly. "But we both agree that dreams are pretty meaningless, just a bunch of random memories and fantasies."

"Nothing erotic last night," he said, grinning, as if he suspected that was on her mind. He took his notebook from his shirt pocket and read the words he had written.

"I'm arranging flowers, daisies, but they won't hold still and there are too many. They keep getting away, and I'm afraid the director will come before I finish. I'm afraid of the director. The wind blows the flowers apart. A storm is coming, gale-force winds tearing the flowers apart, blowing them against cactus spikes. Shimmering against the needles, impaled. The wind is blowing me toward the cactus, and the director is coming. I can't scream."

He stopped reading and gazed at the ceiling again. "Who's the director, Todd?"

"I don't know," she said. "I don't remember any of that."

"How many flowers were there?" he asked, not looking at her.

"I told you, I don't remember any of that." Her voice was too shrill. She took a deep breath. "Barney, dreams don't necessarily mean anything. I thought you'd be the last one to think otherwise."

"Unless they do," he said. "Sometimes, the theory goes, we see things, notice things without making a conscious note of them, but they're in our heads trying to get attention. Not wisdom and truth by outside revelation, but received intelligence from our own brains. And apparently only the dreamer can interpret the dream. All anyone else can do is impose an outside opinion that may or may not be near the mark." He tore out the page from his notebook, held it out to her. "Take it, glance at it from time to time, see if anything surfaces. Okay?"

Reluctantly she accepted the paper.

"Think of the implications of what happened tonight. If the guy who tried to run you off the road is the kidnapper, you've eliminated most of the males from Brindle. Maybe the guy did that really stupid thing the sergeant's been waiting for."

Twenty-Five

At breakfast on Tuesday, Barney looked over the printouts of the digital pictures Todd had taken at the accident scene. He also had the list of names Todd had written of the people she'd recognized there: Shinny, with two men they both had seen around but did not have names for; Ollie, Johnny, Sam, a poor picture of Jacko from the rock shop with an unknown man; one of the councilmen, Albert something, and several others, unnamed but vaguely familiar.

"I'll try to hunt down Dickerson today," Barney said. "It's a good start. Those few can name others maybe, narrow the field considerably."

"Unless that was just a prank, with no connection to anything," she said gloomily. "Some joke. See how fast the Acura can go, where her nerve fails. Ha ha."

"If so, the joker found out that your nerves don't fail. What's on your schedule today? Will you be at the office all day?"

"Sometime or other I have to get my copy to Ruth Ann for her approval. That's it. Otherwise, I'll be there, except for lunch. I'll come home to eat at about one."

He went to the door with her, then stood on the porch as she backed out of the drive and headed for the office. Hours later it did not surprise her to see him lounging near her car when she left for lunch.

"Barney, come on. You can't spend the rest of your life trying to guard me. Get a life, kid."

"Got one that I like just fine. Bum a ride home?"

"This time. I don't usually do hitchhikers."

Eating soup and a sandwich in the kitchen minutes later, she asked if he had reached Dickerson.

"Funny thing about that man," he said. "He seems to have a headquarters of some sort set up in the motel, but he doesn't seem to hang out there much. Someone there suggested that I meet up with him at Ruth Ann's house at two."

Startled, she put down her sandwich, and took a drink of milk. "What's going on with him? Thomas Bird?"

"Don't know," Barney said. "Anyway, if your copy is ready, let's make it a joint expedition. Take your stuff along and we'll both meet him up there."

"I'll print it out here, she doesn't like to read material on the monitor."

She printed the editorial, then retrieved and printed her article about the five missing girls. She had their pictures lined up with the text on each one.

When she finished, they drove to Ruth Ann's house. No

other car was in the driveway. "Maybe Dickerson got busy," she said as they walked to the door.

"I can wait," Barney said.

He didn't have to. Maria opened the door and offered to take their jackets. When Barney said they'd hang them up, she shook her head. "No, no. Let me. They're waiting for you." After they surrendered their jackets, she motioned them toward the living room. Dickerson got to his feet when they entered and Ruth Ann, seated on the sofa, gave Todd a long, searching lock.

"Are you all right?" she asked. "He told me about last night. What a nightmare that was for you."

"I'm fine," Todd said. She glanced uneasily at the sergeant, wondering again why he was here and now wondering why he had been talking about her.

"Has something occurred to you about last night?" he asked.

"Not really. I listed the names of the people I saw that I know, and I have the pictures I took. Several other guys are in them, not well focused, but recognizable, I think."

"Good," he said. "May I see?"

She opened her laptop case and brought out the folder with the pictures and the list of names and handed it to him.

"How did you manage to get the pictures?" he asked, looking at her with interest.

"I stood on the hood of my car."

He grinned and handed the folder to Ruth Ann. She looked everything over, then paused for several seconds. "Maria probably can identify most of them," she said. "Barney, would you mind showing Sergeant Dickerson the way to the kitchen?"

Sergeant Dickerson took the folder back and left with Barney.

"I have my editorial," Todd said and passed it to Ruth Ann, who looked grim as she read it.

"Good. As you said, it just gets uglier."

"And one more thing," Todd said. She handed Ruth Ann the story she hoped to lead with that week.

This time she didn't watch Ruth Ann's careful reading; she stood up and went to the window to look at the town below. When the silence stretched unbearably long, she finally swung around. Ruth Ann was regarding her with a frown.

"No," Ruth Ann said. "It's too inflammatory, for one thing. There's no conclusive proof that they're all connected, for another. It could be a monstrous coincidence, or they could be linked, but you can't just make that assumption without some evidence."

Stunned, Todd returned to her chair. "I believe in coincidences that don't make sense," she said. "For instance, Lisa's being here at least three times when one of them was taken doesn't mean anything. But five coincidences? That's stretching it too far. I know they're connected. You know it, too!"

"I think they are," Ruth Ann said slowly. "I understand that you're afraid for Barney, but his life is not at risk. If that child is alive, hers could be. And we know yours is. At least, let me keep this and think about it overnight. But my first inclination is to say no."

"I believed that you would want the truth to come out," Todd said flatly. "Wrong again."

"I do want the truth," Ruth Ann said, "but I also accept responsibility. Consider what it would do to have that editorial, the hideous things that happen to abducted children—slavery, prostitution, pornography, drug addiction, snuff films—side by side with a story like that one. It would panic many people to no purpose yet."

"Maybe they need to panic a little," Todd muttered.

"In time. In time. But also consider what it might mean to Jodie Schuster if she's alive."

Barney and Dickerson returned then. "Got most of the names," the sergeant said. "Ms. Fielding, I wasn't expecting you, but it's even better this way. Would you mind showing me where you got that flat tire, how far you rolled down the hill?"

She stood up. "Sure. I'm done here. I'll get our jackets." She picked up her laptop, glanced at Ruth Ann, nodded slightly, and walked out to the hall closet. She didn't return to the living room after putting on her jacket, but went to the front door to wait for Barney and Sergeant Dickerson to join her there.

"What I'd like to do is get in your car, and let you go through the same movements you went through that night," the sergeant said. "When we get to the place where you first pulled over, let Barney out, and we'll roll down together to where you stopped again. I'll walk back from there and wait for my ride up at the house. Okay?"

She shrugged and they all went out to the car and got in. She backed up into the continuation of the drive that went to the garage, turned, and made her way down the steep winding drive. At the road she stopped, made her turn and continued.

"I don't know exactly where I stopped," she said after a moment. "It was different at night."

"I understand that," Dickerson said. "Approximately where?"

She drove slower, then stopped in the middle of the road. "About here, I think. I know the curve was up ahead. I didn't like to leave the car at a blind curve. I pulled over quite a bit."

She turned off the engine. "I got out and walked ten or twenty feet, maybe."

"Do it again, if you will."

She took the key from the ignition, slipped it into her purse, got out and walked ahead, turned and ran back. "I didn't get my key out again. That's why I rolled." After Barney got out, she released the hand brake and started to roll down the hill, to the curve, a few feet beyond. "My lights were on the bridge where I stopped," she said. She turned on the headlights, then rolled forward until she could see the reflection on the side of the bridge. "This is about right."

"Great," Dickerson said, opening his door. "Thanks."

"That's why he didn't follow through," she said. "He had no way of knowing what I intended to do, start the engine, or roll all the way down, and in the car I was relatively safe. But he had planned it—loosening the valve meant I wouldn't get a flat too soon, not while I was still in the driveway or near it."

"Or," he said, "it really was an accidental loosening. Or it was supposed to simply scare you off whatever you were doing." He grinned at her. "We try to consider all the possibilities. I'll send Barney on down. Thanks, again."

She watched him in the rearview mirror. He had a long, loose stride and appeared to have no difficulty going up the hill. He vanished around the curve, and a minute later Barney appeared, trotting.

By the time the sergeant returned, Ruth Ann had put the story about the girls in the dining room with the many other photographs and papers on the table. She was again on the sofa when he came back.

"Satisfied?" she asked him.

"I think so. My ride should be along any minute now. Is that her editorial?" He pointed to the typed sheet on the coffee table.

"Yes. Read it if you'd like."

He read it. "She's a good writer. That's a nasty business she's tackling."

"She's a very fine writer and she does good research."

"Why did she get involved in all that business? Curiosity, not an official question," he added quickly.

"I don't think she had any choice. Sometimes you don't."

He nodded. "Yeah, I know." He glanced at his watch. "I'll just go on now and wait for my ride down at the road. Thanks for the use of your house, your time."

Ruth Ann had not moved from the sofa half an hour later when Maria came into the living room.

"I'm going down to Deborah's for spinach and lettuce. Do you want anything from town?"

The Coombs sisters dried fruits and vegetables all summer, and from fall until spring they grew fresh vegetables in their huge greenhouse, a welcomed treat through the cold months. Ruth Ann shook herself and started to say no, then changed her mind.

"Actually, I was thinking of walking down to the office. Something I want to look up. You could drop me and come back later when you're done."

Maria looked her over. "You should be thinking about a nap instead of out running around. Are you feeling all right? You look peaked."

Ruth Ann didn't even snap back at her, which made Maria examine her more closely.

"Give me five minutes," Ruth Ann said, rising. She went to the dining room and picked up the story Todd had left with her, retrieved her notebook from the sitting room, and was ready.

At the curb in front of the newspaper office, Maria stopped and waited until Ruth Ann got out of the car and was inside the building before she drove on. Ruth Ann nodded to the women at work. They all froze at her appearance. Todd's door was closed, as was Johnny's. She crossed the outer room, went on to her office and shut the door.

She had her own filing system, with many cabinets crammed full of her copy from the past. She looked at the list of missing girls and the dates, then opened the file drawer for 1984 and flipped through until December. Christmas, and no doubt Lisa was home for the holidays. She found an item with a photograph of Grace and Lisa lighting the Christmas tree in the park, with Sam standing in the background. Next was the year Lisa brought home her actor husband. She found the mention and the copy of the photograph she had used. And she remembered that ugly scene when Lisa had openly flirted with Johnny in front of his pregnant wife.

Next, a Halloween party and Lisa again. Ruth Ann moved on to 1998, and there was an item about the application for a permit to tap into the water of Brindle Creek for a commercial enterprise; it had been turned down. There was no mention of Lisa, but she had been home, storming about, furious, racing her sports car through town.... And, of course, she had been home the week that Jodie Schuster vanished.

Ruth Ann closed the file drawers, and sat at her desk. Five

out of five times. "Coincidence," she said under her breath. It had to be a coincidence.

In one of her last diary entries, Janey had cursed Joe Warden and Mike Hilliard, extending to their children and theirs to eternity. Even her own child, of whom she had written, "...conceived in bitterness and hatred, rejected all the love a mother could bestow, rejected his mother..."

Hilliard had told her that Joe Warden had murdered her daughter on the night Janey gave birth to Warden's son, and afterward she had not seen Daniel as her own beloved child, but only as a young Joe Warden. She had written earlier that she had sinned and was paying for her sin, that she no longer believed God was going to lessen her punishment. In the later entry, she had written that she did not believe in curses, but prayed God to grant her just this one, to make them all suffer as much as she had suffered.

Daniel, isolated in his stone house, afraid of fire, watching for enemies his entire life; his son, isolated as well; Grace embittered, living on a remote ranch with hired help for company; and now Lisa, in a futile attempt to find love through too much lusting after men. Janey's prayer had been granted, Ruth Ann thought bleakly, down through the generations it was still working.

But what did it mean that Lisa had been on hand when five girls vanished?

There was a tap on her door. It opened and Johnny looked in. "Mildred said you were here. Is anything wrong?"

She stood up. "No. I had to look up something. I'm done."

He entered all the way and closed the door again. Talking fast, with enthusiasm, he said Carol was scouting for land; he had an appointment with their lawyer for Friday; he had been doing research on bindery equipment....

Ruth Ann listened as if from a great distance, and the questions kept rising in her mind: had he ever gotten over Lisa? Did any man ever really get over her? Finally she held up her hand and smiled. "I understand you've been busy. Good, but I have to go meet Maria when she comes by for me."

He grinned and spread out his hands in that peculiar Leone way. "Sorry. I'm full to busting apart these days." He held the door open and they walked through the office to the entrance, where they stood chatting about the weather for the few minutes it took until Maria drove up. He walked out to the car with Ruth Ann, opened the door and held her arm as she got inside.

"Seems like his manners finally took hold," Maria said as she pulled away from the curb.

"Your doing, not mine. I never knew any manners to teach anyone."

"You're awfully quiet tonight," Barney said as they ate dinner.

"Tired. It's been a long day, and I have work I should finish tonight. Working girl's lament."

"I've been thinking. How about if we take off early Saturday and go over to Victor's place, have a little rest out in the lush valley countryside and eat apples?"

"What are you talking about? You'll already be over there."

"Nope. Won't. I'm cutting classes this week. Victor can find someone to fill in for me. You'll be tied up with Ruth Ann Thursday and Friday, but Saturday and Sunday will be ours. Did you ever play Frisbee with two dogs? It gets pretty crazy."

"Barney, cut it out. You're giving midterms this week. Remember? This so-called investigation could drag on for weeks, or even months. What are you going to do? Give up school to stay home and be a bodyguard? I'd quit my job and move to Corvallis before I'd let that happen. There are jobs flipping hamburgers or something." She drew in a breath. "Okay, okay. Cancel that. What I'll do is come straight home from Ruth Ann's house, keep the doors locked, and not even peek out all night."

His mouth was set in a stubborn line as he shook his head. "I know you. You're obsessed with those girls. You even dream about them. If you got a whiff of what looked like a clue to follow up on, you'd be out like a shot to poke around in it."

She shook her head. "Don't be so sure. As of today, I'm letting it go. Ruth Ann is backing off from them, probably afraid of a lawsuit or something, or she's protecting someone. God knows what motivates her. I certainly don't. But I know there's nothing I can do for them or about them. If they come after you, we'll need a lawyer and I'll turn that list over to him and let his investigators do something about it. Trust me, Barney, I'm not about to go looking for a kidnapper or a killer. Not in my line of work."

He lifted her hand and kissed the palm. "Let's think about it."

"There's nothing to think about. Tomorrow I'll tell Ruth Ann exactly what I just told you. I intend to do the job they hired me to do. Period." From the expression on his face, she knew they would come back to it.

Ruth Ann was gazing at the pictures of the five girls, none of them really like another, but so similar. Wanting them side by side, she found her scissors to cut the items apart, each girl with the text on the side. Then, using a clean sheet of paper turned sideways, she lined them up, with each picture covering the text of the next one until only the heads and shoulders were visible. After a minute she found tape and taped them in place that way. So similar, she thought again, and so like Janey.

Startled, she leaned back in her chair. Of course, they were of the same type as Janey had been. Moving slowly, she began to shuffle through the many pictures on the table until she found the one of Janey flanked by the two men who had enslaved her. She cut strips of paper and taped them over the men's images, leaving only Janey, then compared it to the missing girls. She hesitated only a moment, then cut out Janey's picture. Todd could run off another print. She taped Janey's picture centered over the other five girls. One more, she thought then. One more.

Even more slowly, she began to sort through the many pictures she had taken the day Grace and Sam were married. She had yet to find a more appropriate one of Grace and Sam together, but she was not looking for them at the moment. She had taken many pictures of the young people that day. Johnny had been so handsome, twenty-one years old, in his nice suit, white shirt, tie, so grown up, and so young. She found several pictures of the youngsters and studied them carefully until she spotted the one she had vaguely remembered. One that had included Lisa. She had been the flower girl, with a wreath of flowers in her pale hair for the ceremony. There, she thought, that one.

Lisa was not centered in the picture, Johnny was, but Lisa was in the group, thin-faced and blond, with a sullen expression. Ruth Ann drew in her breath, then cut out Lisa's picture, and centered it beneath the others on her collage. She belonged, too. She taped it in place.

Perplexed, she sat back, trying to make sense of the assortment. The missing girls were bracketed by Janey from a hundred years before and Lisa today, she thought. But what did it mean? If anything.

Nothing, she finally said to herself. Coincidence that meant nothing. Synchronicity. Happenstance. There was no way she could imagine Lisa being involved in any of the girls' disappearances. She had been little more than a girl herself when the first one vanished in 1984, and there was no way she could have been in town the morning that Jodie vanished without being seen and noted. People kept an eye on her when she was around. Besides, she added silently, Jodie or any other girl her age would get in a car with a snake before they would trust Lisa.

She was still sitting there minutes later when the cold air hit her. Shaking, she went to the bedroom and had already put on her heavy woolen robe and fur-lined slippers when Maria came in to say she had put on the tea kettle. Hot tea, Ruth Ann thought, or an electric blanket, always one or the other. Huddling in her robe, cold to the bone, she went to the kitchen with Maria.

When the cold hit, Barney went to the bathroom and started filling the tub. He helped Todd get undressed and into the hot water, then undressed and joined her, and held her as she wept.

Twenty-Six

Ruth Ann had watched the changing expressions flit across Todd's face when she learned that she could not run her lead story. She regretted being the cause of her distress, but there it was. The story could not run. Not yet. Still, the child had been so hurt and disappointed, and then disillusioned. She stopped herself. Todd was not a child, but a mature young woman. She smiled. Maria brought coffee to the table and sat opposite her. She had eaten earlier with Thomas Bird, but she usually joined Ruth Ann at breakfast, at least for coffee.

"What's funny?" she asked.

"Just thinking. Twenty-eight is so much younger now than it was when I was that age."

"Ha! Next you'll be saying how much younger seventy is than it used to be."

"The longer I continue past that, the younger it seems," Ruth

Ann said agreeably. "Wait and see." She finished her grapefruit. "I expect Barney will come to check on the thermometers today. If he does, let me know, will you? I want a word with him."

Maria nodded. "He'll be here. He can't believe nothing shows. Maybe he thinks one of us sneaks out and resets it."

"No, I imagine he'd like to think that, but he's too honest. Have you noticed that honest people expect others to be just as honest? I wonder when one outgrows that."

"Probably they're both at just about the right age."

"I'm afraid so," Ruth Ann said. From what little Todd had said about her family, it had been easy enough to fill in the blanks. Her family had been like the *Saturday Evening Post* magazine covers; idealized and fine. She doubted that Todd had ever been directly and personally touched by duplicity beyond the minor childhood and adolescent variety. She had never been forced to take a real stand against real evil. Innocent, Ruth Ann thought then, with near surprise. Todd had come to town innocent.

She finished her egg and toast and poured more coffee to take to the dining room. Time to teach the computer how to double space and then print, she was thinking grimly. She absolutely could not edit copy on the monitor or in single-spaced typescript.

At ten-thirty, when Maria came to tell her that Barney had arrived, Ruth Ann was scowling at a printout. "A goddamn mess," she muttered. She looked again at the screen where the text seemed exactly right, then back to the paper copy, and shook her head. She loathed the computer.

Barney was in the hall, frowning at the thermometer he had installed.

"Hasn't worked, has it?" Ruth Ann said, walking to his side. "It never did before, either."

"Hasn't worked yet," he admitted.

"Come sit down a minute," Ruth Ann said. "There's something I wanted to bring up with you."

He glanced down at himself. He was wearing sweats and running shoes.

"You're fine," she said. She was wearing her old chinos and a wool plaid shirt with frayed cuffs over a T-shirt, her usual outfit at home in cold weather.

She led the way to her sitting room, where she lifted a stack of papers from a chair and motioned him toward it. Then, seated in her own comfortable chair, she said, "You just can't accept impossible things, can you?"

"That word says it all. Impossible. Not possible. And you're right, I can't. I know elephants can't fly, no matter how many movies Disney makes."

He grinned, and she thought with a pang how very young he was. "I'll give you elephants," she said. "But sometimes things that appear impossible turn out to be merely mysterious. Once cause and effect are established, the impossible moves to the other side of the equation, and afterward people are amused at the gullible fools who used to believe it was supernatural or paranormal."

"There are a lot of things people consider paranormal or supernatural today," Barney said, "and researchers spend millions trying to prove them right. For them it satisfies some innate need to believe there's more to existence than what's visible and provable. It's interesting to pursue what drives that need, with a high probability that it comes down to insecurity and fear."

"Eat, drink and be merry, for tomorrow..."

"Exactly."

She waved that aside. "The scientific method works only when you have the right tools to test with, and when you know the right questions to ask. They spend millions and ask the wrong questions, perhaps."

"What are the right questions?"

"I don't know. But let's talk about the cold air mass that settles over Brindle periodically. No one can explain it, or has so far, at least, and it's been happening for a hundred years or possibly longer. It makes some people furious and others afraid. Everyone on this side of the highway and within the loop has felt it, I'm sure. Some much more than others. And some even deny that it happens. Newcomers can find it so unsettling, they won't stay. And that's what I want to talk to you about. Todd is extremely susceptible, apparently. I don't want to lose her, Barney. But neither do I want to see her suffer or become fearful."

He stood up and walked to the window behind her, where he stood and said, "She isn't afraid of the cold. But she's afraid of her reaction to it. She gets despondent, depressed and she cries. I've known her for five years, we've been married for three and a half years, and this is the first time I've ever seen her cry. She can't control it." He returned to his chair. "That's what's frightening about it, her reaction."

She nodded. "I understand. I don't want to debate what is or isn't possible, not today. Another time it will make for an interesting evening, I'm sure. I'd like a rain check for that chat. But there are a few curious things about that air mass. Why, for instance, is it so frequent suddenly? It never was before. Often it didn't happen for many months at a time. And why is Todd so susceptible? See, the right questions without answers. But for now, I think you should consider moving temporarily to one of the house trailers across the highway, or even to one of the motels over there. There are always vacancies in the trailers over the winter months, and she would be close to Sonny and Jan when you're away. But more, with the next editorial, I'm afraid that a lot of people will become increasingly upset with her for arousing fear and guilt. Human nature being what it is, a few people might try to make her life very uncomfortable. It would be good if she was near friends."

Barney rubbed his eyes. His expression was bleak when he said, "You know that someone tried to run her off the road Monday night. She would have been killed if it had worked."

"It's very much on my mind."

"I'm afraid we might have to move over to the valley, not just across the road. I can't leave her alone until this business about the girls is settled, and I can't miss my classes or stop house-sitting those couple of extra days. They're part of the deal I made."

Ruth Ann stood up and paced restlessly through the sitting room, pausing before her parents' portrait, where her father's gaze was no less stern than it had been, but seemed even more penetrating. Facing Barney again, she said, "Both of you come to dinner tonight. I agree that you can't come this close to your final goal and let it drop. Of course not. She is so angry at me right now. We have to talk her into coming here for the next few days that you'll be gone. You know she would be safe in my house, with Maria, Thomas Bird and me all on full alert. Red alert, isn't that what they call it?"

He looked doubtful. "If she'll agree," he said after a moment. "She was pretty upset."

"I know. I know. But come to dinner and let's see if we can't talk her into it."

As soon as Barney left, Ruth Ann went to find Maria. When Leone planned the house, he had insisted on a small apartment that he called the mother-in-law apartment. Ruth Ann's mother had refused to move into it, and it had become Maria and Thomas Bird's domain. Maria was in her own meticulous living room, seated in a rocking chair, mending a shirt before the television with a movie on. She paused it when Ruth Ann entered.

Ruth Ann sat in a second rocker. "I asked them to dinner tonight, and I want to have Todd stay here while Barney's over in the valley this week. She can use Johnny's old room."

Maria nodded. "I'll get it ready. That poor girl. Twice now. She must be scared to death."

"I imagine she is, and I know Barney is at his wits' end with indecision about what to do. Anyway, let's make sure she feels welcome."

She had given up on trying to fathom what was wrong with the computer, and had tackled the printout of her copy, only to find that it was impossible to work with. She put it down in disgust. Johnny called just as she had decided to start trying to pick out a better wedding picture of Sam and Grace.

"It came this morning," Johnny said cheerfully. "A registered letter from Grace through her attorney. We have six months to clear off her land." He chuckled. "And Carol has three sites to show us. Want to come with us to pick out a new home?"

Without hesitation she said she did. That, at least, was something she understood.

When Todd left the office at six, Barney was seated behind the wheel in her car at the curb. She groaned. "Barney, you can't keep doing this," she said, getting into the passenger seat. "I feel like a kindergarten kid with a too-protective parent."

"Sorry," he said. "We're going to Ruth Ann's for dinner. She said something was urgent that she has to talk to you about."

"Oh, God, I don't want to go up there for dinner. I'm tired."

"Well, she sounded pretty upset. I said we'd come up."

She slouched down in her seat. "So, let's get it over with."

She had not lied about being tired. Bone tired, she thought. After the chill of the night before, her sleep had been troubled by dreams that woke her up repeatedly without leaving a memory trace, except for one that involved a roller coaster that plunged downward faster and faster, out of control.

Barney drove up the loop to Ruth Ann's house, and she opened the door for them. "Come in. Come in. It's freezing out there, isn't it? Maria's making dinner. Half an hour, she said, but her time sense is so screwed up that it could mean anything or nothing."

After Barney took their jackets to the closet, Ruth Ann ushered them both into her sitting room, where she had cleared two chairs for them.

"Todd," she said when they were all seated, "I think we have an emergency situation. A personal emergency, at any rate. Grace has made her first move. Today we were served with a notice that we have to vacate the premises in six months."

Todd felt completely deflated by the news. Six months, and then job hunting again. Before she could say anything, Ruth Ann continued.

"Today I went out with Johnny and Carol and we picked out a new site. I intend to move the press. That woman is not going to drive me out of business. So that's the first thing I wanted to get off my chest. But I'm very afraid that she might serve us with a prior publication injunction to prevent the history from being published. And I don't intend to let her do that, either."

"How can you stop her?" Todd sat up straighter.

"By printing it next week instead of three weeks from now," Ruth Ann said. "Can we get it in shape to do that? I should say can you get it in shape? Today I crashed the damn computer again, or did something awful to it, and my copy is a mess, but it's basically written. I need a good printout to edit, and then have you edit."

Todd was thinking hard. Pictures, text, old documents… "When will the paper order be delivered? It hasn't come yet."

"I told Johnny to call them and say we have to have it by Monday. They said no problem. Monday it will be here."

"We'll have to go to press Tuesday with it," Todd said. "Wednesday is the regular print-run day. I'll take a look at your computer and printout and see what went wrong. It's going to take a lot of concentrated work, but, yes, we can do it. I'm sure we can."

"I know this is a terrible imposition for you. But could you bring yourself to stay here while Barney is gone and help get it done? If I crash the damn computer again, I don't know how to un-crash it."

She caught a glimmer of admiration on Barney's face. He nodded slightly as they waited for Todd's response.

"That might be best," Todd said. "We'll need to consult on design, do the layout, decide how to handle the diary and other document entries. Are you sure I won't be in the way?"

"I'm sure," Ruth Ann said. "We have a perfectly good guest room, and you'll be on hand. I've been tearing my hair out today trying to get a printout I can work with. My dear, I can't tell you how grateful I would be. Your final editorial on how to help keep our children safe, and my true history will make for a memorable edition, and the following week you run the lead story about the missing girls. My God, will we shake up this complacent community."

She paused, then said, "Also, I want to tell you the rest of my plans for the new location. In confidence, of course."

When she finished, Barney whistled. "Wow! Cool!"

Todd grinned and stood up. "I'll have a look at your computer and printout."

Maria came to the door and said dinner was ready. In the kitchen, she added, sounding resigned.

Todd looked at her hands. "I'd better wash up," she said.

She left and Barney got up and offered a hand to Ruth Ann. When she rose, he kissed her cheek.

"Nothing else would have worked," he said softly. "Thanks."

"Don't give me any undue credit," Ruth Ann said. "Every word was true. We are going to move the press, and Grace might take that next step."

"Could she really do that? Stop you from publishing?"

Todd rejoined them in time to hear Ruth Ann's answer.

"She could get the injunction, and we would appeal, of course. The whole process would wind its way through the courts, and by the time it was decided in our favor, she probably figures we'd be out of the newspaper business. I doubt that it has occurred to her that I might be ready to move the publishing date by weeks, and then move the whole kit and caboodle. So it isn't going to happen."

"Damn right!" Todd said, and they went in to eat dinner.

After dinner, Todd showed Ruth Ann how to set the double-space command, how to reveal the codes she had inadvertently inserted into her text, and how to delete them again. Ruth Ann made notes as she watched. When it was finished, Ruth Ann asked to be walked through the scanning/printing process. She watched closely, again making notes, and confessed that she felt stupid for not grasping it before. With an apologetic look, she told Todd that she would send Thomas Bird to the office the next day for blank newsprint paper.

"I have to see the supplement in real space or something," she said. "I know you can do layout and editing on the monitor, but I can't see it properly unless it's on paper. I have to do real paste-up. Another step, but I have to do it that way."

Driving home later, Todd felt that she really had been on a roller coaster, plunged into the depths when Ruth Ann had said they had six months, then raised high into the air when she'd revealed the rest of the plan, to have Johnny start his own publishing company, with Todd as editor in chief, with her own editorial assistant. Up and down, she thought contentedly. Up was better.

"That takes care of your being gone for the next three nights," she said. "No problem. I'll be in good hands. Right?"

"Right."

"I wonder if they trick-or-treat around here. Probably not up at Ruth Ann's house, too removed from town. Did you go trick-or-treating?"

"Are you kidding? Next to Christmas, it was the biggest tooth-spoiler around."

"I remember when I was a kid and we went to see *Fantasia*. You know, the Disney film? Remember that scene for 'A Night on Bald Mountain'? When the devil summons up the wraiths and ghosts and such? It scared me so much they had to take me out. I saw it again as an adult and had to admit it's scary. Too intense for little kids."

They were pulling into the driveway and Barney didn't comment. After they were inside the house with their jackets off, he asked, "What made you think of that film now?"

"I don't know. Halloween coming up. You'll be gone. If the spirits start rising, it will be good to be with some people." She had started in a light tone, but as the words formed and were uttered, the lightness vanished, and she realized that she had been dreading Halloween.

"Honey, come on. You're not getting superstitious on me, are you?"

He grasped her shoulders and studied her face, and she said slowly, "I don't think I understand what that means any longer. I used to, but now?"

He shook her slightly. "You know damn well what it means."

"Barney, we have to face the fact that something way, way out of the ordinary is happening around here. That freezing air that comes and goes is not normal, not anything reason can explain. I think this town is haunted. There, I said it, what no one dares say out loud. This damned town is haunted!"

He pulled her to him and held her close and tight. "Good God, you don't believe that. You can't believe that."

Her voice was muffled with her face pressed against his chest. "What you mean is that you can't believe it."

He relaxed his hold marginally and she pushed herself farther back and drew in a long breath.

"I couldn't hear you," he said. "What did you say?"

"I said you were smothering me." She drew back more. "What I'm going to do is veg out in front of the television while you get your gear and stuff ready to take off in the morning. Do you want coffee or something?"

"No. Damn it, Todd. We can't just let it go like that."

She put her finger on his lips. "Consider it unsaid. A passing madness. A random thought that escaped. Go on and do your thing. I've done my yeoman's chores for this week, your turn."

He looked frustrated and angry. She turned away. "I want coffee. The only question is how many cups? For one or for two?"

Without answering, he swung around and headed for his study, and she closed her eyes briefly, drew in another long breath, then went to the kitchen. Coffee for two, she thought. He would come out in a few minutes and either want to talk, or just glower at her, but he would want coffee.

Minutes later, sitting on the sofa, channel-hopping with the sound muted, she was thinking about her words: *the town was haunted.* But she really didn't believe in ghosts, so it presented a problem, she mused. She stopped changing channels when an underwater scene came on with colorful fish swimming in and around a coral reef.

As a teenager, she and several friends out camping had frightened one another with ghost stories, and then had dissected their own stories. Deconstructed them, she corrected. Her argument had been that if there was even one single real ghost, why not millions? Why so few? And what was on their minds? Didn't they have anything better to do than make life miserable for the living? Besides, every day thousands of people died with scores unsettled, vengeance deferred, their tormenters living and unrepentant. Why weren't those dead people being ghostlike and getting even? She kept coming back to her main argument: why so few?

But the spirit in Brindle didn't especially seem to be getting even with anyone; it didn't seem to do anything except bring in a lot of cold air and cause people to feel sad and/or despondent. Not much malignancy there, she thought. What was its point in hanging around?

It didn't do anything in the way of buckling doors, or forcing anyone to jump from a high place, or turning anyone into an ax murderer, or any of the other classic ghostly things. She remembered what Jan had said, a town of Stepford people. People without affect, Todd thought, recalling her psychology class phrase. Or, she added, people without an active conscience.

Another thought followed swiftly: was it acting as a collective conscience because the people showed so little themselves? Was it trying to shake them out of their lethargy, their apathy, their complacency? Or was it responsible?

For the first time, she began to consider exactly what happened to her when the cold air mass struck. All her gaiety gone, her good humor, compassion, everything that made her human vanished, leaving her with overwhelming sadness and despairing. She had thought her emotional response was caused by the cold, but now she realized that it was in addition to the cold, not a result. As if she were being drained of humanity, she thought with a shudder.

On the TV screen a shark had moved in and was feeding leisurely on the schools of jewel-like fish. Those remaining seemed not to notice. Abruptly she turned off the television.

"I can't stay here," she said under her breath. "It, whatever it is, will kill me if I stay."

Twenty-Seven

When Barney emerged that night, he did not bring up the subject again. She knew that if she had brought it up, he would have talked about it, but he was unwilling to precipitate an argument, and if they had talked it would have been low key and nonconfrontational, at least at the beginning. She also knew that it would have escalated into something else. Just as well, she thought. There was nothing real to say on either side.

But, she also understood, eventually they would have to disagree vehemently about something, they would have to have that long-deferred quarrel they both dreaded. She was happy enough to put it off.

She would scream if she admitted to her fear and he came on like an ever-patient parent, soothing, patting, consoling, and in the end telling her to stop being silly. She remembered suddenly how it had been when she had been terrified by the movie many years before, how in the end her father, in a rare show of impatience, finally told her to stop being silly, that she knew very well there was nothing real about the movie, nothing to be afraid of. So far removed from the reality of childhood fear, her parents had been unable to allay hers, and because they could not banish it, they had forbidden it. And she had put it in some deep dark place inside herself, where it had lain dormant until, more powerful than ever, it had escaped into the open once more.

She closed her eyes hard, trying to deny that the present and the past had colluded to terrify her. Now she was the adult who knew the movie was a fantasy, unreal, with nothing to harm her. Her own brain had caused that past fear to resurface, to make the link to the present, and her own brain had to undo it, disconnect that link.

After Barney stacked his gear on the dining table—a box of books, notebooks, binders, his duffel bag—he sat next to her on the sofa, and they watched the news and the weather report. Rain in the valley, scattered showers in the Bend area and snow in the mountains.

"You've checked the chains?" she asked. "You might need them coming home."

"Checked," he said. "And the survival kit, and warm clothes, flashlight. Ready for anything." He turned off the television. "I'll call you when I get to Victor's after school. If anything comes up, you know you can always get through to me."

"Sure. I know that. But I'll be busy. No time for frivolous calls."

"And no wandering around alone. Right?"

"Check."

* * *

It was exactly how Ruth Ann had thought it would be on Thursday. She and Todd were busy from the time Todd arrived at ten until late in the afternoon when Sam dropped in.

Ruth Ann joined him in the living room and sat down with a sigh.

"You look tired," he said, sitting opposite her. "Maybe you should give relaxation a brief trial. You might find that you like it."

"One of these days," she said. "And you look disturbed. What's up?"

"Is Todd around? It concerns her, too."

"In the dining room." He stood up, but she was already on her feet and motioned him back down. "I'll get her." She went to the dining room door and tapped, then opened it. "Sam's here and wants you to hear whatever it is he has to say. Anyway, it's time for a break."

Sam gave Todd a searching look when they returned to the living room. "You created something of a firestorm in town," he said. "That was a pretty brutal editorial you ran."

"Statistics," she said, sitting on one of the brocade covered chairs. "I didn't invent them."

"But you printed them, and people are sore. And some who aren't furious are emotionally shattered. Including Mame. She was just beginning to function again as a nurse. Now this. What's the point? Do you have a point? Besides sensationalism." All traces of his usual geniality and friendliness were erased, his expression hard and remote.

"The point is that they have to acknowledge a bigger world than this little town. A dangerous world for their kids."

"These people aren't evil. They aren't stupid or ignorant. They know about the world, but they don't want an upstart big-city know-it-all coming in to rub their noses in it."

"They know it the way they know peasants in China are suffering from AIDS, or people in Africa are killing one another, that a war is going on in Iraq. They know it in a detached way as if none of it has anything to do with them—"

"What I know is that you've undone weeks of healing work with Mame, and today she's back where she was when Jodie first took off! And some of those other parents whose kids ran away over the years. They had become reconciled, and now they're panicky. Was that your intention? To wreck people's lives?" His face was flushed. "Mame's my patient, and she didn't need to be sent back into a tailspin."

"If they needed something to shake them awake, yes, that was my intention. They should be up in arms, yelling, making a great big stink, demanding real investigations, doing something! I'm not the one who's wrecking anyone's life. Find the kidnapper of that kid, lay the blame where it belongs. It's not my job to hand out tranquilizers, pacify them and keep them quiet." Todd had jumped to her feet as she spoke, her voice had risen and the words were coming in a torrent.

Ruth Ann cleared her throat, and Todd drew in a breath. "I'm sorry," she said to Ruth Ann. "I should get back to work." She walked out stiffly.

Ruth Ann watched her leave, then turned to Sam. "Well, she heard what you had to say, and you heard her. How bad is Mame?"

He had become almost as rigid as Todd, poised as if ready to leap up, just as she had done. He rubbed his eyes, shook his head, and leaned back in his chair once more. "Bad. A nervous wreck again. I'll be keeping a close eye on her for a while. I stopped at Carl's Café for a cup of coffee, and there were a couple of others there. It's not a good situation, Ruth Ann. People are really in a state of nerves, agitated, upset with state investigators prowling around questioning everyone, anxious, angry. They blame Todd and Barney, especially Todd. They want them out of here, out of their lives. They're going to petition Ollie to arrest Barney and lock him up in Bend, under the sheriff's jurisdiction, get him all the way out of town. And they will come to you or, more likely, to Johnny and demand that you let her go."

"Sam, how do the kids put it? It just ain't gonna happen. As for Barney, Ollie can't follow through, not without a scintilla of evidence."

"The way the feelings are running," he said slowly, "some people may begin to remember seeing his truck on the wrong street that morning. They want this chapter closed now."

"So they can go back to sleep," she murmured. "Is that what you came by to talk about? Todd and Barney?"

"Partly." He shook his head. "No, not really. Grace called me last night. She ordered me to appear at her attorney's office this afternoon, to confirm the libelous statements you made about her ancestors. I declined. She said since I have my feet planted in her enemy's territory, I should be the one to let you know that she intends to wrap you up in lawsuits that will break you and put you out of the publishing business. She won't stop until you lose everything you own."

"Well, I won't shoot the messenger this time. But thank you for the warning. I'm sorry you're finding yourself in the eye of the hurricane."

"Just the errand boy," he said. "But, as your physician, I want to mention that you are not as young as Grace is, and you're not as wealthy. She enjoys getting even, but you might not find it pleasant and, in fact, you could be harmed. I saw Mame come unraveled today, and I don't want to see it happen to you. Consider what you have to gain and what you might have to lose if you publish that history, and if you keep aligning yourself with Todd and Barney. I'm not in the center of the storm, but you certainly are. And frankly, you're too old to get so involved. You've been paying your dues for sixty years and it's past time for you to sit back and pass the load to others."

"Strange how for so many years what we're told is you're too young to do this, to go there, or whatever. Blink your eyes and suddenly the message is you're too old for this or that."

"And you intend to go ahead without regard for the consequences? You know Johnny will be affected, too. Ruined financially. Is it really worth it?" He stood up without waiting for a response. "Are you sleeping okay? Good appetite?"

"Yes and yes. I'm fine. Do you want a drink before you go?"

"Too early," he said, putting on his jacket. "Just be careful, okay?"

Ruth Ann continued to sit in the living room after Sam left, reflecting on his warning that she might be hurt, and that Johnny could be, also. A warning from Grace? Or was that Sam's cautionary advice? Finally she shrugged and put it aside. As Sam had said, she was going to do it, consequences be damned.

She spent more time pondering his words about the townspeople and the possibility that someone might come up with enough evidence to convince Ollie that he had grounds to act. Would anyone in town go so far as to frame an innocent man? It filled her with dismay when she had to admit that she didn't know the answer. She had assured Barney and Todd that if he were charged, she would back him personally, and with the resources of the newspaper, but if she was tying up her own money in buying land, building a new plant, and just possibly fighting a lawsuit, what resources would be left?

"Goddamn it," she muttered. Sam was right, she was too old to be worrying about such things. Abruptly she stood up and went to the kitchen. It certainly was not too early for a drink.

By dinnertime, Ruth Ann's copy was all edited, first by her, and then by Todd, who had found very little that needed doing. Ruth Ann was a good writer and an excellent editor, more demanding of herself than Todd would have dreamed of being.

"Let's have three columns, wider than the usual format, but it should be distinctive, different," she said, sitting by Ruth Ann on the sofa in the living room that night. "On the first page, a large picture of Brindle Creek, that picture you showed me of how it looked after the fire. I'll restore the tree, add a few leaves, just a faint yellow, the gray-green sage, all in chiaroscuro, shades of dun, black, white, gray. You know, like the definition. Shades of Brindle."

"That's the title," Ruth Ann said. "The Shades of Brindle. Thank you. I hadn't been able to come up with a suitable title, but that works fine."

Todd was holding her sketch pad, and she stared at the blank page without moving. Shades, she thought distantly. That was just right. In every sense. Then she began to sketch a rough idea for the first page.

Ruth Ann marveled at her ability to show so clearly with a pencil what she had in mind, and she had no wish to change a thing as Todd continued to describe the layout she was visualizing.

"We should be ready for the paper paste-up by Sunday and a final proofreading. Sunday night or Monday I'll get it all on disk. But we can do it, and have it done by Monday night. Then off to Hank on Tuesday. Okay?"

"You're a real taskmaster, or is slave driver more appropriate? But, yes, that's doable and yes, it's okay. If you can make that picture of Brindle Creek work, that would be a fine centerpiece for the front page."

"It shouldn't be a problem."

"Good." Ruth Ann stood up and stretched. "Stiff," she said. "What I want is a long soaking bath and bed. Help yourself to whatever you want." She crossed the room, paused at the door. "Todd, I'm glad you're here. Good night."

A short time later Maria came in, closed the fire screen, then said, "There are cookies, milk, cheese. Make coffee if that's your thing at night. If you remember, turn off the lights when you go to bed. Is your room all right?"

"It's perfect," Todd said. "Thanks. I probably won't be up much longer."

Maria yawned and said good-night.

Todd made a few notes on her rough sketches, then decided there was little more she could do with it now. She closed her sketch pad, turned off the living-room lights and wandered down the hall to her room, Johnny's old room. All traces of him had been removed years ago, no doubt, but it had his twin bed, a bureau with a small mirror and a comfortable chair with a reading lamp. A television had been brought in, probably recently, she thought, turning it on. After a minute she turned it off again, too restless to sit still and watch anything.

She could start on the picture of Brindle Creek, she decided. It would be time-consuming and there really was a lot of work to get done in the next few days. She knew from her magazine experience that it was easy enough to outline the chores, and quite another to actually see them finished. She returned to the dining room and started looking for the picture of the creek. There were many pictures, but not the one she was after. Probably in the sitting room, she thought, and hesitantly went to the door of the sitting room and tapped lightly. There was no answer, but she could see the trace of light under the door. More hesitantly, she opened the door a crack, then enough to enter. The light by Ruth Ann's chair was on, and another pile of pictures was on the table by it. She went to the table and saw her own article about the girls. Frowning, she picked it up. Ruth Ann had cut out the pictures of the five girls.

Another sheet of paper lay face down and she picked it up and saw the girls lined up, with Janey's picture centered over them, and another girl centered below. That one was a snapshot with paper taped over whatever else was in the frame. She carefully lifted the taped part. A group of young people at the table spread for the wedding reception. Johnny? A very young Johnny. Twenty or twenty-one and good looking. And the girl? Thin-faced and sullen looking, with flowers in her hair, blond… "Oh, my God," Todd thought then. Lisa!

She felt her whole body grow rigid, her fingers numb, and

she glanced at the closed door to Ruth Ann's bedroom then quickly dropped the papers back where they had come from and ran to her room. Memories of her disturbing dream rushed back to mind. Too many flowers. They kept eluding her and she had to arrange them before the director arrived. One kept getting away, the others scattered....

She sat down to think what it meant. Janey with her innocent sex appeal; Lisa with her sex appeal and very much aware of it. Jan had said Lisa didn't know a man until she had slept with him. She came back every few years and there was always trouble when she did. Barney said she walked in a cloud of pheromones. Flirting with him in front of Todd. Starting a malicious lie about him. How helpless Johnny had seemed around her, deferring to her. She had been in town at least three times when a girl went missing....

Too many flowers. "Seven," she said under her breath. There had been seven flowers and she couldn't catch them all and arrange them properly before the director came.

Ruth Ann had seen the similarity, and she had not mentioned it. Why not?

Johnny, she thought then. Had he been one of Lisa's early conquests? When she was still a young teenaged girl? He had been so eager to go along with Ollie's theory that Jodie had simply left of her own volition. Fired Todd for the first editorial. It would have stuck if Ruth Ann had not intervened, she was well aware. And Ruth Ann's surprising refusal to allow the news story about the five girls. First she had to give Johnny a plum, Todd thought. His own press where he would be boss. Buying land for it, getting it off the ground this fast. And then, after placating him, she would permit the story.

Thoughts, snapshot memories, bits of conversations all were swirling too fast to be coherent. *Stop it,* she told herself. She knew she was leaping to conclusions.

She thought back to the day Jodie vanished, a Thursday, the day she had spent in Bend shopping for Ruth Ann's computer, then getting it set up and running. Had she seen Johnny that morning? She had gone to the office at about ten or a little after, just to check mail and phone calls, then on to Ruth Ann's house. She had not seen Johnny on Thursday. He seldom got there earlier than she did on Thursdays and Fridays and the fact that she had not seen him meant nothing, she told herself.

Besides, the police had checked out everyone, or were still in the process, making sure they had been where they said they'd been that morning. How would they have checked on Johnny if he claimed he was still at home until after nine or ten? No doubt Carol had already gone to her real estate office before he left. For that matter, what about Shinny? He rarely turned up earlier than she did. Both he and Johnny had been at the highway accident. But so had Sam, Ollie and a lot of others. On Thursdays, Sam's half days, he checked patients at the hospital, then had office hours. Easy enough to confirm that. Or was it?

She shook her head. Guessing. That was all she could do. This must be how it was with the townspeople, eyeing one another suspiciously, then settling for Barney with a big sigh of relief.

Stop it, she told herself again, and thought instead of the picture Ruth Ann had doctored. It was easy enough to spot the physical similarity they all shared. Janey and Lisa also had their sex appeal in common. But what did either of them have to do with the missing girls?

She heard words form in her head: "Lisa was the one who got away." She had come full circle, back to her mental maelstrom in which one question persisted: Was Johnny the director she had feared and dreaded in her dream?

Twenty-Eight

Todd's sleep had not come easily or early, leaving her dragged out the next morning when she joined Ruth Ann and Maria in the kitchen for breakfast. She repeated silently the orders she had given herself the night before. Put it all aside for now. Concentrate on getting the history supplement finished. Wait for Barney to come home and talk everything over with him. In her orders she had repeated *everything* several times. She suspected it would be hard to follow through.

After picking at her scrambled eggs and toast, drinking orange juice and a lot of coffee, she was ready to start work. She excused herself and left Ruth Ann and Maria at the table. As she walked back through the hall, she could hear their murmuring voices, although no one had said much of anything before. She had had nothing to say in the kitchen.

At ten that morning, Johnny called Ruth Ann to tell her that they had had nine cancellations so far.

"I'm not surprised," she said. "Is it going to rain, or will it be snow? Have you heard a forecast?"

"Mother! This could be serious if it keeps up."

"They'll come back. If it's going to snow, Maria has to go shopping soon, before it starts."

"I give up," Johnny said. He sounded very exasperated. "Rain. I'll call you later."

She went back to her pictures, and finally selected one of Sam and Grace by a white carriage drawn by a white horse. He was standing at the side, giving her a hand as she stepped down. At least Sam was grinning in that one, not at Grace, but at someone not in the picture. That would do, she decided, and took it in to Todd.

"She was playing the queen and he was her prince consort," she said dryly as Todd examined the snapshot. "When they left the church to go to the reception, that was their transportation."

"It's great," Todd said. "Just right."

At eleven there was another interruption. Maria came to the sitting room to say that Gretchen Mohrbeck and Ada Mays had come to see Ruth Ann. She had hung up their coats and put them in the living room. She rolled her eyes and shrugged. "I couldn't very well turn them away."

"Next time, force yourself," Ruth Ann said. She went to the living room to greet her visitors. Gretchen was seventy-one and Ada a few years younger, and they both looked their ages. That morning Gretchen looked determined and Ada uncomfortable. She smiled uncertainly at Ruth Ann.

"Good morning," she said to them. "Would you like coffee? It is so cold this morning."

"No, we don't want coffee," Gretchen said sharply, rising from her chair, as if to demonstrate that this was not a social call. Ada looked at her in embarrassment, then studied her fingernails.

"We had a meeting last night," Gretchen said. "The Women's Club in town, and we agreed to demand that you stop those scurrilous attacks on this community, those scaremongering articles you've been printing. They are filthy, not fit for a family newspaper that children might see. Let your sophisticated young woman go back to the city where people feel free to discuss such indecent things in public. This is not such a place. We demand a decent family newspaper, or there will be mass cancellations of subscriptions and of advertising."

"I see," Ruth Ann said. "I promise you that I will take your words under consideration. Thank you for coming, my dears."

Gretchen flushed a dark red and Ada looked more embarrassed than ever.

"Ruth Ann," Gretchen said, "I've known you all my life and I've known you to pull some silly stunts, but I never thought you were a fool. You can't do this to our town and get away with it." She looked at her companion and snapped, "Come on. We're leaving."

Ruth Ann walked to the hall closet with them, watched as they pulled on coats, and then went to the front door to see them out. She sniffed the air. It was very cold.

"As soon as lunch is over and done with, I'll do some shopping," Maria said coming up behind her. "It's going to snow later. Close that door. You'll catch cold."

"Maybe Todd would like to go with you," Ruth Ann said, closing the door. She trusted Maria's weather forecast more than Johnny's. It was going to snow. "She's not used to being cooped up day and night, I imagine."

"I can drop her off at the mall and pick her up in an hour or so," Maria said. "If she wants to go."

Todd welcomed the chance to get out for a break. It was good to move a little, she realized at the mall, not looking for anything, just moving and not glued to a computer.

Maria picked her up again in exactly an hour and a half, and ten minutes after they arrived at Ruth Ann's house, the snow began to fall.

A few minutes later, Todd was standing at the window in the living room watching the snow, thinking of her brothers and the first snow of the season when she was young in Greeley. How excited they all were, hoping it would pile up knee deep, chest deep, hauling out the sleds and skis, ready for anything. She recalled the exhilaration of speeding down a hill on a sled, racing after her brother Tim, the most daredevil of the three boys, with her other two brothers yelling for her to stop. They couldn't catch her and she wouldn't pull off to the side into the snowbank; she was as free and as fast as the wind. If they caught her, they would put snow down her collar, she knew, although in a fair snowball fight, they never won. She had deadly accuracy in her throwing arm. Mandatory softball every summer had developed that. She had turned out to be a very good pitcher. She could hear her mother's not-to-be-argued-with voice telling her she could not sit in front of a computer all summer, to pick a sport, any sport and enroll. The poignancy of the memory shook her.

She heard Ruth Ann enter and glanced at her. "It's so beautiful," she said. "Brindle must look like a Christmas card when the snow accumulates."

Ruth Ann came to the window. "It does. The boys used to come up the hill with their sleds and race down again. They don't do that much anymore. Not this high, at least. Every year one or two of them ended up in the creek."

She was remembering the time that Johnny had ended up in the creek, down by the hotel bridge. Sylvester Coogan had taken him inside his house, stripped off his icy clothes and warmed him by the fire, and later had wrapped him in a blanket and brought him home in his big truck. Sylvester was gone now, she thought with a sigh. So many of her generation were gone now, and the younger ones were not quite the same. She wondered who would take in an ice-coated boy these days and warm him up. Someone would, she told herself. They weren't that different.

Briskly she said, "It won't last long. It never does, especially this early in the season, but while it's here, we're more or less housebound. That hill is impossible with snow on it. Thank goodness Maria got the shopping done early."

"I hope it's gone by Sunday," Todd said. She bit her lip.

"You're thinking of Barney, aren't you? If the road's under snow on Sunday, he can park in town by the upper bridge, and walk the rest of the way. That's what we always did in years past, and would again if we had to go out for anything." Ruth Ann patted Todd's arm. "I think Barney's perfectly capable of coping with a little snow."

There were several phone calls that afternoon, but no one came by, and the snow was piling up. Johnny called to say he was closing the office and going home and did she want anything first. Ruth Ann said no. A short time later, Sam called to say he would be going home early and could easily stop by if she wanted him to pick up anything for her. Again she said no, they were fine.

The most unsettling call was from Mattie Tilden, whose house Todd and Barney were occupying.

"Ruth Ann," she said, clearly in distress, "what on earth is going on there? Three people have called me to complain that the woman in my house is a foulmouthed troublemaker and her husband is a pedophile or worse! For heaven's sake, what's going on?"

Ruth Ann struggled to contain her fury, to keep her voice calm and reassuring as she explained the situation to Mattie. It was a lengthy call and at the end Mattie still sounded doubtful.

"You've known me all your life," Ruth Ann said. "You trusted me with your house. Just trust me a little longer. Todd and Barney are decent, honorable kids. I have every faith in them both. As soon as this is all resolved, I'll call you. I promise."

As soon as she hung up the phone, she erupted in a string of curses that she had forgotten she knew.

All day Saturday, Todd was uneasy. All Hallow's Eve, she thought over and over, but the house remained quiet, and no one came by. The snow had stopped at three inches or a little over, and the town below was like a fantasy image, a dreamscape with no wind to blow the snow from the tree limbs. It glistened in sunshine all day.

"That's what it usually does," Ruth Ann said. "It doesn't melt as much as it just evaporates out here. We hardly ever have slush, and snow seldom lasts long enough to get dirty."

Barney called to say he would leave Victor's house by noon on Sunday. "Be there around five or maybe six, depending on how slow traffic is over the pass. It's raining here."

She told him about parking at the bridge and walking the rest of the way. "You shouldn't try to drive up the loop road," she said. "It would be great if you could go by the house and get my boots so I can hike out with you."

"No problem. Everything quiet up there?"

"Considering that we're snowbound and no traffic's moving, quiet is just the right word. Real quiet."

"Good. See you tomorrow."

"Use a flashlight," she said, remembering how dark that road could be, and how treacherous.

Saturday night Todd was certain she would not be able to sleep, but the house remained still, and she drifted off into a dream-filled sleep before midnight.

In bright sunlight, girls were dancing around a maypole, tethered to it with bright pink ribbons, dancing intricate steps with great precision. Lisa was playing a flute, providing the music to which they danced, faster, then faster, twirling around, forward, back, oblivious that the ribbons were drawing them inward as they danced. Todd wanted to join them, to dance with them; a loose ribbon was fluttering, tantalizingly out of reach. The music became faster still, wilder, and she was racing in her effort to catch the last ribbon. Then she had scissors and her race became frantic as she tried to cut the ribbons, to release the girls. One by one they were being drawn into the maypole, where they became bas-relief figures in ivory against an ivory pole. Janey took her hand and led her away from the spinning pole and when she looked back, there was only a swirling dust devil and the music was the keening of wind in sage.

Todd bolted upright in bed. A faint light came from the bathroom night-light. She had left the door open a crack. She groped for her notebook and hastily wrote what she could remember of the dream: Girls, maypole, flute, Lisa, Janey, dust devil. Everything white, the girls' dresses, their shoes, their hair, the maypole that expanded as they were drawn inward. Pink ribbons the only color. The dream was already fading, the memory losing coherence. She wrote: "Ode on a Grecian Urn." She yawned, lay down and went back to sleep.

She was too warm and wide-awake, not frightened, or even disturbed, just awake. She threw the comforter aside and got up. In her pajamas, barefoot, she walked to the door and left her room. There was no sound in the house as she made her way toward Ruth Ann's sitting room and, again without hesitation, entered and switched on a light.

Ruth Ann came awake instantly when the light streamed into her bedroom. She left her bed, pulled on a robe and went to the door. Todd, in pajamas, was at the table by her chair, moving papers. Ruth Ann took a step into the room, but stopped moving when she saw that Todd's eyes were wide-open, curiously blank. She didn't turn toward Ruth Ann. With a start, Ruth Ann realized Todd was sleepwalking. She remained silent. Todd picked up a slim book, left the sitting room. Ruth Ann followed as Todd went to the dining room and placed the book by the computer. Apparently still blind to Ruth Ann's presence, she returned to her own room. Ruth Ann waited a moment, opened the door and silently walked to the bed where Todd was sleeping. As she watched, Todd moved restlessly and murmured something too low to be heard.

Undecided, Ruth Ann watched the young woman's restless movements for a minute or two. Another nightmare? Should she wake her up, comfort her? Just be there for her? Todd sighed a long tremulous exhalation and seemed to go into deeper, quiet sleep. Ruth Ann withdrew.

She went straight to the dining room to see what book Todd had been driven to collect. Janey's poetry volume. She opened it to a bookmark: "Ode on a Grecian Urn." She read it through, puzzled, and more disturbed than ever. Why that book? That poem? Troubled, she went back to her bed, but it was a long time before she fell asleep.

Todd dreamed that she was in the living room where a low fire burned. Ruth Ann's tall, spare figure was dimly lit at the window overlooking Brindle. She was wearing a pale floor-length robe. Ruth Ann turned, as if she had sensed Todd's presence.

"Come in, dear," she said. "All Hallow's Eve, a night for dreaming. Was your dream frightening?"

"No. In fact, I felt peaceful when I woke up. Thinking of a poem I haven't read since high school. 'Ode on a Grecian Urn.' Keats. Heaven knows why it entered my dream. I have only fragments of it in memory."

Softly Ruth Ann said: "'Thou still unravish'd bride of quietness, Thou foster-child of silence and slow time.'"

"You know it?" Todd asked in surprise when Ruth Ann stopped.

"No, not all of it. Lines. And I read it just recently."

Todd added a line she recalled: "'For ever wilt thou love, and she be fair!'" She shook her head. "Why on earth that came back to mind is a mystery. And for you to have read it recently, a pure case of Jungian synchronicity, I guess."

"Perhaps," Ruth Ann murmured. "Can you tell me something about your dream?"

Todd hesitated a moment. "I can't remember much of it. Barney thinks I'm obsessed by those missing girls, and maybe I am. I dream about them a lot. They were dancing around a maypole and I wanted to dance with them. They turned into the bas-relief figures on the urn, I think, and then Janey was in the dream. I walked away with her."

Ruth Ann gazed into the fire thoughtfully. "Have you been able to derive meaning from the dream?"

"I haven't really tried," Todd said. "I want to read the poem, though. It's as though my brain has it in storage, but won't turn it loose except in bits and pieces. 'For ever wilt thou love, and she be fair!' And another bit: 'And for ever young.' I was thinking of the girls, obviously, so young, frozen in time. And Janey didn't let me join them. It's as if I'm telling myself that I shouldn't fear her. But I'm not afraid of her, not with her dead and gone for more than a hundred years." She had been speaking just as softly as Ruth Ann. Then she said in a normal voice, "I don't believe in ghosts. I don't believe spirits can help or harm the living. Dead is dead."

She had said it, she realized, and added to herself: *Don't be silly. They can't harm you.* Her relief was vast, and she even felt as free as she had as a child racing downhill with the wind.

Ruth Ann smiled at her. "I never imagined that you did believe in such things." She lapsed into silence again, gazing into the fire. She sighed and murmured, "But what is it that tells the geese it's time to fly? What is it that brought on your obsession with our missing children? Why you, an outsider? Why do you feel the chill every bit as much as I do, or even more, since it leaves you despondent and tearful? There are mysteries, my dear Todd. There truly are mysteries."

Todd went to the door, paused before leaving. "How did it happen that you read that particular poem recently?" she asked.

"In the box of Janey's belongings that you found in Sam's attic, there was a book of poetry. That poem had a bookmark, and she had underlined some of the lines."

"The lines I remembered?"

"I believe so," Ruth Ann said. Then in a very distant voice, as if moving away, she said, "Remember the dream, Todd."

When Todd woke up the next morning, it was after nine. She stretched and yawned, thinking it didn't matter if she had overslept. They would finish the history, Barney would come home, and they would go back to their own house. She had hazy recollections of her dreams, first the girls and the maypole, and then a strange conversation with Ruth Ann. She frowned, not getting out of bed yet, rather snuggling deeper under the comforter, trying to sort out the dreams. She had few memories of the conversation with Ruth Ann, and even fewer of the dancing girls, and as she tried to recall either one, it receded and the other interposed itself. Finally she gave up, stretched again and got out of bed. Something to eat, coffee, back to work and wrap it all up, she told herself.

In the shower she smiled slightly, thinking of her fears about

All Hallow's Eve, her childhood fear of spirits rising, of ghosts and specters. She knew she would never mention any of it to anyone, nor would she voice any suspicion of Johnny, or anyone else, as far as that went. She didn't know enough about Brindle and its inhabitants to be any more suspicious of one than another. She felt almost as if she had turned a corner and yesterday's fears and worries now looked foolish and childish. Temporary insanity, she decided, nothing that a good night's sleep can't cure.

In the kitchen she found coffee in the carafe, helped herself to orange juice and made a piece of toast, and then went to the dining table to see what more needed to be done before they started the paste-up. When she picked up the printouts of pictures and captions, she saw the slim book of poetry.

It had been there for days, she told herself; she had simply paid no attention to it. She had seen it once in Janey's box, then forgotten about it. Consciously she had forgotten, she corrected. Obviously unconsciously, she had made note of it. She picked it up and saw the bookmark, opened it, then read the poem, "Ode on a Grecian Urn." She sat down heavily. How much had been dream, how much a real memory? She realized she didn't know the answer.

She put the book down where it had been and shook her head. It couldn't have been there the day before, or any day before. It would have been in her way, she would have moved it.

She was sitting there looking at nothing in particular when Ruth Ann entered. "Good morning. I'm so glad you slept in a little. I was afraid you weren't sleeping well. Have you eaten?"

Todd said good morning. "Yes, I helped myself."

"Good. What I think we'll do is clear off the coffee table in the living room and use that for the paste-up. I'll ask Thomas Bird to make a fire. There's not another clear tabletop in the house, except for the kitchen, and Maria would have our hides if we started to mess things up in her kitchen."

Todd stared at her, moistened her lips, then asked, "Were you wakeful last night?"

"Not at all. Sometimes I am, but not often. Why?"

"Nothing. I just wondered."

"Well, I'll go round up Thomas Bird to start the fire. We'll be done by afternoon, I'm sure."

Todd watched her walk away, then said under her breath: "What tells the geese it's time to fly? Why am I obsessed by the missing girls? Why do I feel the deep chill the way I do?" She closed her eyes, then added: "Was I awake or asleep last night when I talked with Ruth Ann? When did she put the book of poetry on the table? Why did she?"

She got up, went to her bedroom and retrieved the notebook in which she had written about her first dream, adding details as she skimmed it. Then she wrote about the curious conversation with Ruth Ann and, when finished, she regarded it with a frown. She still didn't know if that had happened, or if it had been a dream.

It was all connected, she told herself. Janey, Lisa, the missing girls. It was all connected, even if she didn't know how.

Twenty-Nine

Late afternoon on Sunday, Maria came to the living room, glared at Ruth Ann, then at Todd and left without a word. Galloping chaos, her expression clearly said. Todd was on the floor with her laptop on one side of the coffee table, Ruth Ann on the sofa on the other. Scraps of paper were scattered about on the floor, the sofa, everywhere. Ruth Ann ignored Maria, and after a few more minutes, leaned back and smiled at Todd.

"Done," she said. "Thank you, Todd. More than I can say."

Todd, who had not needed the paste-up, since it was all on her computer, grinned at her. "You've done a wonderful job with it. You should be proud."

"I am." Ruth Ann felt as if a weight on her shoulders had shifted, ready to take flight. When the copy went to the printer, she thought the weight would leave altogether. "Have you ever worked with a paste-up before?" she asked. "You went at it like an old pro."

"In high school. That's how we did the school paper. Then I walked it over to the printer and got out of PE that way. I dawdled a lot, I'm afraid."

Ruth Ann laughed. "In my day, girls didn't have to have gym classes if they chose not to because of their 'delicate condition.' I chose not to." She patted the paper. "I'll go over the copy one more time, but I don't think there's a change to be made anywhere. You're a very good editor."

Todd shook her head. "You don't need an editor. If you do want to change anything, just e-mail me, or call. If it's a big change, I'll come over tomorrow and correct it on the computer. The way the snow is melting, the road will be pretty clear by tomorrow, or I can walk up. Otherwise, it's really ready to hand over."

"Of course it is, but there's always that lingering doubt, a mistake you'll see after it's in print. It's hard to let go."

When Barney arrived a few minutes after six, Ruth Ann excused herself and withdrew to her sitting room, well aware that they needed a little time together.

They had dinner in the kitchen at seven and as soon as it was over Todd said they had to be on their way. Ruth Ann did not urge them to linger. She felt a great tenderness toward them, the way they looked at each other, the way Todd's cheeks were flushed and a light had come to her eyes.

They pulled on coats and boots, Todd got her overnight case and laptop, and they were ready to walk down to the bridge and the truck on the other side. Thomas Bird joined them, dressed in a hooded parka, carrying a lantern.

"You don't have to come with us," Todd said.

"I know. But I want to. I carry the suitcase. Barney can keep the little computer. You have a purse. See? It works out. I carry the light." He laughed and opened the door.

Ruth Ann and Maria waved goodbye, and as soon as they were gone, Maria said, "Now you'll tell me what's on your mind, I hope."

"Yes, now," Ruth Ann said. They went to the kitchen, where she poured herself a second cup of coffee and sat at the table. Maria sat opposite her. Early that morning Maria had asked what was bothering her and she had said later, it would keep until later. She had never been able to hide anything from Maria, she knew, and she thought Todd had suspected there was something to hide that day. More than once she had seen Todd eyeing her as if about to pose a question. Each time she had held it back.

"Last night," she said, "the light came on in the sitting room. I got up to see what was going on, of course. Todd had come in and was looking for something. Although I was standing in the doorway in plain sight, she didn't see me. She picked up a book and walked out with it. I followed her. She put it on the dining table, went back to her room and closed the door. I waited a few minutes, then looked in on her. She was sleeping, apparently dreaming. She had sleepwalked in to find that book. I went to see what she had been after and found Janey's book of poetry on the table. I'm sure she has no memory of any of it."

"Possessed," Maria said. "When people walk in their sleep, they are possessed by spirits who move them without their awareness."

Ruth Ann waved that aside. "I think she knows something

that she isn't aware of knowing. It's fighting to find expression. Everything is coming together through her as if she's a nexus."

"I don't know that word. The shadow is speaking to her because she can hear it even if she can't understand what it's saying."

Irritably Ruth Ann said, "No shadow. Something in her own brain is making a connection, a link between what she's preoccupied with—the missing girls and the history. They are linked in some way and she's the center of it."

"And what makes her brain connect them?" Maria asked softly. "Why her? Because she is susceptible, she hears it without understanding. She has not put a wall around herself. She should go away."

Ruth Ann sipped her coffee. "Last week I thought that same thing. Now I think not. It has to play itself out. Whatever it is that she glimpsed, heard, intuited, whatever, is in her head. It will go with her wherever she is. But I'm worried about her."

After a moment Maria nodded. "You are right. But you mean you're worried for her, not about."

"Yes," Ruth Ann said. "For her."

Boots were by the door, her heavy jacket near his, a few steps farther were her gloves and laptop, his gloves, a sweater, her purse, and by the bed a jumble of clothes in a heap. They had made frantic love and lay in a tangle of bedding, legs entwined, arms going to sleep, hers under him, his under her.

He tried to pull a blanket higher over her, and they both laughed when it proved impossible. The bedspread had to do. "Warm enough?" he asked.

Drowsily she said, "Um."

He drew her even closer and she drifted, not sleeping, not quite awake, content.

Later, shifting to remove the pressure on her arm, she murmured, "I worry so much about you, that long drive, snow on the pass."

He put his finger on her lips. "I worry about you alone out here, and I have all those tapes to listen to. The ones that put you to sleep. It's okay. Besides, we have a great homecoming celebration. I worry that you'll get tired of the same old same old boring sex."

She snorted with laughter, and he did, too.

"I'm hungry," she said a little later. "Pancakes with blackberry syrup, maybe bacon."

While she made the pancakes, he brought out plates, poured milk and, laughing, picked up the trail of clothes and other things they had dropped on their way to bed.

Then, at the table, he said, "I've thought a lot about the missing girls over the past couple of days. Looking for a pattern or something. Besides the postcards, I mean. First, no struggle suggests that they went with someone willingly, and that might mean someone they trusted and knew pretty well. Right?"

"Maybe," she said. "At least some of them. But they were all so slight, a strong man could have swooped in, held a hand over their mouths, carried them bodily to a car. Maybe knocked them out or something like that."

"You're right," he said. "We all assumed they went willingly. Not necessarily so. Then, I considered the population here, pretty static for a long time at about eighteen hundred. I don't know the composition of various families, so I just used statistics. Say a mother, father and two kids for the average family. So already we've narrowed the field a lot. Approximately two to three hundred men in that group, and maybe a third of them either too young to have gone into kidnapping twenty years ago, or too old to continue with it now. Right?"

Again she nodded.

"Pretty soon I got it down to roughly a hundred guys who might fit, assuming it's someone from here, and I guess it must be."

She put her fork down and sipped milk. "We know maybe half a dozen or so of them," she said. "But Ollie knows them all, and they all know one another."

"That's my point," Barney said. "I tried to see it as Ollie must be seeing it. He knows those men, they go fishing together, or hunting, have barbecues together, go to the same church, and he doesn't believe any of them is capable of doing such a thing, so he looks for someone he doesn't know, one who might be capable."

"The state police are checking them all out," she said. "Making sure they were where they were supposed to be that morning, finding witnesses to confirm it. I don't think Ollie can come up with anything, but they can."

"If the guy was smart enough, he might have covered his tracks pretty well," Barney said. "Not everyone has to punch a time clock, or check in with someone each morning. There are ways to be late without questions raised, and impossible to confirm or deny later."

"Two like that work at the newspaper," she said thoughtfully. "Shinny comes and goes when it suits him, and Johnny doesn't keep very regular morning hours."

"And no doubt there are quite a few others in town who fit."

She told him how suspicious she had become of Johnny. "It seemed to be tied to Lisa," she said. "You know, sexpot, Johnny possibly one of her conquests, the fact that she was around at least three times when a girl vanished, Ruth Ann rushing out to buy land, plan a new building, as if to protect him in some way. It seemed to add up to making him a suspect, but only because I didn't include the reasons Ruth Ann is taking that step. That Grace is applying pressure and so on."

"That made you reconsider him?"

She thought a moment, confused. It wasn't as if she had made a deliberate decision to rule him out, she realized. One day she had been so suspicious that she had not even wanted to talk to Ruth Ann very much, and the next day it had been as if the previous thoughts had never occurred to her. "I don't know," she said. "I guess I applied reason."

"Well, I think he is a suspect," Barney said soberly. "And Shinny is, Jacko, a dozen or more others, probably including Ollie, himself. And if you confine it to one girl, I am, too. Honey, we may be in for a tough time in the next week or so. I think in the eyes of people here, I'm the best suspect there is."

"Only until we publish that list of girls and the circumstances in each case, the similarities."

"Again, thinking like Ollie now, those cases are closed. If nothing concrete comes of the ongoing investigation, this case will be closed, as well, and in that event there will always be a lingering suspicion of the new man in town and our life here could become a nightmare. Or, if Ollie can come up with even a hint of evidence he can use against me, I'll be it."

"Xenophobia," she said faintly.

"A pretty strong motivating force. Don't underestimate its power."

She picked up her fork again, but now the pancake on her plate was unappetizing, the syrup muddy looking with flecks of butter. She put the fork down. "Barney, I have to tell you about my dream or dreams last night." She recounted what she could recall. "Then I dreamed I was talking to Ruth Ann and she told me to remember the dream." His expression had gone almost blank with incomprehension.

"Just hear me out," she said and drew in a breath. "I didn't do the sleep labs, but I did study some psychology. We talked about dream theories. One of them is that the dreamer is actually every character in the dream, that some aspect of that person assumes different roles or something. I think I was telling myself to remember the first dream. It's important."

He stood up and took their plates to the sink. "You know dreams aren't prophetic," he said.

"I asked you to hear me out!" she cried. "Just listen." She told him the dream in more detail. "Janey led me away. I don't belong in the group, but for whatever reason Lisa is part of the whole thing. That's what it means."

He returned to the table and took her hand, then loosened his grip when she winced. "Look, you don't like Lisa. And Janey's been dead for a hundred years. Neither of them can have anything to do with Jodie Schuster, or any of the other kids."

She pulled her hand free. "It's all connected," she said. "I know it is."

His gaze on her was searching, somber. "I said I worried

about you, and I do. This obsession is hurting you. You can't let it go and you have to. You've done all you can do, getting the state investigators involved. Now let it go, let them handle it, put it out of mind."

She made no response.

More emphatically he said, "Next week, let's take some time out. You've been working every day for weeks, and we need a little vacation. How about taking the bus from Bend to Eugene on Friday and I'll meet you at the bus station. Get a motel for two nights, relax, listen to music, bar crawl or see a show or something. Just get away from here a day or two."

And put it out of mind, she thought.

Barney covered her hand on the table with his, gently this time. "Second honeymoon, something like that. We're due."

She smiled faintly and nodded. Their first honeymoon had been a weekend at the coast and neither of them had glimpsed the ocean for the three days they were there.

"I'll check out bus schedules tomorrow while you're at work."

She nodded again even as she thought, *but it is all connected. And there's something that keeps eluding me. Maybe a little time away will let me make the connection.*

Thirty

When Todd left work on Monday, Barney was standing beside her car at the curb. "I walked up and retrieved it," he said. "No more snow anywhere."

The wind had shifted, the day had been almost warm, fifty-something degrees, and the ground was as dry-looking as ever.

"You look beat," Barney said, opening the car door for her. "Hard day?"

"Grim," she admitted. She was silent as he drove the short distance home. Inside the house, she said, "Johnny was grim. Cancellations. The special order of paper didn't arrive and Ruth Ann is fit to be tied. Ally didn't come to work today. Hate mail. Mean letters to the editor. Like that." She drew in a long breath. "I want a glass of wine or three."

"Coming up. Dinner in the oven. Sit down and sit still."

"Also," she said gloomily, slumping into a chair, "Lisa is at the ranch, council of war or something, no doubt. I think Hank told Grace about the special edition coming out this week, and Grace called her darling daughter home to help her plot. As if she needs help."

He brought wine for her and beer for himself. "I had a nice chat with Ollie today, just friendly stuff, like am I sure I wasn't on the wrong street when I turned onto the loop road that morning. Nothing serious."

"When it rains," she said, more morose than ever. "God, I wish Seth would check in, or that sergeant. What are they doing all this time?"

"Take it easy, honey. You know they're working. I guess that when Johnny's grim don't nobody smile at the office."

"You've got that right. I imagine they all think the newspaper is going to tank and they'll be looking for a new job any week now. And they blame me, big-time troublemaker."

"They've got that right," Barney said, lifting his bottle in a salute. "Cheers."

He got up to do something to whatever he was baking, and she closed her eyes and drew in another long breath and flexed her shoulders trying to relax too-tight muscles. A moment later the phone rang and she jerked, spilling wine. Barney answered it.

"Yes, she's here," he said. Covering the mouthpiece, he whispered, "Mame Schuster."

She steeled herself and took the phone from him. "Hello, Mame. How are you?"

"I'm all right," Mame said. She didn't sound all right; she sounded almost breathless. "Todd, today at the hospital, an old friend came to see me. We had coffee and talked. Ten years ago her daughter vanished, exactly like Jodie did, with the same kind of postcard a week later. Just like Jodie. She read your articles, editorials, and came to see me. She lives up at Madras now. She said a policewoman asked her questions, and she wants to know if that case has been opened again. No one will tell her anything and I told her not to bother with Ollie. Are they investigating old cases? What's going on?" Her voice had become high-pitched and she sounded nearly hysterical. "Do you know what they're doing?"

"Mame, calm down. Please, calm down. They aren't telling me anything, either. As soon as I learn anything at all, I'll let you know. I'm sorry if I've upset you—"

"My God, you're the only one taking this seriously! You're the only one who even cares. They don't understand that we want to know what happened to our daughters! Sure, we're upset. We have reason to be upset. Not at you. At them, all of them, letting us hang, trying to make us think it's our fault, what did we do to make our girls run away… They didn't run away. They didn't!"

Todd listened to her for several minutes and had virtually nothing to say. There was nothing to say, she kept thinking. There might never be anything to say. Mame told her the names of her friend and her daughter, and she gazed at the two names after hanging up as she repeated the conversation to Barney. "They must be looking into each case," she said. "I guess that answers my question about what they're doing."

He came and put his arms around her, kissed her forehead and murmured, "The world could use a few more determined troublemakers just like you."

* * *

"Marginally less grim," she reported on Tuesday when Barney met her at the office. "You know you don't have to babysit me every day."

"I know. Buffalo burgers. German potato salad. Sound good?" He started the drive home.

"Heavenly. The paper came today and the presses rolled. Johnny took a couple of copies hot off the press up to Ruth Ann. Now she can relax."

"And you? Will you still be going up there on your days off?"

"For a while on Thursday. I'll take file folders and help her organize material and stash it away until she's ready to start her book. I won't stay long, and I'll be home before dark. Satisfactory?"

"Good enough. Promise?"

"Cross my heart."

"And keep in mind that it gets dark early, like now."

It was five-thirty, and very dark. But still not very cold.

When they entered the house, she sniffed the air and exclaimed, "Gingerbread! You made gingerbread! Did you realize that's why I married you? Because you know how to make gingerbread. Where is it? Is it still warm?"

"Maniac. Go wash your hands. It's for dessert, not a minute before."

"What do you think?" Ruth Ann asked Johnny. They were in the living room where a fire was burning. "Looks pretty good, doesn't it?"

"Pretty good," he said. Then he grinned and said, "You know damn well that it looks terrific! Great. Reading it might be a different matter, of course."

"Yes, it might be. Todd's a marvel. It's all her design, her layout, her editing. She deserves a raise."

Johnny nodded absently. He had started to read the text. She watched his expression change from the enthusiasm of a moment earlier to a frown that deepened as he turned the page to the next section.

"Jesus," he muttered when he finished. "Not a lot to be proud of, is there? That's going to rock the town all over again. Grace will go through the ceiling. You know she called Lisa home?"

"Yes. Maria told me. Well, it's done, and we're on the move. So let her rant. Did you make an appointment with the architect?"

"Tuesday. One o'clock."

"Good. We should both be thinking of what kind of space will be needed for two operations, more staff. It has to be considerably bigger than what we have now."

He was studying the photograph of Brindle Creek. "That would be a good book jacket," he said. "Good title, *The Shades of Brindle*." He looked up at her. "You're a hell of a writer, Mother. Congratulations. Let them all rant."

Ruth Ann felt a flush on her cheeks. He had never said anything like that to her before.

Todd finished working before Barney did that night. She stood up and stretched, but at the door to the dining room she saw him still grading midterm exams and she returned to her chair to consider the next few days. Wednesday would be a repeat, she thought morosely, grim and grimmer. On Thursday she would dawdle after Barney left for Corvallis. She would check in at the office at noon, stay long enough to collect mail, and head for Ruth Ann's house for no more than three hours of work. Shop for dinner, eat and go to bed early. Friday, do a little laundry, pack a few things, and be in Bend in time for the three-twenty bus. And then really relax for a couple of days.

It was the strain of cold silence that was hardest to bear. She had not spoken to anyone in town except Mame, Ruth Ann and Maria, and occasionally Thomas Bird for days, and she was feeling isolated from civilization, from human company, so hungry for a friendly word or even a nod, she wanted to scream. Add Barney's absences, she thought, and some days she might as well be in an isolation cell enduring punishment for a crime she was not aware of having committed.

Angry with herself for indulging in self-pity, she stood up more resolutely than before and went to the kitchen to make coffee. Then she was thinking of Barney's words: that life here could become a nightmare. One that neither of them could bear for a long period—cold silence or suspicion, parents grabbing their children to safety if he got near, heads turned away when she did.... She bit her lip in frustration.

She realized how desperate she was to get away for a few days, especially this week when Ruth Ann's history would shake the community even more than Todd's editorials had done. She did not want to be around for the repercussions of the coming edition of the newspaper.

By Thursday when Barney was ready to leave, she felt more depressed than she could remember. She kept thinking, just until Friday, tomorrow afternoon, one more day. Just one day. It didn't help that Barney was dragging his feet, obviously reluctant to go.

At the door, he said, "You'll be home before dark. Remember?"

"Yes, Daddy," she said. "Now scat or you'll miss your class and those lovely grades will go a-wasting."

"I'll call as soon as I get to Victor's house. Be here. Five or thereabout."

"I'll be here. Beat it."

Strangely, she thought only minutes later when he finally left, she was wishing he had found an excuse to stay home.

She entered the office at noon, to be met with more silence. Shinny was at his desk reading the history supplement. He looked at her, raised his eyebrows and shook his head, went back to reading. Inside her own office, she had taken off her jacket and was just starting to open mail when Johnny came to her door, looked in, then entered, leaving the door open.

"You did a great job with the supplement," he said. "It looks terrific. And Mother's text is first-rate. The whole thing is first-rate. How it will play in town is anyone's guess, and we'll find out in the next few days, but I wanted to tell you I think it's very, very fine."

Having braced herself for a tirade, she could hardly speak. "That means a lot," she said. "Thanks."

He nodded, left again, closing the door quietly behind him. She sagged in her chair in relief. He was a good employer, she thought with a bit of surprise. He had her on the carpet in private, but handed out praise more or less in public. After a few moments, she started once more on the mail. Filth. Family newspaper. Not fit for children. Indecent. The words seemed to leap at her, and wearily she pushed the mail aside for another time.

Carrying her jacket, she left her office and headed for Ruth Ann's to find a box of file folders. Ruth Ann had said she had a box, but no memory of where she had put it. In the jumble of boxes and heaps of things in the office, it might take a little time to find them, Todd thought, surveying the untidy room. She located the box under another box of old magazines—it was anyone's guess why Ruth Ann had saved them.

Now ready to leave, she pulled on her jacket, picked up the box, and walked into the outer office just as the entrance door opened and Lisa rushed in.

"Johnny! Johnny, come on out. I have to talk to you," Lisa called.

His door opened and he stepped out, looking wary.

"Johnny, you're a genius! A living, breathing genius! The history is wonderful. Perfect. I want to make a picture. A beautiful, tragic, doomed girl being fought over by two unscrupulous killers."

Johnny blinked several times. "A picture?"

"A film, a movie, a true portrait of the Old West, the way it really was, the heroics, the sacrifices, the beautiful brave girl caught in the middle, used by ruthless men…."

She had rushed across the office as she spoke, took Johnny's hands and pulled him close, kissed him. "You've caught it all. A stroke of genius!"

Todd started to walk past them and Lisa glanced at her and said, "You have to come to the ranch on Saturday. I want digital pictures of the ranch to e-mail to a writer friend. He can produce the screenplay. The ranch will be a big part of it."

Todd shook her head. "Sorry. I'm going to be away this weekend."

Lisa drew back from Johnny and gave Todd an appraising look through narrowed eyes. "I'll pay you, of course," she said coldly. "Whatever your going rate is."

"I won't be here," Todd said and took another step toward the door.

"Johnny, tell her she has to come out and do it," Lisa demanded.

Sounding cautious, he said, "What about Grace? Will she go along with this?"

"For Christ's sake! She'll do whatever I tell her. If she starts screaming, I'll gag her! Send her out." She jerked her thumb toward Todd. "I want pictures this weekend."

"How about tomorrow?" Johnny asked Todd. "Can you make it tomorrow?"

Todd gritted her teeth, then said carefully, "Only if I can be through in time to get to Bend by three. I have prior engagements all weekend."

"No problem," Johnny said. "Get out there around noon, spend a couple of hours, leave the ranch by two. You'll be in Bend in forty minutes from the ranch. Okay?"

"I don't even know where the ranch is."

"Jesus Christ! Why are you making a production of it?" Lisa said in an acid tone. "Get a map, WH Ranch marks the spot, and let's get on with it." She turned to Johnny. "We have things to talk about. I'll want to use some of the pictures in the supplement, and we'll just have to add false fronts to buildings, recreate the old town and old Warden's Place, put horses in the park...."

She swept past Johnny and entered his office.

Johnny hurried after her.

Seething, Todd continued to walk toward the door, where, to her surprise, she saw Sam leaning against the wall with a sardonic grin on his face. She had not seen him enter. He held the door for her and walked out when she did.

"She passed me on the highway," he said. "I trailed along to watch the fireworks, maybe pick up and patch the pieces. One thing you can say about her, she's not terribly predictable. You going to go out there?"

She shrugged. "Johnny's my boss."

"I've got a map in my rig. I'll mark it for you. Won't take a minute."

He held her car door open and she put the box of file folders on the passenger seat along with her purse, and waited for him to return. He brought back the map, then said, pointing, "I marked the turnoff from this direction. Not a bad road, six or seven miles. When you're done, take the other way out and you'll be in Bend in half an hour or forty minutes."

"Thanks," she said as she tucked the road map behind the visor and strapped herself in.

"Poor Johnny," Sam said, closing the car door. "Snared again. Are you going to Ruth Ann's house? Tell her I'll drop in later today. Just checking. She's been overdoing things, I'm afraid. Now I'm off to read the supplement."

"Is something wrong?" Maria asked when she admitted Todd to the house. She held the box of file folders and Todd's purse while Todd took off her jacket.

"Lisa dropped in at the office as I was about to leave. She wants to make a movie, using the history supplement as source material."

"Oh, for heaven's sake," Maria said. "She'll forget it in a month. Did you hear that?" she asked Ruth Ann, who had come from her sitting room.

"Another day, another scheme," Ruth Ann said dryly. "What else did she say?"

"I'm to go out to the ranch and take digital pictures that she can e-mail to a writer friend. Tomorrow."

"You don't work for her. You don't have to do it."

"Well, Johnny sort of told me to," Todd said. "It's okay. I'll spend an hour or so, and then I intend to catch the bus to Eugene and Barney and I will have a little holiday."

"You certainly deserve one," Ruth Ann said. "But I repeat, you don't have to take orders from Lisa, or from Johnny if he's acting the fool and going along with her new scheme."

"Oh, I'll go and get it over with. No big deal. Sam was there. He showed me where it is on a road map, and I don't have a lot to do tomorrow. Sam said he'll drop in later today to check up on you." Todd examined Ruth Ann's lined face. "Are you not feeling well?"

"I'm fine. He's a fussbudget."

"Well, I'll take some of the file folders and get started on the photographs." They divided the folders and Todd went to the dining room and Ruth Ann back to her sitting room.

Later, Todd was thinking of the series of photos she was gathering as the evolution of a park. That would make a good article, she decided. First scrub sage and a couple of pine trees, with the creek in the background and the original way station off to the side. Then a corral with a rough split log fence and a few horses. The ruins of the first building after the fire, the fence gone, no horses… Up to present with grass, more trees, benches.... She came to a picture of the sumptuous wedding table and well-dressed people gathered around it, and put that aside to go with the other wedding pictures.

She heard Sam's voice, but didn't stop working to take part in a social hour.

"Sam, cut it out," Ruth Ann said when he grasped her wrist quite firmly to take her pulse.

"In a minute," he said. "Okay, done." He sat down and she sat on the sofa. "The supplement is marvelous, although I doubt that Grace will agree. Now are you ready to kick back and take it easy for a while?"

She shrugged. "There is nothing at all wrong with me. I do only those things I want to do. What would you have me do? Sit back with knitting and watch soap operas?"

"Fat chance," he said. "But I want you in the office on Monday or Tuesday for a physical. You're overdue. I told you a week or so ago that your heart was racing. Today it's erratic. That can mean trouble. I want to check it out." He pulled a small prescription bottle from his pocket. "I brought a few tablets, to keep that heart steady until we can run an EKG. No, I don't intend to hand it over to you," he said when she reached for it. "I'm going to have a talk with Maria, make her understand that you're to take one at bedtime without fail." He grinned. "I'm also going to tell her to call the office and make an appointment for you on Monday, Tuesday at the latest. I know you too well to trust you to be your own best keeper."

Todd was putting the wedding pictures in order. They told their own story, she thought, arranging them in sequence. Sam and Grace arriving at the church, going in, leaving again, getting into the carriage.... There had been an official photographer, a professional, Ruth Ann had said, who made sure everyone was posed just so, smiling just right. Her own pictures were candid shots, catching the real members of the group, not the artificial ones of the professional. There were several pictures that included Johnny. He had been handsome, young, vulnerable-looking, Todd thought, studying a shot of him with two other young men, and Lisa at the side. Two of the men were gazing at her, one of them Johnny, with a yearning look, while her expression was disdainful, dismissive. There were no pictures of Lisa with girls her own age, just the young men, older men, boys. One of the shots had caught her with Ollie nearby, round-faced even then, but not as heavy. He was looking at her with that same helpless expression. Lisa knew, Todd thought. She knew the allure she had even at that age, fourteen or fifteen at the most. But Janey had been only sixteen when she arrived at Brindle, seven months pregnant. Adolescents, both of them, with that strong sex appeal already working its magic. The words Sam had used came to mind: *Poor Johnny. Snared again.* Another picture of the same group of young men, but this time Lisa was looking away from them, with a malicious smile on her face.

The picture of the wedding party at the outside table, Sam with his toothache expression, Grace triumphant, as if saying, *Look what I caught.* Todd shifted a picture or two to keep the chronology in order. They had gone inside to a more formal reception where champagne was served and the table was even more lavish.

Suddenly Todd sat down hard. She had been standing over

the table arranging the photographs, letting them tell the story of a wedding made in hell.

"Oh, my God," she whispered. "That's the connection." She was staring blindly ahead when the sound of Maria's voice and Ruth Ann's roused her. She had to leave, she thought. She couldn't face any of them right now, not Ruth Ann, Maria, Sam. She had to get out of here and think.

She was pulling on her jacket when Maria came into the dining room a moment later. "I have to go," Todd said. She hurried out to her car and drove away, with Maria standing at the door, watching her with a worried look.

"Something happened," Maria said a minute later to Ruth Ann.

"That's all she said, that she had to go?" Ruth Ann asked. Maria nodded. Ruth Ann got up and walked with Maria to the dining room. Much of the table had been cleared, and a box was partly filled with the folders neatly labeled. Ruth Ann looked at the photographs lined up, Sam and Grace's wedding pictures. But what had spooked Todd? She had seen those pictures before.

Slowly she began to examine them again, one by one, realizing as she did that Todd had laid them out in chronological order to tell the story pictorially. She got to the end, then started over, lingering longer over each one.

Then she gasped and clutched the edge of the table. Maria took her arm and pulled her away, into the living room. "Now sit down. I'll call Sam."

"No. I have to talk to Sonny—Seth—and that sergeant. He left his card. I'll find it, you find Seth MacMichaels's number in the book." She hurried to her sitting room and began to search her old desk.

Thirty-One

Todd was in her kitchen, staring at the notes Barney had made of her dream about the elusive flowers. Too many flowers, one kept escaping. And Lisa fluting while the girls were being reeled in, one after another to become frozen in time. She closed her eyes, recalling the image of Lisa at the wedding table, with flowers in her hair, her malicious smile, and the faces of the men around her, hungry, yearning, vulnerable. Forever the temptress, flaunting her sexuality, forever out of reach, whisked off to boarding school, then to Paris with Grace, down to UCLA.... And when she came home, another girl vanished. They were all Lisas, she thought. They looked like her at that age, adolescent, blond, thin, available. Frozen in time, never to age.

Poor Johnny. Snared again.

But it could have been any one of them, caught, tossed away, mocked. Or maybe she never had let one of them bed her, but made promises that weren't kept, forever tempting, teasing. And he took one after another substitute Lisa, one who was innocent and trusting, who didn't know enough to elude him.

More than anything, Todd wanted to talk to Barney. But not on the phone, someplace where no one would disturb them, where they could try to decide if this was something to take to the state police. What could she tell them? Lisa is the key? And then what? She bit her lip. She knew it was important, but at the same time almost meaningless. She remembered what Jan had said, that Lisa didn't feel as if she knew a man until she had slept with him. She could have slept with practically every man in town at one time or another.

"But she is the key," she said under her breath. Directly linked to Janey, like Janey she had the power to make men—like Mike Hilliard—do insane things. If he couldn't keep her, she had to die. Now someone else was acting out that scenario with a major change. If he couldn't have his Lisa, a substitute Lisa had to die.

She shuddered. Insane. Someone who appeared perfectly normal, driven by an insane fixation on the adolescent Lisa.

When Barney called she told him only that Lisa was in town, and that she planned to make a movie using the history. He made a derisive grunt.

"She wants me to take digital pictures to download on her computer for a writer pal, and that's okay by me, but I tell you, I intend to be first in line to board the bus tomorrow, and I'll be the first one off. You'd better be there, kiddo."

He laughed again. "I'll be the first one you'll see when the bus pulls in. Promise."

* * *

At eight o'clock, the doorbell startled Todd, who was in her office trying to read her e-mail. It was impossible; her mind kept skittering away from the words on the monitor no matter how hard she tried to concentrate. She went to the door, moved the blind aside to peer out, and was surprised to see Jan. She opened the door and looked beyond her. Seth's car was starting to pull away.

"Hi, come on in. What's up?" she asked.

"Things," Jan said, taking off her coat. "Got coffee? I have a few things to pass on to you. Seth will be back in about half an hour."

"What do you mean, pass on? From Seth?" She started to measure coffee.

Jan nodded and took a chair at the kitchen table. "Yep. Unofficially, natch. But he thinks you should know. Are you still planning on running the story about all the girls next week?"

"Yes. Ruth Ann gave me the go-ahead."

"Well, a couple of tidbits you can add. First, that postcard from Jodie? They've been tracing it, and two others they were able to get. Seems that the company that made that series of cards folded about twelve years ago, and those particular cards haven't been available for at least eight years. At least not around here, although there might still be some out in the boonies somewhere if they weren't all sold off."

Todd turned on the coffeemaker and sat at the table across from Jan. "God! Someone stocked up on them?"

Jan shrugged. "Looks like it. Anyway, Jodie didn't buy it, that's for sure, not unless she got it eight years ago."

Todd moistened her lips. "I wonder how many the guy has."

"Good question. The other thing I'm to let slip out is that next Monday the state is officially taking charge, bringing in a special crew with special dogs that sniff out dead bodies. They're going to start on the marsh over by Summer Lake. If nothing turns up over there, they'll take them up to Wild Woods, you know, where they've done a lot of excavating, and then start on backyards around town."

Shaken, Todd got up and crossed the kitchen to pour coffee. Wild Woods, Johnny's mountain resort under construction. A mass grave? Skeletons? "God, I feel sorry for Mame," Todd said in a low voice. "This will tear her apart."

Jan came to her side and took one of the mugs. "Yeah. It's going to be tough. Seth says that the folks they've interviewed, questioned, you know, the ones who got the postcards, they all say the same thing, they just want to know what happened to their kids. I don't know. Is it better to know your kid is dead than not to know anything? That's the really tough one."

They took coffee back to the table. "Is Seth working with the state police? Will he get in more trouble if I use stuff you tell me?"

"Ollie's plenty sore at him, giving him shit work, patrolling the town, for crying out loud, telling people to stop burning trash, keeping peace in the bars. Anyway, Seth's putting in time with Sergeant Dickerson, at the sergeant's request. Todd, I want to tell you, me and Seth, we're both grateful to you for blowing this thing out of the water. Seth says you get the exclusive story when it's over with. And from time to time I'll be a blabbermouth, talking out of school, you know."

"What about Dickerson? Will he be sore if he knows Seth is letting me know things?"

"According to Seth, the sergeant thinks it's about time to shake the tree." She sipped her coffee, eyeing Todd thoughtfully, then said, "Hey, Dickerson was there eating dinner with us tonight when Seth was telling me stuff, and he suggested you might want company since Barney's out of town. Seth wants you to put his cell-phone number on your speed dial, just in case you want to get in touch or something. And Dickerson handed me his card and said you might want to add his. He's out on patrol with Seth, said they have things to talk over. Is it true that someone tried to run you off the road last week?" Her eyes were big, nearly round, her forehead puckered.

"It's true," Todd said, getting her cell phone from her purse. She added the two numbers.

"That's scary," Jan said when Todd finished and put the cell phone away again. "I mean, real scary. Why you? What do you know?"

"Not a damn thing," Todd said. "What do you hear at the store?"

"About what you'd expect. You're a big-city smart-ass know-it-all, a troublemaker, and Barney's probably a pedophile or something. Today, not a peep. It's like they had a bad case of amnesia or something and they're still in shock at seeing all that historical stuff laid out in print, and they don't want to talk about it. Pretend it didn't happen. Collective amnesia, I guess. I knew there was something rotten about this town, and now they do, too. They want you and Barney to beat it, get the hell out of their lives." She looked at her watch and finished her coffee. "I'd better be on the lookout for Seth. He doesn't want to park out front and draw attention."

Todd walked with her to the front door of the house and they both waited in the darkened room, watching for the car. "You and Seth have been great," she said. "Thanks. Just thanks a lot."

"Yeah. Like I said, we're both glad you came along and made things happen. There he is. See you later."

She left quickly and Todd closed the door, then watched from the window until she was inside the car and it drove away slowly.

After checking the windows, making certain blinds and drapes were closed, rechecking the doors to be sure everything was locked tight, Todd rewrote parts of her story about the girls. When done, she leaned back in her chair, thinking of the vastness of the high desert, the countless ravines, gullies, cliffs, innumerable places where bodies could be disposed of and never found. Even with the best trained dogs in the world, it was an impossible task. If nothing came of that search, and the postcards led nowhere, then what? Was that all they had so far?

And her own firm conviction that Lisa was the key, that the missing girls were Lisa substitutes, a conviction based on dreams, intuition, dislike, similarity. Based on nothing. Worthless. She remembered what Seth had said in what seemed a different lifetime: they were all of a type, including Lisa.

It wasn't enough, she knew. Dead end. It would gradually wind down, be relegated to the unsolved cases file, forgotten. Not by Mame and those other parents. They would never find out what had happened to their girls.

She and Barney would have to leave Brindle. She knew they would not be able to continue living here. The community would make it impossible.

Deeply troubled, she had a long soaking bath, wished she had a sleeping pill, and took a book to read in bed. When she turned off the light and finally fell asleep it was not a restful slumber. She came awake more than once, straining to hear. There were house noises, faint sounds of distant traffic now and then, possibly wind in the sage.... Sounds she could not identify. Once she got up to look out the windows, almost certain the sounds were of movement outside her doors. There was nothing to see.

Although she had been angry and resentful at being at the beck and call of Lisa, that morning she decided she was glad to have something to do besides pace while waiting for the three-twenty bus. She put a fresh battery in her digital camera, packed for the weekend in Eugene, drank too much coffee, and by eleven she was ready to start.

She put her things in the car, then went back inside for her heavy jacket. She was on her way to her car again when Barney's truck pulled into the driveway.

She ran to greet him. "What's wrong? What are you doing home?"

He pulled her close and kissed her. "Damned if I know," he said, drawing back. "That's all I could think of when I woke up at six. Just go home, so I did. Victor said he'd find someone to take my class or even take it himself." He looked sheepish and puzzled. "Where are you off to?"

"I told you. I'm going to take pictures of the ranch for Lisa."

"You didn't say at the ranch," he said. "Good God, you promised not to go wandering off by yourself."

"At night, in the dark. It's daylight, in case you hadn't noticed. Anyway, everyone knows where I'm going."

"I'll unload my gear and we'll go together," he said.

She took her suitcase back inside, tossed her jacket into the truck and retrieved the map Sam had marked for her, and within a few minutes they were on the highway. As he drove, she told him about Jan's visit.

"They want me to print it all," she said. "I don't think they're getting anywhere, and this might shake things up so that people will start thinking about the past, remembering things. Or something."

"The postcard business is a start," he said soberly. "Was the guy planning this, preparing from the beginning? Knowing he wouldn't stop with one? Jesus!"

"Something else," she said. "While I was putting away photographs at Ruth Ann's, it struck me that when Lisa was young, she looked like all those other girls, and you know what kind of sex appeal she has. She's the key. Someone was put down by her, denied, snubbed or whatever happened back then. He must fantasize about her, what it would have been like. Then she comes home and it starts all over again. He's taking kids who look like she did. Substitutes for her."

Barney shook his head. "It will never play in Peoria. Guesses. Intuition. Bias at work."

"I know, but that's it."

They had reached Bend, where he turned onto Highway 20 and she opened the map and studied the marks Sam had made. "It's the fifth road on the left. A dirt road, unmarked apparently. We'll have to count as we go."

The desert stretched out to the horizon, fringed with mountains in every direction, the scrub grasses, sage and occasional juniper tree the only signs of life here. In the distance a dust devil swirled. Footprints in the air, she thought. Deer? A coyote, a cowboy, truck? Impossible to tell, but something moved out there and the message was in the wind.

After a minute or two she said, "That's what my dream was about. You know the dream about flowers. She's the one that kept getting away."

"I remember," he said. "Who was the director?"

"I still don't know. But I was afraid of him."

The land was losing the flatness here; Glass Butte was ahead on the right, and there were closer smaller outcroppings of basalt on the left. Volcanic country, earthquake country, tortured land showing every upheaval, every scar. Eerily beautiful, like an alien landscape.

"That's number four," he said. "Next left turn." He slowed down a little and they both watched for the next road.

On the map it appeared to be very close. "There it is," she said after a moment.

Barney had seen it and was slowing down more for the turn. There was little traffic on the highway that day; they had made this much of the trip in forty minutes. That was about right, Todd thought. Sam had said no more than forty minutes out the other way to Bend.

The dirt road was rutted, not the well-graded road she had expected, she thought a few seconds later as Barney slowed more and more on the ranch road. A good road compared to what? The truck was okay, but she was glad she was not driving her little Acura, she decided, as she was jounced around. On the other hand, this was probably how people on the ranch drove down to Brindle from time to time. In her side mirror she could see the cloud of dust rising behind them, sending a signal, here we come, ready or not.

They rounded a sharp curve and now black basalt boulders were close to the road on Barney's side, and the land was sloping down on Todd's.

"It's the wrong road," she said faintly.

"Number five. We both counted."

"It's wrong," she said again. "Turn around when you see a spot. Let's get out of here." Her voice was too shrill, tight with fear.

He nodded and slowed even more. There was no place yet to make a turn. "If nothing opens up, I'm going to start backing out."

The slope on her side was much steeper, the start of a chasm. She could not see how far down it might be.

Another sharp curve and dead ahead the road was completely closed by basalt. It looked as if it had been moved by a grader, and beyond the barrier, there was the chasm.

Barney braked hard. Off to the left in the distance was a tumbled down shack, and the basalt, ten feet high, higher. He opened his window to get a better look at the ground.

At that moment, Sam stepped out from behind the basalt. He was pointing a gun at Barney.

Thirty-Two

"Barney, both hands on the steering wheel, up high where I can see them," Sam said. He was ten feet away from the truck, the gun very steady.

Barney moved his hands to the steering wheel.

"Todd, out of the truck. Walk around to the front. I'll tell you when to stop. Do exactly as I say, or I'll shoot him."

Numb with shock, she looked at Barney, who nodded slightly, then opened her door and slowly climbed down. She walked around the truck, holding on to the side of it as she moved. Her legs felt stiff, unwieldy, each step a torture in slow motion. When she was around the truck, she hesitated.

"A few more steps," Sam said, keeping the gun aimed at Barney. She walked three, four, five more steps and he said to stop.

"Now, Barney, your turn," Sam said. He pointed the gun at Todd. "You see where I'm aiming. Out of the truck, to her side.

Very slowly. Nothing heroic, nothing hasty. Just do exactly as I say."

Barney got out and walked to Todd. At her side, he took her hand.

"We're all going to walk over to that shack," Sam said. "When I saw the truck, I had to change my plans. I'm sorry. It would have been swift, and virtually painless. Now this anguish. I truly regret it. I'll stay behind you, and you start walking. There's no rush. Watch your step. The ground is uneven here. Start walking."

"You killed those girls," Todd said. "You're sick. You need help."

"No lectures, Todd. I didn't kill them. I tried to protect them, to keep them safe. I never killed anyone, and I have to admit that the two times I tried, I proved inept. You've led a charmed life, my dear Todd. I admired you very much. Keep moving. If either of you hesitates or stumbles I'm very much afraid I'll have to shoot."

Barney squeezed her hand several times, and she tried to return the reassuring gesture, but it was a feeble attempt. She was clutching her purse in her other hand and thought distantly what a joke, to hold on to it, as if it mattered.

"I saw too many times what happens to innocent girls," Sam said. "They become corrupt, lascivious, evil. Not my Lisa. I protected her."

Barney squeezed again, harder. She winced, and realized suddenly that he was signaling. Three times. She returned the pressure. One, two, three.

"I gave them all the best of care, a nutritious diet, sunlight, everything the body needs. But they died."

They had covered half the distance to the shack. Ahead, the ground was more open, the basalt stacks farther away. Now, she wanted to cry, *Now.*

He started again. *One for the money.* On her side the basalt was head high, higher on his, tumbled in a heap on both sides. *Two for the show.* He was slowing down almost imperceptibly.

"They didn't appreciate my efforts," Sam said. "Or they turned into whores, promising whatever they could think of. It was happening to them, isolated, kept pure and safe, it was still happening."

Three to get ready. She swallowed hard and drew in a breath. Suddenly Barney yelled, "Go!" and shoved her hard. She staggered, caught herself, spun around, and hurled her purse at Sam as hard as she could throw. At the same time Barney dived at him in a crouching, running tackle.

Todd crashed into the basalt and dropped to the ground before she could stop herself. She heard gunshots and voices yelling. Pulling herself to her knees, she saw Sam on the ground, Barney on the ground near him, and Seth and Sergeant Dickerson running toward them. Other men were coming from behind rocks. Half crawling, half on her feet, using her hands for support, she hurried to Barney. He was rising as she drew near.

He yanked her close, and with both of them on their knees, he held her hard, struggling to get up and to pull her up with him. "Are you all right?"

She nodded. "Are you? Did he shoot you?"

"Missed," Barney said. He drew her closer to the basalt and leaned against it, holding her. She was shaking hard.

"How bad?" Sergeant Dickerson asked, holding the mouthpiece of his cell phone.

"Can't tell. He's bleeding pretty bad." Seth was on the ground over Sam. He had pulled his jacket open.

"Ambulance and the car are on the way." Dickerson spoke into the phone again, then knelt by Seth and Sam. The other men were keeping back, one with a gun aimed at Sam.

Sam opened his eyes. He was as pale as death, breathing in shallow intakes and gasps. He struggled, trying to get up. Seth held him down. "Take it easy, doc," he said. "An ambulance is on the way."

"Have to go home," Sam said, gasping. "Have to get back. She'll be getting hungry. Help me up." He tried to push himself up, then collapsed with a moan.

"She's alive!" Seth said in a strangled voice. "Doc, snap out of it. Doc, where is she?" He started to shake Sam and Sergeant Dickerson pulled him away. He had taken off his jacket and covered Sam's upper chest with it, applied pressure on the bleeding.

"A room behind his lapidary set," Todd said. "In his house."

Dickerson looked at Seth. "Go. Take the truck and go. I'll wait for the ambulance and the car."

"Keys," Seth said. He bent over Sam and found a key ring in his pocket, then motioned to Barney and Todd. "Your truck. Let's go." They ran to the truck and he got behind the wheel. "Direct me," he said to Barney.

With much maneuvering, he got turned around, Barney and Todd crowded into the front seat, and he began to drive. They passed an unmarked car heading in on the dirt road; he stopped a moment, spoke to the other driver, then sped on.

"What's this about a hidden room, or a secret room, or whatever it is?" Seth asked when they were on the highway, speeding toward Bend.

"Jacko said Sam had a special room built for his lapidary equipment, but it's all out in the open in the garage. There's a map," she said after a moment. She was leaning into Barney with her eyes closed. "There are crosses on it."

"That's why you became a target," Seth said. "You knew that even if you didn't know what it meant."

"How did you, Dickerson and his guys get out there?" Barney asked.

"Mrs. Colonna. She said he set a trap for Todd. We sent Jan in to keep Todd's attention while Dickerson had a look at the map in her car. Wrong road marked, dead end. Good place to ambush someone. We didn't really believe Mrs. Colonna, but nothing else was working, so we got there early and waited, just in case." He passed several cars and a truck, then said, "Anyway, Sam parked on a ranch road about a quarter mile away and hiked in. We knew that, because Dickerson had a car on his tail until he turned off. Hiking in made sense if he didn't want his vehicle seen—that's pretty much what we did. Drove in partway, sent the drivers down the road to wait, and hiked in. But there was nothing we could do except wait until he made another move—he could have claimed he was just out looking for rocks. He waited until your dust cloud appeared, then moved in. After that, there wasn't a clear shot or anything until you guys went into action."

Seth was a gun looking for someone to shoot, Todd thought. He had found his target.

"How'd you manage that quick escape act?" Seth asked after passing another car. The other driver leaned hard on his horn. "If Todd hadn't thrown her purse, made him dodge, you'd have been a goner."

"We have a signal for when either of us gets bored at a meeting, or a dumb party," Barney said.

Todd pressed in closer to him and he held her tighter. She was remembering his question from long ago: *Are we bored yet?*

At Sam's house, Seth used a key to open the door and they ran through to the garage. "I don't see any way to get behind that stuff," Seth said after looking over the bench of lapidary equipment. "There's got to be a door somewhere."

Back inside the house, Barney led the way through the back hall, past the bathroom to the end, and opened a door to a broom closet.

He stepped aside when Seth nudged him. After a moment, Seth said, "Here it is." He moved a vacuum cleaner, and felt along a back wall until he found the keyhole, then tried key after key until one worked on the lock. The door swung inward silently.

Todd was right behind him, with Barney close at her heels. Inside the narrow room, the girl was crouched in the corner of a mattress, huddled in a coverlet, her face against the far wall.

"Jodie," Todd said softly. "We've come to take you home."

Jodie pressed closer to the wall, shuddering convulsively as Todd approached her. When Todd touched her shoulder she screamed. Todd sat on the mattress and gently pulled the girl around. "It's all right, Jodie. You're safe now." She murmured it over and over as she gathered the girl into her arms and held her. Jodie sobbed uncontrollably.

"I'll call an ambulance," Seth said.

"Tell them to bring Mame," Todd said. He nodded and he and Barney backed out of the room. Todd held the girl, whispering nonsensical words, stroking her back and shoulders.

* * *

The ambulance came and Mame dashed into the house, as pale as snow, with tears streaming. She seized her daughter and held her as the ambulance crew brought in a gurney. She waved it away, and helped Jodie get to her feet. Then, supported by her mother on one side and a medic on the other, the coverlet wrapped around her, the girl walked out. A state trooper had arrived with the ambulance to secure the premises until the sergeant got his investigators on the scene, but the ambulance was just leaving when Dickerson walked in.

"My guys are with the doctor," he said. "He's still alive." He eyed the narrow room and shook his head. "Jesus, a real prison."

Seth had been prowling about the room, not touching anything. He pointed above the door. High on the wall, the video camera was blinking a red light. "There's a tape recorder under the tabletop," he said in a curiously flat voice.

Dickerson cursed, then seemed to notice that Todd and Barney were still huddled together near the door. "Get out of here," he said. "Go to Mrs. Colonna's house and wait, will you? Seth or I will be along soon."

They fled. Outside, lounging against the truck, Thomas Bird straightened up as they approached. "Ruth Ann asked if you would come by and tell her what happened," he said.

"That's where we're heading," Barney said.

"Good. I'll bum a ride."

They got into the truck and drove the short distance to Ruth Ann's house. She and Maria met them at the door, where Ruth Ann examined Todd's face, then embraced her. "I was so afraid for you," she said. "Come in. You're hurt."

She touched Todd's cheek gently and Maria took Todd by the

elbow and led her to a bathroom, where she cleaned the scrape and applied an ointment.

It stung for a moment, then felt soothing. Todd had not realized she had scraped herself. Now she was starting to feel bruises on her shoulder and arm.

"I'll give you something to put in bathwater," Maria said.

They went to the living room, where Thomas Bird stood in the doorway, listening as Barney told Ruth Ann about it. "I didn't hear Jacko mention that room, or else I simply let it slide right by." He sounded agonized. Todd did not say a word until he was done.

"You told them it was a trap," she said. "Why didn't you tell me? How did you know it would be Sam out there?"

"You told me," Ruth Ann said. "It's in the photographs you arranged. I'll show you."

They went to the dining room where Todd had positioned the wedding pictures in order. "Look at those," Ruth Ann said, pointing.

There was Lisa with her malicious smile, the hungry-looking young men, Johnny. "Look at her hands," Ruth Ann said.

Lisa was holding a small beaded handbag. Todd looked closer, then gasped. Lisa had her middle finger extended, the others curled around the bag.

"And where she's looking," Ruth Ann said quietly.

She was looking at the head of the table, at Sam and Grace. And he was gazing at Lisa with that agonized expression.

"Grace is triumphant," Ruth Ann said. "Sam is in hell, and Lisa is laughing at him, taunting him. It tells the story. Grace must have caught them together, or Lisa told her, and marriage was her price to keep quiet. She could have sent him to prison.

Lisa was fourteen when he came on the scene. I remember how Grace gloated over him for months, her catch, the envy of every woman around—and she wasn't going to let him off her hook, become a laughingstock."

Todd moved aside in order for Barney to get a better look. She felt sick. "He was imprisoning them," she whispered. "Isolating them, using them until they died. That's what he said, they died. There was a video camera, a tape recorder.... He couldn't have Lisa, so he took substitutes. They were his Lisas, one after another, his Lisas." Her voice faltered, failed. She was recalling the line: "For ever wilt thou love, and she be fair!"

"I saw expensive chocolates in his grocery bag," Barney said. "We thought he had a girlfriend somewhere." Then his face tightened and he said harshly to Ruth Ann, "You let her walk into a trap. You knew he'd try to kill her."

"The sergeant said they'd find a way to check out the map he marked, and they would have him watched closely and stake out the area themselves. Seth promised me that he would not let harm come to Todd. I believed him." Then, very quietly, she added, "Sam would have killed Todd eventually. He tried twice and failed, but he would have killed her and he never would have come under suspicion for that, either."

She took Todd by the arm and led her back to the living room. "You've had a severe shock, and this is going to be a hellish weekend," she said. "As soon as the story gets out, we'll be swarmed by the media. You kids were planning on a day or two away. Do it. I have friends on the coast who run a nice bed-and-breakfast. I'll call and tell them you're my guests. Take off for a few days. Come back no sooner than Monday evening.

Possibly the frenzy will have subsided a bit by then. You've been through a very traumatic time and you have to have a rest."

"They'll want our statements," Todd said in a faint voice. "Sergeant Dickerson asked us to wait here. And the newspaper..."

"You'll make statements next week. It doesn't have to be today or tomorrow. I'll talk to the sergeant and Seth. And I believe Johnny and I can manage the newspaper for a short while. Sit down a minute, I'll call Shirley."

Todd had no real arguments. More than anything she wanted to get away for a few days, long enough to dim the immediacy of the last few hours.

A little later, Ruth Ann stood at the door, watching as they walked swiftly to the truck hand in hand. Go soon, she had said, before anyone notices and trails after you all the way. She waited until the truck was out of sight before she closed the door.

Joining Thomas Bird and Maria in the kitchen, she picked up her own big mug of tea, already filled. "Did you put the journal back?" she asked Thomas Bird.

He nodded. "Just where I found it. But there's the broken window. I couldn't put it back." He laughed.

"Good enough. Let them wonder." Earlier she had asked him to go look for a journal, a medical records book, diary, chart, something. Sam was a good doctor, he kept good notes, records. She had suspected that his medical chart or journal would be in the house, and Thomas Bird had gone in through a back window and found it.

She took her tea back to her sitting room. Her computer was on the old school desk, the scanner by it, the printer on the other side. Following Todd's directions, she had scanned the journal, but had not printed the pages yet, nor had she read Sam's text more than with a quick glance here and there. Again, referring to Todd's instructions, she worked on it. Print, then read, she told herself.

She was still at it when Johnny came, more agitated than she could remember.

"Where's Todd? Was she hurt? People are saying Sam tried to kill her. Was Barney shot?"

She told him what she knew, just not where they had gone. "They're both fine, but tired, nervous exhaustion. They're taking a few days to rest."

He paced the living room to the window, back. "Do you think Lisa suspects? Does Grace?"

Ruth Ann shrugged. "No idea. You could ask."

He laughed, a dark and mean laugh. "I doubt I'll be seeing much of either of them," he said. "To hell with them both."

He walked to the window again, swung around, came back. "How much of it are you going to publish?"

"We'll have the basic story tomorrow, a news extra, our first. Tell Hank to be on hand. It should be a tabloid. Someone will have to come by and get it."

Johnny nodded. "Call when it's ready. I'll pick it up and ride herd on Hank."

"I'll write it tonight and it might be late. Then a full story by next week's edition. Eye-witness accounts, the whole works. Todd left with the community regarding her as a viper at their collective throat. She'll come back as a hero." Johnny groaned slightly and she paused.

"She'll become a celebrity, quit to write a book, be hired by a real newspaper."

Ruth Ann shrugged. "Maybe that's true, but I doubt it. She's a newspaperwoman, certainly, even if she doesn't fully realize it yet. As for the rest, how much I'll publish, I haven't decided. I suppose it will depend on whether he lives, how much he talks, who else starts printing it. Are the reporters buzzing around yet?"

"Some. A TV crew is down from Portland, and one from Eugene. CNN is sending a stringer. They can't find anyone who knows anything. God, what a mess!" Then he said, "We sold out the newspaper this week. The TV people want more copies. I think a thousand will go."

"Fame and fortune," she said dryly. "And Lisa thought she would be the one to put Brindle on the map. I suppose in a sense she was right about that." Johnny looked puzzled, but she didn't explain.

Seth arrived soon after Johnny left. "Where are they?" he asked, taking off his jacket. "Barney and Todd."

She told him what she had told Johnny. "They'll be back Monday night. Is Sam going to live?"

"He's in surgery. He'll make it," Seth said. "And Mame's going to take Jodie and the boys away for a few months, someplace warm and sunny where Jodie can be out in the open air. She isn't talking to anyone except her mother. She'll need a lot of counseling. Dickerson's keeping her under wraps, away from reporters. Ollie's holding a news conference," he added, "but the trouble is, he doesn't know squat. I'm referring questions to Sergeant Dickerson, and he's referring them to his captain." He sounded very happy.

Then he leaned forward in his chair. "Mrs. Colonna, how did you put it together? He was so far down on the suspect list, he was like a footnote. That picture doesn't explain anything. Teenagers often hate it when a parent remarries. Maybe they don't express it so graphically, but it's there."

"It's complicated," she said. "You had to know the story about Janey and her imprisonment, the way she was used, her death. Then you had to know about her connection to Lisa, who apparently has the same dark streak that Joe Warden had and passed on in the genes, along with Janey's sex appeal." She noted the flush that rose on her cheeks. "You had to have seen their pictures lined up with the contemporary missing girls. Every piece was needed. Without the history being spread out, especially the marriage of Sam and Grace, nothing ever would have made sense. Without the history I never would have looked at those wedding pictures again. You had to know both the history, and the contemporary crimes. Only two people did, Todd and I. I connected Lisa to Janey and Todd was the one who linked Lisa to the kidnappings. She was the catalyst for everything that followed.

"Imagine Sam some twenty years ago," she continued musingly. She realized as she spoke that she was recalling Leone's lament: he needed museums, theater, charming people to talk to. She pushed the memory aside. "Sam was very handsome when he came here from Los Angeles. And he found Bend and Brindle as they were then. One a dusty little town of fifteen thousand, the other a speck on the map, and not much to do in either. I doubt that he would have had any resistance if Lisa homed in on him. She always did like handsome men." Seth's flush deepened.

"So he was forced to marry Grace. A forced marriage more than a hundred years ago, another forced marriage twenty years ago, both resulting in disaster." She paused, then said, "Not history repeating itself, but parallels. In both instances, a mature, educated man lost all reason when he became infatuated with a teenage nymph. Hilliard had gone to school, studied law, passed the bar exam, and then lost his mind over a fifteen-year-old girl." She shrugged. "Sam, of course, intelligent, after undergoing the rigorous education and training to become a medical doctor, was even more obsessed and irrational. Perhaps knowing about the first one paved the ground for accepting the second.

"Lisa was whisked off to boarding school, to Paris. Out of reach. And Sam moved into the house on the crest and started the renovations. Look up the records, the crew who worked on it. I imagine he had the special room built at that time. No doubt, you'll find out. Likely at first he thought Lisa was pure, virginal, and he knew the girls he kidnapped were. They were his patients. His Lisa substitutes, each one like the girl he'd lost, his forever-young bride… Any of them would have trusted him, the doctor they had known all their lives." More softly, she added, "I pray that none of them lasted very long in that prison."

Seth's expression was grim. "It's a good thing that Jodie lasted, and that there's audiotapes and videos. Jesus, he kept the videos and tapes in a couple of locked drawers, not even a safe. He was that sure of himself. They'll need them, because the history business wouldn't be enough to convince a jury."

"I don't think it will ever go to a jury," Ruth Ann said. "A psychiatric board will judge him criminally insane. Todd said he was trying to protect the girls, keep them safe. Joe Warden said the same thing—he was determined to save Janey, keep her isolated and safe in his stone house. Insane, both of them, all three of them—Warden, Hilliard and Sam."

Seth shook his head. "He was so sure of himself. He didn't make mistakes often. He even had another map in his pocket, one with the real ranch road marked clearly. Switch them, push her little car off the cliff, it would have looked like she took the wrong road, tried to turn around and went over the side. Her mistake. Accident. Case closed. She knew about the room, but Barney didn't," he added. "Didn't Barney hear Jacko tell her about it?"

"Apparently not. She has the instincts of a reporter, hears things and stores them even if they're meaningless at the time. But Sam must have known, he knew she was aware of the room. As soon as he realized she was going to keep the case alive, she became a target."

"That first attempt was before any editorial was printed," Seth said. "He knew she was going to keep it alive. How'd he find out?"

"I told him," Ruth Ann said, her voice heavy with regret. "Or he might have seen her car at Mame's house. I did." But it didn't really matter; he would have known in a short time, she added to herself.

That night, Todd was stretched out on a sofa, her head in Barney's lap, a fire burning quietly in the fireplace. With Maria's herbs in the water, they had bathed together, commiserating about bruises and scrapes. They had eaten steamed clams. The wind was rising, promising a storm on the following day. She loved being on the coast, warm and snug inside, watching a Pacific storm blow in. He stroked her hair.

"I feel as if I've been released," she said drowsily. "Something's gone that was heavy and dark."

"It's really over," he said.

"It's more than that, but I can't explain it. Tell me again why you came home when you did."

His hand stopped moving on her hair, then started again. "A feeling," he said. "A dark and heavy feeling. I just felt as if something was telling me to get the hell out of Corvallis and back to you."

"And you listened and heard," she said.

"I don't know that I heard anything," he said slowly. "No words, no orders. I just had to get out and go home."

"Not just yes or no, black or white. Everything in between, too," she said. "What tells the geese it's time to fly?"

He traced the curve of her cheek with a light touch. "I don't know," he said.

Ruth Ann had read part of the medical journal Sam had kept on the girls. Enough, she thought, more than enough. A soundproof room, everything built in and bolted down, a television that played only the movies he had chosen, books to read that he had chosen, nothing hard, nothing sharp at hand. Nutritious meals that he prepared. When they were good, he gave them candy. But they died in spite of him and his care. And when one died, he had the videos and the audiotapes to sustain him until the need for a new virginal bride overcame him. "For ever wilt thou love, and she be fair," Ruth Ann murmured.

She had stopped reading when she came to a passage that ended: *Exsanguinated.* He had intended to abort a fetus on Saturday morning, but the girl had bled to death from a spontaneous abortion while he was at his office treating patients.

How much of the journal to include in her story? She considered it while standing at her window overlooking the town. Just enough to tell them that their children had not been tortured, she decided. She shuddered, very aware that emotionally and psychologically those girls had been savaged.

Ruth Ann wrote her story. While she waited for Johnny to come pick it up, she used the notes she had made with Todd's instructions and checked for hidden codes and proper columns. It would do. Along with her own story, she would include Todd's original story linking all the girls.

It was very late before the lights of Brindle began to go out. The taverns and bars would be doing good business that night, Ruth Ann suspected, standing at her window. Probably the motels had filled up as word got out that a respectable doctor had been exposed as a serial predator of young girls while the town slept.

She lifted her gaze beyond the town, beyond the highway, to the impenetrable blackness of the great desert, the darkness of the old cemetery. She felt as if something had vanished. Maria's shadow, she mused, without substance, immeasurably heavy, had left her shoulders. Gazing where she knew the cemetery lay, she murmured, "It's over, it's done, Dad." In an even lower voice she added, "Rest in peace, Janey."